HOMAGE TO KLEOPATRA

"An enthralling fictional account of [Kleopatra's] youthful ascension into politics and prominence . . . fine historical fiction that will leave readers hungry for the second volume."
—*Booklist*

"Richly textured . . . an agreeably intelligent and lively read."
—*Kirkus Reviews*

"Fast-paced . . . intriguing . . . consistent and historically accurate. . . . Even those who think they know the queen will discover new facets of her life that will engage both the intellect and the senses."
—*Publishers Weekly*

"A gripping story."

—About.com

"The pages of KLEOPATRA are as entertaining as the scenes of a well-directed movie . . . richly detailed images. . . . Essex breathes life into the ancient world at the dawn of the rise of the greatest Roman emperors."

—Bookreporter.com

"A richly textured novel . . . a stunning, strong, and sensational story of power and lust."
—*Boox Review*

Please turn this page for more praise for *Kleopatra* and turn to the back of this book for a preview of Karen Essex's upcoming novel, *Pharaoh*.

more . . .

"A rich-textured, fast-paced tale that should lead to the latest Egyptian boom . . . incredible fictional biography that contains a fantastic look at ancient Egypt and Rome."
—Harriet Klausner

"A true hidden history. With empathy and mercilessness, Essex has taken complex events and daunting legends and made them not just comprehensible, but thrilling. . . . This authentic, brilliantly reimagined chronicle sets new standards."
—Mikal Gilmore, author of *Shot in the Heart*

"Essex does for Kleopatra what Josephine Tey did for Richard III. She paints a fresh portrait of the woman male historians, not to mention Hollywood, cast as a femme fatale—a cliché. . . . A satisfyingly complex picture of both the woman and the political realities of the time."
—Carol Thurston, author of *The Eye of Horus*

"I was captivated by KLEOPATRA. While entertaining, it also restores important historical truths long ignored about a fascinating woman. A terrific read."
—J. Randy Taraborrelli, author of *Jackie, Ethel, Joan*

"Authentic history and a delightful story mesh perfectly. . . . Essex brings Kleopatra to life."
—Dorothy Garlock, author of *High on a Hill*

"A paradigm shift in thinking about women in history."
—Dr. Mary Bess Dunn, professor of education,
Tennessee State University

"Kleopatra finally gets her due as the brilliant, many-faceted woman she was. Essex's research is meticulous and her prose is as compelling as her subject."
—Susan Ford Wiltshire, professor of classics,
Vanderbilt University, and author of *Athena's Disguises*

KLEOPATRA

karen essex

WARNER BOOKS

An AOL Time Warner Company

Warner Books, Inc., 1271 Avenue of the Americas, New York, NY 10020
Visit our Web site at www.twbookmark.com.

 An AOL Time Warner Company

Printed in the United States of America
Originally published in hardcover by Warner Books, Inc.
First Trade Printing: August 2002
10 9 8 7 6 5 4 3 2 1

The Library of Congress has cataloged the hardcover edition as follows:

Essex, Karen.
    Kleopatra / Karen Essex.
        p. cm.
    ISBN: 0-446-52740-8
        1. Cleopatra, Queen of Egypt, d. 30 B.C.—Fiction. 2. Egypt—History—332-30 B.C.
—Fiction. 3. Queens—Egypt—Fiction. I. Title.

    PS3555.S682 K57 2001
    813'.54—dc21

                                                        00-044930
ISBN: 0-446-67917-8 (pbk.)

Book design and text composition by L&G McRee
Cover design by Jackie Merri Meyer
Cover photo by Barnaby Hall

ATTENTION: SCHOOLS AND CORPORATIONS
WARNER books are available at quantity discounts
with bulk purchase for educational, business, or sales
promotional use. For information, please write to:
SPECIAL SALES DEPARTMENT, WARNER BOOKS, 1271
AVENUE OF THE AMERICAS, NEW YORK, NY 10020

*Volume One is dedicated to the memory of
Professor Nancy A. Walker, and also to
my mother. Without the former's intellectual guidance
and the latter's generosity,
it may never have been completed.*

Kleopatra's Genealogy

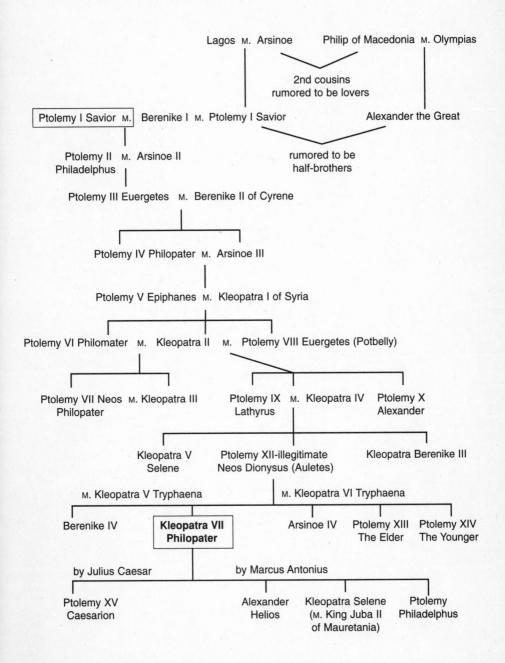

Lagos M. Arsinoe   Philip of Macedonia M. Olympias

2nd cousins
rumored to be lovers

Ptolemy I Savior M.   Berenike I M. Ptolemy I Savior   Alexander the Great

rumored to be
half-brothers

Ptolemy II M. Arsinoe II
Philadelphus

Ptolemy III Euergetes M. Berenike II of Cyrene

Ptolemy IV Philopater M. Arsinoe III

Ptolemy V Epiphanes M. Kleopatra I of Syria

Ptolemy VI Philomater M. Kleopatra II M. Ptolemy VIII Euergetes (Potbelly)

Ptolemy VII Neos M. Kleopatra III
Philopater

Ptolemy IX M. Kleopatra IV   Ptolemy X
Lathyrus   Alexander

Kleopatra V   Ptolemy XII-illegitimate   Kleopatra Berenike III
Selene   Neos Dionysus (Auletes)

M. Kleopatra V Tryphaena   M. Kleopatra VI Tryphaena

Berenike IV   **Kleopatra VII
              Philopater**   Arsinoe IV   Ptolemy XIII   Ptolemy XIV
                                                The Elder   The Younger

by Julius Caesar   by Marcus Antonius

Ptolemy XV   Alexander   Kleopatra Selene   Ptolemy
Caesarion   Helios   (M. King Juba II   Philadelphus
                                     of Mauretania)

Part I

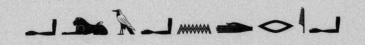

ALEXANDRIA

ONE

There was something about the air in Alexandria. It was said that the sea-god, Poseidon, who lived near the Isle of the Pharos, blew a divine whisper over the town. Depending on his mood, he sent various sorts of weather. In the winter, the air might be arid and unforgiving, so dry that it left old men gasping for breath and wishing for the balmy ether of spring. In the summer, it hung over the city like a sea-damp gum. Sometimes it was but a carrier of flies and dust, and sometimes the harsh winds of the African desert merely returned the sea-god's breeze to its watery birthplace. But this morning, in spring disposition, the god murmured a smooth rhythm toward the jewel-by-the-sea, teasing its way to the land, lifting the tender smell of honeysuckle from the vine, and filling the air with essences of lemon, camphor, and jasmine.

In the center of town, at the intersection of the Street of the Soma and the Canopic Way, sat the crystal coffin of the city's founder, Alexander the Great. The Macedonian king had lain in his final resting place more than two hundred years, his youthful mummy preserved against time so that all might pay tribute to his genius. Sometimes, the Egyptians would pull their sons away from the coffin of the great warrior, forbidding them to say the prayer of Alexander's cult taught in all schools, and scolding them for their allegiance to foreign blood. But the dead Greek had envisioned this paradise, outlining in chalk the symmetrical grid of streets. He had built the Heptastadion, the causeway that reached through the waters of the glimmering sea like a long, greedy tongue, separating the Great Harbor from the Harbor of Safe Return. Alexander's successors, the big-nosed Greek Ptolemy and his children, had erected the Pharos Lighthouse, where the eternal flame burned in its upper tower like the scepter of a fire god, guiding ships safely into the low, rocky harbor. They built the great Library that housed all the world's knowledge, the columned promenades that lined the paved limestone streets and shaded the pedestrians, and the city's many theaters, where anyone—Greek, Egyptian, Jew—could see a comedy, a tragedy, or a special oration. All in Greek, to be sure, but every educated Egyptian spoke the language of the conqueror, though the favor was not returned.

The city was still a paradise, even if the once-great Ptolemies had degenerated into a new species—walrus-size monsters as large as any creatures in the zoo, with appetites just as greedy. Sycophants who happily bled the Egyptian treasury to appease the new Masters of the World, the Romans. Every few years, it was necessary for the Egyptian mob to assassinate at least one Ptolemy, just to remind them that time brings down all races.

But on a day like today, where lovers nestled in shady groves of the Park of Pan, and stalky spring blooms jutted into a gaudy lapis sky; where falls of white bougainvillea toppled from balconies like rivers of milk, it was easy to forget that the House of Ptolemy was not what it used to be. Today, the god's sweet sigh brought everyone into the streets to enjoy the parks and promenades and open air bazaars. Today, everyone smiled as they inhaled the sea-god's whisper. They did not care if it was Greek air, Egyptian air, African air, or Roman air. It had no national character. It simply filled their lungs and made them happy.

The Royal Family, whose ancestors had made the city great, saw none of this. The palace compound by the sea was a lone respite from the city's gaiety, its shutters closed tight against the delicious air and the extravagant day. Workers went about their chores in silence, heads bowed like fearful worshippers. A thick haze of incense hung about the ceilings of the cavernous rooms. All happiness had been shut out; the queen was ill, and the most famous physicians in the civilized world proclaimed that she would not get better.

Kleopatra watched from her vantage point on the floor as the shimmering doors opened and the king rushed the blind Armenian healer into her mother's bedchamber. The girl's eyes, sometimes brown but today green like baby peppercorns, widened as they met the milk-white craters under the holy man's brow. With tattered garments hanging about him like feathers, he hobbled toward the child on what appeared to be two crooked sticks of kindling. Kleopatra leapt out of the way, barely escaping a swat in the head from his saddlebags. She climbed onto the divan where her sister, Berenike, and her half sister, Thea, sat locked in a silent embrace. Though neither moved, Kleopatra felt their flesh harden as she scampered to the end of the sofa and perched herself on its arm.

"Should the little princess be present?" the Chief Surgeon asked the nurse, acting as if the child could not understand what he said. "The situation is grave."

Kleopatra's mother, Queen Kleopatra V Tryphaena, sister and wife to the king, lay listless on the bed, gripped by a strange fever of the joints. Frantic to keep his post, the Chief Surgeon had recruited physicians of great renown from Athens and Rhodes. The queen had been sweated, bled, cooled with rags, massaged with aromatic oils, pumped with herbs, fed, starved, and prayed over, but the fever won every battle.

"The child is headstrong," whispered the nurse. "No one wishes to hear her incessant screaming when her will is challenged. She is a headache. She is three years old and she cannot speak even one sentence of passable Greek." They must have thought she could not hear as well. Kleopatra jutted her bottom teeth as she did whenever she was angry.

"She is very small for her age. Perhaps she is slow to learn," the physician pronounced, making Berenike laugh. The eight-year-old sneered at Kleopatra, who glared back. "Her presence is always disruptive. I shall take it up with the king."

The king—fat, melancholy, and agonizing over his wife's mysterious illness—paid no attention to the physician. "The child is exercising the royal will," the king replied, his glazed, bulbous eyes staring at nothing. "Let her remain. She is my small piece of joy."

Kleopatra glowered victoriously at her sister, who kicked at her with a strong brown leg. Thea hugged Berenike tighter, stroking her long coppery mane, settling her. The physician shrugged. Kleopatra's father, King Ptolemy XII Auletes, had already sent five doctors into exile. Others he simply abused for not curing his wife. If Kleopatra's presence amused him, then all the better. Perhaps no one would be slapped or dismissed or become the target of his verbal spew that day. He was a king famous for his volatile temper. His subjects called him Auletes the Flute Player or Nothos the Bastard, depending on their mood and mercurial allegiance to him. He preferred Auletes, of course, and adopted it as his nickname. Like his subjects' loyalty, his temper was notoriously changeable. But no one doubted that the king loved his sister-wife. It was said that theirs was the first love match in the dynasty in two hundred years. The queen's illness only heightened his choleric disposition.

The tonsured priest praying over the queen raised his slick head, astonished to see that the blind healer was to be given access to the patient. With the attending physicians, he stood stationary, a human shield against the execrable creature.

"Move aside, fools," said the king, thrusting his capacious royal body through the cluster hovering about the queen's bed. "This man is here to compensate for your ineptitude."

"But Your Majesty," protested the priest. "What unholy presence might this conjurer evoke?"

"Strip this idiot of the priest's robe and send him to the mines," the king said calmly, almost lightly, to one of his bodyguards. The priest fell to his knees, his face on the floor, murmuring low incantations to the cold, deaf surface. Satisfied with the effect of his threat, the king winked at Kleopatra, whose glowing child eyes smiled back at her father's weary ones.

Kleopatra wanted the healer to hurry his magic. She longed to see the queen once again sit up, put on her makeup and shiny robes, and take her place beside the king in the Royal Reception Room where the three princesses were allowed to sit from time to time while their parents entertained visitors from faraway places. Though Kleopatra saw her mother only at these occasions, she was awed by her ethereal beauty and by the songs she played on the lyre. Fair and delicate, Tryphaena was not a real person like herself or her father or her sisters, but one of the Muses come down to earth to make them smile.

Out of the healer's saddlebags came small statues of naked deities: one headless, one with fearsome eyes and a hawk nose, one with a crooked phallus. Kleopatra strained to hear the unimaginable secrets he whispered to them as he removed them from the bag. From the bottom of his sorcerer's well he produced a thick cluster of herbs, weeds, leaves, and roots, bound together into a ratty tangle, and called for someone to light it with fire from one of the queen's oil lamps.

"Mithra, Baal-Hadad, and Asherah who slew and resurrected him." The healer raised the torch, summoning the terrible gods of the east. Mithra, Mithra! Kleopatra prayed silently with him as he danced about the bed drawing circles in the air with his smoke stick. "Mother Astarte who creates and destroys. Kybele, goddess of all that is, was, and ever shall be," he invoked.

Suddenly he bent over as if in great pain, spewing guttural noises, thrashing in the air, warring with the unseen forces of the queen's illness. He carried on this way for what seemed to Kleopatra like a very long time. Then he raised his arms, ran to the bed, and passed out cold over the queen's delirious body. Kleopatra willed with all her might that the queen would open her eyes, but Tryphaena, lovely features bathed in the sweat of her fevers, did not flinch.

The king hung his great head as the servants carried the healer from the room. He called for his flute and began to play, offering a desolate melody to the gods in a final bargain to save his wife. Kleopatra wanted to be near him so she crawled to his feet, chasing with her fingers a bright green cricket. The king paused, and Kleopatra hoped he would pick her up. But she realized that he was waiting for the faint strings of the queen's song. They had played music together, he on the flute, she on the lyre, and often passed evenings in this pursuit. When his duet partner failed to move, he began to play once more.

One by one, the old women of the court, relatives whom Auletes sheltered in their dotage, came to keep vigil for the queen. With piteous eyes, they patted Kleopatra's hair, commenting on its lovely sable color, or kissed her forehead as they passed her. She knew that her father did not want the old ladies in the room. Auletes housed the dowagers in the family palace on the island of Antirhodos, so that they had to commit to a boat ride before they could interfere in his affairs. But they could not be kept from the chamber of the dying queen, where they burned herbs and incense and appealed in prayer to Isis, Mother of Creation, Mother of God. Four solemn-faced red-robed priestesses of the goddess came to inspire and anoint the ladies of prayer while the doctors applied compresses to the queen's hot brow and listened to her fevered murmuring.

"Lady of Compassion," cried the women in craggy aged voices. "Lady of Healing. Lady who eases our suffering." As the queen's condition worsened, they made frightful appeals to the goddess's dark side, scaring the small princess, who clutched at her father's ankle with each rancorous invocation.

"Devourer of men."

"Goddess of the Slaughter."

"Lady of Thunder."

"Destroyer of the souls of men."

"Destroy the Fates that conspire to seize the life of our queen and sister."

The Chief Surgeon wiped his hands on his apron. The king put down his instrument. Kleopatra stared at the sandaled feet of the two giants above her, wondering how toes got so big and skin so crusty.

"The queen's blood is poisoned by the high temperatures in her body," the Chief Surgeon said, more confident of his position since the foreigner's magic had failed.

The doctor's assistants walked solemnly from Tryphaena's bed carrying pots of contaminated rags, brown with sweat and dried blood. The surgeon motioned for them to show the contents to the king. Kleopatra got to her knees, sneaking a look at the putrid blood-brown cloths. How could such ugliness come from her beautiful mother?

Trying to avoid the king's face, the Chief Surgeon looked to the ground, where he saw the little princess staring at his large feet. "I have bled her as much as I dare, Your Majesty. I cannot remove the fever. It is up to the gods now when and if we shall lose the queen."

The ladies fell into supplication. "O merciful Lady, Divine One, mightier than the eight gods of Hermopolis. Source of All Life. Source of All Healing. Do not take our queen Tryphaena." Despite their age, they beat their chests unmercifully, fists thumping hollow, sunken breasts.

Kleopatra waited for her father to dole out a punishment to the Chief Surgeon like he did the others. The doctor dropped to his knees and, with the impetuousness of a young lover, kissed Auletes' ringed hand. "Forgive me, Your Majesty, if I have failed you. I would happily pay for the queen's life with mine." Auletes did not respond.

The doctor seemed surprised that he had been sentenced neither to death nor to exile. He recovered his dignity with a nervous cough. "I must supervise the chemistry for the queen's sedatives. Her Majesty must be made comfortable on her journey to meet the gods." With a hasty prayer, the doctor excused himself.

Auletes remained standing, slumped, bewildered, unattended. Kleopatra picked up the cricket and offered it to her father. A sad giant, he shook his head and closed his eyes. Kleopatra settled between his feet, sheltering the cricket with her hands, thwarting its escape.

Fifteen-year-old Thea, the queen Tryphaena's daughter from her first marriage to a Syrian prince, held Berenike in her lap, her cat eyes darting from the little princess on the floor to the king. Kleopatra shuddered. Thea was the image of her mother, but a darker, shadow side. Her black hair fell extravagantly down the length of her back, for she did not yet bind it into the tight knot favored by adult women. Her white, even teeth were perfectly set against her burnished complexion. She had inherited the queen's aquiline nose and triangle-shaped face, but her features were sharper and more acute than her mother's gentler angles. Her contrasts heightened her conspicuous beauty, whereas Tryphaena's softer attributes meshed into a timid gracefulness. Tryphaena, even when in perfect health, looked like an immortal creature merely visiting the harsh world of the living; Thea was clearly designed to live in the earthy, physical world. Though her time had not yet come, her body was developed and at odds with her childish clothes and undressed hair. Her young charms were bursting through the last vestiges of childhood, which she was ready to shed like a snake discards last season's skin.

Thea held Berenike tight, leaving Kleopatra to wonder what it felt like in that closed circle. "I will always take care of you, darling," she said into the child's ear. Thea's words were a song to Berenike, who adored her older half sister; her promises, a salve to Berenike's wounds.

"Now I will never know her," cried Berenike, who was precisely the age at which the queen should have begun to take an interest in her, though it was unlikely that this would ever have happened. Before she took ill, Tryphaena had spent her days playing music, reading books, and having earnest debates with the Sophists. Berenike liked to hunt small prey with her bow, wrestle with her pack of dogs, and chase the little slave brats through the courtyard with her sling.

Thea did not join in Berenike's activities, but was an enthusiastic audience for Berenike's feats, applauding any new progress she made with her weapons. Berenike dreamed of a day when she would be plucked from the nursery to have special audiences with her mother and show her how she could already hit the center of a target. But she had not had a conversation with her mother in more than two months, and her memory of the queen had already begun to dim.

Thea mouthed words of consolation, but she was not thinking about her mother or her stepsister. Thea pondered her own Fate. She was not the daughter of the king. She was not in line for the throne. Once her mother died, she would be sent to one of the outer palaces to live with the meddling old women who wailed in the queen's chamber, until someone in the king's service suggested a marriage to a house in a foreign land. Or until she was sent back to the court of her dead father in Syria, a country now occupied by Tigranes of Armenia, who was at war with the Romans. If the Romans won, which they always did, she might be thrown to one of them as a trinket, a small toy to quench their lusts. That was what she heard the brutal Romans demanded in victory, even from women of royal blood. No, there was nowhere for her to go.

"Ramses looks terribly lonely," said Thea. Berenike's favorite hound sulked in a corner. "I think he is crying for you." Thea deposited Berenike on the floor next to her dog. She walked straight to the stupefied king and took his hand. "Come, Father," she said. Kleopatra tried to hold on to her father's woolly leg, but he slipped from her grip, leaving her little hands empty.

To the astonishment of the ladies, Thea led the king from his post at the queen Tryphaena's bed. Undaunted by the disapproving stares of the wrinkled, fierce dowagers, she steered Auletes through their circle of worship and down the stairs to the level of the palace that housed his private quarters. She took him into his favorite room, the hunting room, and in a voice that she had never before heard come from her body, ordered his attendants to go away. They skittered to all corners of the palace to report what was happening.

Kleopatra sat alone on the floor, screaming words that she thought would make her father return. "Stop your gibberish," yelled Berenike. "No one knows what you are saying, you idiot." But Kleopatra could not stop, could not quiet the desire to bring her father back, to curl into his big firm belly. Berenike stood over her little sister, her long legs tall as smooth young trees. She crushed the cricket beneath her sandal, leaving Kleopatra to stare at the insect's smashed remains.

Thea sat the king down upon the wide, soft pallet of his kills. She said, "I am a woman now, Father. Let me take away your pain." She opened the front of her white chiton and let it slide off her shoulders. The king looked into the wide eyes, identical to those of her mother, his wife, and then to the pair of dark nipples that crowned his stepdaughter's breasts. So like the queen's, but somehow more tangible than Tryphaena's lovely mounds, somehow more conducive to a large pair of rapacious hands upon them. He pulled the trembling girl onto his lap and closed his eyes, letting the heat of her lips dissipate any thoughts that might invade this god-sent moment of solace.

The next morning, the king ordered breakfast for two. Thea lay upon a mattress of animal skins—lion, boar, leopard, bear, and softest of all, panther—lost in the luxurious pile and thick musk smell enveloping her. The king had risen and gone to his bath. She imagined herself Aphrodite after she had lain upon a bearskin with the mortal Anchises in his herdsman's hut while bees circled their bodies, though it was thoughts that buzzed about Thea's head. The day before she had wondered in agony about the destiny the Fates had assigned to her; today she was the lover of the king.

The first time, when wordlessly he mounted her, she believed he would snuff the life out of her with the pressure of his august stomach spreading over her small body. In the morning, she took him by surprise, mounting him despite the burning soreness she felt and making vigorous love to him before he could do the same to her. It was a trick she had learned from her mother. One day she had heard the gentle Tryphaena whisper about the problem of Auletes' formidable size to her lady in attendance, whereupon the lady imparted her best advice to the queen. Before he wakes, take the king's member into your mouth and ensure its sturdiness. Then mount him quickly and he will submit to you in the upper position and not wish to roll you to the bottom. Like Thea, Tryphaena was petite and did not enjoy her time under the girth of the king.

What must the talk be upstairs? And why should it matter? She had ensured her good fortune. She had made herself useful, replacing her mother in the eyes of the king, causing him no inconvenience upon the death of his wife. She was certain her position at court was secured.

A council of crones, the meddlesome great-aunts of the queen Tryphaena, awaited Thea in the late afternoon as she, disheveled, exited the hunting room. They demanded, in the fearless way of women past the years of femininity, what business Thea conducted with her mother's husband.

"I am comforting the king," she replied sanctimoniously, brushing them aside and walking haughtily down the hall.

"Performing a duty of state, dear?" one of the ladies said sarcastically as Thea passed.

"Is there blood on the king's sleeping skins, dear?" taunted another.

"She is ruined now. The daughter of Kleopatra Tryphaena, a king's whore."

"Her mother's husband's whore."

"The state's concubine. Send her to the courtesan quarters for costume."

"A disgrace. No one will have her now."

They waited for Thea to turn to them, to answer their accusations, to seek their help for her folly. But she continued to ignore them and walk down the hall.

"Your mother is dead. She died one hour ago."

Still she walked on. The women stared at Thea's long black mane swaying saucily as the girl marched away from their derision, into her future. Deflated by her dismissal, they gingerly knocked on the door to deliver the news of the queen's death to the king.

"You must call me Mother now, Kleopatra," Thea announced to the small princess. The child watched as the Royal Seamstress slipped a deep blue gown over Berenike's head. Heavy with jewels, the garment fell over the girl, its gems against the plush fabric like shining stars on a clear winter night.

"My mother is dead," replied Kleopatra in very precise Greek. "She died five months ago. She is buried in the royal catacombs near the temple of Isis."

It was the morning of the wedding. The black robes of mourning for Tryphaena, worn a shockingly short time, were to be replaced by ceremonial gowns so rich they were considered part of the treasury. Locked away in the national costume dock, they had been retrieved, refurbished, and altered very quickly for the occasion.

Kleopatra was next to be fitted—a prospect she did not like. The miniature gown of heavy linen embroidered with golden threads rested on the mannequin, looking weighty and dangerous.

"Dear little Kleopatra," said Thea, kneeling to the child's level, conjuring with great effort her most solicitous voice. "Do help your mother out on her wedding day and do as you are told."

"My mother is dead. I saw her body."

Berenike rolled her eyes. Thea widened her patient smile. The Royal Seamstress winced, but did not remove her eyes from the garment she pinned at Berenike's side.

"Our sister is our mother now," Berenike declared, admiring herself in the mirror. "It is very simple, Kleopatra. Thea is to marry our father. When I was small, Thea and I used to pretend that she was the mother and I was her baby. Our pretend game has now come true."

"The aunties say it's all wrong. They say mother hasn't been dead long enough for father to marry," Kleopatra said, parroting what had been said in vicious, hushed tones, knowing she was not supposed to repeat it. "They say that mother is cursing Thea for doing this."

"Do they?" shrieked Thea. "What do they know, those old hags? Are you going to listen to them, or to your mother?"

"You are our sister. Our mother is dead," Kleopatra insisted.

"I am going to put an arrow through you, Kleopatra, if you do not stop saying that," said Berenike, lifting the sleeve of her gown and showing Kleopatra the muscles in her upper arm. "And you know I can do it. I am an Amazon princess and you are just a little four-year-old girl."

Kleopatra glared at the taller girl. Berenike was one to be feared. She had read the ancient accounts of the Amazons' training practices with her tutor, Meleager, who indulged her fascination, as it was the only way he could persuade her to read Greek. Convinced that she was descended from these mighty warrior women, Berenike put herself through the same rigors—shooting, riding, swordsmanship—and now she was as lean and muscled as any of the palace boys she challenged to wrestling matches.

"I have taken our mother's name, Kleopatra," Thea said insistently. "Henceforth, I am Kleopatra VI Tryphaena and I am your mother."

"You are Thea," Kleopatra countered, though this time in the Syrian tongue, a language Thea had heard in her childhood, but which she had long ago forgotten.

"Don't you do that!" Thea ordered. "You will speak to me in Greek or you will be silent."

Pleased that she had frustrated Thea, Kleopatra let loose a stream of dialogue in Syrian, all insulting, all aimed at Thea's face.

"Shut up, shut up!" yelled Thea. "Why do you speak these foreign tongues? What is wrong with you?"

Kleopatra smiled innocently. She did not understand how she knew the dialects; they were like magical gifts bequeathed to her during her sleep. Regardless of the language, Kleopatra looked into the eyes of the speaker and understood the meaning of the words. She was three years and a half before she spoke at all, but by the time she was two months shy of her fourth birthday, she was able to mimic full sentences in Egyptian, Syrian, Ethiopian, Troglodyte, Numidian, and Arabic—the languages of the international cast of slaves and attendants in the palace. She did not adopt the heavily accented Macedonian Greek of her family; rather, she imitated the more refined speech of the scholars who visited her father. Word of her linguistic gifts had spread throughout the city like an outbreak of typhoid, and she knew it, taking pleasure in the fact that her sisters, who had thought her dim, were now made to hear others speak of her with awe.

"You are jealous," said Kleopatra quietly. "Because I am special and you are not."

"How are you special, you odd creature?" Thea seethed through her small teeth.

"I am the first of the Ptolemies to speak the language of the Egyptian people. The first in almost three hundred years to speak anything but Greek. That's what the Egyptians say. That I am an oracle." She saw Thea's mounting anger so she added, "Anyone can speak Greek."

Kleopatra heard everything the Egyptian servants said about her. They interpreted this case of a child of the Greek tyrants speaking Egyptian in a number of ominous ways. Perhaps it was evidence of further Greek oppression; the Ptolemies were breeding a new race of rulers who would pose as Egyptian sympathizers and deceive the populace all the more. Or, more optimistically, Egypt had not fallen to the cultural influence of the Greeks, but the children of the tyrants had finally succumbed to the irresistible Egyptian ways. Kleopatra did not know which was correct, but she liked speaking a language her sisters did not understand.

"No one can stand you, you obstinate creature," Thea said, utterly exasperated. "I wish you were slave-born and could be beaten with a whip like you deserve."

"Where are my nurses?" cried Kleopatra, suddenly afraid that she had pushed Thea too far. "I want my nurses."

"They are waiting for you outside this room, and you will not be allowed to go to them until you do as I say. You have exhausted every nurse assigned to you, you strange and terrible child," said Thea.

"And such a pretty little girl," said the Royal Seamstress in a singsong voice that only made Kleopatra angrier. The seamstress turned to the dress Kleopatra was to wear and lifted it from the mannequin. Then she turned to Kleopatra. "Come here, my pretty princess. Come and try on the beautiful little gown."

"No," said the child, adamant.

"Do you see how she is?" complained Thea. "As soon as she is left with a governess, the sneaky thing runs away, or yells at them in the tongues of the demons. She is not even above biting. The nurses give thanks to the gods when they are relieved of the duty." At present, Kleopatra was in the care of a skinny, sullen Egyptian nurse and two West African female slaves, fleet of foot, who handled her with trepidation.

"You are nothing but bad luck," said Berenike. "I think it was you who cursed our mother with the fever that killed her."

"I did not," said Kleopatra defensively. "The Egyptians say that I am gifted by the gods and that I will rise into the sky and become a star." Kleopatra hoped this was not true. She did not want to be a placid object whose only job was to shine in the heavens.

"I wish you would hurry up and go!" said Thea.

"I will not. Because my father would miss me too much if I left." Even the governesses said that. "I am his favorite, you know."

She had heard other rumors, too:

She was a newborn goddess. She was the savior of the Egyptian people who would wear Pharaoh's crown and drive the Greeks out of the land. That one she did not like, for that meant that she would have to cast out her own father. But she would not stop speaking the different tongues, for Auletes himself said that her gifts were a blessing. My princess is touched by the gods, he would say, for the Lord Dionysus speaks to us in all tongues. That is true, Thea would reply. But surely the princess Kleopatra must be instructed to hold hers.

Now Thea put her clenched fists on her waist and faced Kleopatra in a showdown. "Today is my wedding day. I do not have time to play your games."

Thea called the two attendants into the room. "She must be fitted into her gown, even if she has to be held down." The two women exchanged worried looks.

The seamstress held the gown high above Kleopatra's head. "Come, Your Highness," came the voice from behind the dress.

"Come, Kleopatra," Thea said. "Please do as you are told."

The small princess saw the dress coming toward her as if a monster in a dream, a big garish thing waiting to swallow her whole. She raised her arms, but when the fabric fell over her body it felt as if it singed her skin. Believing that it would set her aflame, she tore the gown from her little body before the seamstress could fasten it. She kicked the seamstress hard on the shin, stepped on the bare toe of one of the slaves, spat at Thea, and darted from the room.

"Go!" yelled Thea, and the two slaves ran after her. Thea, Berenike, and the seamstress followed, Thea ordering the hall attendants to pick up the princess's trail, and Berenike, cursing, hampered by the heavy gown tightly basted to her frame.

The child ran through the corridor like a tiny fox chased by a pack of hounds, flying down the stairs, where those on her trail stumbled over themselves. Running straight to the sealed chambers of the queen Tryphaena, Kleopatra pounded her small fist on the door until her hand throbbed. A tall slave scooped her up in his arms, holding her gently until she gave up her ineffective blows and caught hold of the man's chest hairs, clutching as if to a favored blanket.

By Thea's orders, Kleopatra was sedated with a potent infusion of valerian root that stank like rancid vegetables. Groggy, she was laced into her gown while Berenike watched, wearing the face of victory. Kleopatra noted this but did nothing; before she was completely dressed, she was asleep. Hours later she was carried into the ceremony, where she could not participate as planned, but slept in the soft arms of a big slave woman who sat on the floor in the back of the hall. When she awakened the next day, her half sister was queen.

TWO

Kleopatra, why do you enter the Royal Reception with disheveled hair?" asked Thea. "Thank the gods our guest is not already here. What would he think of a royal daughter rushing about with wild and snarly hair like an untamed thing?"

"He would think, Madam, that the daughter had more remarkable pursuits than attending her hair." Kleopatra could barely contain her joy at the way the condescending response sprang into her mind and out of her mouth before she could stop herself.

"At least straighten your crown," Thea hissed.

The nine-year-old Kleopatra despised Thea; she wanted to knock the golden diadem—the crown of their mother—off her head. She wanted to scratch her pretty face, the face Auletes loved to stroke with his fleshy fingers. She could not stand to be near Thea; the sickly smell of her, thick with the scent of lotus oil, made Kleopatra gag, and she wanted to tell Thea so. But Kleopatra was attended by Charmion, her newly assigned Greek governess, who stood primly at her side. The young woman had been presented to Kleopatra as a lady-in-waiting, in the hope that the more dignified position would discourage the princess's notorious acts of rebellion. Though Charmion was in the bloom of her maidenhood, the stern lines of her face were set like ridges in smooth stone; her posture, impossibly erect. She rarely corrected Kleopatra, but could squelch her outbursts with an admonishing look. Kleopatra did not fear her nineteen-year-old companion, but admired her and knew that she should strive to achieve a modicum of Charmion's restraint. In ambitious and pious moments, Kleopatra tried to emulate Charmion, but with very limited success.

The Royal Family sat enthroned in the State Reception Room, the centerpiece of the palace Auletes had built and dedicated to the god Dionysus. A double-headed cobra, the symbol of pharaonic power, crowned each dais, peeking out over each royal head. Splayed before the royal feet were mosaic scenes from the earthly life of the god. Hovering overhead, a snarling bronze eagle, the emblem of the dynasty's founder, Ptolemy I Savior, flexed his impressive wingspan, almost embracing the royals from above. Visitors to the court could not help but notice that both the king and his younger daughter Kleopatra had noses that resembled the eagle's beak.

The king had explained the significance of the eagle to Kleopatra in one of their history lessons. Kleopatra had official lessons with her tutor, but she preferred learning the story of her family's rule over Egypt from the king, who took her into his lap and drank his wine as he unfolded the legend of the Ptolemies. The king allowed this privilege to Kleopatra alone, who stunned the court by gaining admission to the Royal Reception Room at will and jumping onto the person of the king without asking permission.

The king told his daughter in his most serious voice that there were important things about her family that she had to know, crucial information about who she was and where she came from, so that no one would be able to challenge her claim to rule over the land. "Lagos was the father of Ptolemy I, so that Lagos is the official head of our clan," the king explained. "When people say you are of the House of Lagid, you are not to correct them and say that you are of the House of Ptolemy." The king looked down his nose at his daughter. "I warn you because I know how outspoken you can be. If you are going to be so, then at least be knowledgeable."

Lagos, the king said, had heard a rumor that his wife had been having an affair with her cousin Philip, king of Macedonia. Thinking that Ptolemy was really Philip's child, Lagos ordered the infant exposed on a Macedonian mountaintop. An eagle, however, safely delivered him back into the arms of his mother. "We owe our kingdom to that eagle," the king said to his little daughter, and then asked if she could tell him why.

"Oh yes, Father," she eagerly replied. She loved to please Auletes with her interest in family history. "King Philip of Macedonia was the father of Alexander the Great, and Ptolemy grew up to be Alexander's friend and adviser and general. Maybe they were really half brothers and they knew it!" Kleopatra loved secrets that had to be kept. "Alexander conquered Egypt and he became the first Greek pharaoh. The people loved him because he saved them from the Persian oppressors, who were very bad to the Egyptians. When the high priest at Siwah read the oracle that Alexander was the son of Ra, the people accepted him as Pharaoh and God."

"And Alexander ruled over Egypt until he was a very old man, fathering many children and dying at eighty in his sleep," the king said, taunting his daughter.

"No, no, you are teasing me because you think I'm just a child. Alexander went off to claim the rest of the world for Macedonia, and he left Ptolemy in charge of Egypt while he was gone. But he died of a terrible fever in Babylon when he was only thirty-three. That's when Ptolemy went to Memphis and became Pharaoh, because Egypt cannot be without Pharaoh."

"Very good, my little one. I see that even though I am a king and one of the very smartest men in the world, I cannot trick you."

"And when Ptolemy saw that the Egyptians wanted us to follow their customs, he married his son to his daughter, and they ruled after him, and then their sons and daughters ruled after them. And here we are now, more than two hundred fifty years later, sons and daughters of Ptolemy, on the throne of Egypt." She finished her speech without taking a breath.

Kleopatra had great pride in her family and was determined to prove wrong their detractors. She heard terrible things said about the Ptolemies by palace workers who did not know that she understood their language. The Ptolemies, she heard, were not even real Greeks, but mere descendants of the ferocious, ruddy-faced mountain barbarians of Macedonia. To that, her father instructed her to say that the Macedonians brought vigor and wile to a languishing Greek civilization. "Look at Alexandria—a city that exceeds Athens in its offerings of Knowledge and Art and Beauty. Not built by degenerate southern Greeks, but by Macedonians. Our Mouseion puts Plato's Academy and the Lyceum of Aristotle to shame! Why, the Macedonians revitalized the Greek world, a world that would have died out with those tyrannical bastards who called for the death of Socrates," Auletes insisted, his face flushing with the color of conviction. "Alexander—not some effete Athenian—kept the Greek world alive!"

"I see, Father," Kleopatra said. Then she confessed what else she had heard: The Ptolemies were inbred freaks who misunderstood Pharaoh's custom of calling his wife Sister, and began the shocking tradition of marrying sibling to sibling. "The damned Egyptians are ignorant of their own history," the king retorted, for the great Ptolemy, a historian himself, would not have made such a mistake. But Auletes did not seem hurt by what his subjects said about him, and it made Kleopatra wonder whether her father possessed enough pride. She had just begun to read the books of history Ptolemy had written, and she was sure, from his portraits of both himself and of Alexander, that they would never have tolerated the abuse her father's subjects heaped upon his character.

Some said that the Ptolemies made up the story of the eagle to impress upon their subjects their direct lineage from Alexander, but Kleopatra did not believe it. The busts of King Philip and the busts of Ptolemy I all demonstrated the identical nose—the one that now presented itself on both her and her father.

Auletes was so pleased with the conviction with which Kleopatra told the story of the eagle that he made her repeat it for his guests. Kleopatra hoped she would be asked to perform today, for she had heard the visitor was a Roman. Like her father, she loved showing off for Romans, because they were less educated than Greeks and easier to impress. Kleopatra always paid dearly for her bright moments at court, however, when later, Berenike would find her in the nursery, and when no one was looking, twist her arm and call her a dirty Roman-lover. Now Kleopatra tried to sneak a furtive stare at her sister to gauge her humor.

Fourteen and sullen, Berenike sat next to Thea, sweaty in the corset Thea had cajoled her to wear, sucking on a lock of hair as if she were still a child. Her other hand stroked the dagger she kept sheathed beneath her long dress. Berenike preferred the short, ungirdled chiton of young Greek children, but Thea and Auletes, already cognizant of Berenike's value in the matrimonial market, no longer allowed her to dress like an unruly feral thing. According to tradition, the eldest daughter should be married to her brother, but the new baby, Ptolemy XIII, was still in the cradle. With the present queen only one and twenty, it did not seem intelligent to let the beautiful Berenike linger unmarried. "You must exhibit the qualities of a young queen," Thea told her repeatedly. "I *am* a queen," she would reply as if in a dream, and to Auletes' annoyance. "I am Penthesilea, queen of the Amazons."

Meleager, the eunuch courtier, adviser to the royals, and tutor to the two princesses, sat next to Berenike, though one step lower, according to custom and protocol. A tall, smooth-skinned man in his forties, he had yet to succumb to the paunch eunuchs experienced in middle age. He was said to keep himself fit by dieting with religious fervor, exercising daily at the gymnasium, and engaging in orgiastic sex. He was officious, princely, and cunning, and Kleopatra did not like him. She sensed his condescension to her father, whom Meleager, punctilious about dynastic history, never forgave for being a bastard king.

Auletes briefed the family on the day's visitor, a Roman who had been, in younger days, a high-ranking officer in Crassus's army. Now he conducted diplomatic affairs and had a small import business. "I am told he wants my permission to pass through Egyptian waters with spices from the Cinnamon Country without paying the usual duties," Auletes chuckled. "It is quite possible that I shall grant him this privilege, but I suspect there will be a price for him to pay."

Kleopatra understood his meaning; the king often cultivated visitors begging favor for his intelligence operations in Rome. The Romans had trampled over every one of Egypt's neighboring countries, invading their lands, installing a fat Roman governor, and collecting outrageous taxes to be sent back to Rome. To avoid this unfortunate situation, Auletes depended on a network of spies in

Rome. He apprehended what the Romans might want from his rich land and his ancient treasury, and furnished it immediately, before they had to send an army to demand it.

"It is far easier to bribe a rich man than a poor one," the king continued, tutoring his family. "The rich are of a character to be motivated by money. The poor never lose their bitterness and are more wont to betray. The wealthy have much to lose and restrain such emotion, making them more levelheaded and reliable."

"And what might this Roman do for us?" Thea asked with the sharp tongue of a woman who had grown confident of her stature.

"My dear wife, are we not under threat of Roman annexation? Has Marcus Crassus not introduced a bill into the senate that would make Egypt a Roman territory? Do the Romans not wish to control our grain supply to feed their armies?" Auletes breathed deeply, weary of explaining to his young wife his propitiatory policies toward Rome. "Have the Romans not subjugated every neighboring country, including Syria? Our guest today is a diplomat. Need I say more?"

"We are the descendants of Alexander," Thea said, her face upturned, showing the king her nostrils. "Why do we not use our silver and our gold to raise an army to confront the Romans? Why must we always cower before Rome?"

Kleopatra glared at her stepmother, wondering how she could think she possessed the wisdom to challenge the king.

"You are young and naive, my dear Thea. The Romans fight because they believe it is their right to dominate the world. Paid mercenaries will never defeat such men. The gods, at present, are with Rome. Let us not challenge the gods, but negotiate successfully with those they have chosen."

"The blood of Alexander is sluggish in your veins, my king, while it quickens in mine," Thea said defiantly.

"My dear, your Greek pride could cost us the throne. Do you really believe the Romans will lay down their desire to control Egypt because of our illustrious heritage? We are in trouble. Before he died, our predecessor—our half-witted half brother—wrote a will leaving our entire nation to Rome. The Roman senate has repeatedly tried to use it as a claim on our kingdom."

"And the citizens pulled him out of the gymnasium and slit his throat," Thea yelled. "So much for Roman protection! Roman alliance!"

Auletes raised his hands, fingers shaking like bangles. "The people slit his throat because the corrupt thing was a menace. And thank the gods they did, for had they not, I would not be king, and you, my beautiful wife, would certainly not be queen."

"Majesty," Meleager interrupted. "The murder *was* an act of rebellion against Rome. Whether Greek or Egyptian, the Alexandrian people have a notorious distaste for negotiation with Rome. The rumor that you are going to allow Rome to annex Egypt has spread to every quarter of the city, and everywhere there is unrest. The Greek citizens do not wish to placate Rome, nor do the Egyptians. Perhaps the queen is not entirely wrong. Perhaps it is time to challenge the Romans."

"Have you not heard the proverb, eunuch? 'Whom the Romans wish to make kings they make kings. Whom they will to depose, they depose.' I do not *wish* to be deposed," Auletes said hotly. "I do not wish to be exiled to some ugly black rock in the Aegean while a greedy Roman governor gets rich on the treasures of my ancestors. I like my head very much. I enjoy my fat body very much. And I do not wish for the two to be separated. How they would miss each other!" Auletes rolled his eyes to the back of his head as if undergoing decapitation.

In complete defiance of court protocol, Kleopatra jumped into his lap. He scooped her into his arms and hugged her close to him, brushing her long hair away from her face. He continued, "In the year before this little princess was born, the Roman army crucified the six thousand rebellious slaves who followed Spartacus the Gladiator. They hung the bodies on either side of the Appian Way, lining all three hundred miles of the road. I believe they left them there for six months as a warning. That is Roman vengeance, my dear Thea. I do not wish to see your pretty face rotting on a cross. And I do not wish to see myself hanging next to you."

"May I remind you, Your Majesty, that we are not slaves," said Thea.

"Father, tell us the story of Spartacus," Kleopatra requested, knowing that it made Thea queasy.

"Not again," cried Thea, grabbing her stomach, making Kleopatra wonder if she was pregnant again, having already given birth to two brats, one after the other, the girl Arsinoe, who was two, and the infant boy.

"Six months, my dear Thea," Auletes said pointedly. "Have you seen a body six months after death? A body that has not been embalmed in the Egyptian way but simply left unattended? It's not a pretty sight."

"Will you tell us the story, Father?" the princess asked again.

"I shall let our guest tell the tale, Kleopatra, for it is said that he fought with Crassus against the slave army."

She gasped, eagerly returning to her dais. To the unfettered imagination of the princess, these bestial Romans were unspeakably glamorous.

Kleopatra caught the Roman sneaking a coy smile at her when the king was not looking. She liked having his attention and smiled back. He was robust like all prosperous Romans and wore the thin purple stripe of the equestrian class on his toga. Not a patrician, Auletes had said, but just as rich. Like the rest of his countrymen, his demeanor at a foreign court, though solicitous, had the usual underlying Roman superiority.

"My daughter is most anxious to hear your tales of vanquishing the slave Spartacus," said the king in a merry tone.

"Your Majesty, I come on urgent business that must be discussed before we engage in pleasurable storytelling."

"Oh yes, my advisers have briefed me on your request to abolish the import duties on cinnamon. I am certain we can work out a reasonable and mutually beneficial arrangement," replied Auletes.

"Sire, I have in my breast pocket a letter to you from Pompey."

"From the great general himself?" asked the king, sitting straighter in his throne.

"I have just seen Pompey in Judaea. He is at war with the Jews and requests that you demonstrate your friendship by sending him the supplies and soldiers he requires to subdue that stubborn nation of rebels." The Roman handed the king a letter, which Auletes read to himself. Kleopatra noticed that Thea was squeezing her earlobe repeatedly, a habit she had when she was anxious. The king and queen had already fought much over Auletes' friendship with Pompey after Auletes had given a banquet in Pompey's honor the year before. Auletes had fretted over every detail of the meal, demanding that each of the one thousand guests' gold cups be replaced with a fresh vessel at all seven courses. "How can you celebrate his victory over Syria?" Thea had demanded. "Over our own blood?"

"So that he will think twice about spilling *our* blood, my dear queen, yours and mine and that of our precious children," the king had replied.

Auletes folded the letter in his hand. "Nurturing my friendship with Pompey the Great is of utmost importance to me. You may reply that I am sending immediately the amount he requests in gold and an army of eight thousand."

"But my dear," Thea began, her face at once full of apology and demand, "should we not consider the ramifications from our own citizens before we leap to aid our friend Pompey? This is a sensitive issue. The Palestine was once an Egyptian territory. You see, sir," she said, turning to the Roman, "the Alexandrians have dreadful ways of showing displeasure with the ruling family. A riot, a knife across the throat when one least expects it. I am sure you understand that we must act with their good opinion in mind."

Kleopatra rocked in her seat until she could no longer keep quiet. Who did Thea think she was to openly contradict her father? She knew it was not her place to speak, but she would defend her father anyway. "Madam, Pompey is the most important man in the world. Isn't it an honor that he wants Father to be his friend?"

"At least one person in my family understands both politics and friendship," said the king, looking accusingly at Thea and Meleager. "Even a nine-year-old sees that one must show allegiance to the man who subdued the pirates of the Mediterranean and vanquished the mighty king Mithridates of Pontus."

The Roman saluted the king. "That is what Pompey so hoped, Your Majesty. That the great King Ptolemy would acknowledge his many services to the nations of the Mediterranean and would repay him with a pledge of support."

Kleopatra knew how much her father worried about what the Romans thought of him. She wanted her father to bask in the praise of the great man Pompey without further interference from the pompous eunuch and her ignorant stepmother. Before Meleager or Thea could rebuke him, she said, "Now, sir, will you *please* tell us the story of Spartacus? Were you really there? Did you see him? Did you meet him?"

"Yes, yes, let us proceed with the story of the wicked slave," said the king. "Tell us, good man, what did he look like?"

The Roman, too, seemed anxious to end the business at hand while he still had the king's guarantee. He stood and breathed deeply, the air pulling him to his full height. "Spartacus was tall. Strong. Proud. An Ionian, some say. Others say he was a Thracian, and others, a Macedonian."

Kleopatra beamed. "Father, might Spartacus have been our cousin?"

Berenike grimaced, her first animated expression of the morning; Thea and Meleager laughed condescendingly. Kleopatra was wounded by their insincere tone, by their derision at her mistake, and she despised them the more. "Spartacus was no ordinary slave," she shouted much too loudly, sinking into her throne.

The Roman rescued her from embarrassment, sweeping his toga into his left arm, leaving his right to gesture, telling the story as if to her alone. "We had the rebel slave army outnumbered ten to one, trapped in the mountains of Lucania. Crassus demanded surrender, but the thieves came crashing through our lines, ready to fight and to die like gladiators.

"It was then that I spotted him—as tall as a Titan, and as bold as Poseidon. With a chest like the side of a cliff and an arm like Zeus," he said. "The demon had two of my young officers pinned against a rock. He pushed one of them into the other and slew the both of them with a single thrust of his sword."

The princess held her breath while he continued.

"Three of my men attacked him, striking him in the chest, slashing his knees. But the monster began to fight *again*, flashing his sword about though he could hardly move from his spot." The Roman lifted one side of his toga daintily to reveal a jagged scar on his thigh, a white lightning bolt against his weathered skin. "He cut me here," he said indignantly.

Fueled by the memory, he delivered an impassioned finale to his story: how brave Spartacus refused to give up, still swinging his sword at the men, *still* drawing noble Roman blood; how a Roman centurion of superior size and strength, with a final, mortal blow, spilled the slave's entrails, slicing him from chest to groin. The Roman made an imaginary slash in the air and then raised his arm as if saluting Kleopatra with a sword. "That, my princess, was the end of your Spartacus."

Kleopatra released her breath. Silence in the room. Thea signaled for a slave to fan her. Auletes sighed. Berenike squirmed in her seat, unimpressed. No one spoke.

"Say it again!" squealed Kleopatra, jumping out of her throne and knocking her crown askew against the cobra above her.

Charmion, stiff-backed, motioned for Kleopatra to take her seat. It was one thing for a princess to indulge in the grotesque imagery of Homer, but quite another to listen to specious stories told by these unreliable visitors who embellished the slave leader's capacities. "Sir, I thought that no one knew the identity of the slave, that his men never gave him up, even in death," Charmion said.

"My dear young woman, of course they denied that he was Spartacus. But we knew better. His powers gave him away," he said, clearly perturbed to be questioned.

Kleopatra waited impatiently for a turn to talk. "Father, please may our guest tell the story again? Please?" she implored.

With a nod from the king, the Roman reenacted the scene, this time playing all the parts—the centurions, the slain boys, Spartacus—dying dramatically at the princess's feet, his large body spread over a mosaic of Dionysus entering Thebes disguised as a mortal.

"I should like to have known Spartacus," Kleopatra said to Auletes while slaves helped the guest to his feet and straightened his

garments. He was offered a bowl of wine, which he greedily con-
sumed.

"Is that so, my princess?"

"Yes." She was serious as only a young child can be, wrinkling her
brow with the sincerity of her thought. "I would have taught him
to be more sensible. Didn't he know that he shouldn't defy Rome?"

Berenike, quiet for so long, suddenly sat up in her chair, snapping
at her sister. "Why not? What is wrong with defying Rome?"

"Because he got caught and died. That's why not," Kleopatra
retorted. "No one may defy Rome. That's what Father says."

"Perhaps freedom is a greater condition than life itself," said
Thea. "I know I have always thought as much." She looked pointedly at the king.

"These are questions for the philosophers, my dears. I shall have
to send all of you to the Mouseion to study with the rest of the
scholars," the king said, wishing to change the course of the discussion. "As you are so fond of Spartacus, tell us what would you have
done with the slave if he had turned his lion's courage against *this*
throne?"

"I would have done just as the Romans did," Kleopatra replied
to Auletes' satisfaction, though privately she was thinking that she
and Spartacus might have fallen in love and started their own country. "It would be my duty."

The king posed the same question to Berenike. "And you, daughter?"

"I should have spared the Greek slave Spartacus and crucified the
Romans," she smirked.

The king's black eyes shot out like locusts. "You are banished to
your chamber, Princess Berenike, for insubordination before the
crown and for insulting our exalted Roman guest." Kleopatra was
grateful that the king's anger was not directed at her. His thick lips
were thrust forward as if to entrap invisible food. "You shall not be
fed for two days. Now leave." To Meleager: "Go with her, Tutor, and
bid her to mind her foul tongue."

Berenike marched from the room, leaving the Roman guest unac-
knowledged, and ignoring the peeved eunuch trailing her steps.

Secretly, Kleopatra was full of glee. She made a private prayer to the goddess that Auletes would marry Berenike to a very ugly foreigner, who would force her to put away her weapons, bear his children, and learn one of the many languages she considered beneath her.

"You will excuse the child," Auletes said apologetically. "She is quite contrary. I fear she suffers from a mental disorder."

"A spirited girl," commented the Roman in his best Greek. "Very grand. Very beautiful, if I may be so bold, Your Royal Grace."

Auletes regarded his guest for an uncomfortably long time. "Are you a man who hears the call of the Muses?"

The Roman stared at him quizzically, as if challenged by a clever teacher in an oral exam. "The Muses, Sire?"

"Like Hesiod, I am haunted by those beguiling ladies. Euterpe in particular. The goddess of the flute stalks me, even in my dreams, beckoning me out of my night reverie and into her spell. She is merciless in her pursuit. I am her slave." Auletes sighed dramatically, dropping his great head and folding his hands on his lap. His dark curls fell forward. He threw them back with his hand and continued. "Terpsichore, yes, she too has me in the grip of her enchantment. I am a dancer, you know. A king over men by birth, an artist by nature. A constant conundrum. All aspects demand. All must be satiated."

The Roman had heard the king was a lunatic, a sissy who played songs and danced, but he had no idea that he would have to bear witness to the spectacle.

"I wonder, would you like to hear me play the flute?" Auletes asked the guest coyly, as if introducing the concept of sexual intercourse to a virgin.

"Oh, yes, Father!" Kleopatra interjected, clasping her small hands together. "Please play for us!"

"It is time for your lessons, Kleopatra. Meleager shall be waiting for you," said Thea, not looking at the princess but shooting a luminous smile in the direction of the guest, blinding him with the white perfection of her twenty-one-year-old teeth and the ripe succulence of her reddened lips.

"Your Excellency is a most gifted musician," Thea continued, causing her husband to blush. Causing the *king*, Auletes, to blush, and taking away the attention of the princess's new Roman friend. She is a menace to my happiness, Kleopatra thought, and I have no power to make her go away.

"My dear, you are too kind," replied Auletes. They had rehearsed the scene before countless visitors of the past. Modestly, he added, "My family indulges me."

"Should not Kleopatra join her sister and Meleager?" Thea asked of Charmion. "The children have overstayed their time at court this morning."

Before Charmion could reply, Kleopatra said, "Madam, is it not equally a lesson to be in the company of a gentleman who is friend and kinsman to the great men of Rome?"

The king smiled at his daughter. "The child has a point," he said to Thea. "Meleager sings hymns of praise to the dead. Our new friend has active commerce with the living."

A small victory, the princess thought. Small, but each one significant.

A slave carried in Auletes' flute, an ebony cylinder with ivory inlays and golden keys, holding it like a sacramental relic. The king addressed his Muse. "Cruel lady, Divine Grace, whimsical One, bless me with your gifts so that I may please my god, the Lord Dionysus, with my song." Auletes placed a hand tenderly over his heart. He closed his eyes and recited the details of his vision. "Ah, there she is, dancing before my eyes ever so delicately, luring me into her spell. Always she threatens escape! Inconstant lover! Stay, Lady. Do not flee. Linger with me a while so that I may pay tribute to the god and entertain our guest."

Taking in a copious amount of air, Auletes began to sound a reedy melody, music to entice the god to continue his good fortune. He concentrated fervently, batting his eyelashes when he strained to reach the upper regions of the instrument's capacity, furrowing his brow and bending his knees until his belly rested on his thighs to hit the low notes.

Kleopatra swayed dreamily. Her love for her father swelled, exceeding even her admiration for his gifts.

THREE

The sounds of the king offering his gift to the Greek god wafted through the palace and into the upper chambers. Egyptian, Libyan, Ethiopian, and Nubian servants laid down the tools of their tasks and listened to the music, while in a chamber tucked away at the end of a corridor, it resonated without harmony for an angry Macedonian princess and her besmirched eunuch mentor.

He was insulted—he, the keeper of Ptolemaic tradition. That was how Meleager regarded himself, for it befitted his history as a noble courtier of altered sex. "We have been here as long as the Ptolemies," he told himself. "We are high priests in the temples and shrines, we are advisers to kings, regents and tutors to the royal children of each generation, keepers of the oral history of the family, and arbiters of court ceremony."

In each generation, Meleager's family, longtime aristocrats, selected a special male child to serve the goddess. At seventeen years old, Meleager, the favorite son, entered the mysteries of Kybele. "You are to become the consort of the goddess," his mother told him. "You shall be the earthly representation of the god Attis, Kybele's priest, lover, and servant. There is no higher honor. Besides, it is the quickest way to a high position at court."

All his life Meleager had dreamed of being chosen to represent

Attis, son of the virgin Nana, He-who-is-fatherless, the beautiful youth who offered his masculinity so that he could marry no mortal woman but only the goddess. He was the savior god who was sacrificed by the people, castrated, crucified on a pine tree, and whose very blood washed over the earth and purified the land. The god whose flesh, in the form of flatbread, nourished the people. The most holy god who was raised from the dead on the third day, whose resurrection demonstrated the power of the Mother Goddess. The god who was carried to Rome with her after the defeat of Hannibal to give her honor for the victory.

On a sultry summer evening lost to the past, the young Meleager donned a wreath of violets—the flower that sprang from the spilt blood of Attis—and drank the solution given to him by the priest that made him see hallucinations from the life of the god: his sexual love with the goddess; the sacrifice of his body and his blood; his flesh and blood sprinkled over the crops, and the crops shooting up in response. From somewhere he could not see, Meleager heard drums, cymbals, horns, and flutes, making a symphony to the glories of the god. The music seemed to flow from his own heartbeat, from his own veins. The priestesses tossed their heads to the pounding drums, the priests slashed their arms and chests with knives and shards, and Meleager—drugged, inflamed, impervious to pain— took his testicles in his left hand and, with his right, castrated himself with a sacred dagger. He felt an agony too severe to be described as mere pain, passed out, and awoke two days later in the care of a physician. Death and rebirth, he had said to himself upon regaining consciousness, just like the god Attis. Now his genitals rested in the cave of the goddess as an offering, and he served the court of Auletes.

Meleager believed that it was neither his family nor the Royal Family who chose him for service, but the Mother Goddess herself; therefore, he tolerated the disdain of no one. "I took my evening meal with the princesses and the queen," he would say in response to derision of his kind. "Where did you dine?"

"Alexander himself once took a eunuch as a lover," he would remind those Greeks who criticized the tradition of altering men, those who considered themselves above him because they retained a

few additional ounces of flesh between their legs. They were foolish enough to believe that manhood and pleasure were centered in
those small round saggy things. Was it not the great conqueror
Cyrus—hero of Alexander—who praised the strength and loyalty
of the castrated male? Cyrus observed that castrated horses ceased
to bite, but were not deprived of their strength. On the contrary, in
times of both war and hunting, they still preserved in their souls a
spirit of rivalry. Cyrus found the same qualities in the eunuchs who
served him in battle and at court. Unencumbered by the sentimental attachment to either wife or offspring, the eunuch was free to
offer unqualified fidelity to his master. So what if the eunuch lacked
the ideal manly musculature? As Cyrus said, on the battlefield, steel
makes the weak equal to the strong. There were many battlefields in
Alexandria, and many different kinds of metal. Meleager had chosen the object of his fierce loyalty. He was armed with knowledge
and ready for battle.

Pity the fools who were deceived by the eunuchs' *lack*. Meleager
lacked nothing. He wore extravagant jewels bestowed upon him by
the royals for his service. He lived in lavish apartments adjacent to
the Inner Palace. His view of the harbor was dazzling, his cooks
second only to the queen's. Curiosity-seekers of both sexes admired
and courted him for his boyish good looks, for his sophistication,
and for his access to the Royal Family. Mature ladies of the court
came to his apartments at night complaining that they no longer
cared for vigorous intercourse but sought more delicate pleasures.
Virile and beautiful youths who trained for the Royal Macedonian
Household Troops requested audiences to ask his advice on how to
behave in the presence of the king and often ended up in his bed.
Even members of the king's Order of the First Kinsmen dined with
him, discussing protocol and policy, and then sealed the friendship
in an evening of sexual delight. He experienced passion and he
could give pleasure, even if he could not impregnate.

Meleager had no legitimate claim upon the elongated, regal
young girl who paced his room in anger, yet he knew in his heart
that she belonged to him in the same way that he belonged to the
Mother Goddess. The goddess had selected him for service to this
girl whom she had favored to rule Egypt. He could not attach him-

self to the girl as a lover, for the female Ptolemies usually remained chaste until marriage. He could not claim her as a husband, for he possessed no royal blood with which he might petition for her hand. But he knew that Berenike was the true queen of Egypt, that her beautiful stepmother had less claim to the throne than she, and that by Thea's treachery in seducing the king, she had intercepted Berenike's rightful position as Auletes' co-regent. These things he knew because the goddess had revealed them to him, her servant. But he could not reveal them to the girl because she had attached herself to Thea in childhood and remained blind to her duplicity. Instead, he pretended the same loyalty to the queen in order to stay intimate with the princess. One day, he would reveal to her the goddess's will.

"My father is a fool," said Berenike, pacing. She removed her dagger from its sheath and sliced the air in crisscross motions as she stalked the chamber. "An overblown, Roman-loving fool." Her long dress, open at the sides, followed her, outlining the burgeoning woman's form. The eunuch felt a stirring in his bereft lower region. Already she was taller than Thea, though not as beautiful in the feminine way. Her eyes were bright, angry, vigilant. Her teeth and lips were too large on her young face, Meleager observed, but in years to come, when the rest of her caught up with her features, they would serve her handsomely.

"Your father is king," Meleager replied evenly. It would not do to say disparaging things against the monarch, however impeachable his policies.

"The men in our family are fat and stupid. They say it is because we marry our brothers and that the intermarriage has ruined the men. My father is evidence of this, do you not think?"

It was true; for the last many generations, the Ptolemies had produced idiot men, obese, indulgent, strange. "I shall not speak against the Crown, princess. *History* may substantiate, however, that in recent years the Ptolemy kings have been rather more stout of body than of heart. Yet incestuous marriage has not diminished the caliber of the female. Without fail, each generation has produced a Ptolemaic queen of extraordinary intelligence."

The princess stopped pacing, pointing her knife at the tutor. "You sound as if you are speaking of farm animals. You had better remember that the women in my family are queens of an ancient dynasty. Men do not breed us as they breed hunting dogs."

He might have been angry at the haughty girl, but he was aware that it was he who had instilled in her this pride and arrogance. "Princess Berenike, forgive me for my indelicacy."

"You do not have to be delicate with me, Tutor," she said, still brandishing the knife at him. "But you do have to remember to whom you speak."

Berenike whisked the front panel of her dress aside, exposing the leather garter on her thigh. She placed the knife back in its sheath and sat on a divan, ceremoniously smoothing her gown over her legs. Meleager produced a long scroll that seemed to have the weight of a saber.

"Oh, not more family history. Must we incessantly resurrect the dead? Why am I not free to spend the day hunting?" Berenike asked, contrite.

Meleager continued to unroll the large document, struggling without his scribe present to help. It would not do to have an interloper today. He stretched the papyrus lengthwise to reveal an illustrated chart of the Ptolemy dynasty, with small, painstaking portraits of each royal in the family tree. He braced it on a wooden stand, which held taut.

"You will enjoy today's lesson. We are going to study the female line."

Berenike settled into her seat. "Then let us pay attention to the interesting ones, and leave out the fools who fell to the poison of courtiers."

A rap at the door interrupted the tutorial. The small princess entered, trailed by Charmion. "The princess Kleopatra joins her sister for the lesson," she said formally to the eunuch, escorting the princess to her seat. Charmion and Meleager bowed stiffly to each other.

"Stay with me," Kleopatra urged her governess. She was never more nervous than in the company of her sister.

"Why must you always be a disagreeable baby?" asked Berenike.

"I am not a baby," she replied vehemently. "I am merely smaller than you, and I shall speak to Father about this."

"The world awaits his response to your complaint," Berenike said dryly.

Charmion exited promptly, and Kleopatra, though still afraid, summoned into her face as much spite as she could. She saw the outline of the sheath under her sister's dress and wondered if Berenike would dare murder her, and if so, would the eunuch move to prevent it? But presently, Berenike suffered more from ennui than from anger.

"Our tutor is giving the history of the Macedonian queen," she said. "Which we must learn in the unlikely event that father does not lose the throne, and I actually *become* a Macedonian queen. Proceed," she commanded the eunuch.

Meleager took a breath. "We are going to begin with Olympias, the mother of Alexander."

"Everyone feared Olympias," interjected Berenike. "She wore wild snakes in her hair!"

"Yes, supposedly in tribute to Dionysus. In fact, she wished to frighten her husband, Philip of Macedonia, a devout polygamist who married indiscriminately for political alliance and bred bastards with every barbarian wife he took."

Meleager explained that Olympias's main objective was to see that her favorite son, Alexander, became king. "The Macedonian court was an unruly place, and there was a lot of competition. Philip had an older wife, Eurydice, an Illyrian warrior woman." The eunuch pointed to Philip's senior wife on the dynastic tree. "She and her daughter Cynane used to go into battle with Philip for the sole purpose of killing rival queens. Olympias had to become just as fierce, and quickly."

"No wonder Alexander fell in love with an Amazon!" Berenike exclaimed. Alexander's supposed love affair with the warrior was her favorite part of his legend.

"Alexander was quite used to fierce women. He knew that it was his mother who put him on the throne. They say she had Philip murdered to ensure it."

"Really?" asked Kleopatra, suddenly more interested in the long-dead queen. She did not like to demonstrate interests in common with her sister, but she could never stifle her aroused curiosity.

"Oh yes. Olympias had her way. Greek queens inevitably do," he said slowly, piercingly, aiming his words straight into Berenike's eyes as if he might plant them there. "This is the blood of your mothers. When the king does not rule wisely, or when the proper heirs are threatened, it is up to the queen to see that tradition is carried out, that the will of the gods is done."

"So it is up to Thea to either guide my father's hand in policy or to dispose of him if she cannot?" Berenike asked.

"You think Thea could murder Father? Father is a king. He would kill her!" said Kleopatra, inflamed.

Berenike laughed. "He would have to catch her first."

Meleager hoped he had not been too indiscreet. "Your Highnesses, please do not misinterpret. A queen does not lightly murder her husband. A queen employs wisdom, restraint, and the divine inspiration the gods bestow upon women of royal heritage. Only in extreme cases does a queen resort to violence against her king."

"Is my father's supplication to the Roman Pompey an extreme case?"

Meleager hesitated; Berenike had never asked such direct questions. There was a story he wanted to tell her, but he was saving it for the right time—a time when his liege would make the proper connections. Berenike was only two months fourteen. And he did not want to say it in front of the younger one, whose mind sometimes seemed to drift, but then later would spit out a piece of information that he thought she had neither heard nor understood. Still, she was only nine. "Princesses, do you know the story of Ptolemy VIII Euergetes?"

"Our ancestor who was called Potbelly?" Berenike asked.

Meleager nodded, pointing to the eighth Ptolemaic king. Berenike and Kleopatra leaned forward to see the likeness of the long-dead king, whose belly hung to his knees. Meleager observed that they did not look like sisters. Berenike was tall and fair of complexion like her Macedonian ancestors; Kleopatra was small, and had inherited the olive skin of her Syrian grandmother.

"You can see by the illustration of his person where he got his nickname. I wish to discuss Potbelly's wife and sister, Kleopatra II, a brilliant woman. She would have been your great-great-grandmother." Meleager explained that Kleopatra II first married her older brother, Philometer, and that the two became king and queen. But when Philometer died in battle, certain factions insisted that the queen obey custom and marry her other brother.

"The dreaded Potbelly!" exclaimed Kleopatra.

"Disgusting," said Berenike.

"Nonetheless, she did her duty, and continued to administrate the government while Potbelly indulged his insatiable appetites." The two princesses' eyes spread wide, awaiting lurid detail, but dignity and protocol prevented the eunuch from elaborating. "Suffice it to say that he weighed four hundred pounds and sired many bastard children."

The sisters wrinkled their noses.

"Shortly after Queen Kleopatra II married Potbelly, he decided to rid the kingdom of any vestige of his dead brother, who had banished him to Cyprus. He massacred philosophers, artists, scholars, courtiers of noble Greek birth, anyone who had sworn allegiance to the former king."

"What a horrid man," said Kleopatra, wishing that she could slay the nasty king, for she loved philosophers and artists, the most talkative and amusing people at court.

"That is not all. He then betrayed his wife with her *own daughter,* his niece, Kleopatra III. Whether the king seduced the girl or the girl seduced the king, it is not known." Meleager looked at Berenike, who remained impassive. "Suffice it to say that while her mother was distracted, trying to save the necks of her allies, the disloyal daughter made her way into the king's bed."

Meleager paused to allow Berenike to draw what parallel she might. *The disloyal daughter made her way to the king's bed. The disloyal daughter made her way to the king's bed.* The eunuch chanted this in his head.

"What did the queen do? Did she not have his throat slit while he slept?" asked Berenike, rubbing her sheathed knife. "I would have had the fat bastard murdered."

The eunuch was amused that Berenike misplaced her outrage in the annals of history, but could not find a place for it in her own circumstances. The younger one, however, cocked her pea-size head to the side. Perhaps she had stopped listening altogether. "Just when Potbelly believed he had gotten away with his scheme, Kleopatra II gathered the generals of the army about her and chased the wicked king and princess out of the country. Later, she actually reconciled with the monster. At least publicly. The queen knew that Potbelly could not last," said Meleager. "He died short-ly after his return to Egypt, and Kleopatra II ruled alone once more, dominating her irksome daughter. She ruled for fifty-seven years. A fine reward, I should say."

"A fine reward?" The story left Berenike mortified. "She is less remembered by the people than her worthless husband. Do the peo-ple make shrines to her for her sacrifices? No. But they continue to make jokes about Potbelly, the Malefactor."

"That is because after she died, her daughter destroyed her mother's statues, had her name removed from official documents and histories, retracted her coinage, and put to death anyone who mentioned her."

Kleopatra turned to her sister, who held herself off her seat with her hands as if ready to spring upon a prey. "So Kleopatra III was exactly like Thea."

Meleager felt a chill in his chest. Berenike leapt to her feet and faced her sister. "What do you mean? Thea has put no one to death."

"She took father away before mother was even dead. That is what everyone in the palace says." Berenike's eyes narrowed, and Kleopatra tensed her body, ready to be punched. Kleopatra hoped Meleager would not let Berenike hurt her. But she was tired of Berenike think-ing that Thea was so wonderful, better even than their true mother.

"You are an ignorant child. All you do is eavesdrop on stupid Egyptian servants who know even less than you do," Berenike hissed. "If Thea hadn't married father we would have been sent away. Don't you know what kings do when their queens die? They take new queens and have new heirs with them, and the children of the dead queen are sent away or killed. You are only here because of Thea. She married father for all of us, you stupid child."

Kleopatra felt hot tears clouding her eyes. Berenike was the stupid one if she believed what Thea said. Still, Berenike was older. Might she know something that Kleopatra did not? "Father loves me. He would never send me away."

"So you think," retorted Berenike. She put her foot on Kleopatra's chair and pulled out her knife. Kleopatra threw her arms up to shield herself, but Berenike merely laughed. She pushed Kleopatra's chair backward with her foot, shaking it while Kleopatra's head reeled and her legs dangled helplessly. Then she tipped it upright with a thud, spun around, and put her knife through Potbelly's bloated stomach.

"There," she said, admiring her incision in the scroll. "Lessons are over for the day."

FOUR

"Whenever the Ptolemies get into trouble with the people, they have themselves deified. It's a time-honored tradition," Meleager explained to the Grand Marshal as he adjusted the pointy horse-ears atop the military man's head. They were in the eunuch's apartments dressing for the Grand Procession, the opulent parade in which Auletes would present himself as the god Dionysus. "The Egyptians might despise the Ptolemies, but they still believe that their rulers are their link to the gods, that they *are* the gods manifest in human bodies. The Ptolemies have used that tradition to their benefit for three centuries. It's enabled them to get away with murder—and more."

"It's an exercise of the imagination to see the old flute player as a god," laughed the General. "I'll wager that Dionysus never exceeded two hundred pounds, even after a good feast."

The eunuch smiled. "By the way, the robe of Silenus is stunning on you."

"Are you sure?" The thirty-year-old Graeco-Egyptian had just been awarded the rank of general in the king's Royal Macedonian Household Troops, a position procured for him at so young an age by Meleager. For his trouble, the eunuch extracted the price of weekly nocturnal visits, which the General did not seem to mind.

Indeed, he said he liked spending evenings away from the noise and rigor of military life; liked falling asleep in the quiet palace apartment listening to the waves cuddle the king's private harbor, the sea breezes caressing his skin as he dozed naked in the eunuch's arms.

"Am I not ridiculous in this costumery?"

"Hardly. You're regal. King of the Satyrs, companion to Dionysus."

"If you say so." The General accepted a luxurious crimson cloak from the arms of the eunuch and flung it over his white robe. He stroked his beard. "I think I'll keep the beard, though. I haven't missed my visits to that butcher of an army barber. Miraculous that he hasn't slit my throat by now. I've always envied that about your kind." The Grand Marshal ran his fingertips over Meleager's smooth cheeks.

"Here, let me fix your tail," Meleager said, blushing, scurrying around him. The eunuch reached inside the red wool cloak through a slit in the back and pulled out a long mane of horsehair. He ran his fingers through it, smoothing the coarse hairs.

"This is different, is it not? You behind me for a change?"

Meleager did not respond. Off-color remarks were one thing in bed, another when not making love. The subservient role the eunuch played for the General in the bedroom did not extend outside those chambers. The General stood tall and said in a voice that sounded too formal, "I am flattered and honored, being dressed and waited upon by so noble a personage."

The eunuch patted the General's solid right buttock. "Here, let me sandal your feet. My, how beautiful they are. So slender, so elongated."

"Why must soldiers truss ourselves in this manner? Would we not be more effective if we wore our uniforms? I am growing more uncomfortable, Meleager. Would you call for some wine? Why is Auletes reviving this ridiculous Procession? There hasn't been one in a century."

Meleager adjusted the folds of the white robe, draping them against the ripples of the General's firm chest. "Because he's in trouble. No one approves of the money and the troops he sent to Pompey in Judaea. The citizens are going to call for the king's abdication. They all believe that like his ancestors, he is selling the country to the Romans to keep himself on the throne. And that is why you, a military man, are the procession's marshal. It is quite possible that there will be violence in the streets."

The General put his arm around Meleager's waist and whispered in his ear. "Considering our long-range plans, perhaps we should not do too much to contain it."

Meleager took a deep breath. It was hard to pass up a good opportunity. After all, Auletes' aid to Pompey was a serious misstep. By helping Pompey, Auletes forever abandoned Egypt's claim upon the Palestine. Still, the timing to rid Egypt once and for all of Auletes was not quite right. "We are simply not prepared for the king's demise. His successor, the rightful queen, is not even fifteen. I am afraid we find ourselves in the ironic position of keeping Auletes, whom we abhor, on the throne."

The General looked about his shoulders. "If there is trouble today, which there will be, what with all those drunks in the street, why do we not allow the king to perish? The queen would reign until Berenike is of age, and then we can get rid of *her*."

"No, she is far too capricious. No one expected her to seduce Auletes. She was just a child and her mother was on her deathbed. That's the kind of girl she is. She might take another husband, one not of our choosing. Better to wait until the elder princess is of age, do away with the queen, and let Berenike become Auletes' co-regent. Then he can go."

"I suppose you are right," said the General. "Right as usual. We'll make sure the day comes off smoothly. I know the troops are looking forward to the celebration. They've heard that the wine will flow into the streets as if by magic from giant drums."

"That is no rumor, but truth."

"I suppose a bastard king must do all he can to solidify his claims. Feeding the people and getting them drunk is as effective as anything."

"I'm pleased that you think so, my dear. It was my idea. The king asked me what he could do to appease his rowdy subjects. I told him that we must look to history to see what worked for his more successful ancestors. The Grand Procession is an awesome display of power. It should quiet the rabble, at least for a while."

"My friend, I'm beginning to think everything is your idea."

"Not everything, darling. Some things merely happen. And I like to think that the gods still have a hand in our Fates."

"But in the absence of a firm plan from the Divine, you do not seem to mind being the architect of the Fate of men," said the General.

"The gods are whimsical. I am meticulous. Some things require careful planning."

Kleopatra felt a cool, lemon-scented breeze pass her upturned face, filling her lungs with the life force of the god of the four winds. The day was not yet too warm and the sky was a crystalline blue, so sharp that it made everything seem more vivid and alive, or that is what the princess thought as she teetered on the chariot rings, maintaining her balance and wondering how she looked in her dress. She had chosen to wear the red robes of Isis, the goddess whom Roman women had recently begun to worship with a fervor that their husbands considered dangerous to Roman piety. Kleopatra liked the idea of being considered dangerous in Rome; she hoped that as Isis's representative on earth, she might receive adoration in not one country but two.

So costumed, she stood next to her father on a stallion-drawn chariot of gold inlaid with jewels and ivory. Auletes had had a charioteer install a second, smaller set of rings next to his so that his little daughter could brace herself against his large frame. He allowed her to drive with him, teaching her how to keep on her feet in the chariot rings, how to lean into the sudden jerking movements to maintain her balance, how to relax her body and submit to the fierce jolts of the carriage. Holding her breath, leaning against her father, Kleopatra would force her eyes open against the winds, willing her intestines not to rise up and betray her, while all around her the landscape trembled as if an angry god had called up an earthquake. Out of the tremors she would feel a thrilling shudder rise up from the lower part of her body, slinking along her backbone like a viper, and exploding in her head. "Do not resist," her father would say to her. "Only those who resist fall." She had yet to be thrown.

The horses danced nervously in place, shifting their weight from one hoof to the next, but Kleopatra would not stumble now, while the chariot was not even in motion, and while she and her father were observed by their most illustrious subjects. In full view of his people, Auletes stood tall in the capacious purple robes of the god that rippled in the morning breeze. The Royal Hairdresser had manufactured for the occasion a wig made of the lengthy blond curls of Greek youths, shorn as a sacrifice to Dionysus. The fair hairpiece sat upon Auletes' head, incongruous with his woolly black eyebrows. Crowned with an ivy wreath, he held a gilded *thrysus*, the fennel-stalk wand that the god used as a scepter, dramatically in his hand. He stuck his eagle-beak nose into the air, allowing the curls to fall down his back like a haughty young maiden, while an artist sketched his profile for the coinage he would issue with himself presented as the god.

"I shall have them do a statue, too," he said to his daughter. "I shall have myself preserved for all time as I am today."

"It is time to mount the elephant, Your Majesty," a satyr announced to the king. Kleopatra could not help but notice that his pointy ears were crooked, causing him to look slightly ridiculous. The king's footmen rushed to assist his descent from the chariot, but for the benefit of his audience he pushed them away with his royal foot and alighted unaided with astonishing grace for such a stout man. He reached his arms out to his daughter, who leapt into them.

"Enough of that," said Charmion, whisking her away from her father. "You would not see your next birthday if you were left to your own devices."

"You are like a skittish cat, Charmion," Kleopatra said as she straightened her robes. "You have no love of physical exertion. You are a mind without a body."

"I am a mind who wishes to keep its body."

Kleopatra ignored Charmion's cautious advice whenever possible. "Today I wish that I could be omniscient like the gods, for I want to be in all places at once. Oh, it is terrible to be in the parade, when all I want to do is see it!"

"You have been warned about the dangers today. Do not move from my side. You can see most of it from here," said Charmion sternly.

"I cannot. I am too short." Why was she not tall like Berenike, who had inherited her father's height but her mother's face? Kleopatra was stuck with those traits in reverse. It wasn't fair. "Let us promenade the Grand Pavilion while we have time. That's where all the important people are!"

"No. You will just lose yourself in the crowd, and I shall be to blame when the Procession begins and your float is empty."

"Please, Charmion. I promise to hold your hand and be very, very good."

The Grand Pavilion umbraged Auletes' most significant subjects and eminent foreign visitors under a tent of tautly woven deep crimson linen, held high above the crowd by tall Ionic columns. Just being inside its luxury made Kleopatra feel important. Statuary of gold, bronze, and marble—gods from every nation east and west, and her own deified Ptolemaic ancestors—lined the boundaries of the tent, as if every deus in the universe sanctified the event. The princess studied the scrupulously groomed guests, who struck calculated poses as they talked among themselves. Women, laughing, threw their heads back, flaunting necklaces of creamy pearls or startling red garnets, or sometimes simply their gorgeous powdered necks. Kohl-rimmed eyes fluttered about like nervous insect wings; quivering crimsoned lips heightened the meaning of the spoken word. Kleopatra dropped Charmion's hand and threw her head back trying to mimic their sensual ways, but it made her neck hurt.

"Cousin, you are glorious in red. Heavenly, some might say," said a wry young voice. Kleopatra snapped her head upright to see her cousin Archimedes, nineteen years old, riding a black horse decorated in the purple and gold colors of the king's Brotherhood.

"Cousin! Could it be true, or have you stolen that horse?" the princess asked, praying he had not seen her at her play.

"This very morning a messenger came to my mother's house to

inform me that on this day I was to be inducted into the Order of the Brotherhood of the King. Cousin, I am a Kinsman!"

"My father has always held you most dear," Kleopatra said. Archimedes' mother was Auletes' second cousin; his father, unknown. Auletes retained a soft spot in his heart for any and all bastards. Sometimes Kleopatra fantasized that her father was also the mysterious father of Archimedes. She loved her handsome cousin and wished with all her heart that he was her brother, for then they could marry.

"Report to me, Cousin, what is at the head of the Procession, for I cannot see it all," requested the princess.

"Magnificence and mayhem, my dear. The Marshals are dressed as Silenoi in cloaks of crimson and purple, draped in vines. They are wearing white sandals that all the ladies say will be filthy by the end of the day. And they are led by a particularly handsome military man who is far too young to be a general. The ladies are wondering who got him the appointment."

"How do you know so much about what the ladies say, Cousin?"

"Because where the ladies are, Archimedes aims to be," he replied.

"Never mind the ladies. What am I missing at the front of the Procession?"

"Satyrs and Maenads, six hundred in all, each carrying a sacred object. Very splendid. The Satyrs are smeared with purple and vermilion dyes, and they have put mud and leaves and moss into their hair, which they have grown wild for the event. The barbers in every quarter are starving, my dear."

Archimedes never failed to delight his cousin. "What else? What else?"

"Goat ears and tails adorn heads and behinds. Asses dressed like asses. These fellows are taking their roles as Dionysians very seriously. They are all quite drunk and already chasing the Maenads, who are also drunk. I predict fornicating in the streets by noon."

"Oh, I wish I could see it all," said Kleopatra, feeling very wicked. "I wish, I wish, I wish."

"The wishes of the throne are a Kinsman's command," said Archimedes. He swooped down and offered Kleopatra an arm to mount his horse. She looked around for Charmion, but only saw the back of her head as she engaged in gossip with one of the chatty ladies-in-waiting. Riding sidesaddle and not caring a bit about wrinkling her red robe, she hung on to the steed's mane as Archimedes negotiated his way through the throng.

"I wish I had bigger eyes so that I could see it all at once," she said. The more she tried to take it all in, the more it amplified, spreading out before and behind and all around her. But Archimedes had removed his attention to three tall girls, bare-breasted but for the ropes of braided gold necklaces that dipped into their cleavage. They stood at the head of twelve columns of golden-winged, well-muscled young women costumed as Nike, the girlish goddess of victory.

"Do you recognize those three in the front of the line? They are my father's concubines," Kleopatra said, pointing rudely at the girls.

"How nice it must be to be a king," Archimedes said, his eyes riveted to the red-haired girl in the middle, who at that moment lifted her mane off her neck, making a tunnel for the breeze and raising her left breast ever so slightly higher than her right. Her ringlets fell behind her like a tree shaking its autumn leaves.

"Oh, they fought fiercely with one another for the honor of leading the Nikes. My father finally gave in and let all three have the privilege."

"A wise man," sighed the young Kinsman.

"What a time my father had deciding what necklace, what bracelet, what ring, would be worn by which of those girls," Kleopatra said, feeling very sly and like a grown person, tattling on the king's silliness. She let her voice assume the same inflection and furtive intonation the ladies of the court used in their gossip.

"They are terribly winsome," said Archimedes wistfully. "I should like to see them beg."

"Let us move on," said Kleopatra, annoyed that her cousin would not take his beautiful brown eyes off of the auburn-haired siren. When he made no motion to move, Kleopatra kicked the side of his horse.

"You are not at your most regal, Cousin," Archimedes snapped, trotting past the nymphs. "You'd better behave. The holy ones are looking."

The princess sat up tall on the horse and gave her most solemn demeanor to the priests and priestesses of Dionysus who filled the next cart, their white robes billowing lazily against their rigid bodies like makeshift sails. They were guarded by snarly-haired Maenads brandishing hissing snakes with wild, dancing tails.

The crowd fell silent as the Maenads passed, not from fear of them, but because of what followed—a golden phallus two hundred feet tall, crowned with a shimmering nine-foot star, a meteor in slow motion shooting into the air. It rested on a cart pulled by dozens of men, but the awestruck faces of the crowd turned slowly as if on an axis, following the missile until it moved past them. Boys dressed as Priapus, impish offspring of Dionysus and Aphrodite, scampered in its wake, balancing plaster phalluses as tall as their torsos between their legs and pointing them merrily at maidens.

"Have you seen enough?" Archimedes asked. "Charmion is probably summoning the guard. I shall spend my first night as a Kinsman in prison."

"In that case I shall see to it that you receive generous portions of gruel while you are incarcerated," offered Kleopatra, turning her eyes upward and staring at him out of their corners as she saw Auletes' mistresses do when they wanted something.

"You are very magnanimous, Kleopatra," he said. He smacked his horse particularly hard, and laughed at his cousin when she had to grab his vest so that she did not fall.

The eunuch Meleager had paid fastidious attention to the historical accuracy of every detail of the Procession, but in these more modern and enlightened times, he wondered if the effect of all this ostentation was not a bit lugubrious. Would the spectacle evoke the desired response of increased approval of the Royals? Or might it produce the opposite effect—a joke the gods often played on careful, man-made plans. The choreographer of this opus let it all pass before him as if a dream: Barefoot Ethiopian chiefs carrying elephant tusks and logs of ebony; a thousand camels from Arab lands with saddlebags of saffron and orris; aviaries of peacocks, pheasants, and other resplendent African birds all floated past his eyes like phantasms in a keen night vision. Albino leopards. Giraffes. A rhinoceros, or was it two? Meleager felt like the steward on that great ark from the Jewish holy books; was there any beast of the earth that he had not seen today?

How could one fourteen-year-old princess make her mark amid all of this? And on the masses, intoxicated to sloppiness with pageantry and wine? It was his own fault; he insisted on having the wine flow freely into the streets for one and all. When Auletes had balked at the cost of getting the population of the city good and drunk, Meleager had asked, Is it not appropriate for the New Dionysus to gift his worshippers with his favorite drink?

Now Meleager watched as six hundred slaves coaxed along the unwieldy wine barge. The vessel carried thirty thousand gallons of that blessed drink in a drum of lion skins stretched to maximum strain around a circle of metal spikes. What an engineering feat it had been to get it just right. Despite his worries, he could not help but feel some pride. The men and women, forty in all, who stood inside the drum, laboriously stomped and jigged over the grapes while the scarlet liquid gushed into the street. It was an illusion that they caused the flow, of course, but it was a nice touch. As soon as the flood began, the dignified spectators in the Grand Pavilion became as greedy and anxious as any thirsty peasant. Several wine enthusiasts broke the ranks of the slaves to fill their conical leather flasks, big enough to hold ample drink to weather the long nights of the coming winter.

"Move on, move on," a Satyr ordered one of the gluttons. He picked him up and threw him back into the crowd, where he landed next to Meleager. The man's friends pulled back his head and sloppily emptied a pouch of the elixir into his mouth. The eunuch felt the sticky surplus creep into his sandals and between his toes. By the time Berenike reached these spectators, they would be entirely blacked out from the spirits.

Auletes' subjects were in a jovial mood as their king approached on a swaggering elephant. Under a canopy adorned with ivy vine, fruits, crowns, drums, and masks of comedy and tragedy, the sun highlighted just enough of the gold in his costume to make him appear a great shimmering god. Flanking His Majesty on horseback was the Order of the First Kinsmen, including the newest member, a good-looking, longhaired youth whom Meleager resolved to invite to his next dinner party.

The next sight filled him with loathing. Thea, as Aphrodite rising out of the sea, was not nude, but wore transparent green drapes about her body and tiny conch shells under her breasts. Sparrows and doves, the lascivious birds known to take to the air with Aphrodite, fluttered in golden cages on either side of the queen. Thea's second-born, the infant boy Ptolemy XIII, represented the god Dionysus as a baby. Meleager had argued with Thea about the inappropriateness of her costume, patiently explaining that the product of the union of Aphrodite and Dionysus had been the grotesque Priapus, and that people would laugh at her baby son if they made the connection. Meleager, you are too rigid, she had said. Not everyone is so exacting about the gods.

How fitting, he thought, that the queen chose to represent the whore of Mount Olympus. Then, ashamed, he chastised himself for sounding like any crude person who did not understand the old religions. The Fates had assigned Aphrodite the duty of lovemaking; it was her divine destiny. Aphrodite did not seduce her promiscuous father, Zeus, though it was said he desired her. The same could not be said of Thea.

A ray of light shot into the crowd. Meleager and those about him looked everywhere for the origin, but had to turn their faces away from its intensity. Then he saw the source: On an elephant-drawn float, Berenike stood as still as a statue, holding her shield at just the right angle to catch the sun. She was dressed as Pallas Athena, goddess of war, in her battle gear. Her baby sister, the Princess Arsinoe, firstborn to Thea, shared Berenike's float and her glory, wearing a goatskin and representing the goddess at birth. The float carried all that the goddess invented—flutes, horse bridles, spinning wheels, ox yokes, numbers, small-scale models of chariots and ships. Atop the entire production was a banner with the goddess's motto: "Athena never loses the day." Dozens of maidens in war attire surrounded the radiant Berenike yelling *olulu*, the victory cheer, into the crowd, and a troop of little girls armed with light shields and lances followed on foot like a diminutive Amazon army, echoing the cry of the young warriors.

The princess looked like the goddess herself—fierce, distant, numinous. Her combative nature was well served in the deity's guise; the long limbs, elegant neck, and feral grace all conspired with Athena's warrior persona to create an ineffable grandness. Either ignited by their own happy intoxication, or moved by her regal attributes, or guided by the will of the Mother Goddess herself, the people raised their fists and yelled back.

"*Olulu! Olulu!*" shouted Meleager, to the surprise of his peers, who had never seen the reserved eunuch lose his composure. Meleager saw that suspicious eyes were upon him but he did not care. The shouting rang in his ears, filling him with joy. The response of the crowd to Berenike was an omen from the goddess— a sign of her destiny. He closed his eyes in prayer, his feelings of loyalty to Berenike affirmed.

But his sense of victory was short-lived. On a small float in the shape of the stone boat of Isis, the Mother Goddess of all Egypt, stood the favorite daughter of the king, the red robes of Isis a striking contrast against her dark long hair and her small child's face. She was attended by twenty priestesses, all wearing sacramental black wigs of long springy curls and blood-bright robes. The mass of red hit the eunuch's eye like an assault. He felt his spirit sink into the depths of his bowels as if he had taken sick.

Kleopatra stood at the rear of the cart, holding her thin arms out to the people as if to embrace them, to protect them like the Mother Goddess herself. The crowd, moved by her solemnity, applauded her, and the tribesmen lifted their totems in homage, which they did not do, Meleager could not help but notice, for Berenike. Seeing the emotion she evoked from the people, the child herself thought: *I have a flair for this kind of thing.*

The eunuch Meleager noticed the same. This one will be trouble, he thought. She would never possess the beauty of her stepmother nor the regal bearing of her older sister. She was petite, almost diminutive, but it did not seem to matter. Luckily, she was yet so young. Luckily. For unlike her stepmother, this one had an acute intelligence and could present real danger.

Meleager was driven at the end of the day through the back
streets of the city to the stadium to observe the sacrifice of the
bulls. The bulls would be butchered on the stadium floor, roasted
on the spits, and, along with free fruits and breads and the remaining flow from the wine cart, given away to anyone willing to wait
their turn.

The royal women had abandoned their floats, and Auletes, his
elephant, and the family sat upon thrones that had been transport-
ed to the bleachers. Meleager and a few select courtiers sat under the
royal canopy, the eunuch happy that he had missed the artistic
events though he was a great lover of the theater. He felt genuine
abhorrence when he watched Auletes get carried away at these
affairs. At least on this day when he presented himself to the people as a god, Auletes did not insist on competing with his subjects
for the grand prize. The flautist who had taken first prize also sat
with the Royal Family, his golden Delphic trophy behind him. He
was a beautiful youth with ringlets of marigold hair grazing his
shoulders, and against this blond lushness, startling dark brown
eyes. Tonight, Meleager was sure, the lad would sleep with the king
after being forced to listen to him play the flute. But the eunuch
made a mental note to find the location of the boy's lodgings and
invite him to breakfast. He was not a local and would undoubtedly
love to see the view of the sea from the eunuch's balcony.

Kleopatra sat next to Archimedes, not sure which was more excit-
ing, the procession of the bulls, or her cousin's hot young hand on
her forearm. She did not dare breathe as the bulls—five hundred in
all—moved into formation. Perhaps half an hour passed, but time
seemed to stand still as the animals were led into the stadium, each
one restrained by three men, and escorted by a priest wielding a
scythe and four attendants carrying a large silver vessel into which
the sacred blood would drain.

"It is the most solemn thing I have seen," she whispered to her
cousin.

"The blood of a sacrificial bull must not be spilt sloppily," he replied, "for when the people eat of the flesh and drink of the blood, they consume the god himself."

The late afternoon sun slashed a streak of harsh yellow across the stadium. A choir of priestesses silently entered the field, facing the bulls. All at once they began the invocation to the god: "Come hither, Lord Dionysus, god of the underworld who resurrected his mother from Hades. Come hither, Zagreus, son of Zeus, child who wielded the lightning bolt. Come hither, Lord of the vine, of the crops, of all that is green. The Titans tore your flesh; now we sacrifice you so that you may rise again."

The priestesses flung themselves to the ground.

"Save the bulls and kill the king!" An angry choir of voices from the center of the stadium, opposite where the royals sat, split the reverent silence. "Save the bulls and kill the king!" More voices joined the chant, growing louder—and closer, Kleopatra could swear—gaining ground on the royals. She grabbed her cousin's arm, but he shook her off, jumping to his feet to shelter her with his body, while the other Kinsmen protected the king, queen, and Berenike with their shields.

"Throw the Roman-lover to the bulls!" someone shouted. His plea was echoed by another row of citizens. "To the bulls! To the bulls!"

The row of troublemakers pelted the royals with eggs that smashed against the Kinsmen's shields, a slimy yolk dripping in front of Kleopatra's sandaled feet. A swarm of navy uniforms of the king's troops fell on the upstarts, clubbing them with their weapons. Kleopatra saw the soldiers dragging the pummeled bodies of the rebels out of the bleachers. The king brushed off his purple robes and straightened his blond headpiece, trying to regain his composure. But the General, still in his Satyr's gear, informed the royals that to be safe they must return to the palace.

Kleopatra allowed herself to be hustled away under Archimedes' cloak. Looking back, she saw five hundred scythes reaching for the sky, capturing the hot brilliance of the sun god, Osiris. But she did not get to see the moment when his earthbound brother, the bull-god Dionysus, went peacefully to his Fate.

FIVE

To: Gnaeus Pompeius, General
From: King Ptolemy XII Auletes

My good friend, the gods have presented an opportunity for you to repay my recent act of loyalty. My support of your cause did not meet with the approval of my people. Today I stood within the palace walls listening to the demands of the mob outside—demands to end all diplomatic relations with Rome. The people fear our complicity, fear that I shall invite you to share my throne. My family is confined to the Inner Palace, where we depend upon the loyalty of the Royal Household Troops to protect us. On several occasions, fires were started at the gates. Rumors of an assassination plot against me abound.

Therefore, I appeal to you, my good friend, to come to my aid as I most recently came to yours—quickly and without hesitation. We must demonstrate that the ruling Government of this nation has the support of Rome. Surely the mob would prove no match for a Roman legion, men trained at your own superb hands. To ensure the continuing safety of your most loyal ally, please respond in haste.

"I am ten years old. I am sick of Meleager's dull histories," Kleopatra said adamantly. "It is time for me to study philosophy and mathematics. I also wish to increase my knowledge of Roman politics so that I might better serve the court of my father." She stood cross-armed before the king. Though she knew that the sweet approach would have worked better, she was not in the mood to be saccharine. Her father was in constant danger, and she had to prepare herself to come to his aid. She knew a fair amount about the mechanics of the Roman government, but she needed to know more if she was to fulfill her ambition to be his adviser and diplomat. Thea was queen, Berenike was older, and the king now had two sons who, according to centuries-old custom, would inherit the throne when he died. But none of these possessed either Kleopatra's intelligence or her loyalty to Auletes.

"Besides, Father," she said to the distracted king, "you know that I want nothing more than to study with the scholars at the Mouseion." Long before she apprehended that institution's importance in the world of scholarship, she would sit in the courtyard with Charmion and watch the men of learning in their billowing black robes huddle together like carping crows, arguing about the secrets of the universe. The newest addition to the Mouseion's roster of scholars was one Demetrius, a harrowingly thin Greek philosopher who had recently taught in Rome. A neo-Platonist with secondary expertise in Roman law and literature. A man who might facilitate the fulfillment of her ambitions.

"Well, why not? They're all on my payroll over there." The king sighed. "And the gods know how much it takes to keep them fed and happy. Apparently luxury and erudition are necessary companions."

"If the young princess is to study with the philosopher Demetrius, we must also offer the opportunity to our elder daughter," said Thea.

Kleopatra clenched her arms together waiting for her sister to reply, but Berenike said, "No thank you. I've seen the man. He looks like one of the bats who haunt the home of the dead."

Thus, the next morning, and every morning thereafter at nine o'clock, Demetrius was escorted to the palace. Though the Mouseion shared the same quarter of the city with the palaces and the Library, it was still too dangerous these days for a member of the Royal Family to venture outside the palace walls, even with a guard. Demetrius's black robes hung limply on his wraithlike frame; his hair, as sparse as his flesh, dangled against his scaly scalp. Despite his frangible appearance, Demetrius was a diligent soul, patient enough to read and discuss the dialogues of Plato with a ten-year-old girl. Kleopatra expressed her desire to study Roman history, but the tutor assured her that the young mind must first be steeped in the Great Works, writing of the highest quality embodying the Greek ideals of Virtue, Beauty, Truth, Knowledge, before embarking on the corrupting influences of works written in the Latin, conceived in "that cesspool of a city."

Though she longed to gather knowledge that would help her assist her father, she contented herself with Plato, becoming particularly intrigued with the *Meno* and the problems it posed about the efficacy of teaching Virtue. She could not figure why some people—Charmion, for example, and perhaps this scarecrow before her—seemed inherently virtuous and so willingly did what was right and proper while others—herself included—had to battle their natural tendencies to achieve the Greek ideal. At least she was better than Berenike and Thea, who did not even engage in the war.

"Might you teach me Virtue?" she asked Demetrius as they stood in the palace courtyard before a pond with lotus blossoms like welcoming hands.

"As Socrates demonstrates, Virtue is divinely inspired. All Knowledge—and surely Virtue is a form of Knowledge—is already known by the Immortal Soul. It cannot be taught, but must be remembered by the mind."

"I do not follow."

"Socrates observed that if Virtue could be taught, then all educated persons would be virtuous. Clearly that is not the case." Demetrius's cheekbones were so close to his skin as to make the slightest smile look like an act of torture. The princess beamed. "Might you direct me in the remembrance of Virtue?"

"Does your royal and Immortal Soul have the will and desire?"

"It does, Demetrius. I know it does. I shall remember Knowledge and thereby gain Virtue." She closed her eyes tight, attempting to recall the lost Knowledge of the Soul, but all she could hear was the sharp chirping of a sparrow. "I am getting nothing just yet," she said slyly. "But it will come."

"I believe it will require some time and meditation, Your Highness," said Demetrius. "The wings of wisdom are not necessarily swift."

"That's enough for today." Kleopatra looked up at the clear, cloudless sky. "How I wish I could go for a ride."

"Your Highness, sometimes you seem utterly dedicated to your lessons, but at other times you are entirely distracted." Demetrius put his hands on his hips to demonstrate his displeasure.

"I am dedicated to my lessons, Demetrius, but I do suffer from a strange condition."

"What is that?" The philosopher looked skeptically at the girl.

"Knowledge arouses something in me that I cannot name." She had noticed this disconcerting feeling and did not know what to do about it. She only knew that these days, when ideas coalesced in her mind, she could no longer just sit and contemplate. She felt something that was either excitement or anxiety or both, and only physical exertion would rid her of the feeling. "It makes me want to get up and go somewhere or do something."

"What do you mean?" asked the philosopher. "You must not run away from Knowledge. You will never have an extended thought if every time you learn something new you have to run to the stables."

"Remember yesterday, after we finished reading Sophocles' play *Philoctetes*?"

"Yes. Not two minutes after you read the last line, you were out of the library and begging your father to let you go riding. Impatience is intellectual suicide!"

"Well, I was just so elated that everything turned out for the best, that Philoctetes did not have to spend the rest of his life in pain and alone on that island, that I just wanted to celebrate with a gallop in the fields."

"I do not follow your logic," said Demetrius.

"I felt a spirit rise up inside me. And I just had to get it all out." How to explain to this austere person the exuberance she contained within her small body? How to explain to him—pale skin, brittle bones, all mind—that as much as she loved her studies, she also loved the freedom of the outdoors, and was always torn between the two? That in these long days of confinement inside the palace walls, she was bursting to get away?

"I am not in control of myself at these times," she said, face flushed. "I was entirely out of sorts with the grim atmosphere in that room. I had to escape. I wanted my pony."

"Perhaps you would prefer that we study the great poets at the stables?"

"You do not understand, Demetrius, for you are like Charmion. You are all mental faculties."

"I suppose it is bred into the blood," sighed the philosopher. "Here, let us sit on the bench and rest ourselves." He waited for Kleopatra to sit down on the knobby cypress bench and then lowered himself slowly to sit beside her.

"What do you mean?"

"The women of your family have always been obsessed with horses. At the Olympic games two hundred years ago, the queen of Egypt annoyed all the other horse tamers with her superior steeds. She and her sisters were the great equestrians of their day—much to the chagrin of the Spartans, who tried to have them eliminated from the contests."

"You sound like Meleager, obsessed with Ptolemaic history," she said. "How do you know these things?"

"Because I am a scholar, which I suspect you shall never be. Pity, too, for you certainly have the mind for it. The spirit, though, is rebellious."

"You insult me, Demetrius. I wish to be a scholar."

Demetrius cracked a wry smile. "A noble wish, Your Highness, to be a philosopher queen. But I fear that a life of action is your destiny."

"Espionage is a costly business, Your Majesty."

Hammonius took Kleopatra on his knee, knowing that the girl's attachment to him would strengthen his position and weaken the

will of the king. A large Greek man in his forties, Hammonius wore
his prosperity on his stomach. His robes were of the most expensive linen; his cologne, as fine as the exclusive effluvium made for
the king. He had made his fortune by taking advantage of the
Roman craze for Egyptian goods. By special arrangement with the
king, he purchased merchandise manufactured by the government—
and little else was produced in Egypt, owing to the state's monopoly on industry—at a special price. In return, he spied on the
Romans for the king, bribing them with the king's money in
exchange for information and favors.

"What am I supposed to do? Roman senators cannot be bought
for single coin or a cheap bauble."

"I realize this," replied the king, annoyed. "But must we be so
generous?"

Kleopatra hoped her father would not deny the merchant.
Demetrius was now allowing her diligent study of Latin, and she
dreamed of a day when she might apprentice with Hammonius,
learning how to ingratiate herself to Roman insiders and reporting
the information back to Auletes. Then it would be she and not the
twenty-two-year-old usurper who would sit beside the king and
whisper into his ear.

"These are critical times, Majesty," said the bearlike man. "The
Romans are desperate for money. Their treasury is bankrupt from
waging war all over the world, and there is a terrible grain shortage
to feed their armies. They need money and they need it now or they
are going to find themselves in the middle of another rebellion."

"I know, I know, Rome has once more turned her envious eyes
upon the Egyptian treasury," lamented the king.

"As if we do not have enough problems at home," Thea said.
"Will news from Rome help us when our own people kill us in our
sleep? Perhaps we should spend more money finding out the date
and time of our assassinations."

"The rebellion at home makes the intelligence operations abroad
all the more crucial," Hammonius said slowly, as if to a child. "Only
a greater power will subdue the insubordination."

"Of course, of course." The king sighed, regarding the list of expenditures Hammonius presented. Thea pointed her nose at the paper but did not look at it. "Still, this is an awful lot of money."

"Majesty, have you traveled abroad lately? Do you keep up with the price of things?" Exasperated, Hammonius bounced Kleopatra on his knee as if she were an infant. "Do you think it is easy to get an audience with a Roman senator, even if he knows you are going to offer him a substantial amount of money? These things are very delicate. Sometimes I have to wait in the Forum all day long until I 'accidentally' run into the man I am after."

The king moaned. The queen turned her face away from the discussion. Kleopatra moved herself to Hammonius's other knee, which was not bouncing.

"Many say that this new alliance between Julius Caesar, Pompey, and that rich fellow Crassus is not going to last. This Caesar is a cutthroat whose ambitions know no bounds. He, or at least the men close to him, *must* be cultivated; it would be fatal to ignore him. Alliance with the wrong party would mean—with all due respect and sincere wishes for your health and long life—a guaranteed loss of the throne."

The king signed the invoice and gave it to his scribe to take to the royal bank for a withdrawal. Hammonius followed the scribe, bowing solicitously to the king and his entourage, pleased with his negotiation.

"I do not know who is more dangerous to our welfare," said the king. "The Romans, or the people I pay to extract information from them."

Kleopatra returned to her rooms for her customary two-hour afternoon nap. It was believed that a young princess must not expose herself to the hottest part of the day. Kleopatra rarely slept during this time, but sat on her bed and read poetry, or played with her dogs on the floor, teaching them to do tricks. The girl could not wait until she was thirteen, when the nap would be cut to the traditional thirty-minute adult respite. When she complained that she no longer needed these baby naps, as she called them, she was told by Charmion to enjoy the luxury of a long midday rest while she may. Nonetheless, she was unable to sleep. She lay on the floor with her brindle greyhound, Minerva, tracing with her small fingers the long brown stripes across the dog's rib cage.

Kleopatra knew she had every attribute of the perfect spy. Already she had command of many languages, even the native tongue, though every one of her ancestors had declared it inscrutable. She could tell stories, true or false, and make even the most skeptical listener believe her. She could ride a horse as well as a man, as well as her sister Berenike. She did not get ill in the stomach when she traveled by boat or by carriage, and this, she gleaned from Hammonius, was a most important quality. The king did not favor those prone to the travel sickness. She feared virtually nothing, except that her father would lose his kingdom. Most of all, she desired adventure, but she was always under the watchful eye of someone, usually Charmion, who warned her constantly about the dangers in the streets. None of the royals left the palace anymore. They were afraid, even Berenike, who spent her days in the nursery with the five-year-old princess, Arsinoe, teaching the child to shoot the small bow Berenike had used as a child.

Of course, they did not possess her skills. What use would Berenike or Thea be in an intelligence operation? Face-to-face with an Egyptian rebel, what could Thea do but beg for her life? Berenike would fight and be killed, and what good would that do the kingdom? Kleopatra was different; she could help her father in ways that were entirely impossible for either her self-serving stepmother or her savage sister, ways that would demonstrate to Auletes that it was she who deserved to rule at his side.

The Egyptian girls who did the light household maintenance upstairs, many of whom were Kleopatra's age and size, were furnished with crisp, white uniforms from the palace supply. Just yesterday, Kleopatra had wondered what she would look like in one and had threatened the native servant Sekkie with fantastic stories of torture until the girl agreed to bring her the plain cotton dress of the cleaning ladies and a colorful scarf to turban her head. Sekkie's family had served the Royal Ptolemy Household for many generations, longer than anyone could remember. Her mother was the palace's Head Laundress. Her brothers polished the great copper kettles in the kitchen while learning how to carve meat and fowl, jobs they would grow into upon entering manhood. Sekkie was terribly afraid of being caught by her mother, who had warned her children that there was no room for mistakes while in the royal service.

Sekkie knocked three times—the code they had agreed upon—and slinked into Kleopatra's room, looking both ways down the hall before she entered.

"I am going to reward you for this," whispered Kleopatra as the girl handed her the bundle. "I am going to make certain that you are promoted to my personal body servant."

"Then what you said yesterday is no longer true?" asked the girl gingerly.

"What did I say yesterday?"

"That you would have me tortured and killed."

"I said I would have you tortured and killed if you did not help me," Kleopatra corrected her, slipping the cotton gown over her head. "But you have helped me, and therefore I am going to reward you by having you promoted. You see, if I am to be my father's spy, then you are to be my spy. Do we understand each other?"

Sekkie reluctantly nodded her head.

"How do I look?" With her tawny coloring, the woven basket she carried, and her gift for the inflections of the native speech, she was sure she could pass as a servant. Sekkie took a few cleaning towels from her pockets and tucked them into the belt at Kleopatra's waist to make her look more like one of the upstairs maids.

"You could pass for my sister," Sekkie offered boldly.

"It has all of Rome in an uproar." Kleopatra lowered the vial of oil of carnation from her nose and looked up and over the partition into the next stall. A Greek bookseller was unrolling a scroll. After reading it, he shot a dirty look at the manuscript's owner, a stocky Roman merchant in white robes smattered with the remnants of his lunch.

"You call this poetry?" The outraged Greek read the poem sotto voce, "'Cock fornicates. What, a fornicating cock? Sure enough this is the proverb, the pot finds its own herbs.'"

He threw the scroll back to the Roman, who fumbled it against his chest indignantly.

Catullus. It could only be the infamous one, the Roman poet whom Demetrius had declared off-limits to her impressionable young mind. Kleopatra was dying to read his poetry, but her tutor said that he was a pervert, a catamite, and an anarchist. Now, finally, on this, her third escape to the marketplace, she had struck gold. For the past three Thursdays, while the Household Guard was busy rehearsing its marches, she had slipped down the stairs, into the kitchens, and out the back door, shivering as she called out a greeting in Egyptian to the indifferent guard at the palace gate who had yet to look up from cleaning his fingernails with a knife. With the sun warming her face and the sea breeze pushing her on, she skipped along the Canopic Way to the rambling city of stalls, where every luxury and amenity the world had to offer was to be found, as well as a few items—back scratchers, lice repellent, tooth pickers, tonics for sexual potency—that she had not heretofore known existed. Hoping to overhear treasonous material that she might report back to her father, she trailed peripatetic philosophers—notorious troublemakers—who flailed their arms as they pontificated, their hands like paddles volleying their speeches to the throng of boys who followed them. She listened to languid men playing chess who groused about everything—humidity, dust, flies, taxes—and she spied on merchants as they discussed the politics of the day. Despite her efforts to discover incendiary material, her only victories to date were learning the Ethiopian word for "fuck," and getting a lesson from an old cook on picking ripe melons.

The owner of the perfume stall, wrinkled and sour as last year's apple, eyed Kleopatra suspiciously as she put down the vial of carnation oil and picked up essence of lotus, inhaling it as she tried to eavesdrop on the bookseller's conversation. "Let me see your money, girl," the woman demanded, and Kleopatra produced from her pockets some silver coins. "Oh all right then," she said, too greedy, Kleopatra thought, to throw anyone with coinage out of her shop.

"Smut. Filth. Licentious nonsense. Twaddle!" The Greek bookseller continued to sputter over Catullus's new poems. "What's happened to the boy?" Sighing, hand over heart, eyes fixed on the heavens, the bookseller recited from memory:

> You ask how many kissings of you, Lesbia, are
> enough for me and more than enough. As great as is
> the number of the Libyan sand that lies on silphium-
> bearing Cyrene, between the oracle of sultry Jove and
> the sacred tomb of old Battus . . .

"*That* was poetry. This is dung!"

"My dear fellow, you may not think it's poetry, but it's got all of Rome talking. The muse Lesbia found herself a new cocksman. Now the poet claims she's no better than a trollop. His heart is broken. He cares for nothing, so he slings shit in every direction. He's gone mad; he's even taken on Julius Caesar."

The bookseller took the scroll back from the Roman. "Show me."

Julius Caesar. That name again. He would merit further study. She knew that he had subdued Spain and had been its governor, and that he had a very large army. Hammonius had said he was rivaled as an orator only by the great man Cicero; that he could talk anyone into anything, and often did.

"Right here, see? He calls Caesar an abominable profligate pansy. Says he pokes another pansy named Mamurra."

The Greek read the poem silently; even with his lips moving in an animated fashion, the princess could not make out the words. He looked back at the Roman. "Thought you Romans didn't go in for all that."

The Roman shrugged. "Our Caesar does. He bedded Nikomedes, the king of Bithynia, when he was on his first naval mission. His men still call him the queen of Bithynia behind his back. I should know. My brother-in-law's a centurion in the Tenth." He fumbled in his valise for another manuscript. "What do you make of this one?"

The Greek read it to himself, and then slowly again out loud. "'I have no very great desire to make myself agreeable to you, Caesar, nor to know whether your complexion is light or dark.'"

Kleopatra could not figure out what this poem meant; nor could the bookseller, who looked quizzically at the Roman. "Were these more pleasing in the Latin?"

"The translations are excellent, and if you don't want them, I'm sure Nikias up the street would be happy to buy them."

"No, no, I'll take them," the Greek said, grabbing the manuscripts out of the merchant's hand. "Boy!" he called to his servant. "Get these to the scribe. One hundred copies, and no time for his fancy marks in the margins. I need them straightaway."

"One hundred copies? Of these poems you do not even like?" asked the Roman.

"They're nasty bits about famous people; everyone will want them."

Money was exchanged and the servant took off on foot with the documents. "You may not be getting anything new from me for a while," the Roman said. "I think there's going to be trouble at home. I just might stay on here."

Kleopatra, stomach queasy from a prolonged inhalation of lotus oil, capped the vial with its plug of wax and listened attentively.

"They say that Caesar and Pompey are going to unite their armies and take over Rome. They've got Crassus's money behind them, and believe me, that is more than the treasury of many a country. It won't happen without bloodshed, I'll tell you that."

"Just stay out of it, my friend. Men in power come and go, but men like us need only make a living."

"You are right, my friend. How long can this 'love affair' between Caesar and Pompey last? All of Rome knows that Caesar used to visit Pompey's wife, Mucia, when Pompey was away. He still might, who knows? He put his own wife away after he caught her with his friend Clodius. He said that *his* wife had to be above *suspicion*."

"Even though he's got his poker in this king and that queen, or in this pansy, Mamurra, or in Pompey's wife? You Romans make mockery of morality."

"We learned that from you Greeks."

The two men threw their heads back, laughing so hard that Kleopatra could see the black void of their missing teeth.

"Well it serves Pompey right, being a cuckold," said the Greek, collecting himself. "He's got our king in his pocket. He's got our treasury in his pocket, too."

Kleopatra strained harder to hear what was said. "Are you going to buy that oil or not?" the perfume-monger asked her sharply. "Let's see a bit of that metal, sister."

Kleopatra hurled an angry coin at the woman, turning all her aural powers to the conversation.

"The Flute Player sent your Pompey eight thousand Egyptian troops to help his war against the Jews, and a big fat lump of gold from the treasury. It's got our people mad as Hades. There's going to be trouble here, my friend. If I were you, I would take my money and run."

"What makes you think Rome is safer than Alexandria? The rabble-rousing that goes on here is nothing compared to what we see every day in the streets of Rome."

"I'm just trying to be a friend to you," said the Greek. "I hear rumbling. And when the mob rumbles, things do not stay quiet for long."

From: Gnaeus Pompeius, General
To: Ptolemy XII Auletes, King of the Two Lands of Egypt
My great friend and ally,
Regrettably, my forces are still engaged in the conflict in the Palestine, each man a necessity. Though I have them utterly surrounded and besieged, the Jewish tribes continue to resist, conducting religious ceremonies in the midst of an attack if it occurs on their Sabbath, or some such other holy time. I wonder if they mock me. Until we prevail against them, I must ask that the friendship between us stand as a reminder that if I could respond to your present needs, I most certainly would.

SIX

Kleopatra loved the Delta, the land at the mouth of the river where the Nile splintered into narrow arteries like fingers climbing up the continent. She loved the sudden flash of a flock of heron across the gray skies, or the grace of a lone egret startling the silent horizon. The north country's damp misty air coated her face, plumping her skin. The land was thick and marshy, making it hard to keep a seat on her disobedient pony, Persephone, a very stubborn young filly—a kindred spirit to the princess herself. Persephone was a fine example of the equine species, but there were things she did not like—snakes, mosquitoes, spiders, small rodents with sharp teeth, and most of all, Berenike, who shimmied her big steed, Jason, so close to Kleopatra that Persephone shuddered nervously, almost toppling her rider into the slush below.

"That bratty nag will be the death of you, Sister," Berenike said, riding past.

Kleopatra caught her balance, but Berenike's new companions, two muscular, compact Bactrian girls, quivers in leather pouches slung jauntily over their shoulders, galloped dangerously close to Persephone, their knowing asplike eyes slanting back at Kleopatra as they slipped past.

"Mohama!" she called, looking about for her servant. The desert girl appeared beside her, wild coiling ringlets escaping the Greek-style braids, black ramparts framing her pronounced cheekbones.

"Did you see them? If they are trying to scare me, they will not succeed," she said, masking her fear in front of the older girl.

"Those bitches better not give us any trouble," Mohama said in her throaty, newly learned Greek, her lips spreading high and wide across her face like two peaked mountains. Her eyes were almond-shaped and startlingly yellow; her skin, dark—not as dark as a Nubian, and not as light as the strange fawn color of ancient Egyptian structures, but a shade somewhere in between. An aged bronze. "Do not worry for yourself. My two watchful eyes plus the one in the back of my head are on them."

Kleopatra had taken notice of Mohama a few months earlier when the girl was lighting the lamps in the upstairs hall. Riveted by her height and her strength as she hoisted the covers from the lamps, easily filling them with oil from enormous jugs, Kleopatra approached the slave. "Are you an Amazon?" she asked timidly. The top of her head barely reached Mohama's sinewy neck.

"The Amazons are from the east. I am from the western desert." The girl explained in rather impressive if halting Greek that she was sixteen years old, or so she thought by the counting of the moons, and that she had been captured when she and her brothers attacked Royal Cartographers on a mapping expedition. When she saw that the party was armed, she circled their wagons with her horse, kicking dust into their faces so that her brothers might escape.

"You sacrificed yourself?" Kleopatra asked.

"It was no sacrifice. They had the food."

Over the next several days, Kleopatra watched Mohama at work while considering her usefulness. Though she was not an Amazon, she looked like one, if the renderings Kleopatra had seen on vases and tombs were accurate. Perhaps she also possessed some of the skills for which the women warriors were known—skills Kleopatra's sister and her new companions had perfected. Berenike was older, taller, and meaner than Kleopatra, who worried that her sister's new Bactrian companions might be assassins.

Kleopatra confessed these fears to Mohama. The next day the slave produced from the folds of her garment a curved dagger with an ebony handle inlaid with small pieces of polished ivory. "I have brought the princess a present," Mohama said, holding the gift in front of her. "A Samartian dagger."

"I knew it!" Kleopatra cried, taking the weapon. "You *are* an Amazon. The Samartians are the descendants of Scythian men and Amazon women. They are the best knife fighters in the world."

"I am not a Samartian, but got this knife from a Samartian soldier."

"Stole it, you mean," said Kleopatra, searching Mohama's face to see if the insult wounded. The girl shrugged. "No, the soldier wanted something from me. I gave it to him in exchange for the knife."

"What did you have to give him?"

"Nothing I cannot afford to lose time and time again without losing a thing."

Kleopatra did not know how to respond. Mohama blithely went on. "There is trouble everywhere in the city. The Royal Family is not safe, not even inside the palace. And you might not even be safe from your own sister. If you will allow it, I will sleep on the floor of your chamber next to your bed. But you must sleep with this under your pillow. Whoever enters your room will have to kill me first. Perhaps while he wrestles with me, you can cut his throat. I will show you how."

"Splendid!" said Kleopatra.

Mohama handed Kleopatra the dagger and told her to lie on the pillows and pretend to wrestle with an opponent underneath her. The princess dropped down, carefully holding the dagger with her right hand. She flailed her arms into the pillows, jabbing the dagger into the cushions and kicking with her legs. Suddenly she felt a large foot between her shoulders. Her arms were paralyzed. Mohama grabbed her hair and pulled her head back. She reached around and traced her finger across Kleopatra's throat in a slow, taunting motion. She put her lips right up to the princess's ear and whispered in a hot breath, "There, enemy of the crown. Your head is no longer part of your body."

Kleopatra's heart pounded. She could not move. She could not breathe. It seemed a very long time that Mohama held her body prisoner, hurting her, pulling her hair, straining her neck. She felt powerless to say anything. Finally, the girl released her, helped her to her feet, and straightened her garment. Kleopatra folded her arms around herself, protecting something she could not name.

"Now I'll be the enemy and you be yourself, coming to our rescue." But Kleopatra was frozen. Mohama picked up the dagger and handed it to her.

"If one is to fight, one must be brave. Take the dagger, but please do not use it on me."

The warmth of the handle sent an energy through Kleopatra's body. She felt as if she had awakened refreshed from a long nap and was ready to play. "Yes, I am ready. I am ready to strike a blow against the enemy," she cried, raising the dagger into the air.

"The princess is too full of glee. Killing is a sober business. Perhaps we shall practice without the dagger until you have more skill. I am only a slave, and my neck is not worth very much, but I like it."

Kleopatra giggled and put down the dagger. As Mohama knelt on the pillows, the princess put her foot in the middle of her back, forcing her down. With the full force of her weight, Kleopatra jumped on her back. Mohama's arms flew out to the sides, leaving her in a crucified position. The princess tried to pin her arms down, but before she knew what was happening, they had rolled off the pillows and Kleopatra's back was against the cold tiled floor, Mohama straddling her with her arms pinned above her head.

"There is much for you to learn, Princess. Luckily, you already have the heart."

Kleopatra went straight to the Domestic Supervisor and demanded that the desert girl Mohama be made her personal attendant.

On Meleager's advice, the royal party had left Alexandria before dawn, while the disgruntled mob were still cozy in their beds. Kleopatra knew the trip would be rigorous, but she did not hesitate when Auletes proposed "a little hunt in the Delta" to get away from the dangers in the city, particularly when she learned that Thea, pregnant again, would remain at home.

The party formed a long caravan, cutting an intrusive swath through the hush of the marsh. Carriages of hunting dogs—greyhounds used for chasing hare and the bulkier Indian hounds that worked by smell and by sight for tracking big game—all barked at once, as if in competition for a prize. Twelve carriages followed the king's party; three carrying body servants to the royals and the Kinsmen; two full of cooks and their helpers; two loaded with heavy pots and pewter plates and utensils for feeding the party; and four hauling tents, bedding, and other supplies of the camp. The final, ornate carriage housed the king's mistress and her women, who in accordance with court decorum would remain sequestered waiting for the king's possible visit.

One dozen of the king's personal guards flanked the royals and their attendants. Auletes rode a sleek Greek-bred steed, the kind he preferred over the Nisaean and Arabian breeds, which, though superior in strength and endurance, had large heads that interfered with the precise throw of the spear. Away from the city, the king seemed to forget his urban woes entirely.

"They say that Alexander preferred the Indian hound to the Molossian. He took thousands of them from the palace of Darius in Persia," the king proclaimed over the din of the dogs to Demetrius, invited as a reward for his excellent instruction of the princess. "Demetrius, today you shall see my Indian hound Aura in action."

"Father named her after the dog of Atalanta," Kleopatra said to the philosopher.

"O virgin goddess, great huntress of the Calydonian boar, look kindly on our expedition!" Auletes cried. "O handmaiden to Artemis, bless our weapons, open the scents of the wilds to our dogs, point our spears and bows to the heart of the kill, and cause no man and no animal to suffer needlessly in our endeavors. We shall lay the slaughter on your altar and consume the flesh in your holy name!"

Demetrius's skinny frame jostled in the saddle, his lips frozen in a half-moon smile. The princess knew he cared neither for life outdoors nor for spilling the blood of an animal outside the sacrificial ritual.

"It's in my blood, my friend," the king exclaimed. "The Ptolemies have been inveterate hunters, dating back to Ptolemy the First, who hunted with Alexander."

"Ah, that most legendary hunter from time out of mind," said Demetrius, indulging the king as he had learned to do. "There was no greater hunter but the god Herakles."

"All my ancestors were great hunting men. That is, except Potbelly, who refused to hunt. 'We hunt dancing girls,' he used to say."

The king raised his right arm to the sky as if sanctioning the westward movement of the marsh fowl that flew overhead. "I like dancing girls myself," he said, winking at the philosopher. "But there is no greater thrill than to be face-to-face with the hot tusks of the wild boar. When I was ten years old, I read about Alexander's single-handed slaying of the lion, and from that time on, I could not get enough of the hunt."

Kleopatra took the opportunity to interject. "Father, you raised me on the same tales that you read when you were a boy, and yet you refuse to allow me to participate in the pleasures of the big kill."

"The princess is tortured by the constraints of age upon her person, Your Majesty," Demetrius said.

"But surely Alexander hunted with his father when he was ten," Kleopatra argued.

"Be patient, my little one. You will not be a child all your life."

Kleopatra was alone in the thick of the woods, dressed in a pale green chiton, feet and calves laced tightly into coarse leather hunting boots. She held the same style bow as the Bactrian girls and felt the weight of a full pouch of arrows on her right shoulder. The muddy, narrow path under her feet was imprinted with fresh hoofprints big enough for her to walk in. A large tree had toppled over, its uprooted trunk staring at her like a tombstone. On it grew an odd fungus that looked like a cluster of amethysts, an offering of jewels bursting from something long dead. She dared not touch it though she was curious about its texture.

Leaping from one hoofprint to the next, she came to a giant elm—more mountain than tree—with gnarled roots like dragon toes clinging determinedly to the ground and high branches that disappeared into the hidden skies. Under this timber, a lion stood victoriously atop the hunting net that had been laid to ensnare him. His head and paws were over-large, his body sinuous, his mane puffed, his eyes watery and ferocious. The beast was surrounded by a young man with the crest of a king on his hunting tunic and five Kinsmen on horseback. The king and the beast played a staring game, each entranced with the other's unshakable gaze.

The princess recognized her ancestor. It was he, whose mummified corpse rested in the glass tomb in her city—the city that bore his name. He was with his Companions, those men of history and legend who had loved and served the king from boyhood—Seleucus, Lysimachus, old Antipater, the treacherous Cassander, and beak-nosed Ptolemy. Alexander was splendid—muscled, proud, beautiful. He was not, however, very tall. Kleopatra loved him even more for being short. All her life, she had wished that she could go back into ancient times and know him. She lately had come to believe, in the romantic way of young girls, that he would have been her perfect and true mate, and that history had botched their union. She thought, if only he knew me, I would be his and he would be mine, though Demetrius tried to spoil her fantasy by insisting that Alexander was a devout catamite. Yet here he was, sent to her, she was sure, by the gods.

"Cousin," she said, stepping between the king and the beast.

Alexander replied courteously, as if he had known her all his life. "Cousin, step aside." He addressed the creature. "Beast, lord of animals whose entrails were fed to Achilles by the Centaur to make him strong, prepare to die."

Alexander raised his spear, and the animal leapt like a comet, its belly suddenly Kleopatra's sky. The king tumbled off his horse as he thrust his spear into the lion's gut. He landed on top of the beast, its great paw swiping his face, leaving a bloody stripe.

"Kinswoman, help me," he pleaded, his face and body soaked in the thick, incarnadine red that flowed from the beast's wound.

Kleopatra reached behind for a quiver with her right, but her pouch was empty.

"Grandfather," she said to Ptolemy. "An arrow to save the king!"

From his hunting pouch Ptolemy took a gold-tipped arrow. He placed it in his bow and aimed not at the lion, but at the princess. She struggled to pull away, but her legs were like stone columns planted deep inside the earth. She folded herself into a ball as the arrow escaped Ptolemy's bow. With a sickening crack of her spine, she lost the feeling in her body.

Then she was aloft, looking back at the scene as if through a red-colored glass, her vision narrow now, but intensely focused. Alexander had one foot on top of the lion, whose life gushed out of the deep wound, seeping back into the earth. Ptolemy raised his empty bow to her in a salute. As she soared away, she realized that she was no longer the princess Kleopatra but an eagle.

She woke confused, dry-mouthed, and earthbound, surprised to find herself again in human form, and not sure of the meaning of the night vision. There was no one on the expedition with whom she might discuss its meaning but Demetrius, and he did not believe in omens from dreams.

Now fed, washed, and dressed—shod in tall leather boots, cloaked in a light linen wrap against the morning chill, and wearing a wide-brimmed hat in defense of the soon-to-rise sun—the princess rode the warm, damp Persephone through the morning mist. The king had announced that the "ladies," Berenike, herself, and their attendants, would chase hare with the assistance of two net-watchers, boys who were responsible for carrying, repairing, and guarding the nets, while the "gentlemen and Kinsmen" would hunt, ensnare, and conquer the wild boar. "That is, if we find one," he laughed.

"My father and king," came the husky voice of Berenike. "I am sixteen years of age. My women and I are seasoned in the art of the kill. I am a better marksman than even yourself—a *fact* I humbly submit."

Snickers from the Kinsmen, giggles from the Bactrian girls. It was true, however, that Berenike could outshoot her father. Berenike was as tall as the ungainly king, but lithe and well muscled. Her eyesight, too, was far superior.

If she goes on the big-game hunt, thought Kleopatra, so shall I. She was torn between wishing for the king to reprimand her haughty sister and desiring that he accede to her wishes so that she, too, might accompany the men.

"If the princess Berenike wishes to engage in manly sport, she may do so in her own time and in her own kingdom. In the meanwhile, I am king and I have segregated the sexes on this expedition. And now, a final prayer to our Lady Artemis—"

"The goddess of the hunt is a woman," interrupted Berenike.

"And the princess Berenike is a mortal," replied her father. Before he could continue in prayer, Berenike interrupted him again.

"How is that so, my father, when you bear the title New Dionysus? Do the gods-on-earth sire mortal children? Forgive me, my knowledge of theology is limited in these matters."

No sound was heard but the low blowing of horses' lips, anxious to take to the path. The courtiers, the Kinsmen, the attendants, the slaves, all remained securely moored in their places. Eyes darted where heads dared not turn.

Auletes' thick, black brows knitted together in anger, forming one dark ominous linear hedge across his forehead. "May the Lady of Wild Things set the Calydonian boar upon you and tear you to shreds should you continue to vex the king!"

Berenike remained utterly still, nonchalant at the king's insults. Auletes put the tortoiseshell horn to his lips and sounded the low, braying call to begin the chase. Without delay, the men took off in the direction of the west. Only Demetrius looked back to Kleopatra in sympathy as he turned to follow the king.

Berenike, Kleopatra, Mohama, the two Bactrians with bows and quivers, two slave boys with nets, and two indifferent guards, all sat sour-faced on their horses. Six restless hounds rattled their cages on a cart driven by an old Cilician man, who had been the Keeper of the Hounds until a strange twitching disease impaired him.

Berenike reviewed the members of her hunting party. "Who kills nothing is not allowed to recline at the banquet tonight," she said, looking directly at her younger sister.

"No one reclines around a campfire, Sister, unless he is drunk," Kleopatra replied. She kicked her heels into the hard flanks of Persephone and led the gallop toward the meadows, riding as fast as she dared in a territory she did not know. ·

The haughty dog, Pharaoh, was the first to give course. Berenike overtook Kleopatra, who followed her into a glen. From the top of the glen she saw a little brownish creature running fiercely to keep ahead of Pharaoh. The dog's long legs stretched both ahead and behind his sleek body. Kleopatra was not entirely sure that the animal's paws hit ground. The dog has no equal in grace, she thought. Suddenly, though, the dog stopped dead in his tracks, front and hind legs tumbling furiously over one another. The little rabbit had tricked him by doubling back over his path. The hare ran right past the humiliated Pharaoh, skittering to avoid the hooves of Jason.

"There he goes!" yelled Kleopatra as the hare darted back up the hill and out of the glen. Pharaoh was on his feet again and leading the chase with Kleopatra on his heels. She leaned into Persephone's long neck, so close that she could smell the animal's musky scent and hear her snorting breath. She liked to ride this way, letting the horse govern, unconcerned for herself—not even aware of being Kleopatra at all, but losing that part of herself that witnessed her life. Sight blurred, she became a mere appendage of the beast, who, with its horse intuition, traveled at wild speed, avoiding the rocks and low branches and other obstacles that would injure them.

The rabbit made a mad dash under the stump of a tree, and found himself ensnared in one of the net-watcher's small meshes. Kleopatra halted Persephone and descended. Breathless, quivering, the imprisoned animal's nose twitched wildly.

"There, there," she said to the frightened animal. Pharaoh growled menacingly as she approached the net.

"Back, Pharaoh," she said with all the authority she could muster. "Stay back." Pharaoh backed up two steps but kept his teeth bared. "You won't bite me," she said evenly. The others arrived and dismounted in time to see Kleopatra take the small rabbit, damp from its run, out of the net and into her arms. "It's still shaking," she announced to Berenike. One of the Bactrian girls produced a knife.

"We're setting it free," Kleopatra said.

"Pharaoh is my dog," said Berenike. "The rabbit's fate is mine to decide."

"It is sport, Sister. The rabbit gave a good chase. The little creature has a brave and crafty spirit. Let it be. The philosophers advise it this way."

"The rabbit is lunch," Berenike said, raising herself to her full height, her proud, full bosom as intimidating to the younger princess as her height. "And no philosopher need partake of its meat."

Kleopatra clutched the small, quaking thing to her chest. Mohama took a stance next to Kleopatra. The net-boys looked at each other. The two Bactrians stood behind Berenike, while the guards trotted closer.

"Very well, Sister, release the hare. I shall catch another," Berenike said, laughing, mounting Jason. "This one has already given you his thanks." Kleopatra was stunned that her sister had backed down, until she realized that the hare had shot little black pellets into the crook of her arm.

Berenike turned the steed Jason around and was met by a very different challenge. A boar had stepped from the glade and into the clearing, and stared at the tall princess. Its four hooves were planted firmly on the ground. Berenike pulled so hard on Jason's bridle that the horse reared up.

"Do not approach it, Princess," ordered one of the guards. "Let us back out of here slowly, with our eyes on the animal."

Ignoring him, Berenike held her arm out toward the Bactrians. One of them tossed her a spear, which she caught in her right hand.

"No, Princess!" pleaded the guard in a low, beseeching voice, not wishing to startle the boar. But Berenike drew the spear back. Kicking Jason in the flank, she advanced on her enemy. The boar stood motionless, but when Berenike got close to him, he charged. Startled, Berenike threw her spear so hard that she fell off of Jason. The spear grazed the boar's tusk and dropped on the ground. The Bactrian girls began to empty their pouch of quivers into the boar, a few barely penetrating the tough hide. Berenike rolled away, and Jason, rearing back, intercepted the charge of the beast. The animal gored the horse in the underbelly and retreated through Jason's legs. The horse fell on his side, kicking his legs wildly.

"Jason! Jason!" Berenike yelled his name in anguish, a plea to deaf gods, as his insides came gushing forth, a red flood of death.

Kleopatra thought she might vomit. Mohama held her from behind as she watched the Bactrian girls shoot and connect, the boar writhing each time an arrow drilled his tough hide, but not relenting, not even when an arrow pierced his eye.

A net-boy held an ax in his hand, but was paralyzed to use it. One of the Bactrians took up a spear and approached the undulating beast. Its remaining eye rolled wildly in its head. She held the spear in one hand, teasing the tormented beast, keeping it at bay so that the other Bactrian could load another arrow. Her tribeswoman shouted to her in their native tongue, "Under the neck, my love. The soft spot. The moment my arrow hits! The gods are with you." The endearment surprised Kleopatra, who alone understood what the girl had said.

The arrow flew from the bow and into the beast's ear, jerking its head back, exposing the soft, vulnerable flesh of its neck. The other girl thrust the spear into the throat of the boar, but the animal mustered its final strength to charge her. Weaponless, she fell backward, helpless against the boar's lumbering gait. Mohama tossed Kleopatra to the ground, grabbed the ax from the motionless net-boy, and with a preternatural howl, plunged it into the back of the boar, breaking its spine with a hideous crack. The animal dropped. The Bactrian girl ran to her companion, who lay dazed on the ground. Kleopatra remained on the ground, staring at the dead, bleeding Cyclops. In death he looked much smaller. Berenike was draped over the crimson belly of Jason. She raised herself, exposing her bloody chest to the sky, cursing the gods.

"Where did you learn to wield an ax, desert girl?" the Bactrian asked Mohama as the bedraggled hare-hunting party limped toward the royal encampment. Kleopatra did not like the woman's tone. She waited for Mohama's response, wondering if perhaps the violence was not over for the day.

"I received instruction in the art of the kill from a Persian gamesman in the king's employ," Mohama said quietly.

"I didn't know you could take instruction while your mouth was full." The Bactrian laughed, already forgetting that Mohama had saved her friend from being trampled.

"You can do many things with your mouth full," Mohama retorted. "But very little when your head is empty."

Kleopatra ate quickly and greedily, letting the fat of the meat run down her fingers and trickle all the way to her elbows. The freshly roasted boar tasted greasy and wild. Under the open evening sky, she ate with no self-consciousness, as if she were one of the men. Fresh kill was meant to be eaten this way. She looked up. The stars seemed like a million silver coins tossed about the sky. She was sure that the day's hunts had pleased the gods.

After dinner, Auletes sat with his clan and friends around the fire. Kleopatra was made to repeat the story of the killing of the boar. She kept looking to Berenike to see if her rendition of the events pleased or displeased her sister, but Berenike listened with indifference, probably still mourning the loss of the irreplaceable Jason. Flanked by the Bactrians, she leaned lazily against one and then the other, making it difficult to know if she listened to the storytelling at all.

By the time Kleopatra finished her tale, the fire had diminished to embers. The king drained the last of the wine from his vessel. He raised his arms and said, "And now, to bed."

But Kleopatra could not bear the thought of leaving the cool enveloping night sky.

"Father, won't you tell us a story?" she urged.

"I fear that Calliope, the beautiful Muse of storytelling, has left me a drunken old man. She doesn't like it when I worship too keenly Lord Dionysus," replied the king, waving his wine goblet.

"Father, call upon that fickle Muse and insist that she gift your tongue once again. Your daughters and your subjects await."

The king sighed. "Calliope, Lady who visited the Great Blind One, descend on me, your humble servant who worships your sister Euterpe." Auletes looked reverentially to the sky, took a breath, and keeled backward. "It is of no use. I am drunk!"

"Tell us anyway, Father," Kleopatra insisted, throwing herself on his great belly. "Tell us the story of how you came to the throne!" She loved to hear her father tell the story of his ascent. The details brought her mother—Kleopatra V Tryphaena, the mother of Thea, Berenike, and herself—back to life in a way that her memory could not.

"Help me up, girls," Auletes said. Kleopatra and Mohama each took one of the hairy bearlike paws of the king and pulled him forward. The king inhaled, his dark bug-eyes looking around the circle to ensure that he had the attention of all.

"I am a bastard," he said, slowly, solemnly. "That is the beginning of my story, but, may the gods be with me, not its end. My mother was a beautiful woman, a Syrian princess of royal Macedonian blood, directly from Seleucus, Alexander's great Companion. My father, Laythrus, met my mother while he was exiled at the Syrian court. He did not marry my mother because he was still wed in a loveless match to his second wife and second sister, Kleopatra Selene. He loved my mother and stayed with her as long as he could, but he was called back to Egypt to assume the throne.

"I grew up in Syria at my mother's side. She did not have a tutor for me, but taught me to form my letters and then read with me all that is worth reading. She had a fine voice for reading, grand and dramatic. At the right time, she sent me to Athens to study. And that, my friends and Kinsmen, is where I learned to play the flute.

"I never dreamed I would be king. I was a bastard, an exile, and a musician—hardly a fitting candidate to rule the land of Ptolemy I Savior. When my father died, my lunatic cousin, Ptolemy XI Alexander, became king. He married his elder stepsister to follow custom, and then three weeks later, had her murdered. One day a mob of citizens pulled him out of the gymnasium while he exercised and slit his throat. They dragged his corpse through the streets of the city chanting, 'Who are the king-makers in Alexandria? We are!'

"Well, my dears, we were out of heirs except for me. One day I was sitting in my garden with my beloved mother, reading to her the prayers of Callimachus, when a breathless messenger arrived and told me I was the new king. And that was that."

A polite round of applause was given to the king. He took a deep breath and then a deep drink of his wine.

"And what about Mother? Tell us about how you married her," Kleopatra said.

"Ah, gentle Tryphaena. Many is the night I feel her spirit around me, especially on a starlit night such as this." The king hung his head. The princess Kleopatra sidled up to her father and took his hand. "Do you think she is with us now, Father?"

"Perhaps," the king said wistfully. "She was like the air itself—light and essential."

"If she is with us now, Father, would she not like to hear us speak of her?" asked Kleopatra. "Would that not please her gentle soul?"

"Yes, I suppose it would," said the king. "And I suppose it would please your soul to hear talk of your mother, would it not?"

"It would," replied the princess.

"And you, Berenike?" the king questioned his elder daughter, who had not looked at him while he spoke.

"As you wish, Father," she replied without meeting his eyes directly.

"Well then. Tryphaena. She, too, was the daughter of my father, Laythrus, but of his first wife, Kleopatra IV. Father made a political marriage for her to the son of the Syrian prince, and sent her there to live with her new husband. And that is where I, Auletes, then a young man, made the acquaintance of my half sister. Immediately, I fell in love."

Auletes clapped his fists to his chest and shut his eyes tight. "She was beautiful. The most beautiful. She had an innate artistic quality, much like my beloved mother. When she read poetry, I wept. When she played the lyre, I sang. And when I saw her bathing in the nude, I lusted." He gave a wink to his audience. "But what could I do? She was a married woman, and, regrettably, pious.

"As the gods would have it, ladies and gentlemen, soldiers, hunters, cooks, and thieves, as soon as I became king, Tryphaena's husband—may the gods rest his heroic soul—died in the Syrian war. And poor widowed Tryphaena was left alone in Syria.

"Upon hearing of her untimely widowhood, I went straight to

the Cabinet and I said, 'I am going to take a wife.' And old Menander said to me, 'Well, Auletes, you'd better give yourself a while to make sure the people aren't going to murder you, too, before you bring poor innocent Tryphaena back here.'"

Everyone laughed. The king raised his cup and a boy quickly filled it with more wine. Kleopatra took a big sip from her father's goblet, causing him to laugh more.

"In the spring of that year I found myself quite alive—if not yet adored—and so I sent for my beloved. And she arrived within the month with her little Thea, only five years old.

"The very next year, you were born," the king said to Berenike. "But then we thought the gods had ceased to smile upon us. Five times thereafter, my beautiful queen lost her babies long before their birthing time. In the tenth year of our marriage, the queen made a pilgrimage to the temple of Hathor at Dendara. It was a long and dangerous journey, but she insisted that the Egyptian goddess would bless her womb. I thought her mad and tried to forbid the journey, but there is no interfering in the plans of the women in our family.

"On the very evening she returned home from the journey she asked me to give her a child. I said, 'My dear, you know what a voracious lover I am. Do you not require a period of rest from your trip before I consume your small body in the adventure of lovemaking?'"

The Kinsmen made catcalls as if to avow to the king's prowess. Kleopatra put her head down. She did not like to imagine her father as a lover.

"But Tryphaena insisted that I satiate my lusts. She believed that the goddess had decreed that night for conception. Miraculously, nine months later, this small creature arrived from the bosom of the goddess." He ruffled the hair of the princess, who had begun to cry.

Her mother, Tryphaena, was a woman blessed by the goddess, a holy and pious queen. Why could she not have lived? Why did the gods take her away? And how could Thea have betrayed such a woman? Kleopatra wiped the tears from her face, suddenly embarrassed by her outburst. The hated one! She had forgotten about Thea for one blissful day. The hunting trip had been an example of what their lives might have been without her malignant presence.

"Father, what might have happened to us if you had not married Thea?"

"What do you mean, child?"

"If my mother had had no daughter, would you have taken another wife?"

"I might have, in my loneliness. I am hardly an old man!"

Kleopatra looked at her sister. Berenike sat quietly as one of her Bactrian girls laced her long hair into small braids.

"Father, if you had not married Thea, would Berenike be queen?"

The king shrugged. "By custom, the eldest daughter is named co-regent upon her eighteenth birthday—that is, in the absence of a queen."

"Then it is a very good thing that Berenike loves her stepmother and carries no resentment, don't you think?" Kleopatra addressed the question to her father, but looked at her sister. Berenike had jerked her head forward, yanking her braid out of the Bactrian girl's hand.

Berenike's fair skin was whiter still in the moonlight. Her full lips were as pale as the mouth of a statue. Kleopatra felt a chill and reached again for her father's warm hand. Was this the first time Berenike had realized that Thea, by seducing the king, had sabotaged her own chances of reigning as co-regent with Auletes? Kleopatra had known this fact for several years, and often wondered how it had escaped Berenike, who doted so on Thea. But Berenike resided in her own mythological kingdom where she alone was queen. What would it take to allow Thea's betrayal into her solidly walled mind?

⌣⟶🐊𐤉𐤉▦▯⟝◉◇⟝

The princess could not sleep. The smell of the sharp, citrus incense that kept away mosquitoes and other night-crawling insects sickened Kleopatra to her stomach, while Mohama, breathing monotonously, slept on a pallet not four feet from her bed.

Kleopatra was troubled by the harrowing stare of Berenike when her father uttered the awful truth. What would Berenike do now? Would she turn on Thea, or would she move against Kleopatra, who had goaded Auletes into saying the awful thing?

Tradition stood like a wall between the royal sisters, for no two women might rule together, and no woman might rule without a male co-regent. The elder sister generally married the elder brother and ruled together with him. With these equations indelibly inscribed upon the dynasty, the only sensible thing for the females to do was to find ways to eliminate one another. In that case, Kleopatra had no doubt that she would be the one vanquished.

Kleopatra would offer her theory to Berenike: Now that Thea had a daughter, Arsinoe, and two little sons, she had every reason to move against the other daughters of Tryphaena in order to insure the position of her own children on the throne. Ptolemaic mothers had done as much for almost three hundred years. Had not the eunuch Meleager informed them of that particular habit of their ancestresses?

Was Berenike either naive enough or oblivious enough to think that Thea would support her over her own children? As far as Kleopatra knew, no Macedonian queen in history had ever done that. Kleopatra would make Berenike an irresistible offer—she would happily support her against Thea.

An allegiance of blood, that is what she would propose. The sisters would cut their fingers and mix together the life force. There was no love between them, but there was the bond of blood. The blood in their veins that traced itself back to Alexander and the beak-nosed Ptolemy, whose dream figure bestowed upon the princess the form of the eagle—the symbol of the House of Ptolemy, of their dynasty, *of their very blood*. Their blood bond was stronger than their bond with Thea, who also shared their heritage, but whose blood was diluted by her Syrian father. Berenike, too, was an eagle, not merely a half-member of the House of Ptolemy like Thea. Had Berenike not proved that today at the hunt?

Kleopatra gingerly rolled the linen blanket away from her body and slid from the mattress, stepping slowly around the sleeping Mohama. Delicately but firmly she opened the flap of the tent. The night air had a subtle chill. Two guards, their bare feet outstretched, snored around a lazy fire. All was hushed inside the tents of the Kinsmen, but without, the night creatures sang their nocturnal hymns. The haunting cry of the owl, the chatter of the crickets and other insects of the marshes, the cries of the unknown animals that inhabited the glade—these did not frighten the princess, or so she told herself. A quick prayer to the goddess of night, and she slithered into the dark.

The lamps were already extinguished; Berenike's tent, a square stillness. Kleopatra got down on her knees and slipped inside the flap without making a sound. She knelt in the darkness while her eyes and ears adjusted to the new conditions inside. She saw nothing at first but two empty pallets with white linens tossed aside, beds that should have been occupied by the Bactrian attendants.

She heard a low moan and froze. Someone sounded hurt. Not knowing whether to cry for help or to investigate more, she waited. Another moan, this time lower and more desperate. She remembered how Mohama taught her to attack by surprise from behind, slitting the throat of the intruder. She had brought her knife for the exchange of blood. Could she kill in the defense of her sister? She allowed the thought of her sister's death to enter her mind. If Berenike was dead, the equation of accession to the throne would change in her favor.

Kleopatra crawled farther into the tent and squinted. On Berenike's bed, in silhouette against the white walls, the Bactrian girl who had saved her friend now held the hands of the other high above her head. She was naked, legs spread wide open. Berenike sat between the girl's knees, her dress torn open in the front and her breasts exposed. Her hand, hidden inside the girl's body, appeared to lift her pelvis up and down in a mesmerizing cadence. Berenike's arm was like a handle that controlled the girl's body as she arched herself up and down to the command of Berenike's buried hand. Each time she rose, her full breasts fell to the side. The other girl, who had saved Berenike from the beast with her well-placed quiver, pulled her friend's arms tautly over her head while she called incessantly to the gods. Berenike raised her dress and straddled the girl, moving against her, head thrown back, eyes shut tight.

Kleopatra sat rapt but for a foreign stir deep within the dark and unknowable part of her body. She dared not move, though she found herself unconsciously imitating Berenike's rhythmic movement, while the two tribeswomen bit at each other's lips, spilling deep sighs into the other's mouth. Berenike pulled fiercely at the girl's nipples, as if trying to see how far she might stretch them. The girl bucked under Berenike, who let out a sharp cry. Berenike's head fell forward, and she rocked herself back and forth very slowly. Finally, she fell forward and onto the girl's shoulder.

The unwitting witness slowly backed out of the tent. She had heard about the women who pleased one another without men. She had heard that this was the habit of the Amazons, who only fraternized with men to get with child. She had even heard that the king enjoyed watching such performances between his mistresses who were from the places where this love between women was the custom. Perhaps many adult women engaged in this sexual sport together. Kleopatra did not know, though she had seen vase paintings that insinuated as much. But she now saw that her sister lived in a separate sphere. She had a secret life—far different from the secret life Kleopatra lived when she escaped the walls of the Inner Palace and blended into the marketplace.

Kleopatra crawled back into her tent, relieved to see Mohama still overtaken with sleep, her position unchanged. She let herself back into her bed, pulling the linens up to her chin. She noticed, for the first time, how little space her body took in the large mattress. Small, alone, curling into herself, she pulled the blanket over her head and tried to succumb to sleep.

SEVEN

In the spring of Auletes' twentieth regnal year, while Kleopatra passed her eleventh birthday, a tall, thin man sat in a suite on the Via Sacra in Rome looking at a map of the world. Months before, he had been elected consul, the highest office a Roman of senatorial rank might hold. Already he was Pontifex Maximus, the most illustrious religious official in the land, which entitled him to this convenient office just a brisk walk from his home in town and from his new consular duties at the Forum. He had decorated it sparsely, for he cared not at all about his surroundings. Or his foods or his wines. Or the fluffiness of his beds or the sumptuousness of his sofas. He was not a creature for comforts. His friends and associates had developed all sorts of voluptuous fetishes, which they supposed were the adjuncts of power. For these luxuries he cared not. He liked power, not its accessories. But he did fuss about his garments and his bath. He was a fanatic for the soft caress of freshly pressed linen against smooth clean skin. And he was delighted with the wardrobe of purple-edged togas that came with his religious title, so flattering to his lean physique.

He had offended everyone in power with equanimity, but it had not seemed to matter in the end. He was a fish out of water, the one who swam against the current. Whatever they believed was fine with him. The previous year, he had negotiated an alliance among the extraordinarily rich Marcus Crassus, the awesomely powerful general Gnaeus Pompeius, and himself. Though slightly younger than his two new allies, Caesar intended to exceed each man's respective superiority by the time the game was up. For the moment, however, they were essential. Crassus—may the gods bless him—had mobilized the equestrians in his favor. Pompey made the patricians feel better about him. And the rabble loved him anyway.

It was called the Coalition. With Caesar's preference for sparse, clean language, he characterized it thus, for now no other existing coalition mattered. The arrangement had proved frighteningly simple to manipulate. Pompey charitably ignored Caesar's carnal relations with his wife, Mucia, calling her a latter-day Clytemnestra and promptly divorcing her, while Caesar conveniently left town for Spain. And it was never spoken of again. That was what he admired so about Pompey; he was inordinately proud and vain, but he never held a grudge. In return, what else could Caesar do but reject Mucia himself and marry the melancholy Calpurnia, daughter of his rich supporter Piso? Then he offered his own coltish daughter, Julia, to Pompey. Julia was the love of Caesar's life, the child of his beloved first wife, Cornelia, who died when Julia was just a baby.

Despite the thirty-year difference in their ages, Julia was all for the marriage. "Oh, Father, the general is so, so handsome." That is what all women, no matter how young or old, thought of Pompey, who was a natural with the ladies. He had old-fashioned, grand, formal ways, probably from emulating his mentor, Sulla, whereas Caesar, though only a few years his junior, had the rakish, cavalier charm of the younger set. Women had always loved Caesar, too; loved his facile abilities with poetry and words, his height—for women loved tall men—his dry wit, his impressive lineage, and, last but not least, the way he encouraged their lusts. He was adored for many and varied reasons, though he was hardly a handsome man.

So the girl Julia was pleased with her Fate, and he was glad, for she was all he had left in the way of family besides his sister, and they were no longer close. At the wedding, Pompey had given every indication that he would put his energy into romancing her. And that suited Caesar, who intended to put his energies into surpassing

Pompey in terms of square miles conquered and added to Rome's empire. Pompey looked tired; Caesar felt vigorous. Pompey dominated the east, but the west—Gaul—awaited Caesar and he knew it. All he needed now was the funding.

He felt that he was a new man. Not a *novus homo*, a newcomer to the nobility like Cicero, for Caesar's family was as old as Rome itself. Rather, he was a man for new times, a new man from an old family, a patrician with populist leanings, a member of the intelligentsia who had the devotion of the common throng. He had new ideas, vital ideas, and his opponents were those who clung to the old ways. He had no issue with the old ways, but they were no longer applicable. He had no patience with those who did not share his vision—Cato, Cicero, even Pompey.

Ah, but Pompey had played his part beautifully as a supporter of innovation when Caesar pressed him to do so. Had not he stood with a serene smile before the popular assembly and said before many a stunned senator that *yes*, he was fully in support of Caesar's land bill because it would grant plots of land to his own deserving and loyal soldiers? Pompey had stationed those very same men all around the Forum to demonstrate just how far he was willing to go in support of Caesar. And then, in a beautiful moment, the imbecile Bibulus, Caesar's co-consul, opened his mouth to disparage the bill, and a basket of excrement was showered upon his head by men who quickly escaped. A gorgeous piece of theater. Bibulus, poor fool, went back to his house and didn't leave it for the remainder of his days in office.

But then people began to complain that Caesar had gone too far, and began to call his year in office the consulship of "Julius" and "Caesar." And Bibulus coined the annoying little joke—now in widespread use throughout the city—that Pompey was king and Caesar was queen. No matter. Caesar was content with the role of queen until the king abdicated. Besides, women were perfectly capable of ruling both nations and men, he reminded his detractors. Semiramis had once ruled all of Syria, and the Amazons terrorized the better part of Asia. He would dance on the heads of his enemies. Let them call him Woman.

Caesar had been staring at the map for some time. His elegant fingers swept past the kingdom of Judaea, where Pompey had just made a puppet out of the Jewish king, and reached Egypt. He paused, stroking the country with his index finger from south to north, for that, he heard, was how the Nile River flowed. Stroked it as if it were a pet, a cat, perhaps. A sacred pet. A pet he desired for himself. True, Pompey had the crazy old king in his pocket. True, Crassus had tried to annex it to Rome years before and was shot down by Cicero and the elderly statesman Catulus. But this time Caesar would make contact on his own.

Cicero. Surely he would keep his orator's mouth shut when Caesar collected what he needed from Egypt. Surely he would not take a stand against a simple influx of money into the treasury. By the time he traced the origin of the funds, it would be too late, and Caesar and his men, bought and paid for with Egypt's money, would be far, far away. And by the time he succeeded in Gaul—an outcome he never questioned—public sway would be so strong in his favor that it would no longer matter what Cicero said.

Cato was another story. When Caesar married Calpurnia and gave Julia to Pompey, Cato accused the men of horse-trading in daughters. An aspersion upon his child. An insult upon the House of Venus. A slight to the noble Piso family. And then to say that the senate had installed a king in the castle, simply because Caesar had gotten his way. Every time Caesar had an idea he wished to see to fruition, Cato set himself to pointing out how Caesar ignored the Constitution, weakened the Republic, and usurped the senate's power. Sanctimonious beyond reason, he was like the ghost of one's dead discarded morals—stalking, haunting, reminding one of the way things used to be. He was a symbol of the old ways, the old days of the Republic, the days no one wanted to return to in reality, but wanted to reminisce over and cherish.

Pompey and Crassus agreed that Cato must be gotten rid of, and they had left the details to Caesar. No one would miss his self-righteous breast-beating once he was gone.

"Publius Clodius Pulcher to see you, sir," announced Caesar's footman. He stepped aside quickly so as to not impede the brisk stride of Caesar's guest.

"Busy, darling?" Clodius was a bit shorter, a bit stockier, a bit younger, and from a bit more illustrious patrician family than Caesar. He was every bit as intelligent, too, though hampered by an instability that caused him to crave attention. Not satisfied with the kind of quiet, dignified power that was a matter of birthright, Clodius desired the adoration of the rabble and had no aversion to the use of coarse methods to get it. Caesar had seen him use unnecessary violence against his enemies—violence that would cause a man not engaged in a war to flinch. He had a gang of thugs—there was no other way to describe them—who inflicted pain and humiliation upon any person who displeased Clodius. Yet Clodius had a tender side, sometimes alarmingly so. It was said that he was in love with his sister, Clodia, the city's most beautiful inhabitant and known to be the infamous and inconstant Lesbia of Catullus's poems. The rumor was that Clodius had had a love affair with his sister, from which he had never recovered.

"Never too busy for you, my most excellent friend." A fortuitous arrival. Caesar noticed that he only had to have need of someone for them to appear. He wondered if this owed to his being descended from the goddess Venus on his mother's side. He dismissed the secretaries with a wave of his long hand. "I was just thinking of our friend Cato."

"I, too, think of Cato, though I think ill of Cato. In fact, thinking of Cato at all makes me ill." Clodius laughed at his own joke, exposing his full mouth of unusually blunt teeth and shaking his unfashionable shaggy curls. He had little round cheeks and small, intense blue eyes, which appeared innocent until his laugh gave voice to the nasty spirit that possessed him. Caesar often pictured his former wife Pompeia and Clodius in bed. Lusty Pompeia and the madman who burst into the celebration of the goddess dressed as a woman in order to possess her. Each probably in the thrall of some magical potion to help them lose their heads. It must have been fun. Like Pompey, Caesar held no grudge against his former wife's former lover. Pompeia was beautiful, she was married to Caesar, and

Clodius, like all men, enjoyed the momentary usurpation of another man's power through his wife's vaginal canal. No matter.

"I think Cato's begun to annoy even Cicero," Caesar said.

"For all their like thinking?"

"Cicero told me that he is weary of Cato pretending to be a citizen in Plato's Republic and not a man in the real world."

"So he will not balk and carry on when we rid ourselves of
Cato?"

"I think not. Have you given the matter further thought,
Brother?" Caesar asked.

Caesar appreciated Clodius's gift for chicanery coupled with his
willingness to exceed the boundaries of both law and taste, not to
mention his spritish delight in mischief. It was Clodius who had
arranged for the men to dump shit upon the head of Bibulus. But
Bibulus was a fool and easily humiliated. Though Cato annoyed
everyone, he was still revered.

"I have pondered it," he said, tossing his curls about like a girl.
Clodius was the kind of man who could act effeminate because he
was so dangerous. It was one of the many traits the two men shared.
"I cannot stop meditating on the king of Cyprus."

"I thought we were meditating on Cato." Clodius's plots were
woven like spider's webs, in circuitous strokes, never linear, never
direct.

"I despise the king of Cyprus. Did you know that?"

"Brother, it happened twenty years ago," said Caesar. Clodius
told the story every time he got drunk. He had been kidnapped by
Cypriot pirates who demanded his ransom from the king of
Cyprus. The king refused to pay, and Clodius was so humiliated
that the pirates felt sorry for him and let him go.

"You should have done what I did in that situation," said Caesar.
When young and in the service of the king of Bithynia, Caesar, too,
had been taken by pirates. "I promised that they would die for their
crime and I lived up to my word." For thirty-eight days, he amused
himself with the pirates, demanding that they be quiet while he
slept long hours, writing verse about them, and vowing to crucify
them as soon as he was freed.

"You were sleeping with the king of Bithynia. You knew he

would pay," said Clodius. "I neglected to bugger old Ptolemy of Cyprus."

The king did pay, and Caesar made good on his promise. He was such a gay and sanguine hostage that the pirates were amazed at his vengeance. They died stunned, mouths twisted in horror and irony, protesting as they were tied to the crosses that Caesar couldn't possibly have arranged the executions because he was their friend.

But here was Clodius still seeking revenge. Caesar realized that his policy of never mixing procrastination and vengeance was a good one. He had not thought about the pirates in years. "Poor Clodius. You mustn't carry these grudges. It gives way to a sour spleen."

"I've procured a document from my old seafaring friends confessing that the king was their partner in piracy against the Republic. It's all down in ink—shipments confiscated, duties withheld. Wonderful stuff and so well documented."

"Congratulations."

"I've already shown it around. Enough people—and our Cato is one of them—think it grounds not only for punishment, but for annexation of Cyprus. Obviously the king can't be trusted, so he must be controlled. Of course, Cyprus comes with a large treasury."

"Cyprus is an Egyptian territory. The king of Cyprus is brother, or half brother, to the king of Egypt," Caesar replied.

"So what?"

"So you have managed to get support for the annexation of Cyprus. How does that serve us?"

"The king of Cyprus is rich, rich, rich. And he has beautiful things, darling, jewels, gorgeous plate of silver and gold, fabulous art. We'll take it and display it in the Forum. The people will love it."

"And Marcus Cato? What of him?"

"Who, I ask you, would make a better governor of Cyprus than Cato? I've already had it put into his head that he is the only senator honest enough to inventory the king's treasury without making himself rich."

"I see." Caesar had to admire Clodius. In his own way, he was a genius.

"Who would be more suited to lord over the old hedonist king than that prig, Cato? Oh, what I would give to see him preaching his tedious Republican morals, chastising the king for his excesses. Jumping between the king and his food, the king and his wine, the king and his lovers. The king will be out of his mind with Cato, but will be unable to do anything about it. We'll have all the king's money. And Cato will be many miles away, stuck on that lonely island for at least one year, until your consulship is finished and you've taken your post in Cisalpine Gaul."

"It's quite beautiful. Quite."

"It occurred to me during my morning defecation. Tomorrow I shall devote myself to Cicero."

Cicero was a more delicate issue. "I know you think this crazy, but I have an odd affection for the old man. I don't want anything to happen to him just yet."

"Brother, what could happen?" Clodius giggled. He hugged Caesar so tight he thought he would faint, looked into his face, winked, and turned on his heels. Gathering his cloak about him, he took himself from the room.

Caesar's secretaries reappeared, and he turned his attention to the stack of correspondence Pompey had left for him to attend to. "No one can resist your letters," Pompey had said sweetly. "Not even Cicero." Caesar's persuasive letters were an expedient means of doing business, cutting down as they did on unnecessary talk and travel.

"Read to me again the letter from the king of Egypt to Pompey," Caesar said to the scribe who kept his correspondence.

To My Great Friend Gnaeus Pompeius,

I was very sorry to receive your correspondence from Judaea informing me that you hadn't the troops available to send to my aid, particularly after the army, supplies, and money I sent to support your efforts in Judaea. Again I appeal to our long-standing friendship. The unrest among my people grows. My family is confined to the palace. It is my friendship with my Roman benefactors that raises the ire of my people. Would it not be possible to send a legion to me to demonstrate to the many factions in the city of Alexandria that the king can rely on the support and protection of the great Roman Republic and on the personal support of Pompeius Magnus? I fear that if I do not demonstrate the sanction of Rome, I shall be forced to withdraw from my country, whereupon factions hostile to the Republic shall take command of the government and the army. As long as I live you have my loyalty and friendship. I await your reply.

Urgently yours, Auletes

"The poor fellow sounds desperate," Caesar said thoughtfully. "I believe Pompey *meant* to help him. It's the very least we can do, particularly since we will be taking Cyprus from him. I am sure he gets a pretty penny from the Cypriot coffers. Here, let us write to him and allay his fears. Say this:

My dear King Ptolemy,

I am in receipt of your letter to my colleague Pompey, who is currently on his honeymoon with my daughter, Julia, and is indisposed. I have considered your appeal. You shall have the protection you require from Rome. I shall make certain the senate officially recognizes you as Friend and Ally of the Roman People—a title you have warranted for some time. This decree shall be announced throughout Rome and all her client kingdoms. However, you do understand that protection is a costly enterprise for which the Roman treasury must be compensated. Please send to me the amount of six thousand talents. If it is not possible to procure the amount straightaway, then I can arrange for you to borrow all or part of the sum from my great and trustworthy friend the banker Gaius Rabirius Postumus at a reasonable rate of interest. If this arrangement is convenient, I will have Rabirius deposit the money in our accounts immediately. He will draw up the appropriate papers, and all shall be satisfied until you are able to liquidate the necessary assets to repay the loan. I trust this is a satisfactory and expedient solution to your urgent concerns. I await your prompt response.

Yours, Gaius Julius Caesar

EIGHT

The king was a fool, all right, but he appeared to be a fool who had struck a peculiar negotiation with Fate, a fool who was protected by the gods simply because he was so foolish.

Meleager meditated upon this unfortunate fact as he received a much-needed massage from his body servant. The servant worked the muscles on the eunuch's back while Meleager took deep, exasperated breaths and tried to let his frustrations melt away into the hands of the large man.

With the strange special protection Auletes must have arranged with the gods, he had escaped the turmoil and thoroughly enjoyed himself on his hunt. The bastard king had fled the city long enough to gorge himself upon wild antelope, returning fatter than ever, and to a more peaceful kingdom. When the Vizier informed the leaders of the local *demes* that Auletes had gone on a hunt, the elder spokesman said, "At least he is not feeding himself this week with the public coffers."

Upon his return, the king had made a series of new blunders, so serious that Meleager believed the time had come to rid Egypt of his pitiable rule. Auletes had refused to come to the aid of his brother, the king of Cyprus, when the Romans annexed the territory and confiscated his treasury, despite letters from Cyprus begging for help.

"Your Majesty, the people do not understand why you do not intervene with Rome on behalf of your brother, King Ptolemy of Cyprus," Meleager said. "Cyprus is an Egyptian territory. The stolen money is Egyptian property. Now Egypt will have to negotiate with the governor Cato for the timber we receive from Cyprus for our ships and for the copper for our coins. Rome bankrupts us step by step."

"What can I do? I advised my brother to do what the Romans want him to do—abdicate and join the priesthood of Aphrodite at Paphos. Paphos is a lovely place and right there on the island of Cyprus, not some ugly rock in a black northern sea. In fact, the blind poet, Homer, believed that the goddess preferred Paphos to all other places," the king said with mock enthusiasm. "It would hardly be an unpleasant retirement."

As if his cowardice was not disgusting enough, now the king had given the extortionist Caesar six thousand talents—almost half of the country's annual income.

"I must pay the money, or I will soon find myself in my brother's position, with Cato standing at *my* palace door, making a list of *my* treasures to take away to Rome," the king had said.

"I do not think the people will have much sympathy for Your Majesty's position," said Meleager.

"I have saved my country," Auletes said. "Unlike her neighbors, Egypt is still free." He dismissed Meleager with a tired wave of his royal hand.

Meleager discovered that Auletes had borrowed the money from a Roman money lender, Rabirius. To ensure that Rabirius would be repaid, the Roman senate ensconced a contingent of representatives—"officials"—in Alexandria. The sycophant king set these men up in lavish villas in the city and gifted them with large quantities of servants, gold plate, jewels, and statuary thieved from the old Egyptian temples. The Romans repaid the king by wandering the city drunk, abusing the Greek, Jewish, and Egyptian citizens alike in the name of "Mighty Rome," and terrorizing Auletes' court prostitutes with their savage sexual appetites.

Just when Meleager thought the king had forever alienated his subjects, Auletes soothed the people's anger by declaring a general

amnesty for all those awaiting prosecution. Since the courts in
Alexandria, both Greek and Egyptian, were flooded with civil and
criminal cases, he appeased many with this decision.

"I am wiping the slate clean for my people, who I know possess
pure hearts," the king exclaimed in his last public speech. "Go home!
And thank the gods for your good fortune!"

They didn't thank the gods. They thanked the king. They forgave
the king everything—even the matter of the higher taxes they paid
to satisfy the king's creditors—and went about their daily business,
thereby nullifying, at least temporarily, all the work of the eunuch,
the Vizier, and the General. He should have let the mob murder
Auletes last year at the Grand Procession. Now what? Was the king
so popular that next year, when Berenike turned eighteen, it would
be a chore to bring him down?

The people of Alexandria had no love for Auletes, but they were
easily bought. And the king was the kind of man who knew how to
purchase affection. Was that simply human nature? wondered the
eunuch. Is man's integrity inevitably palliated when his own selfish
interests are indulged?

The eunuch turned over so that the servant could massage his
feet. It had been a long day. He sighed, releasing himself to the pressure of the masseur's hands upon his well-oiled soles.

What to do? Meleager was not a man who took risks unless he
was under the direction of the deities. Perhaps in the morning he
would go to the temple and make a sacrifice to the Mother Goddess
in an appeal for her guidance. *Give me a sign, Great Mother,* he prayed
silently. *Speak your will unto me and it shall be done.*

Two girls, one tall and the color of polished mahogany, and the
other small and peanut brown, stared at their reflections in the mirror. They had chosen the djellaba, the loose, drab dress of the
Egyptian peasant, as their disguise of the day, and had selected the
most unattractive ones that Kleopatra had hidden in her trunk.
Kleopatra grimaced. With her androgynous child's body, she looked
like a common camel boy, whereas Mohama looked like an African

goddess. With an envy that was not entirely chaste, she had stared at Mohama's jutting brown breasts before they were covered by the djellaba, wondering if her own little chest would ever own such imposing twins.

Mohama tied colorful scarves around their heads in the style of the desert people, and replaced Kleopatra's fine leather shoes with the thatched, reedy sandals worn by the palace workers. She lifted up Kleopatra's skirt and strapped a sheathed dagger onto her thin, childish thigh. She armed herself with two weapons, one tucked inside an underarm sling for easy reach, and the other in a sheath buckled to her more well-developed and muscled loin.

Leaving Sekkie as a sleeping decoy in Kleopatra's bed, they scampered down the servants' stairs in the rear of the palace and into the great kitchens, ducking under hanging fowl and small game, past the rows of men still washing the breakfast plates of the royals and their guests, and skipping through the grain pantry, where they stopped to collect baskets for shopping. With Mohama leading the way and Kleopatra assuming the mien of her humble assistant, they were soon out the back door, where workers unloaded produce-cars that delivered fresh food daily to the palace. They quickened their pace, not daring to look back at the indifferent pair of guards from the Royal Macedonian Household Troops who stood at the loading-dock doors.

"Mohama!" one called out with grave authority. The princess's feet stopped in middle step.

"Wait here," Mohama said. She sauntered back to the dock to talk to the man, a husky Graeco-Egyptian with a dark beard. Mohama cocked her head and smiled at the guard, with her hand placed firmly on her right hip. The princess was not accustomed to seeing her slave act coy with men, though Mohama seemed very practiced at this art. After a brief exchange, ending with a loud laugh from the guard, Mohama skipped back to the princess.

"Does he know who I am?" asked Kleopatra.

"Of course not. His name is Demonsthenes. He thinks you are my little cousin. He will believe whatever I say."

"Why is that? Are you so clever?"

"He believes whatever I say because he wants to," she answered cryptically.

They had no agenda for the day, only the desire to escape the court on a day of perfect weather in a city known throughout the world for its welcoming climate. Swollen clouds dappled the blue sky, moving with the sea breezes over the late morning warmth. The smell of jasmine struck their senses as they skipped along the Canopic Way. Free of everything, even her own identity, Kleopatra pranced alongside Mohama's long gait, dodging the loping Egyptian women balancing huge earthen jugs of fresh drinking water on their heads.

Swinging their baskets through the Gate of the Sun, they raced through the southeast corner of the Jewish Quarter to the foot-bridge that crossed the canal and into the more fashionable section of town where Greek aristocrats kept large, white Mediterranean houses built in the style of their homeland.

On the Boulevard of Herakles, a crowd of perhaps a hundred men peppered with a few women gathered in front of one of the larger mansions. Dressed in traditional Egyptian clothing, they moved about like a hive of nervous white-cloaked bees. Some faced the front courtyard, yelling angry words at the closed gates, while others gathered in small groups, talking excitedly among themselves. The horses and carriages and camels that had carried them into the Greek Quarter lined the street.

"Perhaps someone has died!" exclaimed the princess, quickening her pace, trying to ascertain the words chanted by the crowd. As they moved closer, she heard a man yell, "Show yourself to us, you coward!"

"They are calling to someone inside the house," she whispered to Mohama, who did not speak the language of the country that held her captive.

"Murderer! You must answer to the people!" shouted a young man in belligerent but very correct Greek. His dress was of a fine-quality linen belted with an embroidered sash. His sandals were leather. His face was recently shaven and his skin oiled and smooth—signs that he had just visited that ancient practitioner of cosmetic arts, the barber. His skin shone in the moist heat of the noon sun. He smelled of high-quality myrrh. Kleopatra recognized him as the son of Melcheir, the Exegete in charge of public services in the city. An educated Egyptian with command of the Greek tongue. Not the usual sort of person who attended a demonstration.

"This one next to us is the son of the City Exegete, Melcheir. He must be here on his father's business."

"There is no official business here. Let us go quickly," said Mohama. It was the first time Kleopatra had seen her afraid.

"No, let us investigate," the princess countered. "Perhaps we will take information to my father that is valuable and we shall be rewarded."

"If your father finds that we have been in the streets, you will be locked in your room and I will be dead. You know his rules. We must only go to the stables."

"I will protect you," the princess said with authority.

"Celsius. Celsius. Come out, Roman pig." The men shouted the name again and again, the pitch of their demand escalating. "Show yourself, Roman fiend!" an old brown woman said.

"What is the trouble here, sir?" the princess asked the son of Melcheir. She used the native tongue to enhance her disguise.

"You have no business here, girl. Go on."

"Sir, I recognize you for the son of Melcheir. My grandmother, Selinke, was your father's wet nurse," she invented, hoping the man would not deign to know the name of his father's nurse.

The man sneered at the princess. "If you must know, granddaughter of a suckling cow, the Roman intruder who lives inside these gates and feeds his obesity on revenue earned from the bent backs of Egyptian workers yesterday murdered an innocent household cat. We are here to make him answer for his crime." The cat, the man explained, was a princely bluehair from the northern regions above Persia, and a favorite of the Roman's Egyptian cook, who put out a special piece of fish every morning for the animal. "Yesterday the cook was sick and the creature was deprived of his sustenance. He made his way to the dining room crying for his meal. The fat man was hungover from his endless debauchery, and like all Romans, cruel. He threw the creature against a wall and killed it." He returned his attention to the demonstration while Kleopatra translated the story for the incredulous Mohama, who hailed from a land where a cat was not a sacred animal but a nuisance.

A small militia of Egyptians rode toward the assembly at a speed too dangerously fast for a city street, the drumbeat of the horses' hooves heralding their arrival. An outlaw army, thought Kleopatra, one forbidden by the king's orders to gather. She had heard of such ragtag bands—groups of men of vacillating allegiances that organized somewhere out in desert regions or in suburban *demes*. Men who could be bought for any cause that had the funds to pay for their strong-arm services. What were they doing here in the elite Greek section of the city? How had they managed to pass through the king's men at the Gate of the Moon on the south side of town? Had the city tribes begun to organize private militias against the king?

The horses kicked up the dry dust of the street, and Kleopatra took off her kerchief to cover her nose, letting her long brown hair loose like a woman in mourning. The men wore clean white uniforms that could not have endured a gritty morning's ride from the regions outside the city. These were Alexandrians. Egyptian men, heavily armed and riding unrestrained through the Greek Quarter. Bandits, soldiers, who knew?

Mohama grabbed the princess so hard that her arm would have the red, swollen memory of fingers for days to come. "We are getting out of here."

"I can take care of myself," said Kleopatra, jerking her arm free. "If you are scared, you go."

The crowd of protesters parted, making a path for the cavalry. The captain of the militia rode to the gate of the house, reared his horse, and brought the animal's hooves down directly on the wooden barrier, almost jostling it free. "We are not playing with you, Roman. Open your gates and answer to the people of Egypt."

The captain forced his animal again to rear against the gate, this time cracking the wood. Kleopatra felt an invincible pressure from behind thrust her into motion as the crowd, oblivious to the jagged edges, stormed the gate and crashed into the courtyard. Kleopatra looked right and left for Mohama, but the slave was not in sight. Helpless, she let herself be carried along with the mass to avoid being trampled by the men and the horses that held up the rear of the mob.

The crowd was momentarily lost for their next action. Everyone froze in an eerie moment of quiet, looking about for direction after this first victory. Suddenly, three Egyptian house servants pushed the Roman Celsius into the courtyard, surrendering him like an offering at the feet of the captain of the militia.

He reminded her of her father. Dark, obese, hairy eyebrows quivering together in fear. Fat arms his only shields against the pro-testers.

"Get up, Roman." The son of Melcheir spoke to the prostrate man in his punctilious Greek.

The Roman tried to speak, but nothing emanated from his open mouth. His face was drenched with sweat, his thick flesh quivering, his breathing belabored, his throat muscles in wild spasms.

"Go through his house," Melcheir ordered, ignoring the fright-ened man. "Take what you will of the riches the king stole from the people to give to this menace."

The men and women, some on horseback, took flight into the house. Kleopatra did not move, her eyes riveted to Celsius. The Roman tried once again to speak, but appeared to have a sudden agony in his chest. He collapsed over his belly, clutching his heart.

"Get up, I say," the son of Melcheir said in a chilling voice, kick-ing the Roman in the back.

The thud of the man's foot against the Roman's soft flesh scared the princess. She was torn between a desire to defend her father's guest and desperation to keep her identity a secret. She was power-less against such a crowd. Her father would pay the price if the Roman was harmed, but what could she do? Announce to this mob that she was the daughter of the king?

Afraid to witness the Roman's fate, Kleopatra followed the rav-aging crowd into the interior of the house. She heard the crashing of plate and glass and the shrieks of household servants, some who tried to hide under tables and some who joined the fray. A fat-faced man had a young serving girl pinned to the floor, tearing open the front of her dress and laughing at her nakedness. The princess reached under her long djellaba and felt the hilt of her knife. She wished with all her heart to drive the deadly steel into the back of the bully. But the man allowed himself to be distracted by the sight of one of his comrades making off with a bronze statue of the cow-goddess, Hathor, and ran to catch up with him.

Some of the mob had stormed the kitchen and were throwing great jars of grain over the furnishings in the main hall. An old man urinated into a large urn painted with scenes from Egyptian myths, laughing as the yellow arc hit its mark. A militiaman and a kitchen maid copulated on the Roman's couch. The woman's legs shot straight into the air while the man moved furiously on top of her. The woman seemed in a trance, making animal noises, oblivious to the girl who searched her expression for a clue as to how the rabid assault caused such frenzied delight.

An arm went tightly around her waist, holding her intently. Mohama's voice whispered in her ear, "There will be time for that later. Let us get out of here."

Gripping Kleopatra's hand, Mohama led her back into the courtyard, where a group of men had hoisted the Roman high above their heads and were tossing his weight about from one to the other like boys with a bouncing ball.

"Take him to the king!" shouted the captain. "Let us show Nothos the Bastard what we think of his Roman friends!"

The men ran out of the courtyard, bouncing the Roman up and down, his arms jerking away from his body like a puppet whose master has lost control. His eyes rolled about in his head. He made no sound. When the men tried all at once to force their way through the gate, the body hit the top of the arch and fell behind onto the ground with a sickening thump. The captain stopped his horse where the Roman lay. He did not move. One of the men leaned down and picked him up by his shoulders. Still his expression did not change, his eyes open but lifeless.

"He is dead."

"Dead? Do the mighty Romans die so easily? Does fear kill a Roman?"

No one answered the rhetorical questions asked by the son of

Melcheir. The princess stared at the corpse, still holding the dry, cool hand of Mohama.

"Throw him inside and make the king's gifts his funeral pyre. Let us take our grievances to the palace."

Mohama pulled Kleopatra out of the path of the pallbearers and out of the gate as the captain and his militia rode away with the mob trailing behind, some on foot, some on horses, a few on scraggly camels, some in the servant-driven carriages that had delivered them to the protest.

"They are going to the palace," Kleopatra said as Mohama dragged her down the street.

"Yes, and so must we. We must get back inside before the trouble starts. Now come." Mohama took her arm and tried to overcome her resistance, but Kleopatra was not resisting. She could not move. She gagged on the limestone dust kicked up by the horses, her chest racking with coughs as she tried to protect herself from the grimy stuff with the hem of her garment. A horrible acrid smell rose to her nose, pushing the contents of her stomach into her throat. She realized that she'd stepped in a mound of horse manure left behind by one of the militia's mounts. She cursed, kicking the ruined sandal from her foot. Mohama jumped aside as to not become the target of the shit-soaked slipper.

"Come on. You must run, shoes or no. This is no time to act pampered."

When they had gained a safe distance from the house, Kleopatra looked back and saw flames shoot from the interior of the courtyard into the sky like the arrows of the war god.

⌒⚞🦁ⵉ𓏏▦⌐◉⌒⌐

By the time the mob spilled onto the Canopic Way, its number had doubled. Kleopatra wondered if dissatisfaction with her father's policy toward Rome was so great that it caused people to take to the streets, or was this sudden multiplication spontaneous? Did these normally indolent citizens join the ruckus out of boredom with the predictable rituals of their miserable quotidian lives? They infuriated her. They understood nothing of politics, of economics, of the difficult demands of Rome upon her father, whose only goal was to keep Egypt—their Egypt—a nation free from Roman dominion.

Her bare feet pounded the road, keeping up with the older and taller girl. More citizens, some alone, some in groups, fell in with them, shouting obscenities about the king and the Romans. By the time they reached the palace zone, they were part of a frantic, angry parade whose destination was her home and her father.

At the north gate to the palace, Kleopatra and Mohama stopped running, allowing the throng to pass them. Mohama positioned them behind a cluster of oleander trees where they would not be overrun in the mayhem. They squatted down to hide in the shade of the thick foliage and to catch their breath.

"How can the Alexandrians hope to defy Rome?" Kleopatra asked. "Do they wish to martyr themselves?"

Mohama shrugged. "They are hoping that their gods will be with them."

"The historian Thucydides said that hope is an expensive commodity. There is no sense in hoping in a case where there is no hope, gods or no."

Mohama did not answer.

"If the Romans annex Egypt, I am going to tell my father to take whatever position they offer. Priest, king, beggar. Mohama, I do not want my father to die like his brother did. I would rather live in exile in some terrible place."

Kleopatra started to cry. Mohama said, "There is no need to cry. If we are sent into exile, then you and I will tend flocks of goats, or roam the fields at night looking for prey. We will live free like desert nomads. It is a good life for a clever person. So stop your crying. You are with me now and I will never let anything happen to you."

"We would be barefoot and free and running over soft grassy meadows," said Kleopatra, wiping her tears on her dress and smiling.

"That is right. Not dodging camel shit and other dirt on these hard streets of this city."

"Then I could live a very happy life as a shepherd girl," Kleopatra said. Perhaps even happier than as a perfumed, guarded princess.

One hundred yards ahead, the militias had lined up in phalanx style, confronting the smaller, though better armed, palace guard. Demonstrators on foot arrived from all directions. Someone had apparently spread the word to congregate at this hour. Kleopatra looked for Greek faces but saw none.

"I believe we are in the midst of the native uprising that all the generations of Ptolemies have feared," she said.

"Then it is a good thing that we are dressed like them," Mohama said. "Between my skill and your tongue, we will get safely out of here."

"Mohama, why do you not escape?"

The girl looked suspiciously at Kleopatra.

"Why do you not simply run away? I won't stop you. The kingdom is in turmoil. My father is too busy saving himself to even report that you are missing. I would not say a thing. Not until you are long gone."

"Are you mad, suggesting such a thing?"

"Why should you remain a slave? Go. *Go*, I say. Before I change my mind."

Mohama ignored her. "I am not sure if we are better off inside the walls of the residence, or if we should take our chances in the streets where no one knows who you are. Your father will be worried about you, but we cannot go to the king if your chances of survival are greater where he is not."

"I am telling you to go. This is your chance at freedom. Just go. It may be days before you are missed."

Mohama looked about, then turned to the princess. She grabbed both Kleopatra's arms in her strong hands and faced her. "I must say something to you. I do not know what will happen to us today. I do not expect you to forgive me, but only to understand. I am your servant, but I am no longer a slave. I serve the crown."

"What do you mean?"

"I mean to tell you that your father has long been aware of your escapes from the palace. He employs me to keep an eye on you. For your safety. That is why I must forbid you from doing anything that may cause you harm. That is why I do not run."

Kleopatra looked into the cool, duplicitous eyes. A deep burning began just below the rib cage. Her companion in sleuthing and espionage worked double duty for her father. So this is betrayal, she thought.

"I hate you," she said.

"Listen to me," Mohama said calmly and without fear, strengthening the chasm between them—bodyguard and charge. "After I was captured in the desert, I was taken to the Royal Brothel to apprentice as a court prostitute. I learned to speak Greek from the Madam, who took a special liking to me. She groomed me and trained me for one year in the arts of pleasing both man and woman. She said that people at court were versatile in their tastes and one must be prepared for anything."

"You're a whore?" Kleopatra asked angrily.

Mohama merely shrugged at the sling. "On my first day as a prostitute, a man tried to take me from behind and use me as if I were a boy. It hurt me so much that I asked him to stop. He would not, so I got free of him. I broke his arm, twisting his wrist and kicking his forearm with my heel as my brothers had taught me to do. Then, to leave my mark, I bit a chunk of flesh from his face."

Kleopatra tried not to show her admiration for Mohama's ferocity. She squinted to stop herself from smiling.

"I was locked in a small room. For three days I lay on the floor with no food. I thought I was going to be left to die, but the next day, two Royal Macedonian Guards brought me before the Lady Charmion, who interviewed me about my skills in weaponry and fighting, and then took me to the king."

"Why? Why would my father call for you? You are lying to me and I know it."

"It seems that the man I injured was one of your father's Kinsmen."

"And my father did not have you killed?"

"Your father had been looking for a companion for you. He told me that he had a daughter whose ebullient spirit he did not wish to kill, nor did he wish to see harm come to her. He commanded me to make you trust me, and to accompany you on your forays into the city."

Kleopatra felt the hot sting of humiliation. She had gotten away with nothing, fooled no one. Not Charmion, who every day feigned disapproval for her adventuring spirit, but who allowed her to sneak past her watchful eye. Not her father, who pretended to be the fool with her, just as he feigned that role for others. She was neither spy nor Kinsman, but a child, pampered and humored by the grown-ups. Every time she thought she had escaped their hawklike watch over her, every time she thought she was free, she was observed. Like a silly girl, she played the spy while her father, through real spies, kept knowing eyes upon her.

She looked at her companion as if for the first time. Here was a girl who had done the things she had seen Berenike do with the Bactrian girls. Who had done the things her father did with Thea, with his mistresses. Mohama was no longer her ally, but one of them.

"Traitor," was all she could say.

"I know that you will be angry with me," said Mohama in an even voice. She had dropped the veneer of kinship and assumed the voice of authority, the voice Charmion used when she had a purpose, the kind of voice a guardian would use on her charge. "There is no time now for anger or for questioning. We are in danger. Every day when we leave the palace, two bodyguards secretly follow us. Today, they are nowhere in sight."

"This is a plot against my father and we are being sacrificed," said Kleopatra.

"Perhaps. I only know that we have been left alone and that we must get safely back into the palace. Yet I do not know if that is the right thing to do since the palace is under attack."

The princess stared at the orange oleander flowers that shroud-ed the sheltering bushes, knowing them to contain a powerful poi-son, and wondering if she had the courage to stuff one into her mouth. Everyone had betrayed her. No one needed her. She was just a burdensome child—a nonessential, a thing to be tended to while the real business of the kingdom was conducted by others.

At the palace wall, the mob gained ground on the Royal Macedonian Household Troops, who tried to hold the line of pro-testers back with the points of their spears, but were outnumbered.

"Shields!" cried the captain. His men raised their bronze shields against those who threatened to storm the front gates with their horses. "We have reinforcements coming from the king's army," the captain shouted into the crowd. "You'd better go back to your homes and your families, or many of you will not live to see the sun set."

"Out of the way, Greek," said the son of Melcheir to the captain. "It's your king we want, not you. Bring us the king, the Roman lover, and we'll leave you and your men in peace."

"We are the king's men, fool," said the captain. "We will die defending the king."

Kleopatra and Mohama watched this exchange from their safe spot near the thick oleander bushes. "They mean to enter the palace," said the princess. "They are going to take my father and kill him."

Mohama put her arm around the princess, who out of desperation and fear allowed herself to be embraced.

"Deliver the king," the son of Melcheir demanded again. The mob echoed his order.

"Not even if you deliver your sister," the captain scoffed.

The son of Melcheir raised his left hand in a signal. From the middle of the mob, someone shot a flaming arrow over the palace wall and into the gardens. Then another. Then another. The Royal Macedonian Troops answered with a shower of javelins at the source of the arrows. The crowd parted. Those who saw what was coming tried to save themselves by ducking aside, allowing the guard to attack to the middle. Indifferent to the targets of the lethal metal points, they thrust ahead with their spears until they reached the group in the center who controlled the fire.

The princess saw two members of the elite Greek guard seize the fire-throwers, young men not too long at the razor, throw them to the ground, and slay them through the chest with their swords. The Egyptians tried to jump the soldiers, but, better trained than the common demonstrators, they threw the men from their backs and slashed their way through the crowd and back to their own line.

Inflamed, the protesters held up the bodies of their dead and screamed hysterically, "Death to Auletes! Death to the Bastard!"

Kleopatra saw a group of men put their clubs and spears into the firepot, raising their flaming weapons against the palace. "Burn him out!"

"I want to go home," Kleopatra insisted, trying not to let Mohama see the tears swelling in her eyes. "I want my father. If he dies, I want to die with him."

"Follow me. Do not let go of my hand," she ordered in a tone that did not leave room for dispute.

Kleopatra, shoulders cringing with each demand for the surrender of Auletes to the mob, did not look back to see the progress the dissidents were making against her father's guard. Mohama led them to the service entrance of the royal compound on the east side, hoping to find an area safe from the throng, but the palace was entirely surrounded from the east end to the west. Only the side facing the sea was clear—and perhaps it, too, was threatened. The huge gates were open and Kleopatra could see that the masses had infiltrated and overthrown the food-cars delivering supplies to the king's kitchen. The merchants had abandoned their carts and their goods. Lettuces, vegetables, heaps of herbs, grains, and fruits littered the grounds around the loading dock.

Only a small guard stood between the protesters and the king's kitchens, and they were outnumbered. They looked very frightened, eyes shifting past the mob as if hoping for help to arrive. The protesters yelled the same demands. "We want the king! Bring us the bastard Auletes!"

"There is no way in," Mohama said.

"Yes there is," said Kleopatra, surprising herself with the returned confidence in her voice. "We must pretend to be one of the rabble. We'll infiltrate their ranks to get past them. When we reach the front of the protesters, we'll tell the guards who we are and they will let us in. That Demonsthenes, he knows you. He is sweet on you. He will let us back in."

"No. It is too dangerous. Let us go to the Park of Pan and wait until the trouble is over."

"My duty is with my father. I am going in."

Kleopatra felt the heat from the men's bodies and smelled their cheap hair oil as she squeezed by them, eyes on the ground seeking a path through the fray. Finding herself in the front lines of the mob, she hoisted herself upon the loading platform where the guards stood. One of them grabbed her by the shoulders. "Get out of here, you little vermin," he said.

"Demonsthenes," she said. "I am the princess Kleopatra."

"And I am Alexander the Great," he said. He picked her up to throw her back to the crowd.

"Demonsthenes!" Mohama screamed his name. He looked at her. "Please do not hurt her." Kleopatra hoped that Mohama would not reveal her identity. The throng would smash her into shards and send the pieces to Auletes.

"I am the cousin of Mohama," she said to Demonsthenes. "I am sorry I lied. I am a polisher of silver in the king's kitchen. Please do not hurt me."

Demonsthenes threw Kleopatra aside, letting her hit the hard planks of the dock. He leaned over to help Mohama onto the platform, but an Egyptian protester caught her from behind, pulling her back into the crowd.

"Look what we've got here," said another as the man held Mohama. "The king's property. One of the king's cooks. Or maybe one of his young harlots. Let's show the king what we think of his whore!"

Demonsthenes rushed to the edge of the platform and tried to intimidate the protesters with his sword. He squatted down to jump into the crowd to help Mohama, but another guard yanked him back by his clothing. "She's not worth it. We need you. Let her go to her fate."

"No," he said, trying to escape the grip of his fellow soldier.

The Egyptian had Mohama's neck locked inside his arms. Kleopatra looked into her friend's terrified eyes, paralyzed to help her. She had never seen Mohama exhibit fear, but the desert girl who had sacrificed herself to save her brothers now looked back at her companion with the resignation of a deer caught in the hunters' nets. Kleopatra stood up, beating the second guard in the back with her fist. "Help her, I command you," she said.

He knocked her back to the ground. "Shut up, little whore. I'm not losing my best man to save the hide of a common harlot."

Mohama pulled at the arms that gripped around her throat, cutting off her breath. She could not budge the man's tight hold on her. He had lifted her onto her tiptoes. The harder Mohama struggled, the farther he lifted her, until her feet were practically dangling off the ground.

"Help her," Kleopatra yelled again. "Help her or I will have my father kill you."

But the guards were engaged in staving off the other demonstrators who took advantage of the moment by trying to leap onto the platform.

Kleopatra cowered against the wall, pushing her back against the cold granite slab. Mohama stared straight ahead, her face red and strained, her mouth in the grimace of a corpse that had been tortured, and her eyes bulging. Her body seemed completely frozen, as if she was using every bit of remaining strength just to stay alive.

Slowly, the desert girl's right hand disappeared into the hidden breast pocket in her garment. Kleopatra thought Mohama was trying to clutch her dying heart.

It was then that the princess saw the glint of the curved metal blade as it caught a late afternoon insinuation of sunlight. She watched Mohama move in the slow motion of a dream. With a magician's hand, she flipped the knife, reached behind herself, and in a great, deliberate, precise stroke, slit her captor's body from his thigh, through his pelvis, and up to his gut.

Kleopatra looked from the implacable face of Mohama to the face of her victim in time to see him register an almost imperceptible look of surprise, a faint recognition that his fate had been decided. A dark stream of his life's liquid gushed at once onto his white clothing. Surprised, unaware of his assailant, he let go of the girl and looked down to see what had caused the sudden agony. Using his bleeding body as a springboard, Mohama threw herself away from him into the arms of Demonsthenes, who pulled her onto the platform and into safety.

The man fell backward, screaming. He touched his hands to his blood and then raised the red palms to the sky. The crowd, suddenly quiet, looked among their own ranks for the culprit, while Demonsthenes lifted the bolt of the double doors that led to the kitchens and hustled the two girls through.

NINE

Kleopatra followed Mohama up the servants' stairs at the rear of
the palace, her feet throbbing with every step. She stared at the back
of Mohama's dress, soaked in blood, clinging to her backside. The
interior of the palace was remarkably calm. There was no committee representing the king proclaiming gladness at their safety, no one
into whose arms she might have jumped. Kleopatra wondered if
they had even been missed.

Inside the chamber, the rigid face of Charmion greeted them.
"Bathe and dress," she said quietly. "The king will see you after he
is finished meeting with his advisers."

"Is my father safe?" asked the princess.

"At present, it appears so."

Kleopatra allowed herself to be stripped and washed by silent
slaves, dressed, and brought before her father. Without saying a
word, he planted a hard slap on Mohama's brown face, leaving red
streaks where his fingers made contact. Kleopatra observed her own
silence and wondered why she did not speak out for her bodyguard.
She heard with distant ears the even-toned explanation of Mohama,
whose hands did not even touch the swelling scarlet on her face. She
watched as if she were a stranger to herself and to the others as her
father threw his hands up, letting remorseful tears of anxiety and
relief roll down his chubby cheeks.

She lay for two days alone in her bed, refusing the food brought to her, even when Charmion tried to spoon-feed it to her tightly closed mouth. From her bedroom window she heard more shouts coming from the streets, this time in Greek. The clash of swords, the low hum of confrontation, lasted all day long.

"It is the Greeks this time. Our own people," Charmion explained. "A meddlesome philosopher named Dio has organized them against your father. They are upset by the death of the king of Cyprus and the Roman annexation of that Egyptian territory. They fear Egypt is next. They are calling for your father to abdicate."

It was too much for the sick girl to think about. She knew a philosopher at the Mouseion named Dio, a verbose Sophist who spouted aphorisms at the lazy young boys in his tutelage. Kleopatra simply nodded and fell back into her deep slumber. What had become of Mohama she did not know and did not ask. Perhaps the king had given the girl a more important assignment.

On the third day, Charmion brought the news that Auletes would travel to Rome to demand something in return for the six thousand talents he had paid Julius Caesar. He was going to request a show of military support from Rome or else ask that his money be returned.

The princess sat up for the first time in days. "Is my father abdicating? Who will govern in his place?"

"He is leaving the queen to keep the throne, with Meleager and Demetrius as her appointed Regency Council."

"He is leaving us here to die," the princess said, suddenly queasy. Would her father sacrifice all of them, his wife and five children, to his ambitions?

"Nonsense. You talk like a child. If the entire Royal Family goes to Rome, the king will have abdicated, or so it would appear to the people. Your father has arrived at the most intelligent solution to his troubles. The people will not move against the Royal Family if they know they are going to face a Roman legion."

Kleopatra said nothing. *He has sacrificed his family like lambs to slaughter.* She counted herself among her father's victims.

Without warning, her stomach collapsed. It was as if she had been stabbed in the gut, as if someone not present had pushed the knife. There was a word for that kind of magic, though she could not think clearly enough to remember it. Had someone put a curse on her? Motionless, she absorbed the pain in her innards. When she could move, she ran from the bed clutching her middle section, and vomited before she reached the door. Then she saw nothing but black and was not even aware when she crumpled like a rag doll and hit the tile floor.

Out of the dark void came the cold, yellow stare of her sister Berenike, dressed in warrior's clothing, holding an ancient sword above her head. Beside her, the short, combustible six-year-old Arsinoe, a breastplate over her chest and armed with a knife. Berenike ripped her own dress open, revealing only one large Amazonian breast. The other had disappeared and with it the nipple, replaced by a jagged scar. Berenike was poking her sword at Arsinoe, toying with her like she was a puppy, but Arsinoe only laughed, holding her arms out as if praising the gods. Kleopatra looked into the child's luminous eyes. Berenike put the point of her sword into the soft spot on the girl's throat and pushed. The child did not move. Blood poured from her neck. Still smiling, bleeding from the throat, Arsinoe looked down. At her feet, dead, lay Kleopatra.

When Kleopatra came to, she was sobbing and Charmion was helping her back onto the bed.

"I shall summon the doctor," Charmion said, her chilly hand on Kleopatra's hot forehead.

"No. Please." Kleopatra rubbed her eyes, trying to make sense of the vision. "This is not a problem for a doctor, but a holy man or a magician or perhaps a philosopher. Or a soldier or a spy."

"Child, you are ill and delirious. I am taking no chances with you. Particularly in light of recent events."

"If you call a doctor, I shall kill myself," Kleopatra said vehemently, sitting up and grabbing Charmion's dress. "I do not like to quarrel with you, Charmion, because I love you, but I do not like your interfering ways."

"It is my duty to interfere when your judgment is bad," she said, not backing down.

Kleopatra did not argue, but folded her arms. "What did Socrates say about Knowledge?"

Charmion stared at her as if afraid she had lost her mind entirely. "This is no time to make a philosophical dialogue. You are ill."

"Please, Charmion. I am trying to explain myself. Think back to your own lessons. What was the philosopher's position on Knowledge?"

Charmion did not like to be challenged. "He said that Knowledge was a property of the Immortal Soul. That Knowledge is not taught, but remembered. That the process of knowing was but remembering what the soul already knows. Is that the answer you seek? And if it is, then what has Socrates to do with vomiting?"

"Listen to me, and please do not look at me as if I were merely a child. I know that I am a child, but some things I simply know."

"And what do you know this time?" Charmion was not practiced at hiding exasperation.

"I know that I must not stay in Alexandria. I know that if I remain after my father leaves, I will die."

"You are talking craziness, Kleopatra. If you want to make a trip to Rome, you might ask your father without all these dramatics."

"I can't explain it, Charmion. It's like languages. I cannot tell you how I understand the foreign tongues. I only know that when I hear them, it is as if I am remembering a far-off lesson, another life, something."

"I believe you are delirious."

Kleopatra sat on her knees on the bed. "You must listen to me. Without my father's protection, I am not safe here. When we went into the Delta to hunt, the king got very drunk one night and I made him say in front of Berenike that Thea took Berenike's rightful place as his co-regent. You should have seen the look on Berenike's face. As soon as Auletes is out of the way, she will be out for the throne."

"You are unwell. You are submitting to the fantasies caused by fever. I am calling the physician." Charmion gave Kleopatra a look of pity and turned around to leave.

"No. I forbid you to walk out the door."

Charmion, imperious, acquiescing, lowered herself to sit on the bed next to the princess, her spine stark and straight like a reed of bamboo.

"As soon as you told me my father was going to Rome, something came over me. It was like a vision, and as soon as I had it, I became ill. It was as if I saw my Fate, and it was so horrible that I had to expunge it by throwing up."

"And what is that Fate?"

"That Berenike is going to kill me."

Charmion changed Kleopatra's clothes and washed out her mouth with a sweet-tasting liquid. She wiped her face with a cool cloth, rebound her hair, took her hand, and led her out of the Inner Palace. They walked across the courtyard and through the formal gardens to the edge of the compound, where they boarded a small rowboat to the island Antirhodos, where the old ladies of the court resided. Kleopatra took in the fresh marine air, grateful that the waters were calm. She kept her eyes on the oar as the rower dipped it into the pale velvet sea, wondering what Charmion was up to. Kleopatra did not know these old women. They disapproved of Thea, and so annoyed Auletes that he kept them lavishly sequestered on the island in a sumptuous old building, where they could complain of nothing but their inability to meddle in affairs of state and the personal doings of the royals.

The ladies' quarters were thrown into confusion by the unexpected visit. Each wrinkled face fussed over Kleopatra, allowing how much of her mother's charm and beauty peeked from her eleven-year-old eyes. They stroked her cheeks, petted her hair, demanded kisses, and took her from one lap to the next as if she were a little baby. She supposed that to women so old, she appeared no different from an infant.

"The child fears for her life," Charmion said, finally announcing their business. "She received a warning from the philosopher Socrates in a vision. What can you tell us?"

"The philosopher! He comes to us all the time in our dreams," said a tiny lady. Her shriveled arms and humped back made her look like a little mouse hunched over a crumb of cheese.

"He does not like the ways of the world," said another ominously. "He warns us of catastrophes to come."

"The philosopher is a very busy spirit," said Charmion. "But if you are in regular communication with him, perhaps you may properly interpret the meaning of the princess's vision."

The old ladies prepared for the princess a large cup of thick, murky tea, served hot and steaming and in a giant cup that she had to hold with both hands. It was not the kind of thing she felt like drinking on a day when her stomach had already turned against her.

"This smells more like the potion that *killed* Socrates," Kleopatra said, wrinkling her nose.

But the ladies insisted, so she drained the liquid and found its taste not so offensive. When she finished, one by one, the crones passed the cup, each cautiously examining the remains at the bottom. With each passing of the cup, the faces grew more grave. It was generally agreed that the straggling tea leaves displayed a situation of impending doom.

"You must go far away, child. Nothing good will come of your life if you remain in Alexandria past the feast day of the corn goddess," said an old brown-faced woman whose sad, chicken eyes were outlined with far too much kohl. "I was your mother's favorite great-aunt. You must trust me."

"But she is a child, and this is her home," said Charmion. "What am I to do? Send her away in secret to a place where others will care for her?"

"If you love her, see to it," said the great-aunt.

"My father is to make a voyage to Rome next week. Will I be safe if I accompany him?" asked Kleopatra.

The ladies huddled their faces over the cup once more. After staring, muttering, and much shaking of the head, they unanimously agreed that the princess could, should, must, go to Rome.

Kleopatra gave a triumphant look to Charmion. Promising the old ladies lavish gifts from that strange city, the seat of the world's government, she took leave of them.

In the evening, the girl defied the king's prissy Royal Attendants and burst in on Auletes taking his meal with his mistress Hekate.

"Your father wishes privacy," warned a sour-faced man wearing a large plumed hat with a great jewel at the crown of his head holding the feathers together. He looked like an indignant bird.

"My father shall abuse you much if you keep him from the company of his favorite daughter," she said. The king's attendants never knew how to behave in these matters, so erratic was Auletes in his response to his family. But they all knew his indulgence of this one.

Kleopatra did not dislike Hekate. This evening she wore a pale draped silk dress that showed her august neck and the creamy pearl-colored skin of her bosom. She was much more beautiful than the queen, and more regal, too, thought Kleopatra. She wore a sweet-smelling perfume that reminded Kleopatra of lilies, far preferable to Thea's oppressive undiluted lotus oil with which she immoderately doused herself. Hekate was the only one of Auletes' mistresses that he entertained publicly. She was intelligent in the tradition of the *hetairai*, the sanctioned courtesans of Greek nobility. She herself was born of fallen Greek aristocrats, and very graceful.

"Father," said Kleopatra. "I must demand an audience."

Auletes and Hekate exchanged condescending smiles. In the presence of adult women the king treated the princess like a child; when they were alone, he gave her words and her presence full credence.

"Father," she said, with as much dignity and force of will as she could summon in her nervous condition, "it is my wish to accompany you to Rome."

The king said nothing but stared at the princess. His face remained maddeningly impassive.

I must play this right, she thought, but the king gave no clues as to the next step. It would be no use to tell of Socratic visions, of the augury of old women. Auletes would have no patience with such tales. She could not force his will. She must argue well—subtly yet forcefully, and above all, strategically.

"I could be of great use to you, Father. I am proficient in the dialects you shall encounter in your voyage, including the Latin tongue, which, you admit, baffles you by its coarseness."

"My child, I have interpreters in my travel party." Distracted, he ran his fingers along the nape of Hekate's neck. Why was he so preoccupied with a woman he had had many times, and would have many more if he desired? The princess gauged her next step.

"Do you trust your servants so much that you will not doubt their translations?"

Auletes' implacable face turned to one of aggravation, perhaps at the notion that his eleven-year-old child might protect him. The princess perceived that he was anxious to be rid of her so he might become more intimate with Hekate. "Come to me tomorrow, child."

To remain and argue her case was fruitless in the face of his desire for the pale beauty at his side. But Kleopatra stood nonetheless, unwilling to be so lightly discharged.

"Father, if I remain behind, and you have incorrectly gauged the loyalty of your army, you shall have no heirs." It was her best shot, cryptically delivered and, she hoped, well timed. She turned on her toes and walked out.

"Very well," came the voice of the king. The princess stopped, but did not turn around. "Look at me, child."

She turned to face her father, who wore a self-satisfied expression. "Have Charmion see the Travel Steward for your allowance of luggage and attendants. We sail for Rhodes in two days' time. I trust your staff and your little royal personage will be prepared."

Part II

ROME

TEN

Helios the Sun God lay crumpled in shimmering waters at the harbor in Rhodes. The colossal bronze statue, one of the great wonders of the Greek world and the protector of Rhodes City, had come toppling down the last time the gods expressed their displeasure with the island, shaking the earth until every man-made pride had fallen to pieces. The island had recovered, rebuilt its harbor and its businesses, but the god still lay in shambles on the shore, gentle waves lapping at his headless torso, his great bronze crown of sunrays now a tarnished barnacle green.

"Why do they not move the god?" Kleopatra asked. She could not bear to witness the god's disgrace. She looked past the fallen Greek idol to the shops and mansions lining the long, sandy beach, and the whitewashed houses that dotted the rose-covered rocks and mossy slopes above the town.

"Because the people are afraid that if they move the city's protector, the earth will shake again. The priests advise against tampering with it," answered the king as he searched the dock for a greeting party.

"But it is so very sad to see him lying there, headless and ugly. Can you not do something, Father? You are beloved upon these shores."

Auletes, like all members of his dynasty, enjoyed special loyalty from the people of Rhodes. Many centuries before, when the city was besieged by Demetrius Poliorketes the tyrant, Ptolemy I had intervened and run him off. The oppressor was in such a hurry to get out of town that he left his siege artillery, which the Rhodians sold to build the giant statue of the god. For his efforts, the people of Rhodes christened Ptolemy I *Soter*, the Savior, a title he became very fond of and used officially all his life.

"We are here to solicit support and advice, Kleopatra, not to dictate to the clergy," said the king. "The government of Rhodes enjoys good relations with Rome. We are here to learn how to do the same. You shall have to satisfy yourself with the way things are. We shall enjoy the island's beauty, but leave it as we find it."

Chastened, Kleopatra groped for a subject that would recover her father's grace. She did not want to be sent home, nor did she wish to be left in Rhodes in the care of polite, dull Greek women while her father sailed onward to Rome. "Father, is it true that the island of Rhodes has more butterflies than anywhere else on earth?" she asked brightly.

"Yes, and more statues, too," said the king. "But do not be fooled. The island is also infested with snakes. So do not think that you can run off and play like you do at home." The king directed these words not at his daughter, but at the taller girl who stood at her side.

"Do not worry, Sire. There will be no more games." Mohama spoke with easy nonchalance, making Kleopatra wonder if she had had private conversations with the king since that cold hard slap Auletes delivered to her cheek the day of the riots.

For weeks after the incident, Kleopatra had shunned her former companion, fastidiously erasing her from her thoughts, and finally, after days and days of effort, forgetting to miss her. But the morning of the launch, when she alighted the carriage, hounds scampering ahead of her, giant planks shivering beneath her feet as workers hustled the king's goods aboard the ships, Kleopatra felt a whisper of regret that she was leaving Mohama behind. Then she looked up and saw the lone dark-skinned figure standing on the dock staring out to sea, her red traveler's cloak a splash of blood against the drab morning fog. The princess looked angrily at Charmion, who displayed no emotion and gave no apology. The day before, Charmion had suggested that they include Mohama in their party, allowing that she might not be treated well by those who remained in the city. Kleopatra remembered the animosity that had passed between Mohama and Berenike's Bactrian women, but then pushed the rivalry out of her mind. She still stung from Mohama's betrayal and was not inclined to show mercy.

"I never want to set eyes upon her again," Kleopatra retorted. "If you wanted to make me happy, you would bring me the news that she has been enslaved, beaten, and tortured for placing a royal child in danger."

"I believe that she was commissioned by your father to keep the royal child out of danger," countered Charmion.

"Don't tell me that you are going to defend her," said Kleopatra, exasperated. "If we were not in a hurry to travel, I would demand that my father have her hands cut off. Then I would have her returned to her desert tribe where she couldn't even be a thief anymore."

Charmion made no response to this tirade, but gave Kleopatra a captious, almost pitying look. Kleopatra kicked her wooden trunk in anger, stubbing her toe. She yelped in pain like a puppy, ran to Charmion, put her head in the lap of the stern lady, and bawled great heaving tears until she wore herself out.

The next day, the king's party—the Royal Steward, a bodyguard of seven, four Kinsmen, a priest and priestess, cooks and servers, and pets and other animals for sacrifice—ambled up the bridge and onto the ship, looking more like travelers on an adventure than a king's entourage fleeing a rebellion, and Kleopatra's dogs rushed ahead of her to greet the red-cloaked Mohama, nuzzling their snouts against her. Exasperated, Kleopatra followed them, determined to demand that Mohama remain behind. The tall girl petted the dogs distractedly, letting her attention linger on the water, her lovely cocoa skin green with fear.

"I am afraid." Mohama's face looked as if she had just been visited by a terrible phantom. "I have never been on the waters."

"I did not know that *you* had fear." Kleopatra had to struggle to suppress the small secret thrill she felt at being once more in Mohama's company. "You have faced more formidable enemies than the sea, Mohama."

"I have heard of the wrath of the god Poseidon. He will know that I am a child of the sands and do not worship him. He will take his vengeance upon me." The girl's face contorted in anxiety, her brow creased like an old woman, making curvy lines in her smooth, chocolate forehead.

Kleopatra stood very tall and spoke with authority. "Do not be foolish, Mohama. Libya, daughter of Zeus—the goddess for whom your land is named—was once the wife of the sea-god. From him she bore twin sons."

"How do you know that?"

"It is a well-documented fact and known to all educated people throughout the world." Kleopatra enjoyed her moment of conde-scension. She continued patiently, as if pacifying a child suffering from imaginary fears, "Before we sail, my father, the king of the land, will sacrifice a white cow to the king of the sea. Poseidon will forbid the sea-serpent Triton to blow his conch shell and stir up the seas while we sail. My father shall also appease Triton with a pair of small white goats with very tender shanks—a rare commodity for a sea creature. The king sacrifices on behalf of all travelers in his party. You will see. The waters will remain calm."

"Are you certain, Kleopatra?"

"I guarantee it," said the princess, slipping her warm hand against the cool, rough palm of Mohama, lacing their fingers together, and walking hand in hand toward the ship.

⌐⏷𓃒𓏏𓏏𓊖𓂁𓃀𓂝𓂋

The Greek statesman who had earned the privilege of sheltering the king and his entourage on the island greeted the party at the harbor with the news that the Roman senator Cato had landed at Rhodes. "He has stopped here on his way to Cyprus to nurse a severe illness of the bowels that afflicted him at sea," said the Greek, wrinkling his nose. "I trust this will not cause Your Majesty any dis-comfort."

Auletes was outraged that he should have to share the island with the villain responsible for the death of his brother, king of Cyprus. "That man is the reason I am making my way to Rome now," he said. "If not for him, I would have slept on my own mattress last night, not tossed about on that hard bunker of a bed that tortured me until sunrise."

"He is vexed by the doctors, rejects their treatment, and administers to himself the remedies of his great-grandfather," said the dignified Greek. "He has also taken to the extreme use of alcohol, and his condition only worsens."

"Good," replied Auletes. "I shall avoid the monster at all costs."

But as days passed, the king began to think that the Roman might offer him information about the kind of reception he would receive in Rome. Auletes circulated word of his arrival among the Rhodian population and its dignitaries in every way he knew how. He waited two and one-half days for Cato to call upon him, but the Roman sent no indication that he was inclined to meet with the exiled king.

Kleopatra declined all invitations to tour the island, instead sitting with her father in the reception room of the mansion where they stayed, watching him pace like a caged beast, waiting for Cato to call on him. Finally, Auletes swallowed his royal dignity and sent a messenger to Cato to deliver the news that he had arrived and was receiving guests.

To this, Cato did not respond.

Auletes had no choice but to request a meeting. Contemptuously, Cato declined.

"Who is this Roman that he should make my father suffer?" Kleopatra asked. She was sitting on her father's lap late one evening after a long banquet, sipping from Auletes' golden goblet. It pained her to watch her kingly father fret like a nervous serving girl over this Roman swine.

"Who is this Roman that he should insult our king?" echoed the inebriated Kinsmen. The men were sprawled about the dining hall, some having forsaken their couches and sitting directly upon the table amid platters of fruit and pitchers of wine, their boots unlaced, their long legs stretching the width of the table. The wealthy Rhodian businessmen invited to the dinner to meet with the king sat back in their seats, with languid limbs slung over the arms of the sofas. Only Charmion, the sole adult woman present, remained sober and sufficiently erect.

"We have heard that Cato is always drunk," offered the Rhodian statesman with whom the king lodged. Presently, he appeared to share that condition with the Roman. "They say that he yells at his servants if they try to bring him food and beats them if they do not bring the drink fast enough when he requests it."

"He is nothing," said a Kinsman. "His family were still dirt farmers when His Majesty's family had ruled Egypt for generations."

"He has no right to humiliate a king."

Kleopatra could see that the talk, meant to bolster and cheer the king, had the opposite effect. I know my father better than all these men, she thought. She settled into the crook between the king's shoulder and his belly, adjusting her position on his lap, unaware that she absorbed the king's anxiety about Cato into her own small body. Nervously, she fingered his cup, taking another gulp of bitter wine. She had drunk enough to be sleepy, though her fears kept laxness at bay. Auletes seemed neither to notice nor to care that his daughter was getting drunk. He cuddled the girl to his chest, causing her to topple the cup and spill the red liquid upon his linen robe.

She put a repentant hand to her mouth, but Auletes simply laughed and clutched her harder, so that she could feel the quake of his belly rising and falling as he amused himself with her accident. He took the cup from her small hand, drained the rest of the wine, and threw the cup on the floor.

"More!" he called to no one in particular.

A servant rushed toward him with a fresh white robe, but this man he kicked in the chest, sending him toppling backward. The Kinsmen and guests laughed at the calamity, and the stunned servant—stunned, for Auletes was not a cruel man—immediately saw the wisdom in joining in the laughter. He picked himself up, brushed off the fresh garment, and proffered it again to the king, though this time at a distance.

"More wine, fool," said the king, still laughing. "More wine! Not more clothes!"

The Kinsmen again laughed at the servant, who recovered his dignity by snapping his fingers toward the two serving girls huddled in the corner who scurried to fill Auletes' glass, almost tripping over each other. In the rush to please the king, their pitchers clashed, and he doubled over in an uncontrollable spasm of laughter, almost sending his daughter off his lap. Kleopatra, afraid that the two great colliding pitchers would smash her head, ducked into the shelter of her father's gut, bringing more peals of merriment.

"Tomorrow it shall all be settled," the king said, releasing the tight squeeze he had on the girl on his lap. "Tomorrow, I shall meet with the Roman."

Kleopatra sat up as if startled out of a dream. She shook her head to try to clear the drowsy feeling.

"Tomorrow the Roman comes here?"

"No, child, the Roman is not in a position to leave his chambers."

"Has he been censored by his superiors?" the girl asked.

"He has a more compelling reason than that. His doctors have prescribed routine ingestion of laxatives for his flatulence, and he does not wish to leave his chambers in this vulnerable condition. The Roman has invited me to attend him in his quarters," said the king matter-of-factly.

A red-faced Kinsman pushed himself off his chair and struck an indignant pose. "Our king must not humble himself to the summons of an ordinary Roman citizen." The men of Rhodes, who had long been squirming under the Roman thumb, shook their heads in agreement, muttering crass comments about Cato's condition.

"We depart for Rome in two days. Dignity is a small price to pay for Rome's sanction," said Auletes. "I have said before that the gods are with Rome and I am with the gods."

But the Kinsmen and the Rhodians did not see the king's wisdom.

"How is it that you do not understand our situation?" shouted the king. "You are like children. You are worse than children, Brothers, because my daughter is wiser than you."

Kleopatra sat up straight on her father's lap, surprised to be dragged into the argument and afraid to look at the insulted Kinsmen.

"Kleopatra, tell our Kinsmen why it is that Egypt has no Roman governor, despite the fact that every neighboring country has fallen to Roman domination."

Every bleary eye in the room was on the child. "Go on, girl," said the king. "Speak up."

She took a deep breath, "Because King Ptolemy XII Auletes, Pharaoh of Two Lands, son of Dionysus and the native god Osiris, and *my father,* is a friend to Rome."

"Precisely, my child." He ignored his men and locked eyes with his daughter. "Remember this: Always, we are threatened by the might of Rome. Always we must slake the beast. Do you understand that, Kleopatra?"

"Yes, Father."

"Because the one thing that Rome always needs—the true god and idol and soul of the Republic—is the one thing we Ptolemies always have."

They said the word together. "Money."

The Kinsmen laughed, but Kleopatra was worried by the fatigue in her father's eyes. "I shall remember it always," she said. "Tomorrow, I shall accompany you to meet the Roman."

"You are eleven years old."

"I am a princess and I can impress the Roman with my knowledge of the Latin tongue and of Latin literature. I shall be the strictest evidence of your loyalty to Rome, father. He will think that you have paid honor to Rome by educating your daughter in the Roman language and the Roman arts. I shall be your brightest emissary." She stared at her father, avoiding the skeptical faces of his men, who had since grown quiet.

"So you shall," said the king, to the astonishment of all present, even the princess. "I shall let you be my littlest diplomat."

Kleopatra had never seen a more stern-faced old man than Cato. His mouth appeared set in a permanent grimace, with deep crevices slashing downward from the corners. He did not rise upon the royal party's entrance, but remained in his chair with a blanket covering the lower part of his body, so that the princess could not be certain that the chair upon which he sat was not a toilet. With an indolent wave of the hand Cato bid Auletes to approach him. The Kinsmen were mortified by this behavior and desired to move against him, making ominous rattles with their swords, but Auletes signaled to them to be still.

"Who is the child?" the Roman asked, speaking in Greek to the king but staring into the face of the young girl, who stared back at him.

The Roman did not understand that he mustn't address the king first. A Kinsman said, "The princess Kleopatra, the king's second daughter. She is well-versed in languages."

"Is that so?" he said slowly, as if words alone, no matter what their meaning, put him in a foul way.

Kleopatra held her father's hand, anticipating a cue of some kind, but received none. The king stepped toward the Roman. The princess moved with him until they took their seats opposite the Roman. The Kinsmen awaited their king at the back of the room.

"I have considered your position, Your Majesty," offered Cato, apparently oblivious to the customary formalities accorded to a king. "I must advise you to abort this voyage to Rome. You must go back to Egypt and reconcile with your people."

"Marcus Cato," the king began in so agreeable a tone of voice that the princess would have thought he was speaking to one of his favorite pets. "I would like nothing better than to reconcile with my people, as you call them, but I am in an untenable position without the support of Rome. The citizens of Egypt—Greek and Egyptian and Jew alike—are hostile to me for acquiescing to the demands of Caesar and Pompey. My subjects have suffered under the strain of high taxes necessary to pay Rome what Rome requires. This is the cause of their rebellion. Were it not for the demands of Caesar and Pompey upon me, my people would be perfectly content."

"Nonetheless, that does not change my opinion." The Roman

doubled over his stomach, issuing such a loud cry of pain that the king instinctively jumped to help him. Cato, one arm clutching his stomach, raised the other to ward off the king. Auletes took his seat.

The Roman sat up, his eyes turned toward the heavens as if to ask the gods why this ill health had befallen him. "You see my predicament?"

"I won't keep you, my Roman friend," the king said. "I only wish to know your considered opinion of the reception I shall receive in Rome. Might you characterize the mood of the senate?"

Cato said, "My good king, the senate is no more useful than an old man's prick."

Auletes burst into laughter despite the gravity of the situation. "If the senate is of no use, then, pray tell, who governs Rome?"

"It's a monarchy, much like you have in Egypt. Pompey is king; Caesar is queen."

Kleopatra had heard those exact words in the marketplace. She wondered, but did not think it suitable to ask, if, in addition to bedding Pompey's wife, Caesar had bedded the great man, too. She would discreetly inquire on this matter in Rome.

Auletes pressed Cato for more information. Who might he see in Rome to help his cause? But Cato grew weary of company, perhaps because of his condition, perhaps for need of the drink. He said, "Sire, there is a Roman law forbidding a citizen to sell himself into slavery in order to pay his debts, but I believe it is still permissible for a foreigner to do so."

The Kinsmen drew their swords. Auletes rose upon hearing this abominable insult, and the princess with him. She hoped her father's men would take vengeance upon this insulting Roman who talked to her father as if he were a common servant. She would have liked to witness a fight, even at the high cost to her father.

But Cato allowed a crack in his relentless grimace. In a calming tone he said, "I thought our conversation benefited by the insertion of humor, Your Majesty. Believe me, I am trying to save you from what will be humiliation, should you proceed to Rome."

The king waved to his men; reluctantly, they resheathed their swords, but they did not sit.

"Listen to me, Sire," Cato continued. "I am known to be a plain-speaking man. You will never receive more sound advice than this: Go home and raise the money to pay your debt. Do not appear in Rome begging more favor, or this will be a game you play without end. You could turn Egypt into liquid silver and pour it into their pockets and it will still not appease either the senate or Pompey or the vulture Caesar. The leeches who rule Rome will bleed you dry."

The princess was astonished at the Roman's candor. He spoke without fear, knowing Auletes might repeat his words to Pompey, to other senators, to Caesar himself if he had the opportunity. Yet the old grouch appeared to be free of the anxiety that his words might be reported to his Roman colleagues.

"You cling too fiercely to your situation, my dear King Ptolemy," he said gently, almost charitably. "I would not worry so about the annexation of Egypt. Should this occur, it would liberate you. You would no longer have these concerns."

"Yes, I could be liberated—just like my brother."

"I will clarify for you the unfortunate circumstances that occurred in Cyprus. I realize that the actions of Rome and the death of your brother must be cause for some mystification. You see, my enemies in Rome needed to be rid of me. They cannot tolerate a vocal and persuasive critic. The great man Marcus Tullius Cicero is next, of course. They will banish him, somehow."

"What is your meaning?" asked the king.

"It is very simple. Caesar has an agenda of legislation he wishes to pass this year. I am against him in every cause. Therefore I must be got rid of, and therefore, he and his gangster, Clodius, concoct-ed the charges of piracy against your brother, giving them an excuse to send me off to Cyprus to pick his treasures dry. It is my duty, distasteful as it is. At least I shall perform my services without lin-ing my own pockets."

"That is a remarkable tale," said the king.

"I see that you view me with skepticism, but that would be a mis-take. I am not a particularly imaginative man. I do not invent wild stories. Take my advice; to trust either Pompey or Caesar would be a miscalculation. Unlike my peers and colleagues in Rome, I have no aversion to speaking the truth."

"What are my choices?" asked the king. Kleopatra could see that the Roman's honest manner of speaking intrigued her father.

"Return to Egypt and reconcile with your subjects. I offer my services to you. I and my staff will accompany you to Alexandria. We shall meet with the necessary parties and negotiate a settlement between them and yourself. Do you see how far I am willing to go to have you avoid the treachery and bribery you will confront in Rome?"

"And would you not extract your own price for this deed?" asked the king.

"Your Majesty, I am as rich as I ever care to be."

"This is an exceptional offer, my good man, and one I shall sincerely consider. What do you propose my other choices to be?"

"You might take the offer your brother was too stubborn to accept. Submit to the inevitable: Await the news that your country is Rome's next annexed nation. At that time, take up the robes of the priest, save your family, and live in peace. Or perhaps you might negotiate with Caesar or Pompey, whichever decides to march into your kingdom and usurp your treasury. They might allow you to remain on the throne. But surely you are aware that you would be a king in name only."

The Roman sat back and rubbed his ailing stomach. He raised an index finger into the air ominously. "I say this for your own protection. Do not go to Rome with your hand out and your pockets open. There will be no end to the price you will pay."

⌣⬤ⱠⱠ▦ᴗ◉◇ᴗ

"Have I been disgraced or not?"

Auletes did not trust the Roman; yet he believed that Cato's offer to travel to Alexandria was made with noble intentions. The princess did not trust the Roman's motivations, but was not sure that the king should not honor the proposed scenario. The Kinsmen, on the other hand, believed the king had been mocked.

"Send word to Demetrius," the king gruffly ordered his secretary. "Tell him of Marcus Cato's offer and ask him if he thinks such a delicate arrangement might be made without an outbreak of violence."

But upon return to the great parlor of the Rhodian mansion, Auletes received a letter that made his direction very clear.

To: Ptolemy XII Auletes, former king of Egypt

From: Meleager, Regent and Adviser to Queen Kleopatra VI Tryphaena

Enclosed please find a document signed by the Egyptian and Greek tribe leaders of the majority of the *phratries* in the city. The people of Alexandria and of Lower and Upper Egypt have declared you an illegal usurper. You are officially deposed. Your wife, Kleopatra VI Tryphaena, is the recognized ruler of Egypt. You and your daughter, the princess Kleopatra, are banished forever from the kingdom of Egypt and all her territories, including but not limited to territories presently under her domain. Should you be found on the soil of the Two Lands of Egypt, the penalty is death.

Auletes dropped the letter. His body quaked; red crept into his cheeks, his nostrils, his neck, his forehead. "Treasonous bitch!" he spat, saliva flying madly across the room like a burst of hail. "Lying whore, blemish to the memory of her mother."

The king gripped the back of his chair with both hands and shook it, rocking its legs against the tile floor. He picked it up and crashed it to the ground, breaking off one of the legs. His men watched, silent. Kleopatra cowered, waiting for her father to calm, wondering what role her sister Berenike played in the coup.

"To Rome," ordered the king. "To Rome." He brandished the splintered leg of the chair at no one in particular. "If it costs me every cent of my money, I'll see the bitch dead." The king paced about, the chair leg in his hand like a big shank of mutton. "She will be awakened from her thrall by the mocking face of a Roman centurion and his soldiers. And I will be commanding them to treat her no better than a whore to be passed among them."

A cold calm passed over Auletes' face, relaxing his features. "When she begs for death, I will personally cut her venomous throat."

"Father, what of Demetrius?" asked Kleopatra, thinking of the emaciated scholar at the mercy of Thea's cold inclemency. "Surely he will be killed. We should never have left him there. We should have insisted that he come with us. And what about Berenike, Father? Does the eunuch say that she had a part in this?"

The king made no response, his face unusually icy. Kleopatra preferred her father furious, a state of mind that appeared less dangerous than this calculated chill. "Thea sits on the throne, while the eunuch rules. There is no mention of Demetrius. There is no mention of Berenike. But if either of them is aligned with Thea, I shall see them dead, too."

ELEVEN

Mohama threw back her head, dangled the small morsel of fruit above her open pink mouth, and then dropped it in. Aware that she was being watched by every man on deck—the soldiers, the Kinsmen, the servants, the king—she chewed the fruit slowly, rocking the pit back and forth from cheek to cheek. Finally, she walked to the bow, spitting the seed into the water.

An exasperated princess waited for her at the game table. She wished she had eaten the bowl of cherries herself and not brought them to Mohama, who used them to agitate the men. But Mohama had an intemperate love for such fruits, having been ignorant of them for most of her life, and the princess, who had not much appetite, and who had been deprived of nothing, preferred to finish her repast with one chewy date.

It was after lunch. The royal party and companions had removed themselves to the deck to take advantage of the afternoon sun, as if they were traveling on one of the sumptuous Nile barges to which they were accustomed and not a ship that was presently tossed about on the more turbulent waters of Poseidon. Oars were in; sails billowed in the crisp oceanic breeze.

Kleopatra and Mohama were at a game of dice under a white cotton canopy set up on the deck of the ship. The king had been given a marble dice set by a Roman guest at court and was encouraged to perfect his game in preparation for the visit to Rome. The Romans were mad for the game, he was told, and that fact alone intrigued the princess. She had taught Mohama to play it and was often furious because the girl's luck exceeded hers. They had many observers, Kleopatra knew, because Mohama had chosen to wear a dress of sheer linen through which the men could clearly see her large brown nipples made erect by the sea winds.

"It is your turn to roll, and I am standing here waiting. I am out of patience," Kleopatra said petulantly. "You have no qualms about keeping me waiting. I am going to have you flogged."

"I live in fear of that command," said Mohama. Slyly she looked about her to see if she still had the attention of her admirers. She did. She reached into the bowl of cherries and with an extreme amount of time given to the selection, plucked another and held it above her open mouth.

"If you do not roll I am going to strangle you," said the princess. She was tense. Her father had moved them from Rhodes with alacrity, shuffling them—barely packed—aboard the ship. Hearing the news of Thea's usurpation, he had quit talking to anyone, but spent his days muttering into the ear of Hekate, who patted his hand and poured his wine and allowed him to rant while she sat in silent dignity against his angry patter. He had kept his distance from his daughter, who wondered if he had begun to doubt her loyalty, too, though she had never pretended to like or to trust Thea. Perhaps the king did not like that Kleopatra's judgment had proved more acute than his. In time, she trusted, he would allow her to be close to him again. Of this she was sure. Nonetheless, she felt less than settled.

Mohama picked up the rolling cup, shaking it back and forth in the rhythm of her chewing, her hips swaying.

"This is not dance. This is dice. You have eaten two thousand cherries! I am going to turn my back on you right now and go to my cabin!"

Mohama gave Kleopatra a smile of concession and threw the die, her eyes following the six-sided marble pieces as they rolled down the table. When they landed, her eyes bulged and she clutched at her throat.

"Three!" said the princess gleefully. "You lose."

Mohama fell forward onto the table, chin hitting the wood with a loud clump. A dark bile spewed from her mouth onto the gaming board. Kleopatra watched Mohama's eyes roll in her head before it fell to the side. She tried to propel herself away from the spew but seemed to have no strength. She screamed. The king heard his daughter and pushed himself away from Hekate, arriving at the table as Mohama fell to the hard deck. Charmion rushed to the princess, trying to turn her head away. Kleopatra fought against Charmion's embrace and yelled to her father to help Mohama.

The Royal Physician and his man in attendance uncurled Mohama's arms from her belly and stretched her out on the floor. Her eyes rolled helplessly and her limbs were limp, a sweat bubbling on her brow. She was delirious, trying to speak, but was not in control of her tongue. A foam gathered around the opening of her mouth. Charmion again tried to turn the princess's face away, but Kleopatra would not desert her companion. She broke from Charmion and knelt at Mohama's feet while the medical men propped open her mouth and stared into her throat.

The physician looked not at the princess but at the king and said, "What did she eat? Who prepared her last meal?"

Kleopatra put her hands to her mouth. "The cherries," she whispered through her bloodless fingers. The assistant fetched the bowl of cherries, carefully picking it up as if its contents could jump out and injure him. Gingerly he carried the vessel to the doctor, who squeezed two cherries between his fingers, slowly bringing them to his nose. He crushed a few more, inhaled their essence, and then shook his head as if to confirm what he suspected. He sent his assistant below to gather his supplies, among which, he said, was a chemical antidote to the poison he believed she had ingested— deadly little red berries whose liquid would easily be disguised in a cherry.

"We will know very soon if we have saved her," he said. The assistant returned with a box of vials, and the doctor pointed to the one to be unsealed. With a small knife, the assistant delicately cut open the wax seal and poured the liquid into the girl's mouth while the physician massaged her throat.

Kleopatra sat rigid, refusing all hands that offered to help her up. Mohama had ceased to move. Occasionally her foot would twitch ever so slightly, giving the princess a moment of hope in the midst of her fear.

"Who has done this thing?" demanded the king, standing over Mohama's inert body.

Kleopatra raised her face to her father, letting the tears stream down her face. "The cherries were placed in front of me, Father. She is from the desert and had never had cherries before entering our service. I gave them to her because there is no fruit served at the table of the servants."

The king scoured the observers with his wide, angry eyes. "Whoever has done this shall die," he said to no one, to everyone.

The princess realized the king's meaning. "Father, were they meant for me?"

The king raised his beefy fists to the heavens. "Dionysus, god of all that is of the earth, god of the trees, of the vine, of the crops that we eat. Mighty Poseidon, god of these waters upon which we sail. You have spared my daughter but taken from her a loyal companion. Deliver into these hands—the hands of your faithful servant—the lying whore behind this evil deed."

A billowing cloud masked the sun's rays, and the light about the ship grew dimmer. No one issued a sound. The sea seemed to come to a dead calm in answer to the king's words.

"Do you see the skies darken?" shouted one of the Kinsmen. "The gods have heard the king. Someone shall die for this crime."

The king lowered his fists, satisfied that he had been recognized by the deities, but this did not pacify him. He began frantically barking orders: Arrest the cooks. Imprison the serving staff in the cargo. Cast the fruit on board into the ocean. Take the princess to her suite.

To Charmion: Do not leave my daughter.

To the doctor: Do not lose the girl.

The girl. It was as if for a moment all had forgotten Mohama. Kleopatra looked back at the still body of the dark young woman, whose rich color had begun to drain from her face. Her hair was strewn carelessly about her sweaty face like a Medusa. Another Libyan, Kleopatra thought, who made a game of tempting men.

The physician put his ear to Mohama's chest. He took her wrist in his hand and held it there. "The girl is dead."

Kleopatra crawled to the body of her companion, reaching her arm out to touch her face, but before she could complete the gesture, she was lifted into the arms of one of her father's men. The physician's two attendants raised Mohama. Her torso hung limp in the middle as they picked up her shoulders and legs in the flat parts of their forearms like a funereal sacrifice.

The princess screamed Mohama's name as if the invocation would rouse the girl. She put her face into the chest of the Kinsman and prayed, harder than she had ever prayed before. Harder and with more desperation.

Who has commanded this evil, O Holy Mother? Only you can tell me. I offer you everything I have. I offer my life to your will. Only tell me who it is who wishes me dead so that I may stay alive to serve you. I am a small, motherless girl, and my father is only sometimes wise and sometimes foolish. I have no companion now to watch over me. Enlighten me. Enlighten me.

The goddess did not reply. Kleopatra was alone, crying into the tunic of a Kinsman as he carefully carried her down the stairs and into the dank stateroom below. She had believed in the goddess, believed in her own ability to summon her, but now the goddess had deserted her. Perhaps it was her Fate to have died, and the goddess was angry that Mohama had taken her place in the underworld. She cried harder still, praying again, bargaining and reasoning with the deity. *Oh surely Lord Hades is pleased with such a beautiful one as Mohama? Surely she is a more fitting companion to him than I, a mere child? Mohama is more beautiful than Persephone herself.*

Kleopatra turned her face away from her Kinsman, relieved not to be breathing his musky scent. She inhaled deeply, taking in an effluvium as familiar as it was unexpected. Out of nowhere, from the salty air of her empty cabin, her nose was filled with the unmistakable scent of lotus oil.

Thea Thea Thea. The name pounded like a drumbeat in Kleopatra's head. The goddess had not abandoned her, but had sent her an irrefutable sign: Someone in Alexandria had sent an emissary to poison the young royal who would one day grow up and oust

Thea and her offspring from the throne. Who could it be but Thea? And yet, Thea had convinced Berenike as of late to wear the scent, too. So fitting. As far as Kleopatra was concerned, the two had always had the same smell. And now it appeared that they were in collusion. It was more than likely; it had seemed so to Kleopatra for as long as she could remember.

She had always known that they hated her and would hurt her, though she had not known how, and she had not known who would be sacrificed in the process. I will see the two of them dead, she told herself, and I will whisper the name Mohama in their ears as they die.

⌒ ⬦ 𓃭 ⵊⵊ 𓈖 ▦ ⌐ 𓐭 ⌒ ⌐

What could he have done when the queen approached him? At first Meleager believed she had foiled his carefully laid plans, but soon he saw the wisdom in going along with her scheme. Another gift from the goddess, another significant stone in the structure of that intricate architecture he had designed to make Berenike queen. Once again Fate had intervened, showing him the supreme wisdom of the gods, master conspirators divinely gifted for plotting the destiny of the world. Luckily he had always been a religious man.

"I no longer see any use for the king," Thea had said one morning over breakfast. "Do you?"

Meleager did not believe what he was hearing.

"He is gone, is he not? And the kingdom functions as well as when he was here. Better even." The glazed look of victory on Thea's face chilled Meleager. "He is not missed by his people, nor by the queen, nor by her advisers. Not even by his children. The only one who could possibly have missed him accompanied him on his treasonous mission to Rome."

"Your Majesty, you surprise me," said Meleager, swallowing his bread. It sat like a stone in his throat. "Pardon my silence, but this is hardly the conversation I anticipated."

"The king is off once again selling his people to the Roman oppressors. I foresaw this, and I have been building support," said Thea, a wide but close-lipped smile making wrinkles on her smooth cheeks.

"Among which parties, if I may ask?" inquired Meleager, trying to speak slowly and calmly while his mind absorbed the new information.

"The Greek philosopher who has been so loyal to the king has become . . . how shall I say it?" she said coyly, twisting the lone stray lock of her hair and averting her eyes from the eunuch's skeptical stare. "My ally. In intimate conversation, he admitted to me that he had always admired my position on the Roman question, and had always doubted the king's solicitousness to those barbarians."

"Demetrius?" The eunuch could hardly believe what he heard.

"He taught in Rome. He knows of their barbarous ways first-hand. In dreams, the god showed Demetrius that the king was not fit to rule, but that I possessed the qualities necessary to unite the great and diverse people of Egypt under Greek authority and to repel the advances of the Romans if necessary. Though the king would never believe it, the god favors women."

The eunuch knew that it was not nocturnal visions, but nocturnal visits from the queen that had changed the philosopher's allegiance. "How interesting," he said, stalling for time. How could all of this have happened without his knowledge? Under his nose? Meleager tried to conceal his surprise and his concern. Demetrius had been marked for extermination along with the queen. But now, was that wise? Was it timely? How much support had she garnered? How many had fallen to her cloying ways? His mind raced with the possibilities for using this new turn of events to his advantage. To Berenike's advantage. Whom else had the queen seduced? The Vizier? His own General? How many others had been taken in by her lewd charms?

How often had he watched the emaciated Demetrius walk with the king and the small princess in the palace gardens? Why is it that so many men allowed coital bliss to alter their loyalty? The eunuch went over the events in his mind one more time. Demetrius and Meleager were the formal representatives of the king. The queen, already believing she had Meleager's loyalty, had seduced Demetrius, or so she claimed. Now she must believe that no one stood in her way.

These ideas shot through the eunuch's mind like random arrows in a badly planned confrontation. Rarely was he caught without a plan. Rarely did he not anticipate an event and have prepared, at least theoretically, a counterplan. Yet he sat silently while the queen revealed the extent of her deceit, trying not to give away any hint of his surprise, his horror. Listen. Smile. Raise the left eyebrow. Feign innocence. It was all so difficult. Stupefaction did not agree with him.

"Your Majesty, I remain your servant," he finally said. "Now and forever," he added quickly, trying to disguise his agitation.

He reminded himself that the game was hardly over. There would be a way to twist this turn of events in his favor. He must summon the patience upon which he had so relied in the past to get him through the difficult years. Time. Meleager had a long-standing friendship with the element of Time. In his own lifetime, the eunuch had seen events sweep across the landscape with such force as to wipe out great chunks of time. Cities that took years to erect and develop could be wiped out in a day by the right man, or by the determined act of a hostile god. What was time, really? In time, he would have his way. In time, Thea would be brought down, if not by his own hand, then by his own designs.

"Your Majesty, where do we go from here?"

⌒━🐂𓏲𓏲🦅▦⌐▢◇⌐

The day after Mohama was murdered, the princess offered her theory to Charmion: Someone loyal to Thea had stolen aboard ship and acted on Thea's orders to rid the kingdom of Kleopatra—the sole heir loyal to Auletes.

"Why would Thea wish to see you dead and the king alive?" Charmion asked, holding the girl's hand as they sat on the small bed in Kleopatra's cabin, petting it as if she were still a small child.

"Perhaps the cherries were meant for my father, too," Kleopatra answered huffily. Charmion annoyed Kleopatra with her doubt. "Do you not see it, Charmion? Berenike is Thea's ally, and Arsinoe and the sons are her own. I am the only one who might bring her harm, not now, but in the future. I will not be a child forever, despite what you think, and despite the way you treat me. I believe you wish me to remain small because you know that when I am grown, I shall not require your attendance. Then what will you do?"

Charmion sat slightly more erect, a sign that she was hurt by Kleopatra's insult. "Have you thought that Mohama might have been poisoned by one of the many soldiers or servants whom the desert girl tempted but spurned? Men are not as easily toyed with as she liked to think."

"Then I shall demand a full investigation. I shall demand that my father interrogate each of his men."

"I do not think your father would sacrifice a loyal man," Charmion replied coldly. "He is content to believe that this was the work of the queen. You would do well to support that theory in his presence."

"What is your meaning?"

"We do not know the position of Berenike, but she has always been rebellious, and she has always hung on the words of Thea. The rest are children. At present, you are the only heir whose loyalty the king need not question. Your twelfth birthday approaches. In not so many years, you will be of age to be named co-regent when your father removes Thea from the throne."

"You mean that someday I shall be queen?"

"Long ago, the elder ladies made a prediction that I have kept from you. Until this time, you have been too young to understand."

Kleopatra waited for Charmion to continue, withdrawing her hand and tucking it under the covers.

"There is but one descendant of the great Ptolemy who is destined to rule. She is still a girl, but as you say, she will not remain so forever."

The princess absorbed the words. "When did they say this to you? Why was I not told?"

"If it is Destiny, it does not need to be uttered."

"Why do you keep things from me as if I were a child?" Kleopatra moved away from Charmion, rolling over on her side and pushing herself upright. Forgetting that she was aboard ship and sleeping on a hard bed, she let herself drop with the full force of her weight. Her bottom hit the immovable mattress with a force that made her teeth clack together. She tightened all the muscles in her body to take her mind off the fact that in her indignation she had bitten her tongue.

"You are upset over the death of your companion. You will miss her very much. But perhaps this is the gods' way of telling you that it is time for childish games of disguise and intrigue to be put aside. It is time for you to realize who you are and what your responsibilities will be. You must put Mohama and the adventures you shared with her behind you. That is my purpose in telling you the prediction of the crones."

"I will never forget Mohama," Kleopatra said defiantly. "Not even when I am queen." Not even when I am queen. She uttered the words in haste, and then wondered at her daring. Might it be true?

"May the gods preserve her, if the gods are so generous in the afterlife to those of lowly birth. I do not suggest obliterating the memory. Memories, unlike mortals, do not die."

"When did the crones make this prediction?"

"At the time of your birth."

"Does my father know? Does Thea know? Is that why she tried to poison me?"

"The ladies entrusted me with their knowledge because my mother served them. When you were a small child you caused Thea such trouble that the women were afraid she would do something to you if she knew the destiny the gods had written for you. That is why they suggested to the king that I enter into your service. But the king does not know what the crones foretold. The crones do not reveal to men the visions that come to them."

"But why?" asked Kleopatra

"Because that is their way and that is their tradition. They do not trust men, even kings, with this kind of knowledge. Men make sport out of tampering with the will of the gods."

"There is something else, Charmion." Kleopatra recalled the image of her ancestor, Ptolemy I Savior, sitting stone-faced on his horse. She told Charmion about the dream. The path in the thicket of the Delta. The lion. The king. Not her father, but the great man. The youth who had conquered the world. And her ancient grandfather, the young king's best friend and companion and general and perhaps half brother. The one whose sharp, aggressive nose she wore on her face. "Ptolemy shot me but I didn't die. Before I knew it, I was flying above them."

Kleopatra did not realize that she had begun to cry. She put her head in Charmion's lap, letting the woman caress her hair.

"Do you not see the meaning of the dream, child?" Charmion raised her by the shoulders and held her face in her small, cool hands. With one thumb, she wiped the tears from under each eye. "The eagle is the symbol of the House of Ptolemy. In the presence of Alexander, Ptolemy selected you to head his house. Ptolemy reached beyond the grave to inform you of your destiny."

The weight of Charmion's interpretation sat heavily upon the girl. She massaged her brows and the ridge of bone above her eyes to get rid of her headache. "You are making me afraid, Charmion."

"You will know fear. But you must never let it stop you from fulfilling your destiny. Fate marks us all, but its mark upon your life is stronger."

The girl had stopped crying but her chest still heaved. Mohama was dead, Thea was queen, and Kleopatra was terribly afraid. She would be less afraid if she could lean on Mohama's chest and feel her strength—Mohama who had no fear, Mohama who had sacrificed herself to a life of slavery so that her brothers, scavenging food for the family, might escape. Mohama who fought the faceless enemies in the dead darkness of desert nights. Who had spilled the insides of a man who tried to do her harm. Why had Fate chosen Kleopatra to rule a kingdom and the fearless Mohama to be born into a savage desert tribe, only to die at the age of sixteen? What flawed immortal power, what *deus ignotus*, was responsible for such miscalculations? Kleopatra felt so small, so inadequate, to assume the role that Charmion said was hers.

But Destiny was final in her judgments. Kleopatra's girlhood was over.

Kleopatra held her tears at the beginning of the ceremony when a small goat was sacrificed to the god on behalf of the maiden, when Auletes asked the god to take to his bosom the brave girl Mohama who had loyally served the House of Ptolemy and who had more than once risked her life to save a princess.

The king had ordered the captain to dock at Athens, where he sent off all the unnecessary hangers-on, using expense as an excuse, but secretly meeting with the steward, who gravely crossed off the payroll those of questionable loyalty. Only a few personal attendants, the steward, and the Kinsmen would accompany them to Rome; the rest were free to stay in Athens or to return home. But servants who had cooked and served food on that particular deadly afternoon would be turned over to a slave trader and sold in the markets at Delos. "A harsh punishment for so many undoubtedly innocent people," he explained to his daughter. "But the message must be sent that the king and his family are not to be harmed. And that is that."

The king had also ordered the body of Mohama to be given to the sea-god, whom he wished to please by sending such a lovely young girl to his waters. But Kleopatra vetoed his idea and insisted that the girl be given a traditional funeral. She argued strenuously that Mohama had saved her life and was replacing her at the side of Hades. "Only the gods know for certain who took the life of Mohama. If there is any possibility that our Lord Dionysus interceded in a threat upon my life and substituted the life of Mohama, should he not be properly thanked? Should Mohama not be given up to the god whom the king serves? After all, Father, you do carry the god's name." Kleopatra felt like Antigone, arguing for the rights of the dead, but hoping that she would not share *that* young woman's fate. Inwardly, the king was not as anxious as he appeared to get to Rome, and so he relented. "The funeral shall take place at Athens," he said. "And we shall all attend."

Now Kleopatra steeled herself, stepping forward to place upon Mohama's corpse a locket the girl had admired. She held her tears when she saw the edges of the white linen wrapped around Mohama's body take to the flames from the torches. She concentrated on the dwindling fringes of the cloth, silently praying to Zeus, the only Greek deity terrible enough to have made an impression upon Mohama. Kleopatra had once fantasized that the Almighty would reward Mohama's affections by choosing her to have one of his children as he had chosen many beautiful, tempting mortal women in the past. It would have been a great game with them, pretending that Mohama had been impregnated by the Olympian, and not by some soldier with whom she had mercilessly flirted. But as Charmion had pointed out, the games of her youth were over.

Tearless still, Kleopatra watched the hot flames engulf her companion, taking the smell of the burning flesh into her nostrils, letting the heat scorch her cheeks. It was time to cultivate the Stoic control of the emotions associated with great men. If one believed the philosophers, it was not a way to avoid pain, but the key to a life of Virtue and enlightenment. Perhaps that was true, but Kleopatra was surprised that the suppression of tears did not alleviate her grief.

The mourners dispersed, leaving the workers to finish the final details of the business of death, and the king's steward, a spare, finical man, to pay the Athenian priest. Kleopatra interrupted the transaction. "I would like to have a monument erected in honor of the deceased."

The steward asked the king, who wearily replied, "Negotiate a fair price for the stone. I have had a very long and trying week. I am returning to the ship."

"Here is what I wish the inscription to say," said Kleopatra. "'Stop traveler and read what is written. Here lie the remains of Mohama of the Libyan Desert, a Lady-in-Waiting who met an untimely death by poison. She is here honored by the Princess Kleopatra of the Royal House of Ptolemy.'"

"Lovely," said the priest, taking the money from the steward. "I shall have the artisans chisel the letters immediately."

"Splendid," replied the princess, who did not trust the narrow-eyed priest. "I shall return in three hours to admire their work."

"Kleopatra, I am certain that the king wishes you to rejoin him aboard ship," whispered Charmion. But Kleopatra allowed that they did not sail until morning, that they were attended by two of the king's bodyguards, that they had a carriage for hire for the entire day, and therefore, that there was no reason to spend the day on a cramped ship when the city of Athens might play host to them. Reluctantly, Charmion sent word to the king that the princess's party would not return until sundown. "Do not make the mistake of thinking you can turn me into another Mohama," Charmion said, and Kleopatra laughed for the first time in many days.

They spent the day touring the markets, and ate a satisfactory meal of fish, spinach, and olives in one of the town's finest inns. But when the sun threatened its western descent, they returned to the site of the memorial, only to see that the inscription had not been engraved properly. The artisans, apparently confused and hurried, did not name the princess Kleopatra of the Royal House of Ptolemy as the benefactor of the monument. Rather, she was recorded as "the little Libyan Princess."

"What is this?" Kleopatra demanded.

"The Athenians like to call all those from the land of Egypt Libyans," said Charmion.

"We shall have it corrected for the princess," offered one of the bodyguards. "The princess must have satisfaction."

"No, let it remain," said Kleopatra. "I think Mohama is delighted that I have been immortalized as a Libyan." She turned away from the epitaph and into the last rays of the setting sun. "I shall never again have such camaraderie, shall I?"

Charmion winced, and Kleopatra regretted her words. She realized that Charmion was jealous.

"Mohama was a servant who made a better life for herself by caring for your safety," Charmion said slowly, choosing her words carefully. "She was loyal. I approved of her because she had the skills to protect you. I never approved of her ways with *men*." Charmion said the word as if she had just swallowed rancid oil. "But I suppose that is the way with women of low birth."

"Say what you will of her. I shall always remember to judge a person by strength of character, not status of birth." Kleopatra spoke deliberately and sincerely, as if delivering a last-minute memorial address for her friend.

"Like Spartacus, whom you so worshipped as a child?"

"Yes, like Spartacus," Kleopatra said defensively. "I do not fault myself for admiring the courage of the slave Spartacus. Just as I know that not a day will pass that I will not miss my companion Mohama."

"Many days will pass, Kleopatra. You will have greater challenges to meet and greater losses to bear than this one."

"I do not wish to lose anyone else," said Kleopatra. They were alone now, and she let the first tears fall for Mohama.

"I will be there with you," Charmion promised. "You will never have to bear your burden alone." She held Kleopatra by the arm and guided her toward the carriage, away from the monuments to the dead.

TWELVE

Kleopatra woke as the earliest light of day crept through closed shutters. It was her custom to awaken at this time, while most of her family slept considerably later. She liked the morning sun, liked the softness of its first colors as it rose on the eastern side of the palace. At that hour, she and Mohama would scamper down the stairs, through the great hall, and out the palace doors past the yawning guards to see the sun come up from her favorite spot, the wall that overlooked the king's stables. Sometimes they wandered into the stables and talked to the boys feeding the horses, and then exercised the animals in the ring. Sometimes Kleopatra exercised Persephone herself, and sometimes the girls rode their horses along the cataracts into the wild, uninhabited riverbeds to the south of the city gates.

She opened her eyes only to realize that she was not at home. She had passed her twelfth birthday on the tumultuous waters between Greece and Italy, tossing about in the dark cabin while Charmion, stiff as a pylon, suppressed her own illness and kept watch over her by the light of a smelly oil lamp. The trip across the Adriatic had been all torrent and turbulence; the royal party spent the voyage in their quarters, ill and praying that the blustering winds were at least pushing them faster in the direction of the shore. The king, to the annoyance of captain, crew, entourage, and his daughter, reiterated to anyone within earshot, "I hope this weather is no indication of what I shall confront in Rome!" But no one had the authority to silence him.

Finally ashore in Brundisium and grateful to be on solid ground, they rented several carriages for the journey to Rome, traveling through Italy's most desolate landscape, stopping on the first night at a ragged inn. Hungry from many seasick days, they were anxious for dinner upon solid ground, but were served tough, indigestible rabbit, and then given bug-infested mattresses for the evening's repose. Three grimy days enclosed in a carriage, sleeveless arms stuck to the leather seat, jostling along the carpet of huge stones that formed the wide swath of the Appian Way, Kleopatra's only entertainment was wondering what the road had looked like when it was lined with Spartacus and the crucified rebel slaves. "But there is not even a trace of Spartacus now," she said sadly to Charmion, who replied, "Thank the gods."

On the third day, the party climbed the hill to Pompey's suburban villa, where the gates were thrown open, revealing a winding road with tall shade trees planted symmetrically, hovering protectively over the hard-packed dirt. Workers in short mud-colored tunics peppered the manicured grounds, raking, weeding, and trimming the long tongues of grass that rolled like the evening tide up to the massive-columned house. The royals were met at the door by a Greek houseman and were informed that Pompeius Magnus and his bride were presently at another of their homes and would return within the week. He escorted them through the vestibule and into a cavernous atrium, where they walked over a mosaic of the founders of Rome, Romulus and Remus, being suckled by the she-wolf. The princess was given a suite of rooms, the largest chamber for herself, a smaller antechamber for Charmion, and a still smaller cubiculum for their two attendants. She was shown the indoor pools, the baths for the women, the warm room where she was to receive her oil and massage, and the cold room where she was to recover after the ritual before exposing herself to the air. Finally, she was walked through the walled gardens—Pompey's pride—and then allowed to retire to her rooms. She sat primly, watching herself in the mirror as Charmion brushed the knots and dust of travel from her hair, and, disguising her knowledge of Latin, listened to the slaves—who thought she and Charmion were Egyptians—fussing about the room and gossiping about the scandalous sexual displays of their master and his new child bride.

Though the royals had been treated with great solicitousness by the Roman staff, Kleopatra felt confined and tentative in this new place. She tried to enjoy the few luxuries that the barbarians allowed themselves, but she found they did not compare to Alexandria's indulgences. The baths were smaller and less comfortable, and the servants had no idea how to give a decent body treatment. The foods were ill-prepared, and through the long lunches and dinners she had to endure the indecent behavior of Roman women, who, unlike the women they had met in Greece, did not take their meals with one another, but ate alongside the men, stuffing their faces with as much enthusiasm and talking just as loudly. Kleopatra had to admit that since they had left Alexandria, she had become accustomed to being the only female in the dining room, and she liked the attention. But the worst part of a Roman meal was the entertainment, Greek poetry read to them by Roman men of the stage— highly theatrical, she said to Charmion, almost comical. No match for a Greek actor. Then, yesterday, she had shocked the servants by swimming without a garment. She had learned, through her secret understanding of their language, that they considered nude swimming the act of a barbarian woman. How is one supposed to swim wrapped in linen? she wondered. She gathered that Roman women did not swim at all, but simply dipped their covered bodies in the water. How strange, and how useless, she said to Charmion. What would happen to them if they were in a wreck at sea? Would they simply drown for lack of skill? She had so longed to see Rome, to know Romans, to observe them closely and to conquer them. Now she wondered if she was too foreign and exotic a creature to win their affection.

What were they doing here? She worried that Cato was right, that her father was in for a crushing disappointment. Pompey had let Auletes down once before when the king had been desperate for his help. Why did Auletes think the Roman would assist him now? Perhaps the Romans would welcome an idiot like Thea on Egypt's throne, an enemy easily vanquished. What would happen to them if the Romans denied her father?

Kleopatra lay motionless in the bed, wishing that when she rolled to her left she would see the chocolate-colored girl lying next to her, would inhale the sweet smell of Mohama's jasmine perfume filling the cool morning air. Kleopatra did not move. She did not want to see the empty space on the bed. She felt the warmth begin to flood her eyes. She would not cry.

She rose and dressed, slipping past Charmion still asleep in the antechamber, pausing at the portico to look out at the sunrise view of Pompey's estate. She walked straight through the atrium, ignoring the servants who followed her, and out the door, where she picked up her pace. She ran through the arbor, laughing, skipping now, watching the light that intruded through the vines overhead play games with her sandaled feet. Suddenly the arbor was no longer there and she was exposed to the brilliant Roman sunrise, soft and diffuse, bathing her in lemons and violets. She reached her arms upward in thanks for the day and was skipping like a frenzied Bacchanalian when she realized that she had reached her destination and that she was being watched.

Two boys stood before the tall white doors of the stable. She knew they were Persian by the shape of their dark eyes, which looked as if they were lined with natural kohl, and by the language in which they whispered to each other, speculating on her identity. Wordlessly she bid the boys to enter the stable with her. They were only slightly older and slightly taller than she. Nonetheless, she was pleased when they followed her without question.

She paced up the aisle of stalls, peering into each compartment at the animals, but, to her surprise, seeing nothing that suited her. Why does the great man not have a good Greek-bred horse? she wondered. Why only these clumsy-looking monsters that seem bred for carrying a heavy load?

Then she saw him. A steed so black he was purple, the color of ripe eggplant. He was all sinew and steam, with an intelligence in his eyes. They were light eyes, almost hazel, like hers. She had never seen such transparent eyes on a horse. He frightened her much more than Persephone had frightened her in the beginning. This steed was two heads taller than her ornery filly. The steam from his nostrils seemed to come from inside him, not from the collision of the chilly morning air and his warm breath. Yet she had to have him, had to tame him. Had to see if he would respond to her command.

Mohama would have wanted him so.

The boys were appalled when she pointed to the steed. They shook their heads wildly, eyes pleading. She breathed very deeply and closed her eyes. *May the power invested in me by the goddess make them see me as a queen.* Opening her eyes, she spoke to them in their own tongue, amazing them.

"I am Kleopatra the Seventh, daughter of the Twelfth Ptolemy, King of Egypt. I am the descendant of Alexander, conqueror of Persia. I command you to move aside while I mount this steed." The boys fell to their knees, begging the princess not to ride this particular horse. This was no ordinary horse; this was Pompey's horse. If anyone rode this horse, if a *girl* rode this horse, if a *foreign* girl rode this horse and did anything to it, the master would have them flogged, or perhaps killed. The boys' big kettle-colored doe eyes urged her to reconsider.

"Perhaps he will have you flogged, too!" one suggested boldly.

She was not going to back down. She wanted the horse and she convinced herself that Pompey, should he be acquainted with her equestrian prowess and her love of the equine, would wish her to ride his steed. This was no warhorse. The animal had not a flaw, not a mark upon its glimmering dark coat. This was an animal bred for the pleasure and status of its owner, a work of art, a thing of beauty. Kleopatra turned away from the boys and opened the gate of the stall. She would ride the creature bareback.

She approached him slowly as he looked down at her with his great luminescent ovals. Curiosity mingled with disdain. She put her hand to his mouth. After some consideration, he nuzzled his wet nostrils against it.

"Can anyone tell me why my stablehands are kneeling on the

ground like the suppliant maidens while this girl is trying to steal my horse?"

Kleopatra froze. The horse butted her arm with his snout, a signal to continue the petting. She did not respond, nor did she dare turn around. The man spoke a formal Greek, learned at school and polished in diplomatic relations. The voice was that of a commander—deep, assured, mature, beyond reproach. A voice so resonant with authority and intelligence that no one would question the man who possessed it.

It was he, the great man Pompeius Magnus.

"My friend, I apologize," came the rueful voice of her father. "The little thief is my daughter the princess Kleopatra. Please forgive her. She has been known to steal off with my own horse at dawn. She is a lover of the creatures. She cannot resist such a mount."

Kleopatra slowly turned around, eyes lowered. The horse snorted behind her, a witness to her humiliation.

"Your Highness." The man bowed low and then rose to meet her eyes. "Please remove yourself from the stall before you get hurt. Strabo is rather unpredictable."

The princess noted that Pompey had named the horse for his father. She could not be certain if the tribute reflected mockery or honor, since the father of Pompey was generally despised, or feared, or—oh, she could not remember. As soon as she met Pompey's gaze, every detail of Roman history disappeared from her memory. He caused an instantaneous reaction in her of confusion and titillation.

Pompey snapped his fingers, signaling the kneeling stable boys to get to their feet. They skirted Kleopatra as if she radiated poison. One of them secured the gate of the stall while the other inspected the horse as if for injury.

Kleopatra knew that Pompey was well advanced in age, a man of at least forty-six. Yet he had not lost his legendary handsomeness. His hair was thick and tousled about like a schoolboy's; in fact, his boyish face reminded her of Alexander. Though as old as her father, he remained without fat. Tall, very tall. She found herself exhilarated by the sheer size of the Roman. His hair was fair with small glinting streams of gray, and his eyes were pale brown and languid, as if he had not a care in the world. His skin was tanned and leathery but not wrinkled. His face, nose, cheekbones, brow, were what one might call fine.

Auletes stood silent, for once inscrutable—a sure sign that she had disgraced him. Pompey said nothing, but let his eyes dance over her small figure, enjoying now that he had caught the little royal in her cunning. "Your Majesty, I see that your princess is rather shy," he said to her father, not taking his eyes off her.

Auletes did not speak but gave his daughter a look of irony at Pompey's miscalculation of her character.

"We must find her a proper animal to ride."

"If you please, sir," she began by stammering. "I prefer this one. Strabo, so named in honor of your late father, I believe."

"Why, that is correct." He beamed at her as if she were his own precocious child.

"A great man. A great warrior. Perhaps wronged in death." The details of her education—the histories of Rome she so painstakingly had studied—came back to her.

"You honor me with your knowledge of my family, Your Highness. I must find you a pony you can ride while you stay with us. Come, let us review my inventory of beasts."

Kleopatra did not move when offered Pompey's arm. Auletes widened his eyes in warning.

"May I ride your horse, sir? I do believe he will like me."

"I am sure he will love you, but he is a large and cantankerous animal like his owner, and I do not believe he will obey you. I fear he will harm you. And then, my princess, I would not be able to live."

"I wouldn't concern myself about that," Auletes said. "She has a way with them."

Pompey, skeptical, shrugged his shoulders in resignation, giving the boys the signal to saddle Strabo. Kleopatra watched them carefully. She had known stablehands to sabotage a rider. When they finished, she took the reins and led Strabo outside.

The princess got her way, but she did not care for Pompey's horse. Clearly, the steed had but one master to whom he gave his obedience and best performance. He did not try to get away from her. That was a challenge she would have welcomed. Instead, he was slow to the command, unwilling to take his head even when she gave it willingly. Then, when she least suspected it, when she had resigned herself to the careless trot and to the enjoyment of the Roman countryside, he lurched forward, pushing her backward so that she almost fell over behind him. She hoped she was not being watched. She was now in a contest with this conniving beast, a contest they both knew she could not win. Yet she would not let the spectators know who was really in control.

Suddenly she thought of strangers riding Persephone—Berenike, perhaps, who would beat her if she disobeyed—and she began to worry for her horse's safety while she remained in exile. Glumly, she let Strabo gallop back to the stable. She saw that her father and Pompey observed her, so she made the most of the ride in the last furlong, and hoped mightily that the horse would obey her command to stop. Pompey watched her descend upon the stables at a breakneck speed. She was being foolish; the distance was too short for such a spectacle as she put on. But she did not incite his ire as she expected. He helped her dismount, and she blushed when his large hand engulfed hers.

"I have only seen one woman dominate a horse like that," he said. She hoped he thought the redness in her face the result of the ride.

He leaned close to her as if revealing a secret. "Hypsicratia," he whispered. "The concubine of Mithridates." At the utterance of the names of those fearsome persons, the stable boys began to mutter incantations to their native deity. "Mithras! Mithras!" Pompey looked askance at them and they quieted.

"A vicious bitch," he sighed. "I do not miss her." The princess did not like being compared to a concubine, but she met Pompey's eyes, hoping he would elaborate. "Small as you, and always dressed like a boy. She rode with the king, fighting as he fought, tending his horses. Though she was small and she didn't wear the buckskin I believe she was an Amazon. She certainly fought like one.

"Mithridates loved her most, though he had *hundreds* of beautiful women in his harem," he said. He emphasized the word "hundreds," and Auletes raised his eyebrows, wondering if he was diminished in

Pompey's eyes for appearing in Rome with a solitary mistress. Should he have brought women to Pompey? "I saw them, you know, but took none for myself. I sent them home to their fathers," he added, shrugging. Auletes appeared relieved.

Shy again, the princess looked to Auletes for permission to pursue this conversation. She had never before been in the company of a mighty warrior. An Imperator. A Master of the World. She did not know if they enjoyed sharing the details of their conquests. Auletes nodded his consent.

"What happened to Hypsicratia?" she asked.

"She was afraid that many men would want to have the mistress of a man so feared. Rather than risk a woman's Fate, she took poison with her king. They say she died claiming that she chose her lovers, and not they her, and that for her new lover she chose death. At any rate, they both saved me a lot of trouble." He did not seem at all pleased about the victory. "I have their weapons on display in my home. You must see them," he said dryly.

"I shall make a point of it, sir," she replied.

"I had hoped Pompey's young wife would be a good companion for you. After all, she is the daughter of Julius Caesar. Can you not find common ground with her?"

Auletes, lying on the sofa next to his daughter like a bloated fish while she sat up against a pillow, whispered these words into Kleopatra's ear, careful to prevent the servers and the other dinner guests from hearing what he said.

Kleopatra wished she had not partaken of each type of food offered at the Roman banquet. She was not accustomed to the weighty feeling in her stomach, but Auletes said that one must be polite and act like the natives. The first course of the dinner consisted of several kinds of lettuces, snails, grilled eggs, smoked fish, olives, beets, and cucumbers; the main course brought oysters, fish, sow's udders, stuffed pheasant, lamb, and the ribs of pigs, all doused in a coarse fish sauce called *garum* that was strangely sweet and sour at the same time; lastly, there were cheeses, fruits, breads, and small sweet things to finish. None of it was very good, in the opinion of the princess, lacking the subtle flavoring and careful preparation of the food served at home. Wines of many kinds, stronger than Kleopatra had ever tasted at her own court, were poured lavishly—sloppily, even—throughout, laying waste to the austere posture of temperance and restraint that the Romans publicly assumed. Far from living like the hardworking men of the land they pretended to be, they indulged grossly—crassly, she told herself—in princely excess, to the point of having ice brought in from the mountains to cool their wines.

"Father, Julia disgusts me," Kleopatra whispered back to the king. "I do not believe a woman should act like a kitten any more than a kitten should do the reverse. She is appalling." The princess had made her judgment. "Look at her."

The object of their discussion, Julia, only daughter of Julius Caesar, presently was writhing her body like a dancing Arabian slave girl to get Pompey's attention. Kleopatra had heard much talk of the piousness of Roman women, but she had seen little evidence to support it. Perhaps, like the image of the stoical farmer, it was a ghost of the Roman past. Earlier, on her way to the lavatory, Kleopatra had overheard two elderly ladies gossiping over Julia's behavior. They had agreed that in their day, a Roman girl knew how to be useful, how to spin cloth, keep house, raise chickens, maintain the hearth, honor the gods, and advise her husband. "Oh, that one is *useful*," one of the ladies said cryptically of Julia. "For one thing and one thing only," agreed her companion. Kleopatra's enjoyment of their indictments was cut short when the blame for the degeneration of the young people fell upon "that fat Egyptian potentate and others like him," whose debauched ways had crept into innocent Roman minds. Kleopatra wanted to reveal that she had understood their derision, but instead she dismissed it as the prattle of a generation on its way to the grave.

"Does Daddy want more wine?" Julia asked her husband. Pompey lay prone on a dining couch, looking straight into the barely covered bosom of his child bride, caressing her midriff through the gauzy wisp of a dress. She wiggled as she fed him pieces of fresh melon, bitten into tiny morsels by her teeth and then inserted into the mouth of the general, whose eyes rolled back as he chewed.

Seventeen, tall and lanky like her father, she would not be an attractive woman in later years. But presently she had the fresh charm and girlish naiveté that grown men seemed to find irresistible. Pompey the Great was no exception. Kleopatra, who had held his attention earlier in the day, was caught between jealousy and disgust. She had thought better of him. Now she had cause to reevaluate his character. *Senex bis puer*. A handy Roman expression. The old man is twice the fool.

She disliked Julia, but no more than she disapproved of all the brassy Roman women. Earlier in the day, she, Charmion, and Hekate expressed their unilateral disdain of the breed. They listed their objections to the Roman female systematically.

They had no physical prowess outside the arts of seduction.

They did not go to gymnasium, they did not ride, they did not hunt.

They were as loud as soldiers and used abominable language.

They cared for nothing but adorning themselves with gaudy jewelry, bossing their men around, and attracting attention.

The fiercest indictment was the nasty way these Roman matrons treated slaves. At this moment, Julia had taken her focus off Pompey and was chastising an old Spaniard—probably captured years before by her father—for spilling the juice of a plate of olives that he attempted to place on the table. The old man had fallen to his knees to wipe the liquid with the hem of his tunic when another woman, a guest, hit him on the head with her fist.

"Miserable old oaf," she said. "Pompey, you must retire these pathetic creatures that Caesar captured in Spain. When was he there? Was it in this or the last century?"

Pompey simply laughed at her and continued to stroke his wife's body.

Earlier in the week, Kleopatra had winced and had to hold her tongue when Julia slapped a girl for neglecting to secure a lock of her hair in the elaborate coiffure she had just executed. She witnessed this at their "get-acquainted" time, during which she had to relinquish an opportunity to accompany her father and Pompey on a morning hunt.

"Yesterday I rode the animal Strabo," the princess said stiffly, trying to make a conversation. "A fine steed. And so generous of the great Pompey to allow a stranger to mount it."

"Isn't Daddy handsome?" Julia asked Kleopatra when they were alone.

"I have not had the honor of meeting your father," she answered. But she had specifically heard that Julius Caesar was too tall, too thin, and had too little hair.

"Oh, Your Highness," Julia said patronizingly. "I mean my husband."

To be fair, Charmion said, perhaps Julia was trying to make the best of a political marriage made to a man older than her father. Hekate had given a knowing nod of agreement. Kleopatra did not care. She would spend the rest of her visit at the Pompey residence avoiding contact with the goose, even though Auletes thought it in the best interest of their cause that the two young females forge a friendship. They had no common ground; Julia fully dwelled in the lower regions of sensual pleasure that the princess had yet to discover. She had given herself completely to its service.

In truth, thought Kleopatra, what else did Julia have to do with herself? She would never be called upon to rule a people, to administrate a government, or even to solve a serious problem. She was the political tool of her father and the toy of Pompey the Great. Until he tired of either her or of alliance with Caesar. Kleopatra could not decide if the Roman women—boisterous and insistent, always clamoring to be heard—were more fortunate or less than the sequestered women of Greece, who more readily accepted the feminine destiny. She could not decide, and she settled for being very happy to have been born a princess who might do as she liked, for she was not cut of the cloth of an ordinary woman.

Auletes reached across the dining couch, placing his great paw behind his daughter's neck, bringing her closer to him. "My child, I am very frustrated. I do not know what is wrong with Pompey. Have you noticed that he does not leave the house? Would you not think that the most important man in Rome would have business to attend to? I believe he is hiding."

"From what?"

"I do not know. More than that, he refuses to discuss my situation!" said the king.

Kleopatra tried to recede from the smell of wine and fish sauce on her father's breath, but his hand held her firmly in place.

"That is why I wish you to cultivate Julia. She may be able to help us."

Earlier in the day Pompey had given Auletes and Kleopatra a tour of his garden, and appeared to listen patiently to Auletes' arguments for support in regaining the throne. But never did he come forth with an offer of help or a plan of action, even after the king asked directly when he would take his case to the senate. "Would you like to hear me play the flute?" Auletes asked Pompey, trying to prolong his time in the man's company. Pompey replied that he would enjoy that a great deal, but not at the present moment. After the walk, he absented himself to another part of the house.

"I am losing patience with Pompey's evasive tactics," said the king. "He wants to tell me all about his varieties of rhododendron while Thea's behind sits on my throne."

"I know, Father, but Julia is like a small toy. She has no political sway." Kleopatra whispered in Greek, hoping that the Roman woman next to them was either too uneducated or too drunk to understand them.

"And now that bloodsucker, Rabirius, is after me." Rabirius the moneylender had driven to the villa to ask for repayment of the six thousand talents he had lent in order for the king to become Friend and Ally of the Roman People. "You must go ask my wife for it," the king had replied, and then poured his troubles out to the portly man. By the end of the visit, Rabirius had promised to intercede on behalf of the king with his influential friends in the senate, and Auletes had borrowed more money.

Kleopatra fought against the blackout that was coming from drinking so much barely diluted wine. Unsatisfied with his daughter's response to his troubles, Auletes turned on his belly and began to tell his tale of woe to the woman next to him. When Kleopatra regained consciousness, she heard her father say, "And my despicable wife took the opportunity to turn the Regency Council against me. I do not know the fate of my trusted adviser Demetrius, nor of my four other children."

The king spoke loudly to make certain that he was heard by his host, but Pompey remained attentive to his wife and the treats she inserted into his mouth.

"I am certain that the senate will soon hear of my plight and come to my aid, just as I came to the aid of Rome in her plight with Judaea," the king said pointedly in a voice that was too loud.

"Would you like to hear me play the flute?" she heard her father ask the woman sitting languidly on the couch next to him. "Oh yes," she replied. "But not now."

Kleopatra groaned at the rebuff to her father and lowered her head into her elbows. How banal were these Roman dinners. The food she found foreign and not to her liking, nor to the liking of her stomach. The conversation was limited to cheap gossip, recipes for the food served, and the seemingly eternal Roman problems with their lazy slaves. She noticed that the Romans both envied and disdained refinement, calling their upper-class boys who admired the arts and letters of the Hellenes "greeklings," and regarding them as "unmanly." These slights upon her nationality she bore with disdainful dignity, much to Charmion's approval. There was no use in defending Greek achievement to the barbarians.

All throughout dinner the Romans talked incessantly with no mind to concealing the food they chewed, kissed one another on the lips while their mouths were still full, belched loudly, expelled gas, spilled food over themselves and their servers, and laughed out loud at the loquacious poet who sang to them while they ate. Their dining habits were similar to their grasp of most of the world's money and resources—insatiable.

Auletes had now struck up a conversation with the woman who had slapped the Spanish slave. Her husband, waving a goblet in his hand, interrupted them. "Will we have another display of your dinner before us as we did the last time?" he asked his wife. The woman glared at him through her painted eyes as the other guests laughed. "It looks so nice going in but so terribly ugly coming out," he continued.

"It's not as if you haven't treated everyone here to the same spectacle," she said. "I had gotten a bad piece of fish. That is all."

Kleopatra closed her eyes and prayed to the goddess that the woman would not do what her husband had intimated, but the goddess apparently was not listening. As Auletes continued to tell the woman his troubles, she put her hands over her mouth and ran from the room, leaving behind a trail of vomit. Servers scurried to the floor to clean up her mess. When she returned, a slave wiped her mouth while another poured her more wine and still another fussed about her clothing, swabbing away her filth. For these services she said not a word of thanks. All the while Auletes continued his discourse to anyone who would listen, no matter how halfheartedly.

Hekate got up to leave the banquet, stopping by the couch of the princess to wish her good night. "Have you ever seen such a disgraceful display of crudeness?" the elegant Greek woman asked in a whisper.

Since the death of Mohama, Hekate had become a companion and friend. Kleopatra admired Hekate's preternaturally long neck, which she held high above her collarbone. She leaned against Hekate's full bosom, closing her eyes, wishing that she might miraculously disappear. How meager the princess felt in the company of women like Hekate who burst with the essential female charms. Kleopatra noticed her father's easy vulnerability to Hekate's low, soothing voice, her high, full, creamy breasts, and the way her breathing quickened and her eyes upturned when she approached the king with one of her wishes. Kleopatra possessed none of these qualities. She was still small and straight up and down, and devoid of any hope that she would one day be as round and desirable as Mohama, or as slender and desirable as Hekate.

Hekate stroked Kleopatra's hair gently and rhythmically just like Kleopatra petted her dogs. "Would you like to go to bed?" she asked. "I will tell the king to excuse you."

"No, I will wait up with my father."

They looked at the king, who was now trying to plead his case to the oblivious, intoxicated Julia. Pompey had fallen asleep on the couch face up and was making sounds like water being sucked from a cistern.

"He's devised an ingenious method of avoiding me, has he not, sending me off to see the city?" The king was sweaty and agitated, his fat jiggling as the royal party arrived at the gates of Rome. The late-morning sun hammered the black top of the enclosed carriage, but Pompey had insisted that for security reasons the royals must travel in a covered vehicle. "The rabble in Rome has new power," Pompey had warned. "They used to fear us, but no more. Now they boldly harass their betters."

The double gates to the city, one for entering and one for leaving, were three stories tall and guarded by grim-faced, skirted centurions. With sinewy legs strapped to the knee by the leather laces of their sandals they stood in calcified stillness, armed with long javelins, their helmets gleaming like new coins in the noontime sun. The city's walls, the royals were told by their guide, were made of sandstone, four feet thick and impenetrable. Kleopatra stared at the uniformed men who seemed to peer back at her from the wall's many arches on each level.

"How large the men look." Kleopatra was used to the sizable Romans who visited them at court, Romans made bulky by a lifetime of feasting and drinking, but had not seen firsthand the formidable height and mass carried by Rome's military men.

"We are slight in comparison," she said to her father, who sneaked another look at the soldiers from the tiny window.

"Not all of us are slight," Hekate retorted, raising an eyebrow toward the robust king, letting out an uncharacteristic giggle, and causing his daughter and Charmion to laugh.

But when the carriage passed through the towering arch and entered the city, Kleopatra stifled her laughter. Elation settled like a tickling mist over her body. Her dream of seeing the great city of Rome had come to fruition earlier in her life than she had ever imagined. It came under unfortunate circumstances, but still, here was Rome, and she had entered its perimeter.

Once inside the city walls, the temperature rose, and the seats of the carriage seemed to get harder and more uncomfortable. The driver made continual abrupt stops to avoid running into the throngs of pedestrians, or the other carriages, or the merchants' carts, or the tall litter-bearers carrying fortunate persons of means over the heads of the masses.

"A law has been proposed to abolish all carts and carriages from the streets by day, allowing only transportation by litter or by foot," explained the guide Timon, an educated Corinthian slave charged by Pompey to show them the city.

"A few years too late, I would say," the king replied to this news. He looked out the small portal, and a ghoulish face with no teeth and one eye looked back at him. "A coin for a poor old man?" The hollow mouth mumbled the request; the single eye cocked upward, looking to the heavens and not into the carriage at all.

"Zeus!" Auletes screamed. "A giant! Go away, man. Go away."

The princess ducked under her father and stuck her head out the small window. "He is carried on the shoulder of another," she laughed.

"What does the beggar want?" he asked his daughter, fluttering his hands to make the man go away.

"It is just that, Father. He is a beggar asking for coins."

"Well tell the fellow that I, too, am a beggar, living on Pompey's hospitality."

One of the king's bodyguards who followed them on horseback trotted alongside the carriage, kicking the man away. The carriage stopped short again, throwing Kleopatra forward and into the lap of her father.

"What now?" asked the king. "How does one endure this city? How does anyone cope with such crowds, such traffic? I am beginning to see why Pompey does not wish to leave his rural paradise."

"It is the fault of Julius Caesar's new law, put into effect by his man, the tribune Clodius," said Timon, who clearly disapproved. "The law promises free corn to all who reside in the city. Since its passage earlier this year, the rabble have flocked to Rome. No one wants to work anymore. They want to come here, live twelve to a room, and bleed the government treasury."

"An abomination!" said the king. "In my country, the peasants get their daily bread, but they work for it."

Thus far the judgment of the king upon Rome was that it was loud, hot, crowded, lacking refinement, and not at all hospitable to royalty. Though Pompey had put them up at the best of Roman townhomes, it was tiny by their own standards and in the middle of the city, and the royals were simply not accustomed to the noise of a Roman street by day or by night. The king complained vociferously, but he was assured that Jupiter himself could not quiet the streets of Rome. All night long bands of drunken marauders roamed the streets yelling, singing, and terrorizing, threatening to light their fellow night-roamers on fire with their torches if they did not capitulate to their demands for money. The troublemakers made the neighborhood dogs bark, which always woke the princess. By dawn, schoolteachers had already begun their classes, which took place outdoors, so that as soon as Kleopatra settled back to sleep, she was startled awake by a resounding lecture given in Greek on the philosopher Herákleitos or on ethics or Virtue—lectures she might have found intriguing if not for her superior education at the Mouseion. Merchants began hawking their goods shortly thereafter. Carts creaked incessantly, the drivers yelling at one another to move out of the way, and then cursing when their cargo collided as they drove in opposite directions down the hazardously narrow streets.

Despite the danger and the intrigue, or perhaps because of it, the city captivated the princess. Saturated with color, in contrast to the pervasive whiteness of her own Alexandria, houses seemed to be stacked upon houses, with jutting ledges called gutters to capture the rainfall. Unlike the symmetrical perfection of Alexandria, Rome had tiny narrow streets and great wide ones. The people everywhere, regardless of class, were loud and crass in speech; neither inscrutable like the native Egyptians nor intense and argumentative like the Greeks. Everywhere the Romans announced themselves: The exteriors of businesses were decorated with crude murals of the proprietors at their tasks; family portraits were done on the residences asserting the identities of the inhabitants, and long political manifestos were scrawled in hurried penmanship on walls and buildings. Rome and its inhabitants were vulgar, to be sure, but Kleopatra found herself nonetheless infatuated with the display.

Released from the small prison of the carriage now, and strolling down a dank alley at the bottom of Capitoline Hill, she entertained herself with the obscene epigrams that commemorated the various sex acts witnessed in that corridor. Kleopatra read in slightly hesitant Latin, for she was not accustomed to slang:

HERE, I, JULIANUS, TAUGHT MY SLAVE-BOY TO PLAY THE
WOMAN. HE PLEASED ME SO WELL I AM PLUCKING HIS THIGHS
CLEAN AND TAKING HIM INTO MY HOUSE.

"Timon, is it not true that Roman law, contrary to Greek tradition, forbids the defiling of young Roman males?" Kleopatra asked her guide. "That citizens must confine homosexual relations to foreigners and slaves?"

"It is true, Your Highness," he answered. He was a young man, intelligent, and relieved to be in the company of Greek-speaking royals who were happy to share his disdain of the conquering barbarians. "As if one might legislate desire, particularly desire of that kind. People are people the world over. Even the Romans who consider themselves to be so superior and mighty."

"I heard someone say once in the Alexandrian marketplace that there is no language as good as the Latin for telling a dirty joke. Let us walk ahead of my father and the rest so that we may read them," she whispered to him. "Oh yes," he said snidely. "These nasty little ditties are Rome's finest contribution to literature and poetry to date."

They strolled on, stopping for the princess to leisurely read of the adventures of "pokers, quim-lickers, and sodomites," and one lament of a man unable to practice the latter art for weeks due to loose bowels.

BROTHERS, LISTEN TO MY TALE OF WOE.
MY WIFE HAS LONG, VENGEFUL TALONS.
HERE ON THIS SITE SHE CAUGHT ME IN A BOY.
SHE SCREAMED, DO I NOT HAVE TWO BUTTOCKS, YOU BASTARD?
I, THE OLD POKER, TRIED TO PROTECT THE BOY-LOVER FROM
    HER BLOWS.
BUT ALL THE WHILE HE SCREAMED AT HER, TAKE YOUR TWO
    QUIMS AND GO HOME.

"Very good," said Timon. "You only mispronounced a few things."

Kleopatra was not allowed—to her great dismay and despite her good arguments—to enter the public baths, for Auletes said it was unseemly for a princess to bathe with commoners. She did, however, visit the ruins of the temple of Isis, recently destroyed by order of the Roman senate because the religion made the Roman women "too excitable." One senator, grievously worked up over his wife's unmatronly devotion to the goddess, had taken a sledgehammer to the pillars of the temple, leaving the delicate columns in a crumpled heap. Auletes and his entourage were horrified at the treatment of their native deity, the goddess whom they worshipped, the goddess whom Kleopatra had represented in the Grand Procession. "Roman women appear to be excitable enough on their own," commented Auletes. "They don't seem to require the goddess to incite them."

The carriage halted in front of their next destination. "The Forum!" Kleopatra said, eager to see the seat of Roman culture.

"We must exit the carriage," explained Timon. "Vehicles of any kind are not allowed into the square."

"Then it should be declared a holy place," huffed the king.

They descended the carriage into the heat of the afternoon, which was enhanced by a strong humidity. Kleopatra had always envisioned the Forum as a building, or a series of buildings, but it was not. It was a square surrounded by many buildings; at one end, the massive, eight-columned temple of Saturn, built many centuries ago to honor the god-king of Italy. The temple, they were told, also housed the Roman treasury. "See, Kleopatra, that is where all our money will be when they get through with us!" said Auletes.

Roman citizens rested on the edges of three fountains, while others waited for spaces to clear so that they, too, could indulge their hands, feet, or faces in the cool water. Wide colonnades with long benches lined the square. An old bat-faced woman stood in front of painted vessels hawking fresh water and other cooling citrus drinks while a slave fanned his master with a large leaf in the serene shadow of her little booth.

The markets were not in the open air but in two concave hemicycles with arched fronts that faced the squares. Each building had a gallery where patrons might stroll and look in the window, and the princess looked up, hiding the sun's glare with her hand, so that she could see the goods of the merchants displayed behind the open doors.

While the king and Hekate rested in the shade, Kleopatra and Charmion spent hours walking into the shops with Timon, trailed by an armed guard, and purchasing whatsoever struck the princess's fancy. She had wanted to procure fabrics for new clothes, fashionable hair adornments fitting to her new maturity, and shawls for the old ladies who lived on Antirhodos, but she found that the goods manufactured in Rome were primitive in contrast to those imported from Greece and Egypt. She did manage to buy a ceramic figure of a Roman *lar*, a spritish creature who protected the Romans at home, and a brocade blanket that she would put upon the back of Persephone when she saw her pony again.

Thoughts of her horse made her spirits sink. She had had enough of Rome and wanted to go home—to the shimmering sea, to the wide boulevards, to the exquisite pink granite monuments built by her ancestors, to the palace with its luxuries, to the court where philosophers and men of science sat with her father and discussed new ideas. It made her sick to the stomach that the Greek world was usurped, crushed, by these brash Romans, uncouth in so many ways. She decided that she hated this crowded, fetid city made of ugly brick. She hated the rows of apartments stacked on top of one another to house the rabble from Rome's conquered territories. She hated the arrogant men who swept past her in the Forum, followed by armed militias as they left one building and entered another. She hated every sign of the prosperity and might that Rome had built by pillaging the rest of the world. All these things discouraged her, and yet in them she saw a certain inevitability. Here was a race of men who believed that it was their gods-given right to lord over the rest of the world. What fools were her stepmother and sister and their silly, provincial eunuchs who thought that this sweeping force that cast aside the old and painted the future—their futures—could be ignored or demolished.

"Timon, why do all the men in the Forum require such protection to walk the short distance from one end of the square to the next?"

"These men are senators and other men of means. Rome is a terribly dangerous place in these terribly dangerous times."

"Do we require more protection than we have?" she asked.

"No, the Romans are only concerned with murdering one another at present."

After the lengthy shopping expedition, Kleopatra and Charmion met up with the others in their party for a final stroll past the Curia Hostilia, in the northwest corner of the Forum, where the senate often met.

"I cannot go near the place without Pompey!" exclaimed the king, turning away from the direction of the Curia as if he had been told that a plague had been let loose in the building. But Timon assured him that the senate did not meet on this day. "If you would like, you may peer into the great room through any one of the open doors in the vestibule," said Timon.

The long colonnade that led to the Curia was lined with dangling balls hanging from coarse ropes. Pedestrians walked right past the odd-looking spheres, occasionally stopping to admire one, or to laugh at it, or to read the inscriptions that rested on podiums below. Curious, the princess quickened her step. She heard the ever-present footsteps of the guards increase their pace behind her.

When she got within a few feet of the spectacle, she stopped, clutching her arm to her stomach. Timon caught her from behind, steadying her and turning her away from the sight. He turned around and said to Auletes and the others, "Your Majesty, please stay back."

He hugged Kleopatra protectively. "I have become so accustomed to the sight that I have forgotten how horrifying it is to the newcomer."

The suspended objects were not balls, but human heads—severed heads hung as a reminder to those who conspired against the prevailing powers. The skin had turned a putrid green, the mouths twisted in final cries of anguish, eyes rolled back deep into their sockets. Kleopatra raised herself up and broke free of Timon's grasp, riveted before a face that could not stare back. Below it was a simple inscription: "Enemy of the State." Other heads warranted more elaborate anecdotes of their political wrongdoing. Romans continued to walk right past, paying no attention to either the Greek princess or the grotesque sight. It was as if the withering heads were part of a mosaic they had seen many times. Only the occasional curiosity-seeker stopped to read the accounts of the crimes posted beneath the dismembered body part.

None of these heads had belonged to bodies of foreigners. Each had been a Roman, proscribed and executed by a fellow Roman when the political tide had turned against him. This was not a new strategy, Timon said. Heads had been hanging in the Forum for over one hundred years, and over the same issues.

"In the old days, every Roman from the richest to the poorest was a farmer. A simple man who arose early and worked late into the day at his land. Now every Roman believes he should live like a king and have a king's power, too. These are the men who failed in that pursuit, or who interfered with the plans of others."

"I have seen enough," Auletes said. "Please take us back to our quarters." Auletes let Timon and the guard walk ahead. "How can these people intercede in our affairs?" the king hissed to his daughter and his mistress. "Look at the mess they've made of their own nation."

"It is a puzzle, Father. They wish to rule the world, but they cannot even rule themselves. What will be the end of it?"

"No word from home. No word from Demetrius. And Rome sends not one man in the direction of Egypt to help us. Not one man. We are living on borrowed money in this place that the gods seemed to have abandoned to madmen. What will become of us, my child?"

Kleopatra did not answer. What might she, a girl of twelve, do that a king could not do? Auletes sighed heavily as he stepped into the carriage, which tipped toward the princess as her father's weight shook its balance. She recoiled, hoping that the king's bulk would not cause the carriage to topple upon her, crushing her to death in this strange and jeopardous city.

THIRTEEN

Caesar threw back his head and laughed. The senate, he reflected, was like the male organ: flaccid and strong, hard and soft, aggressive and retreating. Rigid and shriveled. Presently, it had two testicles—Cato and Cicero. Caesar had successfully removed one. Now the other must follow so that castration would be complete.

He was alone in his quarters in Cisalpine Gaul—not so far from Rome that it was not constantly on his mind—where he had encamped to make sure that things in Rome went his way before he was too far away to do anything about it, should the political tide turn against him. Eight legions under his command, within a two-day march of the city, would encourage Fortune to remain on his side.

He lay back in the pony-hair recliner that had been carried from the capital for his use. Normally not one for luxury, he liked the way the soft coat felt against his neck and the back of his arms and legs after a long day of work. He rested his body and thought about Cicero. Cicero was basically all talk, but what talk it was. How beautifully executed and impassioned those vitriolic speeches. And how often had he turned his gift for speech and for derision against his friend Caesar. Cicero's passionate verbosity bolstered the courage of the senators who were opposed to Caesar, making them feel stronger, braver, and more willing to oppose Caesar than they really were. Therefore, Cicero must go, at least for a time.

"It has to be a temporary measure," he had told Clodius on his last day in Rome. "I do not wish him any lasting harm, despite his faults."

"He does have those," agreed Clodius, who did not have Caesar's affection for the old man. "Vanity never had a better friend. Politically, he hops from side to side like children at a game of rope. His gift for invective exceeds all his other qualities. And he simply will not shut up, even when I tell him to do so."

"I have to admit that all that is true, but, well, I *love* the old thing." Cicero had so helped Caesar with the composition he was writing on Latin grammar that he intended to dedicate the work to him. He did not approve of Cicero's rather florid writing style; it was so out of date. But it had its own beauty, as things of the past often did. As far as Caesar was concerned, there were but two minds in Rome large enough to hold the subtleties of politics, philosophy, art, literature, science, and rhetoric all at once, and to be expert in each of those aspects of study—his and Cicero's. Of course, Cicero's talents did not expand to the other arena of Caesar's genius, the military. But no matter. He had been brave enough when called upon by his country. Now he would pay for that bravery, but not too dearly. In happier times sure to come, Caesar would make certain that Cicero survived, even thrived, once more.

"What shall it be?" Caesar had asked. "Do you have a plan?"

"Let this be my little surprise, darling. My birthday gift to you. It's the least I can do for your patronage," Clodius said with his usual impish twinkle. Caesar could hardly wait.

Clodius had been a marvelous investment. Not once had Caesar regretted what he did to put the man into the position of power he now held, the Tribune of the People. He recalled Clodius's surprise when Caesar informed him that he would get him elected to the office, which was not open to members of the nobility—indeed, had been created to protect the plebeian class from the senate's absolute authority.

"How do you propose that I run for tribune, Julius, when my name is as old and as patrician as yours?"

"Well, it's the only way you'll be able to veto the senate," replied Caesar. "It simply has to be done. Besides, the lower classes absolutely adore you. It won't be a problem."

For once Caesar had beaten Clodius at his own game, concocting a scheme that even Clodius had to admit exceeded his genius. As Pontifex Maximus, the religious authority of Rome, Caesar arranged for Clodius to be legally adopted by a plebeian. In itself, that was not so much a feat; how many of their noble peers had adopted adult sons to procure an heir? The scandal was that the adoptive father chosen was still a juvenile, and both tradition and the law insisted the father be at least eighteen years older than the adopted son. But the boy was all Caesar could scare up in time for the ceremony. The senate protested the audacity, but they could not overrule Caesar in the matter. He had sprung it on them so quickly that they were unprepared to do anything but watch agape as thirty-year-old Clodius became the son of a boy who had yet to grow a beard. Caesar and Clodius worked together like an Olympic relay team. And now, even though he was in Gaul and such a long distance from the locus of Roman politics, he, Julius Caesar, the aristocrat *cum* man of the people, would still be in control, thanks to his man in Rome, Clodius.

Caesar was relieved to be away. He had feared he would never be able to leave Rome, what with the senate's incessant investigations into his actions. Never weary of talk, talk, talk, the senate had held a three-day debate on whether Caesar's legislation the year before had been passed legally. It was tiresome, and finally he got irritated and told them to sort it out themselves. He had a province to govern—a province where tribes were at war with one another and would soon turn on Rome if he did not subdue them at once.

"You are like old women, Senators," he told them. Like old women, but without that canny wisdom crones acquire once past the hope of arousing the lusts of men.

Once Caesar and his legions marched out of the gates of Rome and toward Gaul, Clodius, on Caesar's behalf, acted with a ferocity and a speed that left them entirely at his and Caesar's mercy—a quality cultivated by Caesar but missing entirely from Clodius's quirky character. Clodius organized the masses who had come to

Rome to take advantage of the free offerings of corn. He united these disparate nationalities of men—these vagabonds with no purpose save putting a little bread on the table—into Neighborhood Associations. Within a month, they had control over every precinct in the city. A prodigy, thought Caesar. An equal.

"We're going to go after Pompey next," Clodius had said.

"In that you must be extremely careful. After all, he is my ally and my son-in-law," Caesar said. "I do not wish to alienate Pompey." At least not yet.

"Don't worry, darling," Clodius had said cheerily before Caesar left. "They'll all blame me. You shan't even be here. How could anyone blame you?"

Caesar was barely outside the city limits when Clodius incited a crowd outside the Forum to harangue Pompey as he judged cases. Pompey was so surprised that he left the Forum. Then Clodius let Pompey's conquered enemy Tigranes out of prison and made him a drinking pal. Caesar knew how irritating this must be to Pompey, for Pompey was terribly proud of the foreign leaders he had imprisoned in the capital.

As a final blow, Clodius sent an armed slave into the senate who attempted to murder Pompey. It was a false assassination attempt; no one wished Pompey dead. But believing he had barely escaped harm, Pompey retreated to his villa in the Alban Hills. Now Caesar was informed that he refused to leave it. He had abdicated all responsibility—he, whom the senate considered their greatest weapon.

Caesar could not quite figure Pompey. His accomplishments rivaled Alexander's: He had conquered Sicily, Africa, and the east; the former two, practically before he had grown a full beard. He was the world's most feared man, certainly more widely feared than Caesar. He had defeated the venerable tyrant Mithridates, who had conducted a campaign of military terror against Rome for generations. He was rich, he was powerful, he was handsome to the point of intimidation, and the world hailed him Magnus. Yet, according to Clodius's letters, Pompey spent his days lingering in his fruit grove, paralyzed by Clodius's acts of terror against him, claiming that he was a private citizen, that Clodius was an elected armed tribune, and that he was powerless to move against him. In the end, Caesar wondered if Pompey had a slight disorder of character.

A great man, Caesar thought, but a limited man. Pompey required a person of power like Sulla, or a body of power like the senate, to motivate him. He possessed leadership qualities, but he lacked the independent initiative of someone like Caesar. Pompey and those of his ilk believed that something had to motivate power, something tangible like a document or a system of government or an army. They did not understand what Caesar understood: that power was its own animator, its own genius. For those who understood its essence, power could simply be summoned. All else fell within its sway, and the flood tide soon followed.

Caesar had one other concern. He had sent a strong letter to Clodius reminding him that his daughter Julia resided at the villa with Pompey. "I am making her personal safety your responsibility," Caesar had said. He let Clodius have free reign because he knew how the man thrilled to these public displays of bullying. But he had his limits. Clodius, sensing this, wrote back with urgency that the girl Julia was safe and would always be so as long as he, Clodius, breathed the air of Rome. Pompey was quite obsessed with the girl and spent his days indoors, not only to avoid Clodius, but also to enjoy the affections of his spry young wife.

How long had it been since he, Caesar, had allowed himself to be distracted from duty by a lover? When he was very young, the king Nikomedes had so intrigued him with the luxuries of a foreign court that, for a time, he forgot all ambition and functioned as a Greek love toy to His Majesty. That ended soon enough. There were others. Servilia in the beginning, when she was young and full of greedy appetites, before she became such an accomplished schemer. His first wife, Cornelia, to be sure. A woman of deep desire, but devoid of artifice. Unusual. He had not witnessed it again in a female, outside the odd provincial, too ignorant or too hopeless to indulge in ambition. A boy here and there, but it never lasted past a day or two. Pompeia. Sometimes he missed her velvety cries in the middle of the night. He imagined Clodius did, too. But to preserve their alliance they had both needed to relinquish her joys.

It had been a very long time since he had allowed himself to be distracted as Pompey was doing at this moment with his daughter. And it would be a very long time until he would again be able to be free for such dalliance. There was so much to do.

Caesar reached down and picked up the most recent missive from Clodius.

. . . I believe you are going to have trouble with the exiled Egyptian king. The king cannot repay his debts unless he can get back into his country, and Rabirius is in a tizzy about it. Rabirius visits the king often to see about his money, but the king's solution is to borrow even more. He keeps telling Rabirius that he must use his influence to get someone, anyone, to act on their behalf. Then Rabirius comes to me. You know how he is, I cannot shut him up and so avoid his company when possible.

At some point, perhaps you should march into Egypt yourself. I know it would be highly irregular, but I believe there would be quite a lot in it for you. Perhaps you should make the offer to the king while Pompey hesitates. I hear he is out of his mind with Pompey's indecision. I have made it known to him that he may call upon me for assistance, which would drive Pompey mad!

The information gathered thus far is from my man on the inside at Pompey's. But he is afraid to be found out and wishes to be relieved of his duties. I fear I have overpaid him and he no longer wishes to disguise himself as a servant.

I have a very busy day ahead, darling, but you will hear from me shortly. It never ends. More later. P. C. P.

"My good friend," began Auletes. "May we speak in earnest?"

Kleopatra cringed, turning her head away from the table and staring at a small fish darting about aimlessly in the fountain. Her father was going to humiliate himself once again and attempt to solicit Pompey's aid in ousting Thea. They sat in the atrium eating a late afternoon snack of fresh fruits from the gardens and drinking wine from murrine cups that Pompey had confiscated from the tent of Mithridates. Pompey did not answer the king, but elbowed Kleopatra to retrieve her attention, pointing to the fawn in the forest scene painted on his delicate piece of plunder. "They say I could get twenty thousand apiece for these on the open market."

"You must be tiring of our company. Do you not think we should make a plan to remove my wife from the throne?" asked the king. "As much as we are grateful for your hospitality, surely you are ready to help us return to our own country?"

"Let me slice you a mango," said Pompey. He cut a thick piece of juicy orange fruit for the king and fed it to him with his own fingers. Probably to shut him up, thought Kleopatra. "Have you tried the varieties of grape?" he asked.

Auletes, mouth stuffed, shook his head.

"The politics of helping you are complex, my friend," said Pompey. "Very complex indeed. I require your patience."

Pompey's Greek houseman walked briskly into the room. "Sir, the guards at the gate have informed me that a guest approaches. I'm afraid it's the orator, Cicero, sir."

"Great gods. What does he want? Why did someone not warn me that he was coming?"

"I just received word, sir. He will arrive within the half hour."

"A man of such fame," said the king. "My daughter has read all his published speeches. In the Latin, of course. She is very learned, you know."

"My friend, I am afraid that Cicero comes on unpleasant business," said Pompey, twisting uncomfortably in his chair. "You see, in January, the Tribune of the People, Publius Clodius Pulcher, passed a piece of legislation that makes our noble Cicero a criminal."

"You must explain this to me, my friend, because my government is very different from yours. We do not change our laws so frequently," said the king.

"But Cicero is beloved in Rome, is he not?" asked Kleopatra. She was intrigued to know why the orator's arrival made Pompey so terribly nervous. Were they not old allies?

"Many years ago, when Cicero was consul, there was an uprising in Rome, led by a man named Catiline. Many say he plotted an attempt to overthrow the entire government, and Cicero claimed to have special evidence of his guilt. Cicero had the conspirators arrested and executed."

"As he should," said Auletes pointedly. "Rebels must be put down. My wife, for instance."

Ignoring him, Pompey continued. "But Cicero neglected to hold a trial. For this, he came under harsh criticism from some, while others supported him and hailed him as Savior of his Country, a name he never tires of hearing. He is very vain, you know."

"But why is he indicted so many years later?" asked Kleopatra.

"Clodius is not very fond of Cicero. He wrote legislation making it illegal to execute any Roman without a trial, and he made it retroactive, specifically so that he might incriminate Cicero and have grounds to get rid of him. Such are the times we live in." Pompey spoke slowly and indifferently, like a historian delivering a history lecture about a long-lost era rather than an active participant in the politics of the day.

"Why is he coming to see you?" asked Auletes. "Does he wish your support?"

"I have already told him that there is nothing I can do. The senate has voted against him. His only two choices are imprisonment or exile. I have advised him to take the latter. When the time is right, I will do what I can to recall him."

"That seems fair," said Auletes, wondering if he would be forever condemned to the same indifference from Pompey.

"He doesn't listen to reason," complained Pompey, eating a grape and spitting its seeds on the floor. "They tell me he's retired his senator's toga for peasant's rags, walking the streets all hours of the day ranting that if he is to be treated like a martyr he will dress like one. He beseeches absolutely anyone he sees, whether knight, senator, magistrate, butcher, or slave, to come to his aid."

That is what your indifference is forcing my father to do as well, thought Kleopatra.

"I have told him that he must be an example and obey the Constitution and the laws of the land. He has spent his entire life defending the very principles he now defies. I am afraid he has gone mad." Pompey spoke evenly, but Kleopatra could not help but notice an air of defensiveness in his voice.

"Sir." The houseman rushed into the atrium and stood nervously before Pompey, as if Pompey would defer to ancient custom and kill the messenger. "The sentinels report that Cicero approaches the house."

"Take care of it, man," Pompey hissed to him. "I am not here, do you understand? I am not here, no matter what."

Kleopatra heard a commotion coming from the courtyard and the footsteps of Pompey's household staff rushing to investigate the disaster.

"Pompey, do not desert me in my hour of need!" The voice came roaring from the outdoors, dramatic, sentimental, and demanding all at once, having as imperious a quality as Kleopatra had ever heard, despite the fact that the speaker was pleading. The footsteps grew louder. "Where is the man I have mentored and held dear all the days of my life?"

The door to the vestibule was open, allowing Kleopatra to hear the houseman say, "Please, Senator, he is not at home. May I offer you a warm bath and a cup of wine before you go back to the city?"

"Out of my way, liar! Hear me, Pompey, who is called Magnus. The animal Clodius had his gangsters sling dung at my person in the Forum! Come out here, Pompey, and see the shit I have endured for the Republic."

Pompey got to his feet. "Do excuse me," he said curtly to the royals, and then ran so quickly from the room that he knocked over one of the prized murrine drinking cups, shattering it to pieces. Leaving Cicero screaming in the vestibule, Pompey headed for the back door leading to the garden. "His usual hiding place," said Auletes.

The orator entered the room. Not so mean-looking as Cato, the princess thought, but just as old and cantankerous. Covered in dirt from the ride, he was dressed in a tattered tunic, and trailed by a younger man. Cicero looked down his considerable nose at Auletes and Kleopatra. "Who are you?" he asked Auletes.

"I am Ptolemy Auletes, king of Egypt."

"Oh, good gods," said the orator, rolling his bleary eyes. He turned around and left.

Auletes put his head in his hands. "Are these the great men whose decisions send thunderous shock waves throughout the world?"

He looked into his daughter's eyes, scaring her with his haggard appearance. She noticed that the skin under his eyes had begun to sag into his cheekbones. "My god, daughter, who is running Rome?"

⌐◄⋏⋏▮▐◢⌐◎◯◢

"Awaken," said the voice. "Awaken, child. Rise."

Kleopatra opened her eyes but saw only darkness. No oil lamp was lit. Only the sound of her cousin's voice filled the void. But it couldn't be him, for he was still at school in Greece. It must be a dream, she thought. He has come to me in a dream with a message. She opened her eyes again and saw the vague silhouette of a man's body.

"Surely this cannot be my little cousin Kleopatra. Kleopatra is a child. Even in the dark I see the body of a young woman."

Kleopatra sat up, pulling her sheet up to her neck.

"It is Archimedes, my love. It is your cousin. I am here." A large, warm, hardened hand laid itself upon her small one and gently rubbed it. "It is I, darling cousin, darling girl. You must hurry and get dressed. The king has summoned you into his chambers."

A dream. A dream in which her handsome cousin had come to Rome and had entered her bedroom. Now she would go on one of night's strange and mysterious journeys with him. She knew she should be afraid, but his voice was as soft as satin and as familiar as the oldest of friends.

"Archimedes? Are you man or apparition?" The girl withdrew her hand and rubbed her eyes. Her cousin lit a candle, revealing his familiar face.

"Cousin!" She threw her arms, almost lifeless with sleep, around his strong neck. "Cousin, you have come to us." He returned her embrace. "Yes, I have come to you, but there is no time now to talk. Charmion will dress you, my darling. You must come. It is an emergency of state and your father requires your presence. Now quickly, into your clothes."

Before she could ask questions, he was gone, and Charmion appeared with a fresh dress. "Do not waste time with speech. Your father needs you. Here is a lamp. Now go to him."

The princess navigated her way down the long halls of Pompey's villa, wondering what had transpired in the night to bring her cousin to her. Was Auletes ill? She crept along the corridors, shrinking from the shadows. As she approached her father's rooms she heard a low mumble of voices. Greek voices speaking in hushed tones. Several men stood outside the door to Auletes' chamber. Men she knew. Men from home.

Princess. Kleopatra. Some bowed, others commented on her growth in the months she had been away. A young lady. Her soft cheek brushed several rough faces. She was caught up in the embraces of her Kinsmen, but no sooner had she received their affection than she was hustled into the room.

"Daughter," boomed Auletes as she met his cheerful face. He appeared to be in the middle of an odd nocturnal celebration. Roman slaves served the Greek visitors trays of hastily prepared food and cups of wine. Kleopatra wondered again if she were awake or asleep, for this was the stuff of dreams. Surrounded by his men, he raised a cup to his child. "Our Kinsmen have brought extraordinary news."

"What is it, Father?" Kleopatra blinked at Archimedes, who kept quiet, deferring to the king.

"Thea is dead," Auletes said slowly, chewing every word as if it were a delicious morsel.

The princess stood very still absorbing the announcement. It was as if all had become silent awaiting her reaction. "Is my father once again king?"

"Your father has always been king," said Archimedes. "Sit with us, Princess, and hear the tale we bring, for it is full of unexpected events. The queen was found slain in her chamber. We do not know the identity of the murderer."

"Who is this hero?" Auletes asked. "We must find this patriot and reward him."

"Your Majesty, we believe it was Demetrius."

"My friend! My savior!" cried the king. "Why did he not join this delegation? Why is he not here to celebrate with us? I have been so worried about him."

"Sire, Demetrius, too, is dead. His body was found the day after the queen's body was discovered. It is believed that he murdered the queen and then took his own life."

"Oh blessed friend!" cried Auletes. "Blessed, blessed man. Why did he do this thing? Why did he not spare himself?" He looked straight at the stricken face of his daughter. "Did he not know that we loved him?"

Kleopatra did not answer. She thought only of the tall, thin man who had become her friend, tutor, mentor, confidant. She did not believe he was gone. Gone the way of Mohama, snatched from her by merciless Fate. Who was next?

"He shall be deified upon my return to Egypt. I shall have him interred next to Alexander himself," the king said. "He is a hero and he died a hero's death. A Titan in a scholar's disguise."

Archimedes stood next to the princess and took her hand. She clutched it tight. It was both strange and familiar, this man's hand in hers. Archimedes turned to the king. "Sire, we must save our grief. There are great complications. We must act with the utmost expediency if you wish to be returned to the kingdom. Egypt is in utter turmoil, but many factions still support you."

"Then return I must. Are you telling me I no longer require a Roman legion to march with me into my city? That I may simply pack my trunks and go home?"

Kleopatra felt her cousin's hand tense. He lowered his voice. "It is a bit more complex than that. You see, in the confusion following the death of the queen, your eldest daughter seized power."

Berenike. The Amazon queen, now the queen of Egypt. Kleopatra shuddered, recalling her vision: the bleeding neck of Arsinoe, her own dead body at the child's feet, Berenike victorious over her sisters. Had she planned it all from childhood? Had she feigned attachment to Thea, knowing that she would use their closeness for Thea's demise?

"Seized? What do you mean, seized? How does a petulant girl 'seize' power?" The king was less shocked than disdainful. "Berenike is a child. Come, let us make arrangements to go home."

Archimedes dropped Kleopatra's hand and moved closer to the king. "She is eighteen, Your Majesty. And she is backed by the eunuch Meleager, the *demes* of Middle Egypt, and the army. The priests of

Upper Egypt and certain Greek factions in the city are still loyal to you. But the situation is grave. That is why I left my studies in Greece and returned to your service."

The king sat back in his chair, exhaling violently, as if expelling all the joy from his body.

Archimedes continued. "Apparently, Meleager has been quietly raising support for Berenike all over the country. He has sent a party to Seleucus, a bastard Syrian prince, to propose that he marry Berenike and bring his army to Alexandria. It is said that Berenike is against the marriage, but Meleager wishes it because Seleucus is someone he can control, someone who would be beholden to him for his power."

The astonished king said nothing. Kleopatra waited for him to begin to rail in his usual manner against her sister, transferring the loathing he had visited upon Thea onto Berenike, but the king merely sat motionless, as if he had been stabbed from behind and was dead.

"Sire, there is much to do. Meleager has sent a delegation to Rome to speak out against you."

"Here? Here to Rome? But he is against all things Roman," argued the king.

"They call themselves the One Hundred. I believe he paid them handsomely to come here. But they are traitors. In the middle of the voyage, about twenty of them left the expedition to join a Cilician pirate hunt for gold. Such is their allegiance to their cause."

"And what is their cause?" Auletes asked anxiously.

"They are headed by a philosopher, Dio, and they intended to appear before the senate to speak out against you, to squelch any assistance for your return, and to ask Rome to back Berenike as the legitimate ruler. They also plan to ask for Rome to sanction Berenike's marriage to Seleucus."

"I am lost." The king threw back his head and began to cry.

"Your Majesty, we do not have even one hour to waste in meditation or regret. Or grief for that matter," Archimedes said. "The One Hundred have already docked in Italy."

"Wretched is the man betrayed by his own family," Auletes said.

"Oh nonsense, Your Highness. Utter nonsense."

Hammonius—friend, merchant, Kinsman, spy, a man not of royal blood but with the wealth of a king—had been silent through the discourse. Gathering his affably heavy body into an erect position, he reminded Kleopatra of the great brown bear in the Alexandria zoo that had been a gift from a Galatian queen. "Let us not admit wretchedness. Let us plot victory." Hammonius raised his ample arms. "Are we ghoulish spirits bringing you bad omens? Or are we your Kinsmen, ready to rally to your cause? Your Majesty, we are men of action. Now let us act."

"You are right, my friend. I must collect myself. Tell me about the One Hundred. Or is it the Eighty?" The king laughed, to Kleopatra's relief. "Who are these eighty traitors and how shall we dispense with them? And who is this Dio? Do you know him, Daughter? Do you consider him a philosopher of any importance?"

Kleopatra did not like Dio. He was arrogant and had paid her no attention when, as a child, she had traipsed after the dark-gowned scholars of the Mouseion seeking access to their knowledge. "He teaches the works of others but cannot be called an innovator or a thinker himself. Nor does he have the compassion of our Demetrius."

Archimedes said, "Dio is the mouthpiece of Meleager, Your Majesty. It was the eunuch who petitioned for him to be brought from Athens to the Mouseion. All the while he was on Your Majesty's payroll, he was secretly publishing pamphlets against you and distributing them through a network set up by Meleager throughout the city. And now he is here, docked at Puteoli, waiting for the senate to schedule a time when he might lead his eighty into the Curia with a list of their grievances against you to plead the case for the reign of Berenike."

"Where will they get with the senate?" Auletes asked with contempt. "Why should the senate back them when I am here as the guest of Pompey?"

"It is believed that Berenike has access to the treasury," answered Archimedes.

It was almost dawn. Auletes looked at the princess. "The lessons of monarchy are not always pleasant."

She shrugged. Auletes stared at his daughter for a long while. "I'm not another Potbelly, you know, killing philosophers just because they displease me."

"Of course not, Father." Did he think her attachment to the scholars caused her to overestimate this Dio's worth? Berenike was a traitor. Kleopatra was first in line for her father's throne. "Father," she said. "It would hardly be like denying the world an Epicurus. Let us act now and without remorse."

"Spoken like a queen." Hammonius knelt before Kleopatra. "May I have permission to kiss your hand?"

Kleopatra extended her hand, allowing the big man to place his soft, warm lips upon the back of her small mitt. "The princess has an infallible ability to judge character."

Archimedes followed Hammonius and kissed the hand of his cousin. But Archimedes was twenty-two years old and tall with very square shoulders and lean, dark arms. Kleopatra quivered when his lips lingered against her skin. He must have felt it, too, because he looked into her eyes as he held her hand and said, "What a princess you are. What a woman you shall be." She blushed and hoped that no one noticed—though how could they not?—and she chastised herself for this display of emotion at such a tense and crucial time. After all, she had just sanctioned a man's death. And on that matter she felt numb, bloodless. Her father and his men were fools if they thought Demetrius could kill anyone. Kleopatra was certain that it was Berenike who killed Thea and Demetrius.

Hammonius brought the meeting back to order. "Your Majesty, I know a man. He is not a particularly good man, but he is a powerful man. A man of action. An effective man. I believe we might take our dilemma to him. I believe he can help us."

"Tell me, Brother," said the king, interested, "is there a Roman who might come to our assistance? I have found them to be entirely inert. I would be happy to contribute to the purse of one who has no fear of action."

Hammonius looked about the room. "All here are beholden to secrecy. Swear it now upon your lives and the lives of your families. Whoever betrays his brothers in this matter will surely die. The man who will save the king is despised in this home."

"Here is what I think of your choice of husband, eunuch."
Berenike stepped aside. Three of her women dropped the strangled
corpse of Seleucus, the Syrian bastard prince, at Meleager's feet. The
young Arsinoe stood next to her tall sister, laughing at the spectacle. The astonished eunuch beheld the dead man, his neck purple
and bruised, his head dangling loosely from the rest of his body, his
lifeless face contorted in surprise and agony.

"Did you really expect the queen of Egypt to accept this saltfish-
monger?"

"You have known him three days. How is it that you believe you
can murder whomever you do not like?"

"I am exercising the ancient right of queens to choose and even
to murder their husbands." Berenike laughed, her grin a radiant half-
moon. "I remember all your lessons, Meleager. As you taught me,
in the days before Theseus disrupted the natural order, the Greek
queens of old selected a new king every year, sacrificing the old one
up to the goddess for the fertility of the soil. I simply sacrificed this
one a little early."

The little girl Arsinoe radiated the same lustrous smile in the
direction of the eunuch, as beautiful as Berenike's, though more
chilling in the younger face.

"Those are ancient myths, Your Majesty," he replied, careful not
to stare too long into the dead man's eyes, for it made him shudder.
"Not instructions for the living."

"Then you should have made that more clear in your lessons,"
she said triumphantly. "Please rid us of the body," she continued.
"And never forget that I make my own policies. I have chosen my
husband. He is Archelaus of Pontus, whom I met when I last visited that country. He is brave, he commands a large army, and he is
handsome beyond compare."

Archelaus of Pontus? How could this dazzling girl's judgment be
so demented?

"But Your Majesty, he is the illegitimate son of Mithridates, the
enemy of Rome. Have you forgotten that one hundred of your

most esteemed countrymen are in Rome at present petitioning the senate on your behalf? What will the Romans think when they hear that you married the offspring of the man with whom they were at war for three generations?"

"They are not paid to think."

Meleager tried to modulate his voice. "I must urge you to choose another Syrian. The Roman Gabinius is soon to be rewarded governorship of Syria. He may wish to be involved in your selection of husband."

"He will be denied that privilege. I have already told you my position on the matter. I expect Archelaus within the month. Please make arrangements for the accommodations for his men."

Berenike stepped over the body of Seleucus, turning her back on him so fast that her dress fluttered behind. The three women followed, leaving the corpse of the dead prince for Meleager. Little Arsinoe—how old was she now? Seven?—skipped behind the mad queen and her cutthroat entourage.

It had all been done so sloppily. He himself had planned the disposal of the queen and the philosopher. After speaking to Demetrius and hearing his guilty tirade about his betrayal, his "mistake," Meleager realized that the adultery was a godsend—that he could have both of them eliminated and make it appear that the philosopher, in a moment of forlorn remorse, had murdered the queen and had then gone back to his chamber and taken his own life. It would have been so neat. No untidy, unexplained details. No one to blame but the dead.

But Berenike was one step ahead of him. She came to him, eyes blazing with passion and madness, and told him that she had solved all their problems. She had killed them both. Now there was only Auletes and the little troublemaker who stood in their way. But do not worry, she had taken care of them, too. The sister of one of her women had been taken aboard Auletes' ship as a scullery maid. Before she left she was given a special cargo. A little something with which she might season their food.

It might have all worked out even then. There was only one problem—the queen was mad. Meleager, who had given his life, his very manhood, to the goddess, had been directed by that mysterious deity to arrange for a lunatic murderess to sit on the throne.

Meleager fell prostrate on the cold floor of his apartment, his nose flat against the tile, ignoring the fact that he lay next to a dead man. "Why have you forsaken me, Lady?" he sobbed into the floor. "Why have you done this thing?"

What use was it to ask the gods the question they inevitably refused to answer—why me? He cried for what seemed to be a long time. Finally, in the chaos of his memories, he saw a pattern emerge, an order, perhaps. Not his order, but a Higher Order. So what if he did not like or approve of the outcome? The goddess was under no obligation to make everything turn out in his favor. He was but a grain of sand in the desert, a minor player in a drama that began long before he was born and would continue long after he was forgotten. He did not have the whole picture; he saw only a few tiles in the mosaic. The Ptolemies, Egypt, Rome. The goddess had commissioned him to make certain that Berenike IV became queen. He had done that. So what if he, too, had paid a price?

He had come to the end of his service. As soon as he realized it, a great relief settled over him, like a warm bath after a long ride in the desert. It was as simple as that. The complexities he had pondered and woven all added up to this one thing. He had been given a Divine mission to see Berenike queen and he had completed that mission. What happened now was neither his concern nor his responsibility.

So that when he went to his private box of carved ebony from the Numidian forests and extracted the dagger, he did not waste even a moment in regret. He had lived an extraordinary life. He called for his servant to draw a bath; while his man fixed the temperature of the water, Meleager would write a letter to his mother.

He had already suffered the worst imaginable pain and survived. This time would be easier. He would be efficient and effective, just as he had been in all facets of his life. He had played his part with dignity and, if he did say so himself, exemplary aplomb. It was time to bow out and let history take its course.

Auletes, Hammonius, Archimedes, and the princess met with the Tribune of the People in his home on the Palatine Hill, because Clodius could not be received in the home of Pompey. It was just the four of them. That was the arrangement. No weapons, no body-guards. No one entered Clodius's house armed. Kleopatra was allowed to come because there was no time to argue with her, and because Auletes was afraid Clodius and his men would exchange private information in their own language.

The house was encircled by guards, soldiers armed as if for war, who interrogated the king's party upon arrival, checked the men for weapons, and then, at the command of the host, stepped aside so that the royals might walk under the great arched door and into Clodius's vestibule. The house was neither as new nor as splendid as the home of Pompey, for it was a smaller city house built in the days when the empire of Rome had not extended so far and Roman patricians were not yet enjoying confiscated treasures from around the world. But it contained an impressive collection of Greek statuary and pastoral floor mosaics of Italian farm life that Kleopatra found charming. Compared to Pompey's villa, it seemed old-fashioned, almost quaint. Nothing about the surroundings betrayed the power of the head of household.

"How is it that you have brought a child to our meeting?" Clodius inquired. He stood to greet his guests and then offered them seats on divans draped with worn tapestries.

"My daughter is my chosen heir," said the king, letting himself fall into the stuffed cushion of the sofa. "It is our custom to rule king and queen, side by side. The princess Kleopatra is being tutored in the ways of monarchy. She speaks many languages, including your own. She is a valuable diplomat."

Clodius bowed to Kleopatra but the amused look on his face remained. He looked smaller than the other Romans she had met, and was fairer of complexion. His Greek was precise and impeccable. For all his reputation for terror, he was one of the cultured greeklings so despised by his fellow Romans. Yet beneath his curly coiffure and his childlike straight white teeth, Kleopatra sensed the demon that drove him.

"What specifically might I do for you, Your Majesty?" he asked the king after food and drink were delivered to the guests. "After all, you are the guest of Pompey the Great. What might I do that that good man cannot?" he asked in a mocking tone.

Auletes did not intend to go into his problems with Pompey, for he was all too aware of the tension that existed between the men. "A delegation of traitors has docked at Puteoli and intend to speak out against me and my cause. I want to be rid of them before the senate gives them a hearing. Despite the friendly mask they wear at present, they are the tools of a deeply anti-Roman faction. You will serve me, yourself, and your own country if you do away with them."

"As tribune, I am here to serve the Roman people," replied Clodius. "Give us a minute." He sat quietly for a while, occasionally raising his eyebrows, breaking an impish grin, and tossing his shoulders about. The king did not know what to make of this, but Hammonius put his meaty hand up, a signal for the king to surrender to Clodius's idiosyncrasies. Finally Clodius took a deep breath as if he were coming out of a trance.

"Your Majesty, I have spent the last days in meditation upon another cause. I believe we might join our purposes and deliver a double thrust upon those who so vex us and our loved ones."

"Let us hear your thoughts, my good man," said the king.

"It seems to me that we are both caught up in matters of protecting our families. You are preserving the throne for your daughter, the future queen, and I am in the midst of a delicate situation concerning my beloved sister, who has fallen upon hard times."

"Go on, man, go on." So close to the promise of action, Auletes could barely contain his anticipation.

"My beloved sister, Clodia, has had the misfortune of becoming the obsession of the rabid poet Catullus. He has written pornographic poems explicitly describing his sick fantasies about her irreproachable person."

Could it be true that Clodius's sister was the muse of Catullus's erotic poetry? And if so, was Clodius the brother with whom she had the notorious incestuous affair? Kleopatra felt a wild elation but contained it; it would not do to reveal her love of Catullus's poems to the brother of the revered and then scorned Lesbia. Kleopatra's mind seized onto the idea that she could use this encounter with Clodius to catch a glimpse of the renowned beauty—or even of the poet himself.

"How does a poet fit in with my needs?" the king asked impatiently.

"Oh, the poet has nil to do with it, really. No one pays attention to him. But you see, my sister was cursed by the gods with an inordinate beauty, too captivating for mere mortal men to endure. One look at her and they seem to go mad. 'If only I could turn them to stone,' she cried to me only yesterday. 'Then they could not harm me!'" Clodius fluttered his eyes as his voice took on the shrill high pitch of a female.

Clodius had the attention of the king, who waited patiently for a revelation that would unite Clodius's complaint with his. "My sister was taken in by a lying dissolute, Caelius Rufus. She gave him an astounding sum of money and all of her jewelry so that he could promote himself politically, but instead he sold the jewels to pay his gambling debts."

Clodius squinted his eyes and rubbed his palms together. "I went to him to demand my sister's money, but I found him in his usual morning stupor. He cowered in the corner and wept, 'Oh Clodius, please do not hurt me. I am but a poor man. Clodia promised me I could keep the jewels. She really did. You know that I would never do anything against yourself or your family.'" Clodius used the same shrill voice in imitation of his sister's lover.

The king simply stared at the Roman.

Clodius resumed his masculine voice and began to lay out his scheme to do away with Auletes' enemies, wreak vengeance upon Caelius Rufus, and murder the philosopher Dio who stayed in the city, the guest of the wealthy knight Lucceius.

"Here is what we shall do," said Clodius, his eyes staring into space. "Next week Clodia is to make her annual sacred pilgrimage to Delos. And from where does the ship leave? Why, Puteoli, of course. Now do you see it, Your Majesty?"

Clodius would lure Caelius to Puteoli with promises of a last minute meeting and reconciliation with his sister. "But alas—he shall arrive just in time to have missed her boat. Meanwhile, we will have disposed of your enemies. Then, when Caelius arrives, we shall frame the murder on him."

Clodius jumped to his feet and did a little hopping dance before the king. "And that is just the beginning!"

Auletes turned to Archimedes. "I feel as if I am trapped inside the strange plot of one of Menander's comedies." He loudly cleared his throat. Kleopatra could see that he had wearied of listening to the complexities of Clodius's plot. Auletes came to his feet. Automatically, Hammonius and Archimedes joined him.

"Surely you aren't leaving?" asked Clodius with a hurt look on his face. "Don't you want to hear the rest of the plan?"

The king shook his head. "For the gods' sakes, man, just kill them."

With those words, the king left. The stunned members of his party apologized to Clodius and fixed when and where they would deliver the money. Kleopatra followed her father out of the house, wondering if her father had completely ruined her chances of meeting Catullus's muse. But the king simply got into the carriage that had brought him to the house, sat himself down, and fell asleep.

FOURTEEN

How do you like adventure when it is not merely play, Cousin?" Archimedes teased, the mirth in his brown eyes cutting through the morning's damp chill. Kleopatra resented that his good cheer came at her expense and she glared back at him.

"Is riding a horse three days through this endless Italian fog such a great adventure, Cousin?" retorted the princess. "I have had more excitement in the marketplace of Alexandria."

She was very tired and cranky and regretting that she had argued so passionately to be present. They had arisen long before dawn, having spent the night at a tawdry inn usually frequented, Hammonius said, by criminals and soldiers. The beds were hard and the meal inedible. Breakfast was a piece of bread taken on horseback. The lower part of her back ached. With each bounce of the horse his backside collided with hers, causing a pinch of pain in her sacrum. Though they had slowed their pace because of the fog, she longed to dismount and sit on a soft cushion. The soggy air made her colder than she ought to be. She craved a warm cup of weak wine and her own bed.

It was past daybreak but a murky haze still hovered over them. The torches of the bodyguard fractured the shroud of darkness, cutting a shadowy path along the empty highway. Though she could

smell the salty ocean air, she could not see as far as the shore. They
were told that the road would take them all the way to the port at
Puteoli, but in the engulfing fog, the road appeared to pave itself a
few feet at a time as the torches revealed it.

The entire scheme had been finessed with Pompey's blessing, but
without him knowing of Clodius's involvement. Kleopatra noticed
that in the months they had stayed with Pompey, he had put on a
considerable amount of weight. She had ceased to blush in his presence. Still, though, Julia frolicked before him like a nymph and,
nightly, he fell into her ocean. Auletes explained to Pompey what
would transpire, carefully eliminating the name of the architect of
the plot. Pompey listened patiently as if weighing the king's words
carefully. "I know nothing about it," he finally replied, giving his
dispensation.

The king caused great anxiety among his men by insisting that
he witness the deed. "I am spending a great deal of money on this,"
said Auletes. "I wish to see the faces of the traitors before they die.
I shall call upon the gods to take them to the bowels of Hades—
away from the company of poets and philosophers and lovely
women and into the depths of eternity where they shall live among
the shades of criminals and slaves." At that moment, Kleopatra
began her own campaign to accompany the men on their grim purpose, a campaign the king immediately squashed. Kleopatra did not
relent, but created for Auletes fantastic scenarios of her own vulnerability should his mission go awry, leaving her alone among the
Romans. "I am your heir, Father," she said. "What might they do
to me if you do not return and your clandestine purpose is discovered?" She laid the argument out logically as Demetrius had taught
her to do, pointing out the sequence of events that might lead to
her demise. If anything happened to the king, she would be left in
the hands of Pompey, who was the enemy of the man who had
designed Auletes' grim mission. Would Pompey take revenge upon
her for her father's alliance with his most egregious rival, Clodius?
Auletes regarded her skeptically, but she added, "One thing is certain. If the mission is not successful and my father does not return,
I shall certainly not be rewarded."

Finally, Archimedes interceded. "I will take full responsibility for the princess's safety, Your Majesty, if you allow me the privilege. I will lay down my life to protect her."

Kleopatra could not stop the squeal that escaped her mouth. She threw her arms around her cousin's neck.

"Let us hope it does not come to that," the king said, relenting.

Kleopatra released her cousin and turned to thank her father, but his disapproving stare stopped her. She had forgotten that she was no longer a child, and it was unseemly for her to have behaved this way.

"You will not regret changing your mind, Father," she said, suddenly somber.

"It is never too early to learn the lessons of power." Auletes sighed. "But you, young man, are responsible for her safety. Her safety—but your duty to the princess stops there," he added pointedly. He looked at his daughter to see if she took the warning, too. She bowed her head to her father.

Now the king was resplendent in his alertness. He rode ahead of his men and his daughter with a small guard arranged by Clodius, who assured them that they did not want to travel Italy's roads unaccompanied. The assassin, Ascinius, rode behind them dressed in dark clothing that matched his cimmerian countenance. He did not utter a word. Clodius had warned them not to be deceived by his bleak demeanor; his methods were impeccable and his loyalty beyond reproach. Kleopatra reckoned him a man to be feared.

Just when she thought she could no longer hold herself erect on the horse, they arrived at the docks. The royals were quickly sequestered inside a shack built for the dock master and his family, who had vacated for the day by order of Clodius. The hut smelled of fish and sea rot.

"But we will see nothing from here!" protested Kleopatra. "And the odor is putrid."

Her father's quiet glare silenced her. She perched herself atop a wooden table under a small round hole from which she could look out.

"There is the vessel to Delos," explained Archimedes, pointing at a small sailing ship. Kleopatra wished he would put his arm around her shoulder as they looked together to the sea, but he did not.

"And there is the ship of the One Hundred." It was a larger boat, with tall sails and, below in the gallows, long slits for oarsmen to propel the craft should the winds fail them.

From the small opening Kleopatra witnessed the unfolding of Clodius's great scheme. She watched as Clodius kissed a cloaked woman before she turned to board the ship headed for Delos. Her disappointment at not seeing the face of the beauty overtook her and she tried to escape the careful watch of Archimedes and sneak out the door, but he caught her and sent her back to her roost. Moments later she was gratified when the infamous one turned as she reached the deck to wave a final good-bye to her brother, revealing the notorious features that had dazzled so many.

Clodia's womanliness could not be restrained by her bulky travel clothes. She was graced with perfect proportions. The full mouth, red from the sea wind. The high cheekbones and dark slivers of shiny onyx eyes. The elongated neck and full chest tapering into a dainty waist. Long legs hidden under a skirt that protected her from the sea air. The luminescent skin—flawless, at least from the distance, but what woman has driven men to ruin without the feature of a perfect complexion? The dainty wistfulness as she waved a languid hand at her brother. Most of all, the nose, small, pinched to aristocratic perfection, resting indifferently in the middle of her face without interrupting the grace of her other features.

Kleopatra would never have such a face. It was her most vivid thought. Already her nose was too big and her eyes, though hot with intelligence, were not large nor dramatic enough to compensate for that feature.

Two sailors took in the plank. Clodia disappeared and the ship left the dock.

Glum at her own prospects, Kleopatra lowered herself upon the table and went to sleep.

⌒⬦𓃀𓏤𓏤𓊖⌐𓇳◠⌐

"If I had been a weaker man, I would have wept at the sight of the familiar faces." Kleopatra hopped upon the lap of her father, dodging the goblet Archimedes put into his hand. "Let me tell you a tale of betrayal and revenge."

They were men he had trusted. Men he had made rich by his generosity. Men with whom he had hunted, dined, whored. Harpalus, the mathematician to whom the king had given a large stipend to come to the Mouseion and study. Lycus, the philosopher Auletes invited to the palace time and again to discuss theological issues. Icarius, the importer of spices, who was just awarded a monopoly on nutmeg and cardamom. Nestor, the whoremonger of the Fayum, who provided the Royal Brothel with some of its most unusual talent. The admiral Periander, whom Auletes suspected—but could not be sure—was one of his bastard sons by a court governess. How else did the ingrate think he got the officership so young?

"Daughter, I almost wept to see who had deserted my cause and joined with Berenike and the eunuch. But I knew that I had no time to waste in grief. Ascinius went before me and his men followed close upon the rear. Quietly, we entered each cabin. I pointed at the traitors I recognized, and in the blink of an eye, they were done. Just like that. Still asleep, the most of them, but I picked each of the condemned up by the scruff of his nightshirt and said, 'This is my final gift to you, traitor. Give my regards to the ghost of my wife.' And then . . . " The king slid his hand across his neck. "We did our business and then vanished as if into thin air. The others aboard are still asleep, the lazy bastards. What a surprise awaits them when they awaken.

"The One Hundred are now down to sixty," he continued, stroking his cup. "How lucky are the twenty cowards who deserted to hunt gold with the pirates. Traitors though they be we cannot begrudge them their lives. The gods decide who stays and who goes, eh?"

"What is happening now, Your Highness?" asked Archimedes. "Should we not flee this location before we are found out?"

"No, no," said the king, nonchalantly. "Clodius has it all planned out. We mustn't interfere. Open the shutters here and behold what he has wrought."

From the open window, they saw a man kneeling on the dock,

frantically waving his arms at the ship that carried Clodia, the beautiful Lesbia, to Delos. He beat his chest, appeared to curse the heavens, and then threw his body flat upon the rough wood of the dock and beat its boards with his fist.

"Who is that crazy man on the docks?"

"That is Caelius Rufus, the thief who stole the jewels of Clodius's sister. Clodius told him that she wished to reconcile with him, and as a token of sincerity, she had a very heavy purse to leave with him," laughed the king. "So he is a little sad to have missed her boat. Now, observe the genius of Clodius in action."

Hammonius emerged from the ship of the One Hundred with a Greek sailor who pointed at Caelius splayed upon the dock and yelled, "There he is, the one who murdered the Alexandrians. Grab him." Stunned, Caelius sat up, having no choice but to submit to the sailors, who took him into custody.

Suddenly, like a deus ex machina, Clodius appeared.

"Now watch," said the king. "Clodius shall say that Caelius is a gentleman and a nobleman and demand that he be released to his custody. And Clodius, being Tribune of the People, shall be obeyed."

The sailors let go of Caelius, who fell into Clodius's arms, leaning against him, weeping.

"And to think, Father, the Romans always accuse the Greeks of being devious," Kleopatra said.

Days later, to the delight of the king, the philosopher Dio mysteriously died of poison. But Auletes' pleasure, like most of the joy in his life, was short-lived. The very next morning, Pompey came to the king with a very solemn face. "You are always welcome in my home, my good friend," said Pompey. "But for your own safety and the safety of your daughter, I must insist you leave."

"But what of my cause? I have not even had an opportunity to speak before the senate, and as far as I know, no one has solicited their support on my behalf," he said pointedly. "I have no country. I have nowhere to go," he wailed.

"I shall take up your cause when the time is right," replied

Pompey. "The senate is rather distressed with you, my friend. A date was set to hear the grievances of the Alexandrians, but when the time came, not one man showed up. It was then discovered that twenty among them had been brutally murdered, and that they had fled Italy. No one has spoken of charging you with this crime, but Rome is thick with the notion that you are responsible. It is being regarded as an act of tyranny."

Kleopatra said nothing, but thought of the tyranny of Julius Caesar, of Clodius, of Pompey himself. What hypocrites were these Romans, doing anything they liked and then hiding behind Republican ideals when it was politically convenient.

"The timing is not good for you," Pompey continued. "The senate is nostalgic for a more democratic time. The ways of a monarch are feared here. I'm afraid the senate is not in the mood to favor you. We must wait for a more auspicious time."

"My usurping daughter sits upon the throne. I have no country! Where am I to go? Am I forever banished from my kingdom?"

And I, too? wondered Kleopatra. Perhaps she would not grow up to be a queen as predicted, but would live with her father herding goats on some uninhabited patch of land in an inhospitable sea.

"Your Majesty," interjected Archimedes. "Perhaps there is a safer and more neutral place where you might wait for the tide to turn in your favor. Leave Hammonius here to attend to your business and remove yourself to calmer waters."

"Your young Kinsman is right," said Pompey. "The Egyptian question is always a topic of debate in the senate. But now is not the time to force the issue one way or another. Remember the fate of your brother, Ptolemy of Cyprus."

With that ominous reminder, Pompey excused himself on the pretense that his wife waited for his presence in the garden, where they were to take a tour of their spring flowers. "May the gods be with you, my friend," he said. He kissed the hand of the princess. Kleopatra knew they would not see Pompey again, that he would avoid them until they were packed and gone. She imagined him sneaking a look to make certain that they rode away from his villa and were gone for good.

As soon as Pompey quitted the room, the king let out a long, slow, frustrated growl. "These Romans have taken everything from me and given me nothing in return but a debtor's certificate. I may as well be a dead man. I am nothing without their assurances. I will not go until I have satisfaction!" insisted the king.

Kleopatra thought her father sounded like an obstinate child who demanded a thing that would be harmful to him, but a thing he wanted anyway.

"Your Majesty, there is a rumor about that your host is organizing a group of thugs to do street battle with Clodius," whispered Hammonius. "There is a man, Titus Annius Milo, an undercover associate of Pompey, who has just purchased a team of well-trained gladiators. It is said that he will use these men against Clodius's mob. The city streets are already rife with violence. Get out while you may."

"We must go somewhere where we will be safe, Father," said the princess. "Pompey was either threatening us or warning us. I do not know which. But I would very much like to leave Roman soil."

"My dear child, the entire world rests upon Roman soil," said the king dryly. "We shall go wherever you like. I leave it to you and your Kinsmen. I am going to withdraw myself now and enjoy the warm and cold plunges of the Roman bath while I still may."

The king swiftly departed, leaving the princess and her advisers to watch his bulk sway from their presence, his great ass waddling like a goose.

"What shall we do?" Kleopatra turned to Archimedes. She hoped her cousin would offer a solution.

"You are one day to be queen, my cousin. Perhaps the decision should be yours."

Archimedes' eyes twinkled at Kleopatra. She thought he might be teasing her again, treating her like a child. She would not offer a serious idea if he was going to strike it down with laughter. She said nothing, waiting for him to reveal that he had been joking.

He looked at her impatiently. "Now come, let us put our rather brilliant heads together."

FIFTEEN

The air is alive with the breath of the gods. Can you not feel it on the inhale?" The king took in a great swallow of air, puffing out his chest. He exhaled like a horse, blowing his lips and neighing.

After punctilious deliberation, Kleopatra had chosen the Lydian city of Ephesus as the location to wait for their future to unfold. She had remembered from her history lessons that Herodotus had praised the Ionian founders for settling in places that had the most beautiful climate and scenery in all the world. She knew that they would be welcome there. The city had burned to the ground on the night of Alexander's birth and had been rebuilt by the great Ptolemaic queen Arsinoe II and her first husband, Lysimachus. Kleopatra had heard that the city rivaled Alexandria in temples, museums, libraries, and brothels, and was alive with foreign and Greek peoples, merchants, holy men, seers, prostitutes, and scholars. Not to mention, as Hammonius pointed out, that the ancient temple of Artemis, the city's most famous attraction, was also a world bank in which the Ptolemies had stashed a goodly sum of their gold.

Auletes was so pleased with Kleopatra's decision that he told her with a wink that she would henceforth rule the kingdom. "What a pleasure to ride through the streets without fearing for your very life. If I never see Rome again I shall remain a happy man."

Auletes had not again mentioned the incident at Puteoli. It was as if the memory of the slayings had vanished along with the lives of the dead. "My dears, we shall not be lazy here," he said, patting the white slender hand of Hekate. "We shall spend our days attending the lectures at the academy. Why, we are in the birthplace of Herakleitos. The home of Artemis. Ah, back to civilization."

"Rome!" sighed Hekate. "What a terrible place. There is not even a theater. Not one. A disgrace."

"Pompey has plans to build a theater," said the princess. "He told me so himself."

"Pompey has many plans," said Auletes. "But Pompey does very little. Thank the gods for Clodius. No wonder Pompey despises him so. And no wonder Clodius hates him."

"Men of action inevitably look with disdain upon the lame," Kleopatra said.

Overwhelmed with affection for the princess, the king leaned over and kissed her on the cheek. She could not recall when he had done such a thing, when he had been so joyful, and she felt a twinge of conscience. The king had no idea what conspiracies were at that moment forming in the mind of his blossoming adolescent daughter.

She was taking a chance with her father's goodwill but she believed it worth the risk. Charmion was in on it, in on one of her schemes for the first time. Charmion had been through the rites years before and did not approve of one so young participating. But Kleopatra reasoned that it was better for her to enter into the Mysteries now, before her time came, when the coupling would cause no child to be born. It would not do for a future queen to have a child sired by a masked Bacchant undoubtedly not of royal blood. The family dynasty did not need more bastards, and unlike when the men sired them, women doing such a thing was met with inevitable disgrace.

"But you are thirteen," argued Charmion. "You must wait until you are older."

"I do not wish to risk impregnation."

"There is never any cause to fear impregnation if one is careful. I will give you a small device to insert to protect you from such a thing. You know about these things, Kleopatra. Why do you use such faulty reasoning with me?"

"I am myself deified, and the daughter of the living god on earth. I do not believe you should stop me." A different approach. She spoke with complete assurance but held her breath. Charmion rarely fell for intimidation tactics. Yet she sensed the woman's vacillation. Charmion welcomed anything that would closer align the princess with the gods, but she feared that she was too young to participate in the frenzied ritual and the random coupling that followed.

"Then why are we not asking the permission of the king?" Charmion asked.

"The king fears for my safety, that is all. He would heartily approve of the journey to religious enlightenment. Besides, no one may be initiated after the age of twenty."

"That is seven years away." Charmion's eyes narrowed. "I know why you are doing this thing."

"I am doing this thing because I cannot do it in Alexandria. There I am a princess and I represent the goddess Isis and such a ceremony would be fraught with meaning. Here in Ephesus, I may remain anonymous and demonstrate my devotion to the god."

Kleopatra finished her speech, thoroughly pleased with the reasoning and delivery. The truth, however, was closer to what Charmion guessed: The women of Ephesus were enthusiastic devotees of Dionysus, and the only time they captured Kleopatra's imagination was when they spoke in furtive tones of the mad Bacchanalian rites. Normally, they were very dull. When she was made to, she kept company with the Greek women in the home in which they stayed while they quietly attended to their chores. Spinning. Spinning. Spinning. Supervising the kitchens. Spinning again. Adorning themselves. Taking exercise. The isolated lives of these Greek females, away from men, from the city, from the pulse of the Greek marketplace, bored her to distraction. But when the talk turned to the god and to the Mysteries, their voices quickened, neck muscles quivering, hands fluttering like leaves in the crosswinds. With eyes wide, the women would look over their shoulders to see if husbands—lords, masters, and interlopers—lurked about, listening to the secret ways to worship the god. For it seemed that once men were older, once they were given the key to enter the wider world, they let go of their devotion to the god Dionysus, and it was left to the women to serve him. King Ptolemy XII Auletes was an exception. But he was not simply the god's keenest advocate; he was the god. And, being more histrionic than most members of his sex and a musician, too, he was more inclined than most to serve Dionysus.

Now his daughter discovered the wellspring of his faith. She observed the excitement in the women, and she wished to know the cause of the stimulation. And she wished to participate in the anonymous coupling that followed. She was weary of her own ignorance of that mystery. She was young, but was she not precocious in all other aspects of life? What is so special about the Mysteries? she asked one of the women as she watched her busy fingers at the loom. The woman stopped what she was doing. "Child," she mouthed through rounded lips, "it is the essence of life."

When the time came, Kleopatra loosened her hair and ran barefoot through the night and into the cavern with the others. The cave was dark and lit with torches, making shadow figures above her. The damp coastal air, acrid inside the holy place, hung about her like a wet second skin. A goat with horns was tied to the altar, jumpy with the presence of the others and the premonition of its destiny. Kleopatra stared into its nervous yellow eyes. She had already drunk too much wine from the bowl that was passed around the circle of initiates, and she felt light in her body but heavy in her head. She was frightened. This was no place of worship such as her father had built in honor of the god, no elaborate, painted room in a palace. This place was primeval and hidden from sight, the kind of place where an uncivilized thing might transpire and no one would stop it.

A Maenad crone with tufts of silvery hair placed a tortuously woven crown of ivy on Kleopatra's head, making her even more aware of her tingling scalp. She drank a bowl of foul-smelling liquid, a mushroom broth meant to give her better communion with the god. It was like drinking mud; that, or some fluid of the dead, something not meant for human consumption. The vile substance mingled with the wine in her stomach. She belched up a putrid combination of the two.

A cramp snaked its way through her intestines and made her double over. She felt her ears close to sound, as if a gate inside her head had dropped, shutting out the world and locking her inside her body. She wondered if the god punished his followers—inquisitive mortals wishing intimacy with him, wishing to know the secrets that lurked below earth's surface, the mysteries that made flowers bloom and vines grow.

Time passed, or did not, and Kleopatra became aware again of her surroundings, of the voices of the Bacchants invoking the name of the god in a hollow chorus that sounded as if it came from a deep tunnel. The sound became song and then became pure sound again, neither word nor name, but a hum that gained power as it merged with the echo of the cave and the bleating of the goat. Kleopatra joined the chorus, chanting the name of the god time and again, letting her sounds converge with the whir around her, becoming one with the others, an isolated princess no more, but now reduced to a dizzying vibration.

"His name is the Word." The priestess made the initiates repeat the phrase over and over. Kleopatra moved as they moved, around and around the fire, around the bleating goat until the hum became motion. But she could feel nothing. She heard the high pitch of the animal's cry and then saw the blood spill. Someone pushed her from behind. She fell forward, and the incarnadine liquid of the animal warmed her toes. Hands patted red prints over her dress, over her face. She yelled and continued to yell, spreading the warm liquid over her body.

Then she was running. No longer in the shelter of the cave but in the dark blanket of night. Running with the women, their hair loose and trailing behind their fleeting bodies like trains of a gown, their only cosmetic the goat's blood. Running barefoot, naked skin electrified by the shock of wet grass. Slowing as the grass turned to sand, slowing, slipping. Suddenly the cold water of the sea tickled her ankles, her knees, her neck, until she was immersed, fighting against the water to follow the torches the women held high above the waves. And laughter. So much laughter. Not echoing now as in the cave, but loose and dissipating as the sound of their fervor hit the diffuse ocean breezes.

Feet off the bottom of the sea, stomach falling, breath going out of her body, she was lifted onto a strong, wet shoulder. She felt as though she were breaking in two at the waist and kicked her legs up, almost falling headfirst back into the ocean. The abductor leaned back, the two of them tumbling into a wave. She, lost, scrambled to evade him, but he caught her from behind and carried her like a baby out of the water. She did not know whether to struggle. She wanted to push away from him, but if she did, she would remain untouched by the god and untouched by man. She gave in to the strong arms and closed her eyes, licking the salty water that trailed from a lock of her hair pasted to her face.

Then she was down, a spiky patch of grass a bed beneath her back. She opened her eyes but it was dark. They had moved away from the shoreline to a desolate place behind the temple of Artemis. He was but a shadow figure, a spirit kneeling over her. He stood up tall to look at her. The moonlight illuminated his painted horrific mask, gigantic purple lips turned down, the image of the god's face in displeasure. His body was lean and muscled but hairless. An athlete, she thought. Had she once seen him in the games? Did he know her identity? She closed her eyes again and heard the rip of linen as he tore her robe apart.

"You are just a child," he said. His voice was young, not thick and low like the older men, like her father or the Kinsmen. Or Archimedes. He was not much older than herself. But he had passed that crucial time and was a man, for his penis stood straight out in front of him.

He entered her like some kind of hot swift weapon, wounding her, touching a place deep inside where she was sure no one belonged. She locked eyes with him. That was the only way she got through the pain. She was feeling now, but wishing that the numbness would overtake her again. She kept looking into his eyes, hypnotizing them both as he writhed on top of her, twisting and thrusting. Nor did he stop looking at her; neither knew any better than to play their roles without guile. He hurt her again with the intrusion of his flesh, so she screamed the name of the god. He looked frightened, pained, but he too invoked the god's name until she realized that she was not only chanting with him but riding his rhythm. She ceased all resistance and locked her legs around his bare buttocks. There was nothing now but this, nothing in the world but the motion and the pain and the rhythm. Swallowing the word as she gasped for new breath, taking in the smell of the wet ivy crown, of the salty, sweaty boy on top of her, of the strange musky odor that came from herself.

But then—was it moments or hours into the act?—he choked on his breath and began to move faster and deeper into her. She kept with his rhythm, obeying a driving agitation from within. Suddenly, he uttered a loud snort and then a sigh. His eyes rolled into his head as if he were about to die. He arched over her, sighed again, and collapsed upon her. She screamed the name of the god, moving now with ferocity, for all his weight was upon her. She kicked and screamed against him, calling the god, calling the name of her slave, calling Mohama, calling for Charmion. Nothing. She wondered if he had died right there on top of her in the service of the god.

And then she passed out.

The next morning, close to dawn, Kleopatra awoke in the arms of Charmion's slave, a tall, silent Numidian man who spoke only to Charmion in his halting Greek. Filthy and bleeding, her head spun as it fell back over his crooked arm. She tensed her neck muscles to still the whirlpool behind her eyes, but the insides of her head continued to move on their own accord.

The tide had gone out and the beach was covered with the slime of the sea. The initiates lay on the shore, their naked bodies wrapped in seaweed, as if a mermaid had come in the night and dressed them. Her partner had disappeared. She would never know who he was.

Wordlessly, Charmion took off her clothes and bathed her gently, sponging away the sand, the caked and crusty debris of the body's ecstasies. She led the princess to her bed, pulled the covers over her and said, "The princess is a woman now."

They never spoke of it again.

From: Hammonius in the city of Rome
To: Ptolemy XII Auletes

I hope this finds you well and happy in Ephesus, and thank the gods you are not in Rome. The last months have seen violence beyond our measure. Pompey got tired of being the victim of Clodius's mob tactics and has formed a mob of his own under Milo. This week, they clashed in the Forum, and Cicero's brother Quintus almost perished in the fray. He hid under the bodies of two dead slaves until the atmosphere calmed. Cleaning crews are still mopping up the blood.

Your Majesty, it is the strangest thing. After one year of lethargy, suddenly Rome's most powerful men see profit in reinstating you and vie for the honor. Pompey (imagine a stance from him!) has petitioned the senate to restore you himself. I suppose that having Milo's gladiators at his disposal has made him once again brave. They say he is tired of things in Rome and longs for another eastern campaign. It is also speculated that a victory in Egypt would provide a nice counterbalance to Caesar's impressive conquest of Gaul and Briton.

Meanwhile, Caesar has sent letters to the senate saying that he will gladly take the burden of Egypt from their shoulders. Everyone knows that he acts due to pressure from Rabirius. The two of them see nothing but money. Not wishing to be left out, Crassus has also petitioned to go to Egypt with an army to restore you. Crassus is very jealous of the military glories of Caesar and Pompey. Though he is extremely wealthy and getting on in years, he is determined to compete with his fellow Coalition members for military greatness. He has so much money that it is likely that he will get his wish.

Finally, my king, one of the gods interceded on our behalf. Yesterday morning, the statue of Jupiter was struck by lightning, which the Roman diviners took as a great portent. As you know, they report all sightings of lightning to the governing bodies, who act or decline to act that day according to the omens. The striking of the statue caused great concern. The Board of Fifteen, led by Cato—who is back from Cyprus—marched solemnly to the oracle, where the Sibylline Books were consulted. In them was found the most

unusual advice: *Restore the king of Egypt, but do not use a multitude of force.*
From the oracle they marched in procession to the Forum, where Cato read
the words aloud. By the end of the day, it had been translated into Latin and
posted throughout the city. Still, no one had a satisfactory interpretation.

Cicero—back from exile, his new house full of blond-haired slaves sent as
a gift from Julius Caesar—is the one who solved the Sibyl's conundrum.
Cicero has advised that the military man Lentulus, an honest man, should
escort you back to Alexandria, but must leave you outside the city and march
in with his troops. Then, when he is certain the city is secure, he should bring
you home. Force would be used to take the city, but reinstatement would occur
afterward in a peaceful manner. The senate is pleased with the plan, so that
when you return home, you will have the orator to thank.

You will soon hear from Lentulus, and you must quickly acquiesce to
whatever he proposes regardless of price. (Count yourself lucky—Caesar,
Pompey, or Crassus would have demanded more for their services.) You have
often said the gods are with Rome. It appears that they are also now with you.

Please give my love to the princess. Tell her to prepare for the voyage home.

⌣⟶🦁𝄃𝄃▮⌐◎◇⌐

Kleopatra was lightheaded. She had fasted the night before to
purify herself. This would be the first time she paid for a sacrifice
out of her private purse, and the first time she would make the kill.
She wanted to be certain that the goddess Artemis knew her precise
intentions and did not confuse her prayers and offerings with those
of the king.

The temple was empty except for the princess and the young priestess. The priestess washed the lamb with holy water while the princess
remained in silent meditation, trying to mask her fury with words of
supplication. After weeks of anxiety waiting for word from Lentulus,
her father had been contacted instead by Gabinius, the Roman governor of Syria, who had demanded the usurious sum of ten thousand
talents for marching his troops from Syria to Alexandria and toppling
the government of Berenike. Auletes, frantic to return home, agreed.
Now the king complained daily of an ulcerous stomach, for he did not
know how he was to make peace with Julius Caesar over the earlier
debt, much less raise the money for Gabinius.

Kleopatra knelt before the immense statue of the goddess and prayed with a new fierceness. *Lady Artemis, goddess of young women, of maidens, of the creatures of the forest, accept this small sacrifice. I beseech you to expand the riches of Egypt. If you so bless my kingdom, I promise that when my time comes, I will not sit on the throne like my ancestors, draining the country to keep myself in power. I will not walk the floors at night like my father, wondering how to fulfill the extortionists' ransom on our country. I will succeed where they have failed.*

Why did the gods allow one who had served them so well as Auletes suffer this endless humiliation? Kleopatra and her father had waited and waited for Lentulus, Auletes becoming more and more dejected by the day. What had happened to this Lentulus, this honest man, she asked the goddess, whose name had inspired so much hope? Why was he replaced by the greedy pig Gabinius?

Divine Lady, do the gods not exceed the Romans in power and strength?

Hear my vow. Lady, I will never retreat from this position: I will happily face death rather than live a life devoid of dignity. This I swear before She who hears and knows all. Death before humiliation. Death before supplication before the might of Rome.

She fell prostrate in front of the statue, hugging the hard tile floor with her body, murmuring the promises over and over. Tears streamed onto the goddess's feet until Kleopatra's face rested in a cold wet puddle between Artemis's heels. Exhausted, she raised herself upright.

"Are you ready, Your Highness?" asked the priestess. Wearing the short hunting tunic of the goddess, she did not seem much older than Kleopatra. She was an unmarried Greek woman, an anomaly in a country where women had no other function than to wed. Unlike the Romans, who demanded chastity from their priestesses, the Greeks only demanded chastity from the priestesses of the chaste goddesses.

Kleopatra caressed the white wool of the animal and looked into his unsuspecting, watery eyes. How could anything be so soft? She had heard from the Arab people that the softest fabric on earth was from the chin hairs of a particular kind of mountain goat raised for the sole purpose of donating its wool to blankets made for their king. She would have to procure such a thing herself someday, for she loved such luxury.

She stopped touching the animal. She was queasy in the stomach, either from lack of food or from the pressure of the vows she had just made or from anticipation of what she must do to the small lamb.

"Your Highness looks a little sick," said the priestess.

The color of humiliation invaded her cheeks, giving her away. She was not able to hide her emotions from the woman. This would not do. No, it would simply not do to have commoners, even if they were priestesses of the goddess, able to read her thoughts. She must be even more mysterious than the mystics. She looked away from the priestess and, without pause, pulled back the head of the lamb. Ignoring the way his soft wool felt between her fingers and the last bleating gasp of protestation, she slid the knife across his throat. The kill was not easy. She had to use more strength than she had anticipated as she ripped across the supple neck of the small creature, closing her ears against his cry and her eyes against his stunned expression. The blood came spewing from the neck vein with such force that the priestess had to push the bowl forward to catch it. Kleopatra watched the blood spill into the bowl like a long red tongue. She dropped the animal and looked straight ahead, not wanting to meet its open lifeless eyes.

Damnation to Gabinius. Damnation to Pompey. To Rabirius. To Cicero. To Julius Caesar. To all those Masters of the World who had caused her father and her people so much pain. Those barbarians who made the descendants of Alexander lie down and weep. *Goddess, holy virgin who rules over vast lands, watch over me. I am of Alexander, of the highest and most noble Greek blood. We are your subjects, your chosen, your people. Abandon these Romans who steal everywhere from us, our money, our poems, our art, and our very deities. Do they not call you Diana? Who is Diana but a Roman fantasy, a Roman bastardization of something pure and Greek? Lady, I ask you to consort with your fellow deities and protect us, the original and true people who serve you.*

The priestess raised her head from her posture of supplication and looked into the eyes of the princess. "Your Highness, the goddess has received your prayers and your sacrifice. Whatever you ask is done."

Part III

THE TWO LANDS
OF EGYPT

SIXTEEN

Berenike IV Ptolemy, you are accused of murdering your step-mother, the usurper Kleopatra VI Tryphaena, and of illegally assuming the monarchy. Further, you are accused of the murder of the philosopher Demetrius and of the eunuch Meleager. How do you plead? Guilty or innocent?"

"Meleager committed suicide," Berenike corrected, her black robes of mourning stark against the chilly marble podium for the accused. She had cut off her chestnut brown tresses as a funereal offering to her husband, an enemy of the state whose body had yet to be buried. Shorn of her hair, stripped of her weapons and her adornments, she seemed, to Kleopatra, more powerful. As if peeling her down to her essence revealed the source of her strength.

"That is not a plea," the magistrate shot back at her.

Kleopatra sat next to Archimedes, craning her neck around his shoulder to see her father's face. The king witnessed the trial from his usual box seat surrounded by those whom the general Gabinius had told him were his supporters—including the Roman money-lender Rabirius, who had insisted on coming to Alexandria to be sure of collecting his debt. Draped in commodious Greek robes, Rabirius's rouged and flabby cheeks were framed by unreasonably long curls, still imprinted with the crease of his crimping iron. He sat next to the chiseled military man Gabinius, the pair looking curiously like a long-married couple who had aged in opposite ways; one given to cosmetics and bloat, and the other, gaunt, his skin as brown and spotted as an antique scroll.

Berenike cocked her head like an amused coquette. "Does it matter how I plead? This trial is a mockery staged for the amusement of my father. I will not plead. I choose not to plead at all before the bastard king."

"I will give you another chance to enter a plea and to save yourself. Berenike IV Ptolemy, how do you plead before this court?"

Berenike ignored the magistrate and addressed her father. "What a fool you are, Father. I know about the money you paid the Roman to arrange my demise. Do you think you were the first Ptolemy he approached to fill his pockets with our gold?" She waved at Gabinius as if acknowledging a long-lost acquaintance.

She continued, "Let us dispense with this travesty. Father, hear this: Gabinius and I have been in close communication since before he left Rome for his governorship in Syria. The Roman wished me to marry a co-regent from Syria so that he could extort money from us regularly. And I did, Seleucus, a worthless royal bastard much like yourself. But he was coarse and ignorant and not fit for my bed so that I had to dispense with him. But still, Gabinius was willing to do business with me, as long as I was willing to pay. You do know how that system works, do you not, Father?"

A low mumble slithered through the crowd, but was silenced by the booming voice of Gabinius. "Will no one quiet this girl and her lies? Your Majesty," he began. "Surely you will not allow the words of a traitor to vulgarize these proceedings."

"The defendant may continue," said the magistrate. "Unless the king wishes to object."

"No, no," said Auletes. "I am quite interested in this testimony. Do go on."

Gabinius sat down, exasperated, grumbling loudly to his neighbors, who were more interested in hearing Berenike's version of the events than his low-pitched indignation.

Berenike, her outstretched arms making a shadowy curtain, told of how she decided to choose her own husband, Archelaus of

Pontus, handsome, fierce, and the illegitimate son of the great tyrant Mithridates. Archelaus came to her with a dowry of his own, his militia. Still, Gabinius was happy to ally with them, though Pompey, when hearing that Berenike had married the bastard son of his former enemy, expressed his displeasure. "Did you wonder, Father, why your host in Rome remained inactive in the face of your pleas? Did you never think that he was waiting to see which of us could supply him with the most blood money?"

Auletes did not show emotion as Berenike ran through her accusations, but sat placidly, his hands folded in his lap, and his face attentive but inscrutable. Kleopatra wondered if he was judging the truthfulness of her words, or if he was by now numb to tales of betrayal and intrigue.

Berenike, voice full of knowledge, taunting her father, explained how her relations with Gabinius finally soured: The Roman heard that as much as ten thousand talents might be extracted from the desperate Egyptian king for his reinstatement, money that, if not readily accessible from the treasury, might easily be furnished by Rabirius. "When he realized that Archelaus and I did not have access to *that* kind of capital, that he could not perform the slow bleed of the leech on us, the friendship, shall we call it, came to an abrupt end. Then he cut off my negotiations with the Roman senate by trumping up charges that I was conspiring with pirates in the Mediterranean to form a fleet that would attack Rome."

"A good story," she said to Gabinius. "I congratulate you on your imagination."

Turning to her father, she continued, her voice colder now and full of confidence, as if she were not the one on trial but the prosecutor in a guaranteed victory. "I assure you, Father, if I had had better access to our treasury, you and I would be in different seats today. As it is, you have the money. Or, rather, you have the *money-lenders*." Berenike smiled disdainfully at Rabirius, who rebuffed her gaze by raising his bulbous eyes to the ceiling. "That is why Gabinius ignored the senate's decree giving Lentulus the commission. He began the westward march across desert and marsh only because you agreed to produce ten thousand talents. And now, I leave it to you to do just that."

"This is an outrage! Silence the girl," yelled Gabinius, jumping out of his seat, words and spit flying from his mouth like sleet. "She is a treasonous bitch who thinks she can save herself by indicting me. Your Majesty, let us leave this room. Let us not suffer the insults of a traitor."

"The blood of my husband is on your hands, Roman," Berenike fired back. "May the gods see that you have the same unhappy Fate as Archelaus."

No authority rose to stop the altercation. Kleopatra could see that the magistrate, his smile shiny like a crescent dagger, was enjoying the exchange.

"Enough of this," the king said finally. He stood, facing Berenike, pointing an accusing finger at her. "Your very soul is stained with your husband's blood. His and that of many others. Loyalty has never figured into your character. You attached yourself to your stepmother, a woman you loved all your life, and when she became inconvenient to you, you did away with her. I will never forgive Thea, and I will never forgive you. I cannot hear you out, Daughter. You speak the words of an enemy."

"Ah, Father, as if you could recognize a friend," Berenike said quietly. She looked at Kleopatra, her eyes deadly cold. "Behold, Sister, a premonition of your Fate. You were always an ambitious child. I am warming the seat of the condemned for you."

Kleopatra said nothing, but averted her eyes from her sister. "Do not listen to her," whispered Archimedes. "The condemned never wish to suffer alone."

"Are we not ready to pronounce the verdict?" sighed the king.

Berenike threw back her head and began to cackle like a crone, her laugh bouncing off the marble floor and echoing through the room. Kleopatra made two shells out of her hands to protect her ears from the unholy noise, but she only muffled the sound. She tucked herself under Archimedes' shoulder and he held her close.

"The court finds Berenike IV Ptolemy guilty of the murder of Kleopatra VI Tryphaena, of the philosopher Demetrius, and of the eunuch and Prime Minister Meleager. The court finds Berenike IV Ptolemy guilty of illegally seizing the throne. Therefore the court finds the accused guilty of three counts of murder, and of treason against the crown, all of which are capital crimes."

Berenike continued to laugh through the reading of the verdict. When the magistrate finished, she wiped her watery eyes and stared at her father, a look of triumph on her face. Was this courage or madness? wondered Kleopatra. What kind of person celebrates receiving the grim gift of death for their crimes?

"Does Your Highness wish to have a final word?" asked the magistrate of the king.

Kleopatra wondered if her father might exonerate her sister—not dismiss her crimes, but lessen the sentence to exile. Berenike was a full-blooded daughter, the firstborn of the king and his beloved, dead Tryphaena. If Tryphaena had lived, none of this would have happened. Tryphaena, gentle, lamblike, caring only for music and thought. How had she begotten Thea, whose fault this was entirely? Thea had infected Berenike, Kleopatra thought, infused her dirty ambitions into the child Berenike's susceptible mind. Perhaps Kleopatra needed to be grateful to Berenike. Perhaps if she had been the firstborn, Thea would have cast her poisonous intentions onto her, and she would be sitting in Berenike's place. She had never thought of that, and she wondered now if that might be true. Perhaps the gods were good to Kleopatra as Auletes always swore they were to him. Thinking of her mother, Kleopatra was certain that the king, too, would remember the delicate nature, the lovely face of his long-dead first wife and palliate the punishment doled out hastily to their daughter.

Auletes took a deep wheezy breath and blew the air out through his lips. "I am still weary from my voyages abroad," he replied. To Berenike, who still looked at him defiantly, he said, "I shall see you dead in the morning." He rose, gathering his white linen robes about him like a cloud, and floated from the chambers.

Not wishing to spend another moment in the same room with the condemned, Kleopatra took Archimedes' hand and quickly followed her father, who waited for her to catch up to his side. She did not look back at Berenike. She did not know if she would ever see her sister alive again, but she did not want to meet that mad gaze, the gaze that implied that she, Kleopatra, presently the king's favored child, was also a candidate for the king's proscription.

"Father, do you believe the things Berenike said about Gabinius?" she asked, searching her father's face for remorse over condemning his own flesh and blood. But she merely saw the face of a tired man. The sacks under the king's eyes hung low, his mouth turned downward. "Do you think Gabinius was in an alliance with her at one time?"

"It is not inconceivable, my child. Who among the Romans we have met is a loyal man? Anyway, it hardly matters," said the king. "Tomorrow we shall put the past behind us for good."

Berenike was executed before their eyes. Kleopatra was startled to learn that she was to witness the death of her sister. She thought the king would spare his children the spectacle, but Auletes announced the news stone-faced, his features so rigid that Kleopatra knew he was not to be challenged. She had never watched a person be executed, much less her own flesh and blood. That evening, she listened to Auletes consider the traditional Greek means of putting to death—hemlock, casting the criminal off a cliff or into a pit, even the brutal cudgeling that was customary in the execution of slaves. After much discussion, he decided that the first was too merciful, the second, unseemly for a royal, and the third would leave him with a reputation for cruelty. After all, he wanted to be as fair to the condemned as possible. So that the next morning as the sun crept its way into the courtyard of the magisterial building, the remaining children—Kleopatra, Arsinoe, and the little boys, five and three— stood silent in dawn's roseate glow, waiting for the executioner's sword to decapitate their sister. "A lesson," said Auletes to the lot of them, including Kleopatra, who was not allowed to sit with the Kinsmen, but had to forsake the comfort of Archimedes' strong arms and stand next to Charmion. "A lesson and a warning."

Defiant to the end, Berenike, pink-skinned and lustrous in the morning light, stared directly at her father as if she awaited the arrival of a good meal or a swift new pony rather than the sword upon her neck. In her long black robes, she looked, to Kleopatra, like the moon goddess; as if she might rise from the platform of the condemned and drive her white chariot across the sky, wiping out the sun's light with her cold blanket of darkness.

When the executioner raised the sleek, gleaming instrument of death, Kleopatra tensed her feet, legs, and stomach muscles so that she would not lose her balance at the sight. She believed that she must see this thing through, must watch every gruesome detail of it and survive it, remaining distant, glacial to its horror. Kleopatra told herself over and over that she had never cared for Berenike—had despised her in youth for her alliance with Thea, detested her even more for her betrayal of Auletes. That Berenike deserved to die in this horrible way, that the king must punish, must send the message, must smite his enemies or risk another rebellion. She even told herself that her father was killing Berenike for her sake, so that Berenike would not harm her in the future. That attending her sister's execution was, strictly speaking, an act of duty. That she must not flinch; that she was present in an official capacity.

That this could never happen to her.

Kleopatra could not suppress the sickness in her stomach, the rise of bile into her throat, when she saw Berenike's eyes pop wide upon the impact, as if they were trying to free themselves from either the pain, or from death itself. She willed the putridness back into the pit of her belly and blurred her eyes so that all she saw was an awful gush of red. The little princes, chubby and bleary-eyed, turned into the skirts of their governess when Berenike's head toppled forward, but Kleopatra noticed that Arsinoe, a pretty but distracted girl of ten, did not recoil. Arsinoe had spent her childhood at the feet of Berenike, listening to her stories, learning her ways. How did the girl numb herself for this event? Kleopatra could almost detect a tacit smile. The executioner quickly covered Berenike with a black cloth, and Kleopatra lowered her eyes to the ground, remembering that last grimace on Berenike's face. Nineteen years old and already having led a rebellion, Berenike IV Ptolemy died smirking and alone, one husband murdered by her own hand, the other killed in battle, her faithful Bactrian attendants having committed double suicide in prison.

Auletes hugged Kleopatra, and then embraced his other children one by one, as if to demonstrate that he held no malice toward them. Kleopatra watched as he took the small boys into the folds of his robes, remembering that as they sailed back to Alexandria, he had said, "We must not despise the little ones. They've committed no crime but to be born to a traitor." She had nodded in agreement, looking out to sea, but recalled Arsinoe, as a child of eight, gleefully following Berenike around like a pet. She thought: Even after this, he is naive about the potential treachery of his remaining children.

The execution, a private affair for family and officials only, was followed by a parade for the king down the Street of the Soma so that his subjects might welcome him back to his kingdom. Gabinius's army led the procession, glimmering in the slats of bronze armor that bound their chests, their tall helmets beacons in the sun, their only vulnerability bare legs, but those as solid as any stone column. Berenike had faced this legion, Kleopatra thought, had stood at the fort at Pelusium on the eastern border of Egypt and watched this glistening force of destruction march in her direction, herself and her bridegroom their primary targets. Perhaps she *was* mad. Most certainly she was mad. Yet, with nothing but the force of her madness, or some internal sense of power, of entitlement, she had negotiated with the Romans she so hated, and when that negotiation failed, she had raised an Egyptian army and faced her enemy. Kleopatra heard it said that when the Roman legion marched into Pelusium, they were so impressed with the size of the opposing army that they threatened to turn around and go back to Syria. Perhaps Gabinius bolstered their courage by handing out coins at the fortress gates. Berenike was a traitor to her own father, that much was incontestable. But she had lived and died by her own aberrant convictions.

The king—smiling and remorseless—rode in an open carriage in the midst of the army as if he commanded it. Gabinius and Rabirius paraded with the king, the latter hanging on to the king's robes, as if waiting to catch any coins that might magically fly from his purse.

Despite the grim event that had begun the day, the mood was festive. It seemed that all of Alexandria had turned out for the event.

Egyptian vendors sold water, wine, and beer to the spectators, while their children hawked small trinkets—cheap bangle bracelets, phony signet rings, toy crocodiles on wheels. Kleopatra, riding Persephone behind her father's carriage, noticed that many people were drunk for the occasion, carrying big smelly leather flasks of wine that spilled the liquid down the sides of their mouths as they drank.

Kleopatra could not believe that the population had changed its mind about her father. Perhaps two years of chaos had reconciled them to the king and his policies. Or perhaps her father had arranged for supporters to appear. Both were likely. And perhaps the citizens had to get intoxicated to go along with the charade. She wondered if she would ever be reduced to paying for her subjects' approval. It appeared to be a family tradition.

Exhausted after the parade, Kleopatra tried to excuse herself to go to her chambers, but her father did not wish to be alone.

"We are very busy today. One must be tireless, young lady," said the king, who had many times excused himself from his duties on the excuse of fatigue. Today he seemed younger, resilient, as if energized by the death of Berenike. Kleopatra wondered how he had so easily erased from his mind the image of his firstborn dying a bloody death by his own command. Perhaps he was merely cloaking his grief behind this facade of vivaciousness.

"Your Majesty," said Archimedes. "The young cavalry officer Marcus Antonius wishes an audience with you."

"Marcus Antonius. Do I know the man?"

The princess's heart quickened. "Father, do you not remember what we heard about him in Rome? He was the friend of Clodius who had an affair with his wife, Fulvia. When Clodius found out, Marcus Antonius went to Greece to study oration, but the real reason he left was because Clodius was going to kill him!"

"From what impeccable source did you hear this idle gossip?" asked the king.

"From Julia. She said that Antonius is a favorite of Julius Caesar. And that he is the most handsome man in all the world. And that he is the most famous lover of women, too. And the bravest soldier. And the most daring horseman and swordsman in the empire. I think Julia loved him, though she could not say so in her husband's house."

"That sort of loyalty would seem extreme when practiced by a Roman woman," said the king dryly.

"The princess does have several facts correct regarding Marcus Antonius," said Archimedes. "He is handsome, for a Roman. And brave. Have you not heard of his many services on your behalf?"

Archimedes looked around for interlopers. He leaned closer to the king and the princess, explaining to them that Gabinius's troops were, despite the impressive show they put on for the population of Alexandria, an undisciplined bunch with no particular loyalty to either Rome or Gabinius. They had refused to cross the desert into Egypt even on Gabinius's command, preferring to stay in Syria to loot and drink. Gabinius was paralyzed, but Antony took command. He spun fantastic stories of the untold riches and exotic sexual pleasures that awaited the soldiers in Egypt. "He is most eloquent, they say, a natural teller of tales. He convinced the troops to make the long and waterless march through the deep sands."

"Does this Antony believe these mythic stories of our country?" asked Kleopatra, wondering if Antony was just another Roman come to Egypt to fleece her father. "Does he think my father is like Darius the Persian?"

"I do not know, Cousin, though that is what many Romans think. But Antony's sheer enthusiasm and his own willingness to endure the hardships of the march shamed the lazy soldiers into crossing the waterless desert."

"Then he is remarkable, is he not?" said the king. "The gods shall be with such a man."

"There is more, Sire. When Gabinius's men saw the multitudes of enemy soldiers awaiting them at the fortress at Pelusium, they tried to turn around. But Antony roused them by leading the charge. He made them ashamed of their cowardliness, and they followed him into battle. That is why Your Majesty is at home today."

So it was this man's courage and not Gabinius's gold that motivated the men. "Is it possible that there is one Roman who is truly brave and good?" Kleopatra asked. "One we can depend upon for action?"

Archimedes paused. "He wishes to take up the matter of Archelaus's funeral with you, Sire. It seems that he was a friend of Berenike's late husband."

"What? You tell me of this man's good qualities and his services on our behalf and then you tell me that he was a friend of my most egregious enemies?" the king said, offended.

"Oh, please, Father," cried the princess. "Marcus Antonius is a powerful man. If already he has performed such services to us without knowing us, think of what use he may be to us if we befriend him?"

"Of course we shall meet with the man. But I am warning you. I will not be overruled!"

There was no sight more arousing to a girl of fourteen than Antony at twenty-seven. Kleopatra could not look directly at him, nor could she turn away. She met his eyes—brown, lambent, and as penetrable as rich soil—swallowing her as if she were a fresh seedling. They were deep-set beneath a broad, lordly brow, and full of merriment despite the solemnity of the occasion. Though she longed to gape at him, she could not manage more than a furtive glimpse in his direction. It was as if he knew it, too, and could read her embarrassing thoughts. He stared as much as she shied away, forcing her to look again at the aquiline, fine nose, the cheekbones like proud peaks, the acute cleft in his chin, the broad neck with muscles like taut rope. His red cloak hung carelessly over one massive shoulder. He wore his tunic girt low about his narrow hips; a sheathed sword hung at his side. He had removed his breast armor, so that Kleopatra could see the muscles in his chest distorting the folds of his garment. He was so majestic of body that she wondered if he had been fathered by a giant, a Titan. The girlish titillation caused by Pompey, even by Archimedes, became a shattering earthquake in the presence of Antony. She could take no more and quickly dropped her eyes to his feet, quivering at the sight of the leather straps of his sandals snaking up his sharply hewn calves.

"Your Royal Highnesses," he said, bowing low to the king and his daughter. "Welcome home." He waved his arm around the room as if it was he who had invited them there.

He is reminding us of our debt to himself, Kleopatra realized through her infatuation. The man was both beautiful and crafty. A deadly combination in a woman, thought Kleopatra. How much more dangerous in a powerful man?

"Thank you for hearing my plea on behalf of the Syrian Archelaus. I realize that he caused you some harm, but in the end, is it not better to demonstrate charity? You have won, Your Majesty. You have prevailed. Archelaus was once quite the favorite of your friend Pompey. Did you know that? Pompey rather admired him and bore him no grudge for being fathered by Mithridates. I do not suggest that Pompey condoned the marriage to your daughter and the actions against yourself. Only that death does inspire sentimentality in old friends. Pompey may not take kindly to Archelaus being humiliated in death. After all, none of us, no matter how bold, wishes to be haunted by those who have gone before us."

Antony let the king ponder the complex situation while he explained that in better times he had received the hospitality of Archelaus in his native country. "I was his friend, though here, Fate called upon me to fight against him. Let us remember the lessons of the poets. The gods do not reward those who deny proper burial to the fallen."

Antony's manner was friendly yet deferential, but Kleopatra had difficulty concentrating on what he said. His cloak draped negligently around him, and each time he wished to make a point, he cast it behind his shoulder, shrugging off its weight. His arm in motion was beautiful, strength radiating in each small gesture. *He is the living god*, she thought.

Auletes weighed the argument, twirling the hairs of his left eyebrow unconsciously as he did when he was thinking. "I suppose it would be no great concession to agree to your request," he said, to the great surprise of the princess. Could this man have her father spellbound, too?

"Particularly since you have performed such services for us and without even knowing us, or asking for a reward."

"Only a dignified repose for the body of a friend," Antony corrected.

"I hear, my boy, that you shamed your men into crossing not only the desert, but the Serbonian marsh, where no drinking water is to be had. My people call that land the breathing hole of Typhon. I am not certain I would have crossed it myself, even to recover my own kingdom!" The king winked at Antony as if the two of them were longtime friends.

"What is thirst compared to justice? I was able to convince them of the rightness of the cause. It was not so much a challenge," Antony replied. "The soldier finds his purpose in the willingness of the commander to endure suffering."

"You please me, my dear boy. Your argument is sound, your speech is persuasive, your Greek excellent, and your cause a compassionate one. Yes, you please me. I would that you were my son."

"I am flattered, Your Highness," Antony said. "But if I were your son, you would no longer like me so. I have caused displeasure to more than one father. But if you will permit, there is another favor I would ask of you."

"And what is that, my young warrior? Name it. My kingdom is yours."

"The prisoners, Majesty. The rebels held in the jail. I understand they are to be executed tomorrow."

"Correct. Who does not do away with his enemies has no tomorrow. You are a man of the world. Surely you know that," huffed the king.

"I have interrogated the prisoners myself, Your Majesty," he said, smiling, his highly arched nostrils spreading to meet the rise in his cheekbones. He was polite, solicitous even, but always appeared to know that he was going to win the argument. "Many are the victims of confusion that ensued in the wake of your exile and the death of the late queen. They're rather simple opportunists, fallen prey to the flowery words of the persuasive eunuch Meleager. More to be pitied than harmed, I think. I believe you will gain more by demonstrating clemency. Besides, your daughter executed the late queen's supporters, saving you the trouble. The last of them, the General, died in battle with Archelaus. I have here the list of the proscribed and the dead." He handed Auletes a long scroll of names, those fallen to Berenike's sword of vengeance.

"I follow the example of my spiritual father, the great Julius Caesar," he continued as Auletes read the list. "He always says,

'Antony, the fearful govern by the sword, the great by mercy.' Your Majesty has no more cause for fear." He looked not at the king, but at his daughter, who this time boldly looked back, trying to force down the red that crept up her neck and into her cheeks.

Auletes paused, wrinkling his forehead. Kleopatra did not know if her father found this young Roman's words threatening or persuasive. After a few moments, Auletes nodded his head agreeably. "I shall rest in your word. It shall be as you wish, young man."

"May the gods bless you, Sire," Antony said. "And now, I am off. I thank you for the honor of speaking before you."

"No, no," said the king. "You must not leave us. You are one of us now. I will show you the very soul of Egypt. The tales you told those greedy soldiers about the pleasures of our country are not mere fantasies for those who are my guests." He winked at Antony.

"It would give me nothing but pleasure to remain in your service, but I have been summoned by Julius Caesar, who requires my immediate appearance in Gaul. He has appointed me commander of the cavalry."

Kleopatra's hand involuntarily covered her mouth, her hopes squelched. She hoped he either did not see the gesture, or if he did, she hoped the proper interpretation eluded him—a fact she doubted. His flitting eyes seemed to touch every surface of her body and mind. She did not wish him to leave. Why didn't her father say something to make him stay, this powerful Roman they now had in their audience? This man with the wicked eyes, the sharp wit, the vast chest. This Titan who threw about the names of his elders—names that made ordinary men quake—as if they were his friends. Julius Caesar. Pompey. They *were* his friends. Father, she wanted to shout, please do not let him go, for here, finally, is the Roman who will help us.

"I am in despair that we did not have the opportunity to converse, Princess Kleopatra," he said. "We shall meet again, I am certain."

He must have seen the disappointment on her face when he had announced his departure. Undoubtedly, he could take for granted the fact that women wanted to know him, to have him turn his easy charm in their directions. For all her practice at cloaking her feelings, this man saw right through her, and now—she was sure—was taunting her for her silly, girlish crush.

She wanted to say something entirely haughty to make him believe that she had not given him a thought. Instead, all she managed was to murmur that she did, indeed, hope they would meet again. Then she committed the unpardonable gaff of blushing.

What was the use in trying to mask her feelings? She had already spun elaborate fantasies about this young Herakles: She would sit at his side during long dinners, watching the candlelight flicker on his bronze face, offering him every delectable variety of food—marinated quail, roasted boar and fishes, figs, wines from their vineyards, beers from their breweries—and even, if her father was not looking, slip, with her slim fingers, a date into his mouth. She would conduct tours of their city designed to impress him with their wealth and sophistication, taking him to the Library, to the Mouseion, to the zoo to see the great black panther her father had just imported from Armenia. She would engage with him in his own Latin, demonstrating her command of Roman literature, including the more erotic rants of Catullus. In her mind she had already envisioned the devilment in his eyes as she read to him the sensual escapades of his debauched countryman. She would *tolerate* the journeys he would make with the king to the palace prostitutes and to the brothels in the Fayum where Antony would experience the pleasures of the flesh in which she, a princess, might not indulge. She would summon him to the courtyard to see the ponds with lotus blossoms like welcoming hands, the aviaries of crimson canaries, chattering parrots, and fluttering creatures with gossamer wings and a barely audible song. She would tell him how, from her bedroom, she could watch the waves lick the beaches of the Royal Harbor, and hope he imagined himself there with her. When he drank too much with the king, she would admonish him with a smile and give him a powder for his hangover. Despite her young years and her childish body, she would charm him, and in the end, she would make him love her.

But these would have to remain girlish fantasies. With a low bow and an unsettling smile in her direction, he was gone.

SEVENTEEN

Caesar sat on the rubble of the fallen siege wall sunning himself. The autumn air in Gaul came earlier than in Italy and could be so pleasant. His legions labored below, busily cleaning up the residue of a battle fought and won, packing the remaining bags of grain into giant sacks, counting the horses, repairing the leather ties that held together their armor, loading the battering gear into the baggage carts. How could he be a happier man? Whether Fate or himself governed events, Caesar did not know. He suspected that Fate recognized his talents and his efforts and decided to play in his favor.

He had waited for this moment for many years, the moment when he could breathe easily, assured that he had once and for all subdued this rebellious nation of feral tribes. It had been five long years in the making, but he had earlier that day received word from Vercingetorix's men that their leader wished to know the terms of surrender. Caesar quickly sent back his orders. *Lay down your arms and come to me.*

Now the giant of a man walked toward him, young, so young still. How old could he be? Thirty? An Alexander, but with the height the Greek general had lacked. Unarmed, surrounded by his men, most of whom were crying. But not Vercingetorix. He had

polished his silver-and-bronze armor and wore it proudly. How nice
it would look on display in Caesar's home in Rome.

The blond man quickened his pace as he made his way directly
to Caesar. His men dropped back, linking arms to hold one another up as their leader prostrated himself at Caesar's feet. Then he
looked his conqueror straight in the eye. "I told my men to kill me
or to surrender me to you. I am not dead, therefore I am begging
your mercy. Not for myself. But for them."

Thank you, Mother Venus, Caesar said silently to his ancestress.
For here in the suppliant position was his nemesis, the man whose
insolent rebellion had caused him to slaughter hundreds of thousands of Gauls. His Hannibal. A Titan of a man a full head taller
than the tall Caesar, his muscle triple the size of Caesar's lean
physique. A man whom, under other circumstances, he might be
curious enough to see what gifts were hidden under his battle gear.

"Vercingetorix, get up. You are no earnest suppliant," said Caesar.
"You ask for mercy, but what mercy have you shown me?"

Caesar pulled himself up taller to his full six feet, preparing to
speak from deep within his gut, so that he would be heard by the
mile-long, pristine rows of soldiers that stretched in front of him.

"You used our friendship to seduce me into a false sense of security. As soon as I left your country, you rode from one end of this
land to the other urging your countrymen to betray me. When they
would not join your cause, you encouraged them by—what methods? You cut off their ears, tortured them, poked out their eyes,
branded them with a burning sword, until they agreed to join your
madness.

"You are indeed a savage. But you are a fortunate savage. I shall give
to you more mercy than you demonstrated to your own people."

"My life is yours to do with as you wish," replied the man. He
displayed no emotion, not even irony.

"Put him in chains," Caesar said indifferently to his men. He
called to Labienus, his second in command, and ordered him to
seek out among the prisoners the members of the tribes of the
Avernii and the Aedui.

Caesar watched as his officers pulled the longhaired savages out
of the ranks of the imprisoned, some cowering as if they believed

themselves singled out for additional punishment. Now they would see the mercy of Caesar in action. Caesar balanced himself atop the fallen wall, making a strong triangle with his legs. He raised his arms to speak and smiled at the speed at which the hush fell over his audience, Roman and Gallic men alike.

"Listen to me, you men of Avernii and Aedui—you allies of Rome intimidated into joining the rebellion by this animal's hideous tactics. In your hands I place the keys to peace and harmony with Rome. I say to each one of you—go home. Go to your wives, your children, your elders, and tell them of the mercy of Caesar. Tell them that today, Caesar could have killed each treasonous prisoner who made Roman soldiers suffer and die. Instead, he released you to return to your loved ones. Go now in peace."

Caesar took in the satisfying hum of the prisoners as the news of his unexpected clemency traveled to the back of the lines. He allowed himself to be helped off the rock by one of his men, squaring off to face the still-impenetrable face of Vercingetorix. Well, he would show him, wouldn't he? "Now, each of my men, officers first, will select a personal slave from your ranks. Vercingetorix, you will turn your head and watch the process."

Caesar knew this tedious selection of slaves would be a long and dreary procedure, one during which he himself would get bored, but tired as he was, he wanted a definitive end to this conflict. He had spent the winter, the spring, and the summer listening to the sound of dying. Perhaps the weather god was the cruelest dictator of all.

In the winter, Vercingetorix had set fire to every farm or town or village that he could not defend, trying to starve out Caesar's army by burning all the local crops and killing the animals. In retaliation, Caesar built a massive siege wall around Avaricum, the one city the Gauls pleaded with Vercingetorix to save. Caesar's men were exhausted, having traveled through mountain passes, clearing six and eight feet of snow as they walked. They were out of grain and living off animals stolen and slaughtered as they marched through the relentless white mountains of a Gallic winter. Both Caesar and his men were past their patience. They had subdued this nation once, and now the rebel Vercingetorix was forcing them to do the job again.

So what choice did he have when his soldiers—rabid, angry, hungry, and made even more bestial on their unbroken diet of wild meats—entered the town of Avaricum and began the slaughter? Never had he, a man of war, witnessed such mayhem and bloodshed, such ritualistic and thorough extermination of a town. Half dead already with winter's ravages, his men finished nature's job on the townspeople, tearing out the guts of men, women, children alike with their cold metal weapons. They stopped neither to save the town's assets for their own, nor to quench their sexual thirsts. Their needs were beyond money and lust. After the massacre, the body count took two days. Thirty-nine thousand, two hundred twenty-seven, if he remembered correctly.

That is what this creature before him had driven the soldiers to do, this thing now asking for mercy, this Vercingetorix, with his army of two hundred thousand vandals and hoodlums.

Caesar thought that the Avaricum massacre would send the message, but it had the reverse effect. The Gauls became even more determined. Desperate for victory, they started their burning campaign anew. In the spring, Caesar marched his men through fields of ash where farms, meadows, mills, and markets once stood. By the onset of summer, their clothes and weapons were burnished black with the ashen remnants of Gallic civilization. Vercingetorix, unmoved, had retreated to the city of Alesia, atop the summit of a hill, impregnable—or so he thought. Had he not already borne witness to the fruits of Caesar, the master builder? Was his hope so great that it deterred his judgment?

Caesar's men cheerfully accepted the challenge of constructing the fortifications. And he was so proud of the product—a circular siege wall, ten miles long, fourteen miles in width, to the best of his approximation. Three tiered circles around it so that there was no way in and no way out. It was his magnum opus.

He confiscated all the food that the Gauls tried to sneak into the city. He estimated that he could starve the town into either death or surrender in thirty days or less.

After two weeks, Vercingetorix opened the gates long enough to push out all those who were unfit for battle—the women, the children, the old men. In tattered rags, bones jutting like thorns, they came to Caesar for quarter. But how could he take on the responsibilities of his enemy? He felt certain that Vercingetorix was trying to take advantage of his reputation for mercy. He told them to go back to their men and demand that they take care of their own.

"We cannot go back," said one bold woman, whom Caesar could tell had been quite beautiful before her starving body began to feast upon itself. "The warriors have said they will dine upon our babies if it means keeping themselves alive to fight you."

Caesar took this into consideration, but refused them nonetheless. And so they camped under the fortifications, the old and the young, and the women who cared for them, sheltering themselves from summer's burning sun, and tortured his men with the sound of their babies crying themselves to hungry deaths. The low moans and curses of the old men, the whimpering cries of the mothers and the girls, the vows of hatred against all things Roman, the rotting smells—these things so discouraged the more sensitive of his commanders. Every time one more would die, the women would beat their chests—why did women of all cultures do this strange thing?—and curse not Vercingetorix, but Caesar. Starvation had made them irrational.

Who should pay for these crimes but this beautiful, implacable savage?

Vercingetorix did not flinch as the Roman soldiers eyed the Gallic warriors greedily like customers in a whorehouse. Tullian, a cavalry officer known for his homosexual predilection, had placed two of the youngest, fairest of the soldiers side by side, looking from one to the other, trying to choose.

"Labienus, please tell Tullian that he may have both of those young men. I do not wish him baffled by the choice," Caesar said, looking for a response of some kind from Vercingetorix, who scowled but remained still. After all, what were Caesar's men to do? The Gauls had sentenced their own women to death by starvation. The few that remained were scrawny and dying. Still, they made him think of *her*. In his dreams, which came all too frequently now, their dying bodies had her face.

Julia.

His only child, the coltish girl he so loved, was dead. And Caesar was not even there to witness her demise, to hold her hand, to apply the ointments to her fevered brow, but was at war with these barbarians. He had been given complete reports of the event; still, he had a difficult time believing she was gone.

She had died trying to give Pompey an heir. Pompey, devastated, prepared a grand funeral ceremony at his property in Alba, but a mob of citizens showed up at his house and demanded the girl's body. Stole it, really. They took the corpse from the house and performed the ceremony in the Field of Mars where all Rome might attend. They told Pompey to his face that the daughter of Caesar belonged to the people and not to him. That, Caesar would like to have seen. He was told that the funeral pyre was spectacular. The mourning, city-wide. All in tribute to his only heir. Clodius, poor dead Clodius, had arranged the spectacle.

Julia, dead. Clodius, dead. Murdered on a lonesome stretch of the Appian Way by his rival, Milo. Intoxicated by violence, Clodius had gotten out of hand, stirring up trouble in the city to the point where the senate had threatened to put off the coming elections. Antony, running for quaestor, put a stop to it. He drew his sword on Clodius and promised to kill him if he did not change his tactics. When it came time to choose between Clodius and Antony, Caesar was decided. Clodius was the past, Antony the future. No one rivaled Antony in battle, no one, not even Caesar himself. Milo merely took care of an ugly job, saving Caesar from the necessity of turning forever on an old friend. The tear Caesar had shed upon Clodius's death was merely nostalgic.

And now Crassus. Poor old Crassus, desperate to compete with Pompey and Caesar, had marched into savage Parthia, where he and his men—his son included—were mercilessly slaughtered at Carrhae, that same place where the Jews believed that their god had spoken to the prophet Abraham. Crassus's head was brought to the king of Parthia, a monster known for his perverted productions of Greek plays, who used the unexpected gift that very evening as the head of Pentheus in a production of *The Bacchae.*

"Everyone is saying that Crassus was the Isthmus of Corinth," reported one of Caesar's secretaries. "The bulwark of calm that prevented the two great seas, yourself and Pompey, from crashing."

Caesar considered the metaphor. Was it apt? He did not know if he was anxious or not for that prediction to manifest itself into truth. Perhaps not just yet.

According to the reports, Pompey was giving all his attention to his new wife, Cornelia, the young widow of Crassus's slain son. It was said that the two of them strolled about Pompey's beloved gardens with garlands draped around their necks, celebrating their union as if neither had a dead spouse to mourn. A disgrace. Caesar admitted that he was more than a little agitated that his Julia had been so quickly replaced.

Was Pompey trying to insult him? Since Julia's death, Pompey had been so competitive. Or so it seemed to Caesar. Caesar conquered Briton; Pompey built a magnificent theater. Caesar vanquished Gaul; Pompey imitated Clodius and began to feed the masses with free grain. Now Pompey had turned his back on all the violence in Rome, quitted office, and gone back to hiding in his gardens. But he couldn't fool Caesar; he was trying to force the senate to appoint him dictator.

And that would not do.

Caesar rose, feeling the familiar lightness in his head, the all-too-frequent blackness before his eyes when getting to his feet. It was already late afternoon, and he had forgotten to eat again. Though food had been put before him, his thoughts were too distracted to focus on consuming a meal.

The soldiers had selected their slaves. The rest of the Gauls were enchained to one another by the foot, twelve to a chain, to be led behind the baggage carts all the way to Rome, where they would be sold at the slave auctions. The best of the remaining lot were put into wagons—gifts for friends and allies of Caesar in Rome. No women. That was a problem. How many of his friends had requested a blond barbarian to add to his household? Well, he had sent them so many already.

"And what shall we do with Vercingetorix?" asked Labienus.

Caesar looked at his enemy. "Oh, he is coming back to Rome to be paraded in chains in my Triumph parade. The ladies will enjoy it so."

Caesar headed toward his camp, Hirtius falling in next to him. The two men walked in silence. As methodically as ants, Caesar's men carried the remains of the town out of the gates and loaded the plunder into large carts. Pottery, tapestries, goblets of silver and bronze, barber's tools, water dishes, even chamberpots. Whatever might fetch a price in the markets at home. Caesar counted forty-two carts of soldiers' gleaming armor, medals, and jewelry, as well as horses' ornamentation and adorned saddles. With the gold and silver and the possessions of the townspeople, it would be an impressive show. But it was never enough for the insatiable appetites back home.

What next? Rabirius was forever pestering him to go to Egypt and collect the debt from the old king, now that he had been reinstated. *He's spending the money he owes us restoring temples and buying back the goodwill of his people,* Rabirius had complained in his last letter. *Can't you do something about it?* Antony's tales of Egypt's bounty had been impressive. Though the senate would be against it, perhaps he should go there and claim it all for Rome. The senators opposing him would balk at the expanse of his power, but Caesar guessed that when he sent them their share of Egypt's treasures, they wouldn't send anything back.

"I have compiled the statistics you requested, sir," said Hirtius. He was Caesar's favorite secretary, quiet, unassuming, intelligent enough to know the mind of Caesar, but not ambitious enough to exploit that fact. "In all, we have subdued eight hundred Gallic towns and villages. The loss of life of the rebels totals one million, one hundred ninety-two thousand, as nearly as I can figure it."

"Thank you, Hirtius, I estimated as much." *More men than lived in the city of Rome.*

"Do you think it a good idea to release those figures in the report?" asked the secretary. "They are rather startling. Particularly for those unaware of our circumstances here."

"Yes, by all means," said Caesar. After all, was it not a Roman ideal that no war should be abandoned until it was won? Besides, Caesar guessed that the numbers would thrill rather than revile his countrymen. "My reputation for mercy is beyond reproach."

EIGHTEEN

Kleopatra walked alone down the great hall toward the Royal
Reception Room in search of her father. Though he no longer liked
to be bothered with the details of administering the government,
she often sought his counsel when she did not receive satisfactory
advice from the new prime minister, Hephaestion, or when she was
unsure of her own judgment. But the last time she approached the
king about money for one of the temples, he threw up his hands so
fiercely that she shied away.

"I am not a well man!" he yelled. "My spleen is heated, my bowels loose, my liver chilled, and my chest burns like a Roman furnace
day and night." Auletes, indeed, did not look well. During the four
years since his return from exile, his consumption of food and drink
had doubled. He was larger than ever and had begun to wheeze as he
walked, as he sat, as he ate, and even as he talked. "I am becoming
Potbelly, am I not? Fat as one of those large African beasts that are
born in the water." A hippopotamus, replied his daughter with as
solicitous a voice as she could muster. Auletes frightened her in this
temper, not because she feared what her father would do to her, but
rather what he would do to the kingdom. With every groan, he moved
closer to the day when he would be incapacitated. Kleopatra sometimes found herself torn between waiting for that day and dreading it.

She was seventeen, and had been so for the better part of the year. Small, still slim as a stable boy, she had learned to compensate for her lack of height with knife-sharp posture, and for her lack of mature features with scrupulously applied cosmetics. Instead of jumping on her horse first thing in the morning, she bathed quickly, allowing time to be dressed in a newly designed wardrobe of draped white linen that flattered and elongated. Her long wavy hair, streaked by the sun, was swept into a swirling hive at the nape of her neck and fastened with a smart ivory comb dotted with diamonds from African mines. To her cheeks, Charmion applied a powdery mix of cinnamon and ginger, brown enough to blend with her skin, for Kleopatra did not wish to look red in the face like the painted Rabirius or one of the court prostitutes. Charmion reddened her lips and palms, darkened her eyelids, and inked her lashes. With a steady hand, she rimmed Kleopatra's impatient eyes with a fine band of kohl. All the while an attendant massaged almond oil into the princess's hands, forearms, and feet, finishing with a brusque chamois cloth.

Thus, with her adolescence painted away, Kleopatra began her long day.

This morning, dread was her only companion. Every time she brought up the debt to the Romans, Auletes acted like a petulant slave child who did not wish to do his daily chores. I have executed my enemies and now it is my friends who so torment me, the king would complain. I cannot spend any more money placating the Romans. They are laughing at me, just as they laughed at Potbelly. And then he would waddle from the room, leaving the troubles of his kingdom behind, and leaving his daughter to wish she might so easily exonerate herself from duty.

Composing the speech she would make to the king, Kleopatra motioned to the guard to open the double mahogany doors and strode breezily, unannounced, through the opening. Below the great eagle over her father's throne sat Auletes—his robes wide open, a naked youth stretched across his lap like a baby. The boy's penis was firm in Auletes' hand, his head thrown back, his mouth open. Little gasping noises escaped from his lips. Auletes frantically pressed his head against the back of the throne, while he thrust himself into the boy's bottom. Kleopatra stood agape. They seemed not to notice her. A water boy, a spritelike Egyptian of perhaps eleven, crouched on the floor next to the table of wine. He glanced at Kleopatra and then hid his face in the tablecloth. He probably fears that he is next, she thought. She turned away and walked out, the sounds of their ecstasy serenading her exit.

At least he's written his will, she thought, quickening her step in the direction of the Prime Minister's office. Six months earlier, the scrupulous Hephaestion had urged Auletes to name as his successors Kleopatra and her younger brother. Ptolemy the Elder was still just a child, but, theoretically, her future husband. Auletes issued a Proclamation that they be known as *Philadelphoi,* deities, lovers of their siblings.

Kleopatra suppressed a smirk when she heard the wording. She hardly knew her brother. Custom, nonetheless, was custom, and Auletes arranged succession according to tradition. He then invited Kleopatra to accompany him to the small palace where his other children lived to announce the contents of his will. They were reared by a staff who brought them to official ceremonies several times a year, but Kleopatra and her father had no real contact with these offspring. The king, Kleopatra suspected, considered them remnants of his life with Thea, and probably feared that betrayal was a characteristic that ran in the blood. Why should he trust them when his entire family history bore witness to that possibility?

Arsinoe, fourteen, was a creature of both Thea and Berenike. Berenike had raised the girl, intoxicating her childhood with the legends of the warrior queens. Arsinoe was very like Berenike—muscular, aggressive—though shorter and even less attached to the earth. But she was buxom like Thea, and Kleopatra felt a deadly chill of memory when Arsinoe sat in her father's lap and stroked his face seductively. Ptolemy the Elder was ten years old and demonstrating the unfortunate tendency to fatness of the males in the lineage. His tutor, the painted and bejeweled eunuch Pothinus, attended him solicitously, praising his every word, even if he was merely quoting an overused verse of Homeric poetry, and encouraged Arsinoe to praise him as well. Kleopatra had been warned about Pothinus by Hephaestion, who judged him grandiose, foolish, and ambitious.

"There is nothing worse than ignorance followed by action," Hephaestion had said, "and I fear that Pothinus subscribes to that pattern of behavior." Ptolemy the Younger was eight, but already aware of the position to which he might someday ascend, and fully attached to the elder two, who told him they would conquer Syria for him to rule while they presided over Egypt. Still in the nursery, he wore elaborate clothing and bid his nurse call him Ptolemy XIV, king of the Seleucids. Lost in a dream world, these children knew nothing of the functions of the government. Kleopatra noticed that Arsinoe indulged the tutor and her brothers, all the while turning shrewd eyes to her older sister, letting Kleopatra know that her eager compliance was mere sport. The boys will forever be a burden, Kleopatra had thought, and Arsinoe, trouble. Another Berenike— fierce and ambitious, but ignorant of the world's realities. Kleopatra sat motionless in her chair, assessing this bizarre assembly of characters—her father and his rotund sons, identical replicas of descending sizes; her sister, a master of connivance, playing the temptress for her father, the solicitous nursemaid to her brothers, and the precocious pawn to the eunuch. It was as if every censorious judgment against the Ptolemies had been painted into this living tableau before her. Kleopatra had begun to feel dizzy and cut the visit short with complaints of a headache.

Auletes attempted to deposit a copy of his will with the Vestal Virgins in Rome, but the terror reigning in the streets of that city thwarted his effort. He sent letters and gifts to Pompey, begging him to ensure that Rome would support Kleopatra and Ptolemy the Elder as monarchs in the event of his death. "Remember the little girl who so skillfully handled your horse? She is a woman now and reigns at my side. She is astute in matters of policy, and is an invaluable diplomat as she speaks and reads many languages." He sent dozens of these missives, always with gold, or with extravagant jewels for Pompey's new wife, Cornelia, whom Kleopatra assumed was another young plaything like Julia. When she discovered the truth— that Cornelia was herself a scholar and learned matron—she suggested to Auletes that he send her a generous gift from the Alexandria Library. This Pompey responded to, undoubtedly at Cornelia's insistence. He sent Auletes a letter guaranteeing that he would be responsible for the safekeeping of his will and for its implementation in the "terrible event that the gods take Your Highness from us." Auletes had the letter translated into Greek and demotic Egyptian and posted throughout the land.

Once Auletes had Pompey's assurance, he abruptly withdrew from his duties. He attempted to escape the ravages of his age and condition by daily indulgence in wine and in the pleasures of young lovers, lured by gifts of jewelry for the ostentatious, rare manuscripts from the Library for the intellectuals, and idle promises of future political power for those who were ambitious. Finally, thought Kleopatra, he has succumbed to the pattern of iniquity established by his ancestors. Was it the destiny of the men in the family to spend their later years wallowing in decadent sport while the kingdom was run by women and eunuchs? So be it; she was up to the task.

With a resolute gait, she strode into the office of the Prime Minister, waving at him to sit when he rose to attend to her, and dropped carelessly on his sofa. "My father is debauching himself again with a boy from the gymnasium. I did not think it a good time to bother him with our concerns."

Hephaestion smiled. He was a handsome forty-year-old eunuch who dressed conservatively and moved with the slow, tranquil pace of a priest. It had taken Kleopatra many months to learn to trust him. She had found his manner of silently observing her disquieting. But after he had watched her conduct herself in the arduous two years after she and Auletes had returned from exile, he came to her one day and said, "Surely you realize that none of the king's advisers any longer seek his opinion. If you wish, I will henceforth direct all matters of state to you." Kleopatra had been stunned at his candor and merely stared at him. "You do realize you are running the kingdom?" he had asked, his sincere brown eyes defying her to disagree.

"Yes, I realize that," she had replied. "I did not know whether *you* realized it as well."

"Very good," he had said, pleased with her answer.

"But what of my father? Do we ignore him now and treat him as a senile old man?"

"No," the eunuch had replied almost tenderly. "We furnish him with all the respect of his office and his age. You must always remain loyal to your father and treat him with dignity and warmth.

"But, Princess Kleopatra, when you make decisions regarding matters of state, I advise you to let your blood run cold."

Now the eunuch smiled at Kleopatra's report of Auletes' excesses. "At least he is not vexed with worry as we are. I rather envy him. He is clearly not a bitter man."

"When you are an old man, you, too, shall be allowed to wallow in depravity, but at present, I require your good mind," Kleopatra answered. She appreciated his humor but was too occupied to acknowledge it. "Let us face the facts: My father is a spent man. He has worn himself out trying to hold on to the throne and trying to appease all parties. He only wishes now for a bit of pleasure in his dotage. Though he says his doctors tell a different story, I know he is not well. His days are numbered," she said, numb to her own words.

"I concur with your assessment," said Hephaestion. "But it does not alter the situation."

"Read it to me again," she said.

The eunuch retrieved a small scroll from his desk. He opened it.

My Dear King Ptolemy, I hope you have forgotten neither your old friend and benefactor nor your outstanding debt to me. I have taken the matter up with my colleague Julius Caesar. As you may have heard, Caesar has finished his governorship in Gaul and will soon return in glorious victory to Rome. I have sent him notice of the aforementioned matter. He is reviewing it and will shortly make a decision as to what action may be required to collect the unpaid funds. I trust that you will send a substantial portion of the money owed immediately. My attempts to help you have cost me dearly. I look forward to your expedient response. Yours, C. Rabirius

"Concise and to the point, I would say," said Hephaestion. "Pay up or face the most feared man in Rome."

"What of Caesar? Why should he collect the debt for Rabirius?"

"Why? For a portion of the money. Your Highness, Caesar is a dangerous man, a renegade. His men are excited from their recent victories and believe themselves invincible. Your father's man Pompey also has a huge army he might raise at any time. I believe these men will soon clash and one will emerge as king."

"And if that happens?" asked Kleopatra.

"Allow me to pose this question: Who will help us if Caesar defeats Pompey? We have done nothing to cultivate Caesar. Everyone knows Auletes is Pompey's ally. What will become of Egypt if Caesar and Pompey come to blows and Caesar prevails? It is hardly an impossible scenario. All Rome fears it. What will Caesar do with Pompey's friends and allies, particularly those who, like your father, owe thousands of talents to the Roman moneylenders? It is not pleasant to contemplate."

"So what must we do?"

"We do not have control of the treasury, so we must go to your father and convince him to send a portion of the money owed to Rabirius. We don't want Caesar coming here and taking the money by force."

"Where do you propose we get this money?" she asked. "Those who are against my father will rise up again if we raise taxes."

"That may be true. But whom would you rather confront? The opponents of Auletes or the ten-legion army of Julius Caesar?"

"We will never really appease Rome, will we?" she asked. She had vowed that she would find a way out of this, had promised the lady Artemis, spilt the blood of the lamb, and made her covenant with the unseen powers of the earth and sky that this would not be her Fate, this fretting and groveling over the demands of Rome. But how to avoid it? Roman boots had trampled over half the earth. Why should Egypt be any different?

"Your Highness, I do not mean to induce melancholia. I believe the native people will support whatever you do. The king has made many improvements in the country since his reinstatement."

"They always support us until we take food from their mouths," she answered curtly, fuming over the memory of Rabirius's tyranny over Alexandria, his long curls matted with pomade, his feet turning outward like a duck when he walked. He cut an altogether ridiculous figure for one who had caused so much harm.

Even worse than Rabirius's drain on the treasury was Gabinius's legacy to Alexandria. After Berenike's trial and execution, Gabinius had gone back to Rome, leaving behind his army of mercenaries, allegedly to protect the king, but really to protect the interests of Rabirius. Undeterred by the reestablishment of the king's authority, the Gabinian soldiers went on looting the town at will. The men made Alexandria their personal whorehouse, raping the native women wherever and whenever they pleased. When threatened with punishment, they simply laughed and replied that *they* were now the law. For six months they had conducted a reign of terror over the city.

"I am utterly beholden to Rabirius, that miserable scrod," the king would grumble, searching for a solution. "And Gabinius, the pirate, whose army of cutthroats will be at me if I move against Rabirius. What can I do? Without those two criminals, I would never have been able to return home, and they are never going to let me forget it."

To appease Gabinius and Rabirius, Auletes had been forced to appoint Rabirius to the high position of Minister of Finance, giving him access to Egypt's revenues and her treasury. In return, Rabirius used Egypt as his playground and her resources as his toys.

It was the then sixteen-year-old Kleopatra who finally outsmarted them. She was not about to be intimidated by the preening fool, the man Cicero once disparaged in a speech as a "thieving dance-boy in hair curlers." She had Auletes put Rabirius on watch. They discovered that he had lowered the wages of the workers in every government-owned factory and kept the remainder of the money for himself. He stole the workers' share of the goods and loaded it on ships sent back daily to Rome. He had become the most despised man in Egypt. But he was still a friend of Julius Caesar, and he still had the support of the Gabinian soldiers.

One day in her bath, Kleopatra had an epiphany. Suddenly, she was furious at the dashing cavalry officer who had made such an impact on her. All at once, the plan by which Antony had used her father and her country unfolded. He had promised Gabinius's army wealth if they crossed the desert. He took the credit and the glory for leading them into a victory. Undoubtedly, he also took a large sum of money from Gabinius for his services. And then he absented himself to make it possible for the soldiers to steal whatever they pleased.

So that is his game, thought the princess. She felt humiliated that she had been taken in by his good looks and seductive ways. She and her father and the mission to restore him were no more to Antony than to any other Roman—an opportunity to line their pockets with Egyptian gold.

She arrived in her father's office barely dry. "Father, you are going to secure the loyalty of the Gabinians."

"But how?" asked the king, wearing his most bemused, defeated expression.

"How do the Romans secure their soldiers? They give them land and money. You must give each man a parcel of land, the size according to his rank and his record. And you must encourage them to stop raping our women by giving them permission to marry them. If you provide what the Roman generals provide, they will be beholden to you as they are to their own commanders. For all the boasting of the loyalty of Roman soldiers, they are bought and paid for like any other men."

"My child, you are an oracle," said the king.

The Gabinians readily accepted the king's offer of housing and money, and several announced their desire to be married to women of the city, both Egyptian and Greek. Like all other immigrants since Alexandria's inception, they, too, were eager to be seduced and assimilated into her promise.

Shortly thereafter, the factory workers rose up against Rabirius and ran him out of town. Kleopatra would never forget Rabirius bursting into the Royal Reception Room—pomaded hair stringy around his fat, wet face, his ridiculous painted robe stained with perspiration—begging for protection from "the filthy Egyptians." They had greeted him at the gate of the linen factory where he had come to pilfer a portion of the goods; armed with knives and clubs, they attacked him. "I was hit on the shoulder with a terrible stick by a dirty little man," Rabirius had exclaimed, "and I have bruises. Bruises!" Kleopatra had giggled when he lifted his short robe to reveal an ugly purple knot on his thigh, stifling her laughter when Hephaestion calmly offered to shelter Rabirius in the jail until he could escape Egypt on the next boat to Rome. Without alternative refuge, Rabirius had reluctantly agreed to live in prison for several days. The last Kleopatra saw of him was his fat bottom swaying contemptuously as he lumbered out of the room.

Though the menace himself was gone, Rabirius's legacy remained. Hephaestion collected reports from each of the forty-two metropoli: Every state in the nation had been ravaged by the years of revolt and the recent visit of the Roman army. The young men are dead from the war, the eunuch explained. Taxes continually rise to pay the debt to Rome, and the food and merchandise produced have been stolen either by the army or by Rabirius. With implacable calm, Hephaestion informed the king that while his restoration had stopped the war, it hardly had benefited the people.

"Why do you trouble me with these things at a time when I should be merry?" The king scowled, his lower lip puffy like the underside of a caterpillar.

While Auletes pouted, Kleopatra absorbed the realization that her father's kingdom would have to be won not just once but time and again. With the optimism of a child, the king was always satisfied with small gains, as if history had not imprinted upon him the lessons of his own experiences; as if the Romans would forgive such a substantial debt. As if his own subjects did not despise him and would suddenly stop searching for any reason to send him off into exile again. Next time, she might not be so lucky. She might be murdered in the palace, left behind by her father to face the mob, or even be asked by the leaders of the city's tribes to betray her father, at which point she would become their puppet queen until they could rid themselves of her, too.

Kleopatra persuaded her father that he must act quickly to solidify his claims on the throne by restoring the temples and monuments of the gods that were pillaged by the Roman soldiers and by Rabirius. She told him firmly, reciting to him as if he were a little boy, the same words he had spoken to her in her youth: The Egyptians honor those who honor their gods.

"But I have just returned to my kingdom," he had said. "Must I leave it so quickly?"

"Father, all of Egypt is your kingdom," Kleopatra had replied, and then handed him an itinerary carefully made by Hephaestion. The king was to travel down the Nile, leaving behind hefty donations to the temples as a reminder of his beneficence.

While Auletes was away on his mission, she and Hephaestion came up with a number of ways to compensate for the iniquities visited upon the people by Rabirius. The farmers were to receive a more favorable division of their corn crop; the duty on Lycian honey, adored by Egyptians and Greeks alike, was lowered from fifty percent to twenty-five; conditions were improved for the workers in the Nubian gold mines. Kleopatra and Hephaestion worked many long days and nights to bring to fruition these improvements. The strategy had been impeccable. The priests at Karnak, a powerful political force in Middle Egypt, had expressed their gratitude by commissioning native artists to depict Auletes in Pharaoh's dress vanquishing his enemies.

Now, for the first time in many years, an air of calm rested over both the city of Alexandria and the country of Egypt. Rabirius had been prosecuted in a Roman court and fined for his excesses in Auletes' kingdom and for illegally holding office in a foreign government. Yet the parasite was still trying to collect his blood money.

"Well?" Hephaestion's modulated but firm appeal interrupted her contemplation. Kleopatra suddenly felt as old as her father and just as worn. The enormity of their problem settled over her like a shroud. "Let us request a formal meeting with the king. We can do nothing in this matter without his permission."

The king had already taken his supper and was seated in the gaming room with Hekate at his side. At his feet were two boys who looked like, but were not, twins. With skin that was not brown or black or fair but instead pale yellow, they were wrapped in shiny red triangles of cloth. Their faces had the same angular three-sided shape of their dress. They sat cross-legged on the floor, shoulders touching, each leaning against one of the king's calves. He stroked their fine, silky black hair as he sat staring into space. Hekate sat very erect, pretending either that they were not there, or that she did not object to their presence. Kleopatra found herself torn between irritation at her father and concern at the ashen color of his face.

She began gently, though in a firm tone. "Must we discuss the affairs of the kingdom in the company of such unfamiliar faces?"

"Oh, do not mind them," said the king. "They speak only some singsong language that no one understands. Not even you, I'll wager. They do not care for official business and such."

"Very well. Hephaestion has read to you the demand letter from Rabirius?"

"Yes, yes," said the king curtly.

"And what action do you recommend?"

"Send him some money. Or if you would like to meet Julius Caesar, do not send him some money." The king laughed at his joke. "For myself, I should like to meet Caesar. I hear he is a splendid conversationalist and an art lover. I should like to play my flute for him."

"The doctors recommend that you do not play anymore, Your Highness," said Hekate quietly. "It takes away your wind."

"Nonetheless, I would happily play for Julius Caesar. Perhaps he would forgive the debt if I enchanted him."

"Father, I do not wish to meet Julius Caesar under such circumstances. Hephaestion believes we must send Rabirius a payment, but only after we have gathered support from the people."

"Do what you wish," Auletes said. "You are queen."

Kleopatra looked at the Prime Minister and shook her head. So this is what it had come to. Her father had lost his mind and he no longer recognized her. "Father, I beg your indulgence. You are king. I am your daughter. There is no queen."

"No queen?" Auletes replied as if he had just been given startling news. "We shall have to remedy that. I thought I had married you."

"Father, I am Kleopatra. I am your daughter, not your wife."

"I once married my daughter."

"Yes, Father, that was Thea, the daughter of your wife and my mother. I am neither your first wife nor your second."

Kleopatra tried to conceal the alarm in her voice. She looked at Hekate, who lowered her eyes. What was she to do? Her father was no longer her father but some madman who did not even know her. She felt the protection she had enjoyed all her life as his most favored and loyal daughter drain away like water out of a tub, leaving her empty and alone.

"You are how old?"

"I am almost eighteen, Father," she said.

"Already eighteen years old? Very well. As of tomorrow you are queen." He shrugged, saying to Hephaestion, "Draw up the papers. Bring them to me in the afternoon." And then to Hekate, "Oh, I am tired. I want to be carried to my bed."

The queen held the coin between her index finger and thumb, admiring the favorable way the craftsman had dignified the prodigious profiles of herself and her father. Was there any possibility that her face was as lovely as it looked on the coin? She feared not; she had too often held a mirror to the side of her face and appraised herself from that angle. But the artist had managed to capture the intelligence in her eyes, the dramatic levity of her cheekbone, and the enticing, upward curve of her lips. *In the thirtieth regnal year of King Ptolemy XII and the first regnal year of his co-regent, Queen Kleopatra VII,* it read. Cheek to cheek, they stared forward, as if into the future.

She flipped it again, catching it in the cup of her palm and bouncing it a few times. No one, she was sure, would notice her handiwork, her alchemy, except the foreman at the Royal Mint. And he was a reasonable man.

Once Kleopatra's joint rulership with her father was made official, she requested that the government issue a coin with the images of her and her father to announce to his subjects that his daughter now ruled at his side. But Hephaestion brought her the grim news that the treasury's supplies of bronze and silver were severely diminished, due to the extortion of Gabinius and the machinations of Rabirius. There is simply not enough metal, Hephaestion explained, to issue coinage at this time. The supplies are almost twenty-five percent lower than in previous years. Perhaps later, he said, when we have solved some of our financial problems. She did not like the way that her first command as queen had been summarily dismissed. That evening in her bath, breathing the aromatic steam, skimming her hand over the oil-slicked surface of the warm water, Kleopatra came up with the idea. She leapt to her feet, almost losing her balance on the slippery marble floor of the tub and startling the bath attendant. She allowed herself to be wrapped in a towel, dancing, almost, in bare feet while she reviewed her inspired idea for possible flaws. They would issue the coins, but with less bronze, twenty-five percent less, to be exact. She brought the plan to Hephaestion the next day.

"How can we do that, Your Majesty," he asked, "when the coins are weighed for their worth?" He looked at her as if surprised at her naiveté; as if she were a child with an unreasonable demand who had manufactured an impossible, silly solution just to get her way.

"It is simple. We will stamp the worth of the coin on the coin itself. Just as we stamp our image, we will imprint the worth of the coin directly into the metal. Then no one will be able to contest the worth. It will also save considerable time in the trading process. No one will have to weigh anymore. They will know what the coin is worth because we will tell them."

"But that has never been done," he replied politely.

"Precisely. Then there is no law against it."

The man looked astonished, but whether in admiration of her or fear that she had lost her mind, she could not guess. She continued, "A coin of forty drachmas will be stamped forty drachmas. But it will weigh thirty. In this way, we will make a full twenty-five percent profit on every coin we issue. The surplus can be used to make a payment to placate the scoundrel Rabirius."

Hephaestion did not answer, but rubbed his palms together slowly as if he were praying on the idea. "It has never been done before, but it shall be done now," he said, offering her his characteristic modest smile, as if a broad grin would crack open his unlined skin. "Your Majesty, the gods enlighten you. I hope you are aware of that gift. I believe you are specially blessed. I shall remember to honor that as long as I am in your command."

"I am aware of the goodness of the gods," she said. "But if you really wish to please me, you should offer me a more extravagant smile."

Thus edified and feeling terribly like a queen, Kleopatra went into the Royal Vaults and extracted her mother's ring of the Bacchant, a heavy, gold-sculpted rendering of the god, naked and at his most manly and beautiful, his tousled curls capped with an ivy crown. She liked wearing the ring of the last true queen of Egypt, as she liked to think of it, and to have that link to a mother whose voice, features, and demeanor she could not recall, even in dreams. Perhaps the ring would please the ailing Auletes, bringing back pleasant memories of his first wife, whom he had lost not long after his daughter was born. In the past month, the king had forsaken his sexual indulgences as well as his duties and had taken to his bed. Kleopatra visited her father daily; sometimes he knew her, sometimes he mistook her for others long dead.

Hekate hovered over Auletes day and night, holding his hand for hours and hours as he lay gasping for breath, laying soothing herbs and presses on his forehead. When the king did not show improvement either in mind or in body, Kleopatra called a meeting of the physicians and demanded to know why they could not revive her father, who was not an old man.

"He has fevers, Your Majesty," the Royal Physician replied. "Yet his liver is excessively chilled. The traditional cures have not worked. There is not a physician or a scientist at the Mouseion that we have not consulted. We have brought in the native women to administer the secret healing herbs of Egypt. We have also written to our colleagues in Athens and Rhodes for advice."

"By the time we receive an answer that compensates for your lack of knowledge the king will be dead," she said curtly. But she knew the truth. Auletes was a spent man. The long years trying to placate all the disparate factions of his kingdom and his family, the familial betrayals, and, most of all, the humiliation he had faced time and again at the hands of the Romans had defeated him utterly.

Kleopatra flipped the coin into the air, catching it in her palm. She clutched it tightly and smiled. She would bring it to the king directly. This symbol that his lineage continued into the future would cheer him. He had held the throne of his ancestors in the face of his family's rebellion, his subjects' displeasure, and the Roman menace. The coin was the greatest evidence she could show him, other than her abject loyalty, that his life had been a success.

"How is the king today?" she asked the physician she met coming out of the king's chamber.

"He is in most decent spirits, Your Majesty," the man answered. "He ate a splendid breakfast of dates, quail eggs, and milk, and then called for an orange. He insisted upon peeling it himself. I believe he is mending. The gods are good to those who serve them."

The king lay in his bed, his head propped on an immense silk pillow. His perspiration had discolored the patch that haloed his head, making a mock crown. His eyes seemed out of symmetry. Though Hekate swabbed his forehead repeatedly, his face glistened, giving him an ethereal countenance. What could that physician have meant by his spirits?

When Hekate saw the queen she began to rise, obeying the protocol for her new status, but Kleopatra silently stopped her with her hand.

"Father," she began in an uncharacteristically perky voice. "Look here what I have." Auletes attempted to focus his eyes on the small, metallic orb that she held in front of his face.

"Look, Sire," said Hekate. "It is the coin of the joint rulership between our new queen and yourself. How handsome you look, Auletes. It is a wonderful likeness."

The king squinted. "Yes, it is, by god. Look at me. How fine I am. But do you not think I am portrayed as too fat?"

"Not at all, my darling," Hekate said. "You are pictured at the height of health and prosperity. It is a fine tribute to you and to the queen."

"And how lovely my wife looks, though she does not appear herself at all."

"It is a likeness of myself, Father," answered the queen. "Kleopatra, your eldest daughter."

"But why do you wear the ring of my wife? Have you stolen it from her? Where is she?"

"My mother is dead. She died when I was but a child."

"Ah, so it is. Come close to me."

Kleopatra sat on the enormous state bed beside the supine figure of her father. Hanging above them was the eagle of Ptolemy, nesting directly above, serving as a canopy over the ailing king. The beast's sharp beak curved ominously, pointing its tip at Auletes' belly. Kleopatra had never before been on the bed of her father. Would she someday sleep in this room? How could one get a good night's rest when the eagle threatened always to swoop down and hit the bed's tenant in his most vulnerable spot?

Auletes' hand was limp and hot. She smelled the odor from the wet poultice that covered his liver. Kleopatra's first instinct was to withdraw her hand, but she let it rest in his palm. He closed his hand around hers, immediately causing her to perspire, whether from the temperature or from nervousness, she did not know. "You are Kleopatra, as was your mother and her mother. Or so it says on your new coin."

"That is correct, Father."

"You are not an impostor or a usurper, are you?" he asked wickedly. She did not know if he joked with her or if he was still in a confused state.

"I am not an impostor. I have remained true to my father the king even when his wife and his other daughter and his own people turned against him," she said, wishing she did not have to make this bedside defense of herself.

"The name Kleopatra means 'glory to her father,'" he said. His eyes were now focused intently on hers. She believed she felt heat emanating from them. "Swear to me that you will honor that name always."

"I swear it, Father. I shall care for you always and never desert you or fail to heed your wise counsel. The kingdom suffers from your sick leave. Every day I pray to the gods that my father recovers quickly, that one morning I will awaken to the sound of his flute."

Hekate smiled her approval for Kleopatra's patronage of her father, while Kleopatra wished that there was even a modicum of hope behind her words; that her father were himself and that together they could attend to the thousand details and problems of government as they had in what seemed now like times long past.

Auletes sighed, his chest rattling like the annoying toy of a child. He tried to catch his breath, shaking Kleopatra off the bed with his convulsion. Hekate quickly called to the servants to hold the king upright to expel the poison that had arisen from his lungs. She took

Kleopatra to the foot of the bed and whispered, "Your Majesty, forgive my interference, but I fear for the life of the king."

"Hekate, you are family to us. Nothing you do on behalf of my father's health can be construed as interference. Speak your mind."

"The fever has settled on the king's brain. The Royal Physician says that the king improves, but the medicine woman has told me that once the brain absorbs the fever, nothing can be done."

"The physician told me as I entered the room that the king is on the mend."

"The physician wishes to abdicate responsibility for the king's illness. Behind his back, the old woman and I have administered all the remedies known in our family for many hundreds of years, but we have failed him. I wish to die with him, Your Majesty. What am I, a courtesan, without her king?"

Kleopatra understood the meaning. A middle-age courtesan was admired if she successfully parlayed her love into lifelong financial security, and despised if she failed to do so. She suspected that Hekate would not have manipulated such an arrangement, believing it beneath her dignity. "Hekate, has the king not provided for your future?"

"I did not request it," she said.

"You have been a most loyal and tender friend to my father. Another woman might have abandoned him or ridiculed him for his recent foolishness. But you have given him love. Whatever the Fate of my father, I promise you a pension for life to supplement the king's many gifts to you. If you desire it, I shall arrange for you to return to your family in Mytilene upon the king's death."

"You shall be a queen unlike any other, known to all for your compassion." The older woman knelt before the girl whom she had known since before her eleventh birthday.

"Hekate, please," said Kleopatra, helping the woman to her feet. "The king needs you."

Hekate returned to her nursing post. Kleopatra took a moment to watch the delicate hand sweep a sage-soaked cloth over the king's heavy forehead. The king smiled sweetly like a small boy given an unexpected piece of candy before his dinner.

He closed his eyes and breathed peacefully.

NINETEEN

Kleopatra squinted into the rising sun. The farmers who lived in misshapen mud huts along the banks of the Nile had already hung out their wash, and it fluttered in the torpid morning breeze, the first movement of air she had felt in days. Clusters of palm trees with fronds like worn-out combs swayed softly against a pearl-blue sky. Papyrus, brown and dry as beavers' tails, choked the shoreline. Despite the subtle wind, there was an unearthly stillness to the river at sunrise. Kleopatra was accustomed to feeling dawn stir the city back to life, and she felt unsettled in this static land where, beyond the verdant stripe that lined the river, the solemn dunes of the desert lolled toward an eternal horizon.

Though it was barely May, summer had descended upon Egypt, but this year without the spring rain that relieved the relentless heat of the land. The river looked deadly low. If the rain did not come, if the river did not rise and flood the crops as it did yearly, there would be famine. Surely the people feared it, and surely they were in no mood to receive the daughter of the Greek monarch who had appointed the Roman Rabirius—the swine who, two years ago, had raped them of their last good harvest. Kleopatra added these thoughts to her list of woes, letting the weight of it settle into her viscera along with her other anxieties.

The royal barge, long, flat, and sleek, sailed at a languid pace through placid waters, but Kleopatra felt the boat's motion in the pit of her belly. She had not taken food in two days, and her stomach was empty and queasy all at once. Her hands shook from the fast; her head felt light, as if it might ascend to the heavens without the rest of her body. Two tall servants stood beside her shaded chair on the deck, fanning her with feathery plumes, but the heat had penetrated well beyond the skin and into the very core of her body. No amount of hot breeze would unseat her burden. As the wind teased her face, she wished it would lift her and carry her away to join her father, who at this moment was probably playing his flute for the gods. She was certain that her father's spirit was precisely where it wished to be—free, finally, from the untenable dilemmas of politics; weightless, at last, no longer bound to soil dominated by Rome.

The last several days had been unreal, time she floated through by steeling herself against the tide of sorrow and panic that descended upon her at Auletes' death. She could not reveal the slightest weakness, the smallest insecurity, the tiniest inkling that all was not well within the palace. When a stray emotion threatened to surface, she tensed her body fiercely to scare the grief or the fear away. She had yet to catch a full breath since the moment she was informed of the king's demise, and now her body was exhausted and her mind relentless.

On that evening, she had dressed hurriedly and run to her father's chamber, Charmion ahead of her lighting the hall with a heavy oil lamp. The first thing she heard was a low, murmuring sob. Hekate was on her knees at the bedside, gently beating her breasts with her fists, crying an almost inaudible lament. The king's eyes were closed, his face at rest, his hair slightly damp. He looked as if he had just expended himself in one of his licentious pleasures and slept the deep and remorseless sleep of the hedonist. His tranquil face was in odd juxtaposition with the angry stare of the Ptolemaic eagle above him. Kleopatra moved toward her father, but was stopped by the large hand of Hephaestion upon her shoulder. "We must talk," he said.

"My father is dead," she said angrily, shocked that he would choose the hour of her grief to address official matters.

"Yes, I am sorry. Tonight, before I rest, if I rest, I shall pray to the gods for his soul. But at present, the dangers to you and to the kingdom do not allow us to express the normal emotions." The eunuch's voice was filled with the authority that Kleopatra did not, at this moment, possess. Her source of authority lay dead, his burly arms folded across his stomach. Kleopatra wanted to go to him, unfurl his arms, and curl inside the woolly shelter of his chest as she had done as a child. Just once, just one more time before he was gone forever.

"Please listen to me before something of irretrievable harm is done," Hephaestion said, breaking protocol and taking her firmly by the shoulders with his hands. "Your life depends on it. You are not two months a queen. The coins announcing joint rule with your father have not yet reached the provinces. You have no official support outside your father's status as king."

Kleopatra stood silent, unprepared for both the death of her father and for the news that she was queen in name only. She had spent her life preparing to embrace power, but her will and vitality seemed to have disappeared along with the spirit of her father. How easy it had been to assume power when her father was alive, when the force of his years and his title and his heritage were pushing her on. How would she manage alone? Where was Archimedes? Hammonius? Why did they not come to her now when she needed them most? She longed to cry upon the shoulder of a Kinsman, but the only person before her now was this inscrutable eunuch demanding her attention.

"We are going to pretend that your father lives," he said to her astonishment. She looked again at her father's body. "You must stifle every emotion and carry out this ruse."

Kleopatra listened as the eunuch informed her that she was not going to mourn the death of her father, but rather, was going on a crucial diplomatic mission. He had already arranged for her to leave the next morning for Hermonthis in Thebes. Buchis, the sacred bull at the temple of Amon-Ra, had died, and a new bull was to be installed in the holy place. Kleopatra did not speak, but looked skeptically into Hephaestion's genial brown eyes for any sign of treachery.

"To the Egyptians, the bull is the living soul of the god. He is the symbol of the Thebiad region. He is not a Greek deity like the Apis bull at the temple of Sarapis, but a god of the native people from ancient times. He is a reminder to them of the days when all men feared even the name of Pharaoh. By leading the procession, you will secure the loyalty of the priests and the politicians of the Thebiad. While you are gone, I will open discussions with those who wield power in the city."

"Are these sinister methods really necessary?" asked Kleopatra. Was Hephaestion succumbing to the eunuch's archetypal delight with intrigue? "Or are you trying to get rid of me for your own purposes?"

Hephaestion dismissed the accusation by refusing to address it. "Your sister Arsinoe and the two boys are in the thrall of the eunuch Pothinus. Do not be fooled by his ridiculous, garish exterior. He is as conniving a creature as we've seen at this court. I have been watching him for years, and he knows it. He intends to rise to power through your sister and brothers, which of course calls for your demise. The moment he knows your father is dead, he will begin a campaign against you."

Kleopatra cursed herself. How had she become so vulnerable? How had she imagined she would retain power after her father's death? By magic? Had she been so busy with her duties that she had failed to keep an eye on her siblings? She still considered them children—surely not allies, but hardly formidable enough to be dangerous. At least not yet.

"Your brother is ten years old, and when he becomes your co-regent, Pothinus and others of his choosing will govern as his Regency Council. He is a boy and they can have their way with him. You are of age, and may make decisions by yourself. With you out of the way, they could have eight years of uninterrupted power. You are the only challenge to their authority. They know you have run the kingdom in the last months, and they fear you.

"But if you are strong, if you demonstrate that you have the loyalty of those who served your father, they will have to respect your position."

"How can we keep my father's death a secret?"

"I have instructed the doctors to declare him quarantined," said Hephaestion. "They are issuing a Royal Order that no one be allowed into the chambers of the king except themselves, who bring food and medicines."

Two physicians entered the room waving smoking incense burners, releasing an acrid, wicked scent. Kleopatra covered her nose and mouth with her hand. "Why this horrible smell?"

"To deter the curious," Hephaestion said, a tiny smile cracking the tension in his face. While Kleopatra took short, shallow breaths, Hephaestion explained that an expert embalmer was on his way from the Necropolis. Should anyone burst into the room, the king would have a lifelike appearance. Pothinus and the nurses of the children were being informed that deadly diseases lurked in the room. At the sacrifice for the king's health in the morning, the priests would predict horrific fates—instantaneous disappearance of the tongue or untimely death by plague—to those who intruded upon the king.

"How can I leave the city at this time? Is it safe?" She had learned to trust Hephaestion without question; intuition, her best adviser, had told her to do so. Now, panicked, feeling as if the very floor under her feet might at any moment give way and betray her, intuition vanished, leaving a vacuum quickly filled by insecurity and a desperate, futile desire to change the unfolding events.

"You must go. You will be the first Greek monarch to perform this ceremony in the three hundred years your family has occupied Egypt. Can you think of a better way to consolidate support among the native people? Must I remind you of the very words you uttered to move your father to act? The Egyptians honor those who honor their gods."

Without spending a decent expanse of time at her father's side while his spirit escaped his body, without repeating the proper prayers or incantations for the dead, without shedding a tear for her king and father, Kleopatra left his chamber to prepare for her voyage.

The royal barge sailed deeper into the mysterious land of Upper Egypt, so far away from the Greek city of Alexandria that most considered it another country. Auletes, like most of his dynasty, was often called King Ptolemy of Alexandria and the Two Lands of Egypt. And that was how he had viewed himself—an Alexandrian first and foremost. Yet here was Kleopatra, sailing farther and farther from Hellenism and into the strange country that she hoped would accept her as queen. She stuck her index finger under her dark black wig and scratched her sweaty scalp. She wore the robes of the goddess Isis, the deity with whom the Egyptians associated their royal women. Her sleek linen dress was long and knotted at the breast, with tiered, draping folds. The wig's two long curls snaked down either side of her face. She prayed that she looked dignified and grand, and not like the ordinary Egyptian girl she passed for in the days when she used to run wild in the marketplace. In the morning, without her cosmetics, she still looked so young. She hoped that her heavy face paint, the goddess's elegant robe, and the gold filigree bracelets lining her arms would prevent her girlish face from betraying her. My power is yet so fragile that it must be painted on, she thought.

How strange it would be two weeks from now to attend the king's funeral as if he had just died. She remembered her charades of the past, masquerading, play-acting, but that had been all in fun. Now she must apply skills acquired in childish adventures to her new position—that is, if she managed to hold on to it.

She was presently the sole ruler of the Two Lands of Egypt, although no one but herself, Hephaestion, and the embalmer knew it. But both her father's will and many thousands of years of tradition prevented her from remaining in that position without a male consort, despite the fact that she had effectively ruled alone for the past year. Never mind that her brother was a mere child controlled by an ambitious, meddling eunuch, and that her intelligence had kept the country running while her father whiled away his last days in senseless pleasures. Those were the facts, but would Egypt ever accept a lone female sovereign?

Fate, show me your purpose, she prayed, closing her eyes, the whisper of sultry air from the fans grazing her face. *Why have you delivered me to this point in life without mother or father, forcing me to govern when my father's interests left public affairs, if you were not preparing me for a life that would test my abilities? Surely I am not destined to stand by while preposterous eunuchs and misguided children ruin the land conquered and made the center of the earth by my ancestors? Isis, Lady of Wisdom, illuminate the path that Destiny has cut in all the possibilities of my existence.*

Her meditation was interrupted not by a reply from the goddess, but by an adviser, a retired Greek governor from the Theban region who now served as a diplomat. He sat beside her and began to brief her on Egyptian custom and history. He was sent on the trip by Hephaestion, who had assured her of the man's impeccable understanding of the darker recesses of Egypt's arcane culture, so she listened as carefully as she could to the story of the ancient drama into which she was about to step. She would have to play her part convincingly, he said, for nothing set off the rebellious spirit of the Egyptians like sacrilege. Now, how much did she know about the ceremony? She stared blankly at him. He was entirely gray—of hair, of pallor, of brow. Even his lips had a slate-colored pall. Like the black lips of a dog, she thought and almost laughed.

But out of the grayish mouth came words. Words that she must pay attention to despite the heat that crushed her concentration like a vise. Did she know that the Egyptians believed that the holy bull, Buchis, was the living soul of the sun god, Amon-Ra? That Ra was King of the Gods, who lit the dawn every morning when he opened his eyes? Who shut light out of the world every night when he closed them? He awakens in the east, said the official, whereupon he is dressed by the other gods. He steps into his golden barge that sails across the sky, warming and lighting the earth. At night, he turns into a ram, passing through the Twelve Gates of Night, each representing one hour, and arriving in the underworld to visit his son-in-law, Osiris, god of that subterranean region. But Ra must cross a snake-infested river to get to the land of the Dead, so the clever god turns his barge into a great golden snake to deceive the reptiles. That is but one version of Ra's journey into the darkness to restore the light, the diplomat said, with big stony eyes. Another is that every night, the god wages war on the great serpent Apophis, monster of Chaos, so the peaceful order of daylight might once again prevail over the earth.

"I see," Kleopatra replied, letting the details of the story pass by her, along with the hot, punishing air that hit her face and neck but offered no relief. "What does this have to do with the procession of Buchis?"

"Buchis represents the Great Father, Ra. Your Majesty will ride with the bull in Ra's Sacred Vessel."

"Such a thing exists?"

"Oh yes, it is housed in the temple of Osiris at Karnak, the one so recently restored by your father's generous donation."

"Then I shall be welcome here?" she asked hopefully.

"I would not say that, exactly," he replied, hesitating, raising his thin eyebrows. "They may not welcome you. They never do. But of course they will not *harm* you."

He excused himself to retire to his cabin, for he was no longer acclimated to the desert temperatures, he said, but had been spoiled by the gentler clime of the city by the sea. "Also, Your Majesty," he added, "I am no longer young." She watched him shuffle away, leaving her to her own internal consternation, fueled by Egypt's inglorious heat.

"Osiris!"

The oarsmen invoked the name of the god as they approached his house of worship at Karnak, and Kleopatra shook herself awake, adjusting the wig to make certain it was not crooked. Having fallen asleep for a brief moment, she stood now, holding on to her chair for balance, for she was still lightheaded. The gray adviser rejoined her on deck, and she hoped she would not fall into his frail arms if she fainted.

On the east bank of the river she saw the temple, larger than any Egyptian monument she had ever seen. Surrounded by high stone walls, like most of the temples of Egypt, its precinct reached beyond the sphere of worship and into the community. The tops of its colossal columns and the flat-roofed buildings within the temple complex rose high above the walls. Nearby, there would be shops where local craftsmen sat at looms making Egyptian cloth, where beer was brewed, where any number of local goods were produced and sold by the temple priests. Before the main entrance, a long courtyard ended in a glistening rectangular lake, the sacred waters where, the adviser told her, the priest bathed three times a day to purify himself before entering Amon's inner sanctuaries. From the heart of the temple shot four obelisks, granite phalluses penetrating the still blue sky like a tetrad of insistent lovers. They had been placed in the temple, the diplomat explained, by pharaohs of old, the tallest being the work of one named Hatshepsut, dead now for probably more than a thousand years.

"The top of the obelisk used to be lined with gold to attract the rays of Ra," he said. Of course, she thought, imagining how the sight must have dazzled, shimmering wildly before the mortal eye. Inspiring awe and not a little fear. "Who was this king Hatshepsut?" she asked.

"The Egyptians say she was a woman who dressed like a man and ruled the kingdom," he said. "But you know how they exaggerate. Undoubtedly, Hatshepsut was a man. You can see him on temple walls, naked, as a young boy. He had a beard and phallus. If he was a woman, he was a strange one indeed. He built a mortuary temple over there." He pointed to the west bank of the river, where the hard, dry Theban mountains jutted into the sky. "It is called Djeser-Djeseru, which means Most Holy of Holies. It was once a magnificent tribute to Hatshepsut's power, but now it is being reclaimed by the terrible sands of the western desert." He waved his arm toward the tall, dry slopes. "That is the great valley where the old pharaohs built their tombs and were buried with their riches. It is all gone now, the treasures taken by thieves, and the tombs by Set, the Egyptian god of the desert. To think, Your Majesty, a million people lived here in Thebes in those days. Then it was called Waset. We Greeks named it Thebes. Now, not even eighty thousand live in and around it."

Kleopatra turned her attention to the east bank. Despite the splendor of the temple, the shore was cluttered with rubble. Buildings had crumbled, and new makeshift structures were built right next to the piles of unremoved debris. A civilization on its way out, Kleopatra thought. Once great, once the pinnacle of power, culture, all that was large and bold in the world, and most of it now lay in heaps of ruins. Yet the region still had political sway and could cause great headaches. During the rule of Kleopatra's grand-father, Laythrus, the Thebans had started a rebellion that was responsible for the destruction of many quarters of what remained of the city. Men and nature had been trying to vanquish Thebes for more than a thousand years and yet it still stood, no matter how shabbily, like an old man whose only joy in his waning years was to cause trouble for the young. How majestic were these native monu-ments. She wondered if the civilization that had long ago con-structed these magnificent temples was remarkably different from the lazy, embittered body of citizens now employed by the Greek monarchy.

Though under their domination, this land had yet to be con-quered entirely by the Greeks. The Greeks had layered their civi-lization over the conquered, or so they believed, but here was the Mother Country, still looming so many hundreds of years after Alexander had declared himself its king. Suddenly Kleopatra feared that Hephaestion had miscalculated, that the Egyptians would mock her for dressing as their goddess, for daring to preside over their most sacred ritual. She, the latest, the youngest, of the despised Greek usurpers. Was there any possibility that Hephaestion was in conspiracy with Pothinus? Was she sent into a hostile territory only to be sacrificed? She wondered if the gray adviser standing next to her was indeed an enemy. She scanned him for signs of betrayal, but when she caught him trying to stifle a yawn, she relaxed.

Kleopatra saw two naked children swimming in the river, small ochre-skinned boys frantically paddling their thin arms to get to the shore. On the dock, a small assembly of peasants dressed in color-less linen tunics had gathered to greet the queen: women with flat piles of hay atop their heads, little girls bearing flowers, old people bent from years of farming, all clustered together, a small, animat-ed hive. News of her arrival had preceded her, perhaps through the bureaucratic channels, perhaps by means of Hephaestion's private spies. It was a small crowd, precisely what she might have expected to gather on such short notice. Nothing to fear. Perhaps this ancient ceremony that was to take place in the morning was no longer so important as Hephaestion believed. Perhaps she would be allowed to politely play her role in the pageant and go home.

The barge glided without incident into the small harbor, with uniformed dock workers tying its wet ropes to metal spikes. The humble-looking throng parted, making way for a procession of tonsured priests and priestesses from the temple, their shaved heads bobbing slowly as they walked in a straight line like an army of ants. The temple officials dropped to their knees, the shiny tops of their heads glaring like bright buttons in the sun. The rest of the congregation followed, falling to the ground.

Kleopatra gave her arm to the adviser. She was uncertain that she might walk without help. She was so tired, so dizzy, so hot, that she was not sure she could face even this small, suppliant gathering. As the queen's feet touched shore, a young man, a local Greek-speaking Egyptian official, raised himself. Afraid to meet her eyes, he announced to her staff that he was to have the honor of serving the queen as interpreter. Kleopatra made a demonstrative wave of the hand, indicating that she intended to speak for herself in the native tongue. The man did not understand her gesture, and retreated from her, hands shielding his face as if he thought she was going to slap him.

She had wanted to use her command of Egyptian to placate, but already she had alienated the arrival party. She played nervously with the fabric knot at her breast, rubbing it as if it were a charm. Realizing that she was demonstrating nervousness, she quickly put down her hand. No one spoke, no one met her gaze. Why had she agreed to come here? Without Kinsmen, without friends. Without Charmion, even, who had to remain behind to safeguard the truth of the king's condition. There was no one to come to her aid. The little gray man just smiled at her, waiting for her to act. There was no one on whom to depend. No one but herself and She whose costume she wore. *Speak through me,* she prayed to the Lady of Compassion. *Let my words be yours.*

Finally, she took a deep breath of arid air, so full of heat, so devoid of moisture that she thought she might choke. She felt hollow and powerless, her arms limp, her throat constricted. Though no one looked at her, she sensed their anticipation. Where was her strength now? Hoping her voice would not falter, Kleopatra took another gulp of desert air, and said, loudly and in Egyptian, "I have no need of an interpreter. I shall address my subjects in their native tongue."

The kneeling clergy raised their heads, careful not to meet her eyes. She heard the murmur of surprise work its way through the Egyptians, who wondered if the Greek oppressor queen had tricked them by pretending to speak their language.

Thrill shot like an arrow through Kleopatra's empty stomach. She would be the first to tell them in her own words, without translators, what she wished of them—that is, if the goddess blessed her and she did not faint in the heat.

The chosen representative of the city of Thebes, an elderly priest, quietly presented himself, revealing an arrival gift, a bronze necklace with an amulet of the goddess in the simple draped garment that Kleopatra presently wore. He knelt before her with his head lowered, holding the offering by its ends with his large, wrinkled fingers, presumably so that she could inspect it before she accepted it.

"Rise," she said. She asked one of her attendants to take the necklace and to place it around her neck.

The priest met her eyes. Nothing subservient in the man despite the fact that he had been on his knees before her. "Your Majesty speaks the language of the people?" he asked, wrinkling his polished forehead. "Is this true, or is it the god's magic?"

Or is it a Greek's deception? That's what he wants to ask, she speculated. Did I learn a few words to be polite, or to deceive them into thinking I could speak the language?

"I am the queen of Egypt, am I not?" she retorted, perfectly imitating his inflection. She smiled at her own ability to replicate another's accent, even in foreign languages. She was pleased that she had spent so much time cultivating this particular talent. Not one of her ancestors had done this thing, not Ptolemy the Savior, not his visionary son Philadelphus, not any of their brilliant, power-loving wives, not even Alexander, who brought the nation of Egypt and much of the rest of the world to its knees. Kleopatra let herself absorb the thought just as she let the sound of her voice uttering perfectly formed Egyptian words sink into the consciousness of the people on the dock. They had long ago made up their minds about their Greek oppressors, had long ago learned to hate them, to sabotage them whenever possible, to identify the lot of them as insatiable leeches plumping their bodies and their treasury with the blood of the native people. But her command of their language gave her a power that her ancestors had never possessed—the power to surprise them, the power to woo them. Hadn't she spent years and years alongside the Egyptians in the palace, listening to their talk, learning the contents of their minds? As ill-prepared as she felt for the death of her father, and for this voyage into Egypt's hot, mystifying interior, she realized that she was more prepared to face the Egyptian people than they were to face her, for she was a new breed of Greek queen.

She took her time to speak again, and when she did, she lifted her voice a little, trying to project to the crowd while conveying a levity, an irony that she knew they did not anticipate and would not know how to interpret. Finally, she said, "Naturally, I speak Egyptian. I would think it odd if I did not speak the language of *my* people."

If there was power in knowledge, there was even more power in surprise. A collective gasp escaped the mouths of her audience, though no one was bold enough to look at the queen but one old crone, skin like hide, with a straw doll hanging from her neck, who was startled enough to look up and into her eyes. Before she could help herself, she blessed the queen with an ancient, toothless smile.

The temple of Amon-Ra was two miles down the river from Karnak in the ancient Theban site that the poet Homer called the hundred-gated city. And so it must have been in those long-gone days, Kleopatra reflected as she caught her first sight of the tall columns of the temple in the high, hot early afternoon sun. Their giant diagonal shadows struck a hard geometry across the massive courtyard, where temple sweepers in white turbans looked insect-size against the mammoth, painted pylons. Statues of long-dead pharaohs lined the many entrances of the holy place, their implacable eyes looking west toward the rocky cliffs of the desert. The temple was not twenty yards from the dock, so that as soon as Kleopatra stepped off the boat she was immediately in the sharp shade of these dead monarchs, dwarfed in the pool of their huge outline.

"All of these are Ramses the Great," said the Greek adviser, sweeping his arm. "Or so it is believed. When he became Pharaoh, he erased the names on his predecessors' monuments and replaced them with his own. Almost every statue in Egypt proclaims to be Ramses. And who is to argue with these great slabs of stone?"

Kleopatra was to spend the rest of the day at this temple, undergoing a series of rituals to prepare for the ceremony of escorting Buchis fourteen miles downriver to his home and eternal resting place, the Bucheum. She would sleep that night within the forbidden walls of the shrine to Isis—forbidden to all who were neither clergy nor royalty. A great honor, she was assured by the adviser, only given to the highest of holy persons and deified royalty. Oh yes, very important to stay the night in the shrine, echoed the priestess who greeted them. She asked Kleopatra to dismiss her small entourage, for they were not allowed within the temple walls. Reluctantly, Kleopatra said good-bye to her party, including the gray adviser. The priestess and her attendants escorted the queen inside the shrine, whisking her past an enormous sacrificial slab, upon which she could not help but envision her own neck being slit during the night—a delicate Greek prize offered to the mighty Egyptian god.

The southern temple of Amon, she was told, was the temple of love. Originally dedicated to Amon-Min, the fertility god, the walls of its inner chambers showed the god in all his manly glory, possessed of an enormous, alert phallus. In ancient times, Amon-Ra used to sail down the river in his Sacred Vessel to this temple to be reunited with his harem, whereupon he would impregnate a goodly number of his women. In more recent times, this ritual was reenacted during the Opet festival, which followed the annual flooding of the river, when Osiris was reunited with his sister-wife, Isis. The statue of the god was taken from his shrine at Karnak and placed in a golden boat. After the short voyage to his southern home, he would rest with Isis in her shrine for fifteen love-drenched days before returning upriver.

Kleopatra was charmed by the rituals of the Egyptian religion, but she was so hungry that she could not focus on the details of the stories. She hoped that she would soon be offered a refreshment; instead, the tour continued into the sanctuary of the Sacred Boat of Amon, a chapel built by Alexander to honor his newly adopted divine father, with wall paintings of the Greek king honoring the Egyptian gods. Finally Kleopatra was taken into the Birth Room, where the reigning pharaoh who built it had depicted himself as an infant with Isis as his midwife. Brusquely, the priestess called for the purification rites to begin, which included mandatory fasting until the ceremony of the bull was concluded.

Lightheaded and nauseous, Kleopatra knelt for hours on the thinnest of cushions in the dank air of the inner temple, while the holy men and women read from the sacred books. Every time she sat back on her ankles to give her wretched knees a rest, the presiding priestess, now adorned in a ceremonial wig—a fountain of snaking black curls—gave her an admonishing look, as if to defy her earlier victory with the people on the dock; as if to say to her that she had a long way to go to reach the heart of this country.

Sweaty and starving, Kleopatra was relieved when the priestess announced that it was time to bathe in the holy waters. Wrapped in linen, she was taken to a small pond in a dark room in the temple, where she glided gratefully into the granite bath, only to realize that the waters were not warmed, but kept chilly and still by the stone. Faint, she suppressed the desire to call for help. It would not do to let them know her limitations. She wondered if the Egyptians were taking the opportunity to torture her, to make her pay a singular price for the occupation of many generations of her family; for the luxuries of the Ptolemies extracted from the stooped backs and empty pockets of the native people.

At the end of the long day, Kleopatra was anxious for sleep, which she thought would come easily despite the day's travails. She announced that she would prefer to spend the night with her staff aboard the barge, but the priestess explained that sleeping in the shrine of Isis—so that the goddess might inspire her dreams—was the most important element in the rigorous purification rites. The priestess silently guided her to a small cell with a mattress on the floor and a shrine to the Lady Isis at the foot of the bed. Kleopatra took one look at the makeshift bed and winced at the bedding, longing for her capacious bed at home, stuffed with the softest feathers of young geese. With barely a nod in her direction, the priestess closed the door, leaving her alone in the darkness.

Nothing to distract me from the goddess, she thought as she lay down. Except the worry that one of the Egyptian clergy might sneak in and kill her in her sleep, ridding their nation of at least one Ptolemy. She tried to cast the sinister thought aside, but as soon as she got comfortable, the linen shift began to make her backside itch. She decided to ignore the sensation, but every time consciousness threatened to slip away into night's mysteries, either the lumpiness of the mattress or the harshness of the nightgown, or the precariousness of her political position, brought her back to her waking mind. She knew full well the softness of fine Egyptian cotton, the firmer caresses of carefully woven linens upon the skin of the body. Why were they making her sleep in this agonizing garment?

Craving sleep, yet knowing it would not come, she rose, opening the door slowly, quietly, cognizant of the smallest creak breaking the silence of the sleeping priestesses in their cubicles. Barefoot, Kleopatra went to the goddess's altar. The room was still lit, torches casting a numinous glow in the quiet night. She took a tall candle from the altar and decided to investigate the older parts of the shrine that she had not yet seen. Down a narrow corridor, cold tiles casting a chill into her bare feet, she slipped through an opening and into the shadows. Holding the candle up to the wall, she found herself in a dead stare with a pair of furious eyes. She jumped back, and the candle lit the rest of the stone tableaux. Like a spirit, a woman's figure floated above hundreds of drowning men, heads bobbing frantically above the waves hoping for a reprieve from the female terror lurking above.

A tall shadow rose on the mural in front of her. She let out a small cry, but could not make herself turn around.

"Lady Kleopatra?" came the disapproving voice. Kleopatra turned to find the youthful priestess staring at her with folded arms. "Can you not sleep without the presence of your retinue? I am sorry to have caused you anguish." The formal cadence of her speech palliated any nuances of sarcasm, but Kleopatra gleaned the insubordination and wondered how one so young had the courage to so address a queen.

"The Divine Lady did not allow sleep," the queen said with controlled flippancy. "Perhaps she wished to inspire my waking mind and not my dreams. I would like to ask you some questions about the temple. What is your name?"

"I am Redjedet, named after the glorious queen who gave birth to triplet kings." Redjedet's bald head gleamed against her candle as she made a patronizing bow. Earlier, in her wig of elaborate black curls, she looked older and very beautiful. Now, unadorned by hair, the strong lines of her face, the broad nose, triangular cheekbones, and eyebrows like black arrows made Kleopatra think of Mohama, though the young woman was not so tall. Her square shoulders, though, and her tawny luminous skin, made her seem more substantial than her modest height.

"These murals are astonishingly beautiful," Kleopatra said, wondering if the priestess shared a touch of Mohama's warmer qualities. "What is their meaning?"

"They were carried here by ferry from the temples of the old city of Amarna, which was long ago swallowed into the desert. They are portraits of queens who ruled the Two Lands of Egypt. Like yourself, they also served the goddess, and so have been preserved in her shrine."

"Who is this ferocious one?" Kleopatra inquired, looking back into the angry eyes on the wall.

"Beautiful Queen Nitocris, wife of a pharaoh who was murdered by traitors. She built an underground banquet room and invited the murderers to feast. Then she opened secret flood gates and let the waters of the Nile drown them." Nitocris's head was thrown back, eyes wide with madness and vengeance as she watched her enemies perish in rushing waters.

Kleopatra walked deeper into the dark room, her candle illuminating a different pair of eyes, black, serene, inexorable.

"The great Nefertiti performing Pharaoh's duties," Redjedet said. Nefertiti wore the *uraeus* on her forehead, the cobra that was the sign of her pharaonic powers, ready to strike her enemies. Bare-breasted, scimitar drawn, she held an enemy by the hair, prepared to decapitate him. "The time depicts her life after his death, when she alone was king."

When she alone was king? Kleopatra paused. It was not possible for an Egyptian queen to rule without a male consort. That is why she and all her ancestresses had to marry their own brothers, in imitation of the Egyptian ways.

"Why do you call the queen a king, Redjedet?"

The priestess looked quizzically at the queen, as if impatient with her ignorance. "When the Lady on this wall ruled the Two Lands, there was no king. The king was dead. She had to be king. Egypt needs kings. Egypt needs Pharaoh," she said pointedly.

Kleopatra wondered at this Egyptian logic, hoping that hunger and fatigue had not made her lose command of the language. In many nations a queen may be a ruler, but only in Egypt could a queen be a king. In some parts of this strange land, would they call her King Kleopatra?

Without speaking, Redjedet departed, leaving Kleopatra alone. She hurried down the tight corridor, its sweating stone walls threatening to scrape her elbows, until she followed the priestess into a room that was no larger than a tomb.

Redjedet lowered herself to the floor, holding her candle against a faded painting beneath their feet. Kleopatra stepped aside in order to view its entirety. The cow-goddess, Hathor, suckled a pharaoh, who received Divine Powers through her milk, while the vulture-goddess, Nekhbet, and the cobra-goddess, Buto, watched. The pharaoh wore a long beard and the double crown, red and white, of the Two Lands.

"I do wish I could decipher the old Egyptian letters," said Kleopatra.

"Some say it is enough that you speak to us in our tongue," the young woman said, giving no indication that she consented to the opinion.

"The inscription says 'Hatshepsut is the Future of Egypt,'" Redjedet explained. "'No one rebels against me. All foreign lands are my subjects. Everywhere Egypt bows her head to the King.'"

In one portrait, Hatshepsut was wearing a royal woman's clothing; in the others, the traditional costume of the pharaoh. "Was Hatshepsut not a man?" Kleopatra asked.

"I have heard the Greeks say as much. King Hatshepsut was a woman who ruled the Two Lands. It is said that she married Pharaoh when she was twelve years old. When he died, she became king. Egypt needs *kings*," Redjedet repeated impatiently. "That is why Hatshepsut appears as king in the paintings. In Egypt, there is no queen. There is only Pharaoh's Consort. Queen is a Greek word."

"You are certain of this? That Hatshepsut was a female?" Kleopatra asked skeptically.

"The reign of Hatshepsut was predicted in an oracle made in this very chamber when she was a young girl. It says in the inscription that on the third day of his festival, Amon himself here proclaimed that Princess Hatshepsut would become the ruler of Upper and Lower Egypt. Hatshepsut had the approval of the gods. Only then did she have the approval of the priests of Egypt."

Kleopatra stared at the strange symbols, trying to make sense of their lines and figures. Did the priestess not understand the message she was sending to the queen? That Egyptians, not once but several times, had readily accepted a woman as Pharaoh, without the sanction of a male partner. Was Redjedet aware that for centuries the Ptolemies had followed the Egyptian ways, or what they had assumed had always been the Egyptian ways? Kleopatra wondered if Ptolemy the Savior—unable to communicate directly with the Egyptians—had misinterpreted Egyptian custom. More likely, Kleopatra suddenly realized, he had interpreted the Egyptian customs to suit the ways of the Greek monarchy, in which women, no matter what their royal lineage, were always dependent upon a male consort.

"And you say these pharaohs, these *kings* at one time or another ruled Egypt alone?" Kleopatra asked again, not wishing to reveal her own intentions, but wishing for the priestess to clarify the issue.

"That *is* why they are kings. Egypt must never be without Pharaoh, or the gods will not be pleased." The priestess looked up at Kleopatra. The candle lit her face from below, making deep shadows beneath her eyes. "Pharaoh may not please the *people*," she said.

"But Pharaoh must please the gods. We are here only a short time. The gods are forever."

Redjedet stood, but did not release Kleopatra from her stare. I am being challenged, Kleopatra thought, but I do not know how or why. Is she telling me that the Egyptians will accept me as Pharaoh? Kleopatra stared back at the formidable creature, whose black eyes were as beautiful and as inscrutable as those of Nefertiti. She may not be any older than I am, Kleopatra guessed, but she has exemplary self-possession. The kind of self-assurance it would take to capture the loyalty of the people of the Thebiad and use it to her benefit back in Alexandria; the kind of composure Kleopatra would need to wrest power from her brothers' cunning courtier. The kind of strength she would need to rule a nation on her own.

"Will you pray with me before the statue of our Lady, Redjedet?"

"The one who serves the goddess also must serve the queen," she said coldly, quietly, her first concession to Kleopatra's position.

Kleopatra and Redjedet knelt before the smiling goddess, the Lady of Compassion. Redjedet lowered her head but watched Kleopatra from the corner of her eye.

"I am praying for the abundance and happiness of the Egyptian people," Kleopatra said. Redjedet turned away, unbelieving, and Kleopatra looked into the tilted eyes of the goddess. Straining her neck, she waited until the goddess seemed to invite her prayer, until she was swallowed into the deity's enormous eyes.

"Do not forget to pray for your own family," Redjedet said caustically, erasing any advancement Kleopatra hoped she had made with either the priestess or the goddess.

She felt anger rise, but held her temper. "In my mind and in my prayers, the people of Egypt and my family are one and the same," she replied. She sat back on her heels, turning to the young woman. "I want you to understand what I am saying to you, and I want you to spread the word to whomever you think must hear it. If I have the support of the people of the Thebiad, I promise you, with the goddess as our witness, that I will never act in conflict with that fact. The Egyptian temples shall profit from my rule all the days of my life. So help me Isis."

"As the Romans have profited from the reign of your father and his father and his father?"

Kleopatra had to force back the desire to call for her guard and to have this young insurgent arrested and flogged for insubordination. She summoned as much control as she could on an empty stomach, with nothing filling her insides but anger and fear. Trembling, she kept her voice very low. "If not for my father and his father and his father, you would be nothing but the toy of a Roman soldier's lusts. Only by my father's design can you still call yourself an Egyptian and not a Roman's slave. But we are not talking of my father, who is presently very ill. I am speaking of myself, and of my assurances of prosperity to those who demonstrate their loyalty to me."

"Well then, so be it," Redjedet huffed, with so little conviction that Kleopatra knew she would spend the rest of the night wondering whether she was heard and understood, or whether she would be slain in her sleep.

☞ ⛏ 𓏏 𓆓 𓇋 𓊹 𓐎 𓂧 𓂝 𓈖 𓏭

The Sacred Vessel of Ra was not a slim wooden riverboat, but a golden snake; the bow, his glimmering cobra head, the stern, a sleek, pointy tail. The low arcing belly of the asp sank into the water, which this morning was a dark orange. The serpent's eyes were giant orbs of silver-veined turquoise that focused warily ahead on the shiver of amber that the boat cast through the river at sunrise. Oarsmen were already aboard, as was the bull, Buchis, chosen for the unusual black spots dappling his white back, his horns dipped in gold to attract the sun. He was restrained in his pen by leather straps, but he stood still, his big brown eyes facing the opposite shore as if he anticipated the sight of his new home.

The queen had been awakened long before dawn from her few moments of rest. Sleepless, famished, Kleopatra was sure her body had begun to feast upon itself; her already slight frame had dwindled, and as she waited for her dress, she ran her hands against the hollow of her abdomen, feeling a new sharpness to her ribs.

Now on the deck of the vessel, she awaited the full sunrise, the holy time when she would preside over the crossing of the river. The oarsmen dipped the long golden paddles into the water. Slowly drifting into the Nile, the vessel began its voyage down the river to the small city of Hermonthis, home of the Bucheum. The bull was behind the queen, and she was flanked by the high priest of the temple on one side and by Redjedet on the other, their shaven heads floating through the morning mist like stellar orbs. Neither holy person looked in the direction of the queen but stared ahead at the river as if their glaring eyes lit the path of the boat.

The heavy crown of Isis—a silver sphere cradled by the bronze horns of Hathor, the cow-goddess—pressed against Kleopatra's wig, giving her a headache. She had to strain her neck muscles to prevent the horns from going askew. Surely, she thought, it would take the divine powers of a goddess to tolerate this headdress every day. She stood deadly still, focusing on her posture just as Charmion had taught her to do as a child, until finally the snake glided round a gentle bend in the river, revealing the small cluster of buildings that was Hermonthis. Both the eastern and western banks of the river seemed to have a strange foliage cluttering their shores. Kleopatra had never seen anything like this white flowering brush that relentlessly covered the rich dark lining of the slow-moving river. It was as if she were entering a new country, where nature yielded an unfamiliar bounty.

As the forms on the banks became clearer, her knees weakened and her already shallow breath caught in her throat. No one had prepared her for the multitudes that were present for the ceremony. No foreign species of tree choked the banks, but thousands of people, dressed in their finest white garments, laundered into stark whiteness for the event. Where in this desolate land—uninhabitable but for the fertile strip of life along the banks of the river—had this magnificent assembly come from? Kleopatra wished to be joyous but could not repress the thought that her small escort, following the snake boat in the royal barge, would be defenseless against the crowd should they turn against her. She remembered Redjedet's comment about the Romans prospering from her ancestors' rule. Not so long ago, Kleopatra had been stranded outside the palace gates listening to the Egyptians call Auletes a Roman-lover. She had watched a Roman sacrificed at their hands. She tried not to think of the lifeless face, of the limp body of the Roman Celsius, dead in his own courtyard after killing a cat—a foreigner's gaffe that had so inflamed Egyptian ire. But the man's image kept coming back to her, along with her father's serene death countenance. Auletes would be of no help to her now. No one could help her now. She, alone, was queen.

The inflexible Redjedet registered no surprise at the great crowd that covered everywhere there was space to stand. The priest also did not alter his expression. Their lack of response made Kleopatra shiver.

As the boat sailed closer to the crowd, Kleopatra was relieved to see the uniforms of Greek military governors from the neighboring states, as well as local Egyptian authorities and the banners of Temple Councils from every *nome* representing their districts—though in this part of Egypt, nationality was no guarantee of loyalty. The officials filled special tiered seats that were set up on either side of the river so they could watch the bull-god cross the water to his hallowed destination. Sitting cross-legged or squatting in front of the bleachers were the peasant farmers who had been given a morning's reprieve from working the land.

"We anticipated a count of thirty thousand," the priest whispered into Kleopatra's ear as the boat slowly turned, heading straight for the Bucheum. "But I believe there are even more."

Surely I will not be attacked on this sacred day in front of so many witnesses, Kleopatra thought, holding her breath, searching the face of the priest for any sign of betrayal. But he merely looked ahead, letting the sun warm his leathery brown skin. She eyed Redjedet's red robe, wondering if its ample drapes sheathed a secret knife that might be used against her. She looked again at the multitude—thirty thousand people who despised the Greek tyrants—and fell against the priest's arm. "Are you ill, Your Majesty?" he asked.

"No, it is merely that I did not sleep well," she replied, with more composure than she thought possible.

The small brown priest was not much taller than the queen. He took her arm and leaned very close to her. "The point is not to sleep, Your Highness," he said in Egyptian. "The temple is the place where Pharaoh comes to be united with Ka, his divine spirit—the spirit that gives him Divine Right to rule. If the union is successful, no sleep is necessary." He turned away from the queen, letting his profile soak up the warmth of the sun god emanating from the east, closing his eyes, ending any possibility of conversation.

What was she to think now? She had been put to the test, and she had no way to gauge whether or not she had passed. If Kleopatra had been united with Ka during the night, the spirit had left no evidence. She was exhausted, empty, and terrified. Her stomach ached, her head felt as if a pair of invisible hands was squeezing her at the forehead and the nape of the neck, and her limbs were limp and useless. She could barely hold herself upright. She joined the high priest and Redjedet by turning her own face upward into the rays of the sun god, praying that she, too, would be blessed by his heat. She could think of no source of power to call upon but the Divine Lady, the Lady of One Thousand Names. *Take away my fears*, she prayed.

Instead of grace, she was struck with the worst kinds of visions. Even if she succeeded here and procured the loyalty of the Thebans, to what wickedness would she return? The revelation of her father's death and her treachery in concealing it? The Royal Macedonian Household Troops or the Gabinian soldiers bribed into serving the government of Pothinus and her younger siblings? Hephaestion killed, or, worse, shown to be in conspiracy with the others? She might already be exiled from the city. She would not know until she tried to return. And to what was she returning? A eunuch's dagger in her back? A hostile army at the palace gate? There was no sense in pursuing these horrible possibilities, yet she could not entirely block them from her mind. She took slow, deep breaths to push the fears away, but the hot air threw off her equilibrium even more.

Lady of Compassion, she prayed again. *As Athena, the wise one, came to her beloved Odysseus in many disguises, always sending him the help he needed, mentoring him, befriending him, guiding him through the darkest moments of his journey—come to me now.*

Was my father wrong to make me believe that the gods were good to those who honored them? Lady of Compassion, I am your daughter and this is my journey.

Come to me as Athena came to her devoted Odysseus. Please do not forsake me, Mother of All.

The waters of the Nile, bluer now in the morning light, rushed past the boat like rough-cut sapphires. Feeling the weight of the goddess's crown, Kleopatra balanced herself against the priest as the boat rocked into the harbor. She stood at the steps of the barge, blinded by the sun, waiting for the Egyptian military escort to help her descend, feeling safer once an officer's warm, strong hand was on hers.

Despite the shaft of sunlight and the weightlessness in her head, she discerned the silhouette of the tremendous temple, the smooth pillars, the stark, bleached courtyard beyond, and the cavernous black windows that gaped like dark open mouths. Thousands of people waited at the gates to the sacred place, all dressed for the ceremony, a brilliant blanket of white against the vibrant reds and blues and greens of the painted pylons, with only a narrow path cut through the middle for the procession. Kleopatra realized that she would have to walk past them all. She closed her eyes against the harsh morning light, grateful for the momentary respite of blackness, feeling safety in the moment, and wishing she did not have to move from that spot.

Slowly, her dizziness tapered into clarity. With the escort leading her, balancing her, she descended the boat on a painted golden bridge hooked into the side of the vessel, its other end planted firmly on the shore. Kleopatra took very deliberate steps, feeling the planks beneath her feet, planting each foot firmly before the other, walking into the mass of Egyptians. She heard the bull snort as his hoofs hit the bridge, his step quickening as he descended behind her, and she hoped that he would not break his leather restraints and crush her from behind.

Steadily, she walked on toward the gates of the Bucheum. The shadows of its columns reached her, giving her eyes temporary umbrage from the brutally direct sun. The temple was huge, built high against a dry cliff that housed the mummified bodies of the many hundreds of sacred bulls who had presided over the temple through the ages. Kleopatra was close enough now to see the eyes of the people in the crowd upon her—dark, curious ovals drawn like magnets to her face, but dropping quickly like nuts from a tree if she met their glance. Redjedet walked behind her, next to the bull, and Kleopatra heard the priestess whispering low murmuring sounds to calm the beast against the presence of the people. The guard before her called out to the crowd to widen the path to the temple. Though she knew that this courtesy was for the animal and not herself, she was grateful, for she was certain she would pass out cold if she had to walk through such a narrow passage, through such thick walls of human flesh. Through a body of people who probably did not care if she made it through their ranks alive.

She looked behind her to see if her own attendants were anywhere in her sight, but all she saw was the bull, his golden horns reflecting the god's rays. Oh she was foolish. Why had she come on such short notice, so ill-prepared, so vulnerable? Well she would simply not do it. She was queen and she would prevail. The bull can lead himself, she thought. I am going back to my ship.

A congregation from the temple approached her. Male and female alike, they were costumed as soldiers of the god, their metallic breastplates blinding her, their muscular legs, wrapped tight under short brilliant white skirts, marching toward her. Some wore the headdress of the fierce and warlike lion-goddess, Sekhmet, lips frozen in a snarl, eyes wide and angry. Armed with golden bows and silver swords, they headed straight for their Greek queen, the last eight of them carrying what appeared to be a golden, slatted battering ram.

Kleopatra thought she might run. She turned around, but Redjedet was guiding the lumbering bull forward, blocking any escape. The Egyptian army strode directly up to the queen, its members flanking her sides until she was face-to-face with the giant, shimmering rammer. They turned the cylinder upright and stood aside. It was not a weapon, but a ladder, painted with a sparkling metallic alloy, and hung on both sides with garlands. Kleopatra stared at the strange object until the priest invited her to ascend it. She hesitated, wondering if they were putting her on this podium to stone her to death, or if this was part of the ceremony. She looked everywhere for her adviser, for her guard, but in the brilliant sunlight and in her dizzy condition, she could find no familiar faces. She was aware that all eyes were upon her. In the silence, she could feel the anticipation of the crowd. Praying for a sudden inspiration by which she might save herself, Kleopatra grabbed the sides of the ladder. Buoyed by the firmness of the wood, she carefully put one foot in front of the other as she climbed each small step. When she reached the top, she looked out over the swarm of people.

The sun struck her face like a blast of fire. She clutched at the top of the ladder and shut her eyes so tightly that her face shook, willing away the urge to give in to the heat and faint, when she realized that the sun was not draining her power, but fueling it. She turned her face upward like a flower and let its rays soak into her skin. She shivered as the heat ran down her body like lightning, and she felt so electrified that she let out an inaudible laugh. Laughing inside for the first time in so long, she let her lips fall open so that even her mouth could capture the blessings of the sun.

Suddenly, through her moment of joy, she heard the thunderous voice of the high priest crack the muffled hush of daybreak.

"All Hail King Kleopatra, Daughter of Isis, Daughter of Ra."

The Egyptians began to chant her name. Kleopatra. Kleopatra. The priest cried out again in Greek. "All Hail Kleopatra, Daughter of Alexander, of Ptolemy the Savior, Lord of Alexandria and the Two Lands of Egypt."

Kleopatra heard her name repeated by the crowd, first in the rows of people so close to her that their shadows crossed the steps of the ladder, and then, again and again through the layers of spectators. Soon the name Kleopatra seemed as if it were being chanted from the very walls of the temple, from the ground beneath her, from the banks, both east and west, of the river. She was surrounded by the sound of her own name as it waved through the crowd. It filled every breath of the hot desert air, and she felt embraced by the very sound of it.

Kleopatra, Kleopatra, Kleopatra. Glory to her father.

Slowly, cautiously, Kleopatra opened her eyes. The priests and priestesses, the lesser clergy, the sacred clerks, the officials both Egyptian and Greek, the peasant farmers, the military men, even Redjedet—all but the bull himself—were bowed low to the ground.

Part IV

EXILE

TWENTY

Sons of Marcus Calpurnius Bibulus, welcome to Alexandria."

Kleopatra received the young Romans in the Royal Reception Room favored by her late father, defying Hephaestion's warning not to entertain important foreign visitors without a representative from her brother's Regency Council. Let them find out about the Romans' visit from their elaborate network of court spies, she had said.

Kleopatra had made no changes in her father's government since the announcement of his death, but at that time, the lines of power were drawn. Pothinus the eunuch came into her office as she sat with Hephaestion making arrangements for the king's funeral. Pothinus costumed his late-middle-age girth in voluminous painted robes, adorning himself with more silver-and-gold jewelry than the prostitutes in the Fayum. He clanked as he walked with the four attendants—two scribes, two slaves—who followed him at all times. On this day he was accompanied by a larger retinue that included Achillas, a commander of the army, a clever and handsome man with swarthy skin and white teeth, whom the queen did not quite like, and Theodotus, a small-minded Samian academician with a mouth pursed like old prunes, who now tutored the young Ptolemy brothers. Kleopatra wondered why Samos, the fair isle that gave the world Pythagoras, the genius architect Theodorus, and the fabulist Aesop, had long ago ceased to produce original minds.

The queen gave all leave to sit in her office, relieved when the motion terminated the jingling of Pothinus's ornaments. Ceremoniously presenting her with a copy of the deceased king's will, Pothinus said nothing, but waited for her reaction.

"All Egypt and much of Rome have seen this document, Pothinus," Kleopatra said wearily, returning her attention to the review of the king's death certificate. "Unless you've doctored it, it contains no surprises."

"Your Majesty, we've come to see about the wedding."

"Who is this 'we'?" she asked, looking at Achillas, who had the audacity to smile at her. Theodotus could not meet her gaze. I will have trouble with him, she thought.

"We, the Regency Council of your brother and bridegroom, Ptolemy XIII the Elder."

"By whose authority have you appointed yourselves Regency Council?"

"By our *own*, Your Majesty. *We* are the Chancellor," he gestured to his own person. "And the guardianship of an underage king does fall under our sole jurisdiction."

Kleopatra was well aware of the eunuch's power but was still annoyed when she looked to the Prime Minister, who apologetical-ly nodded confirmation of this fact of the government's structure. She knew she was stalling for time, her mind racing for the best strategy to establish herself as this fop's superior.

"Where are the proper formalities, Chancellor? You burst in upon my grief on the day of my father's death without offering the consolations of the gods? I will see about having such an impious man in my government."

"How unkind of me." He sniffed, sat erect, and composed him-self. "May the gods carry the king swiftly across the River of Death on a winged chariot. May his earthly blessings follow him to the House of Eternity. May he justify himself to Lord Osiris, King of Life-Ever-After, and board the Divine Ship to the Underworld. May his eternal glory forever stay in the memory of those on Heaven and Earth."

"May he safely reach the port of the land that loves silence," Theodotus interjected nervously. "May the Lord of Brightness receive his Divine Essence—"

"Thank you both. May the gods bless you for your fervent prayers."

Achillas suppressed another smile as Kleopatra interrupted them. She saw this and silently cursed his audacity. Was he trying to form some covert alliance with her? These days, her instincts in reading the motivations of others were rarely wrong. She rebuffed his complicit gaze, giving him no indication that she had picked up his signal.

"Your Majesty, may we focus on the interests of the living?" Pothinus asked condescendingly, his small black eyes opaque as onyx beads. "Ptolemy the Elder, heir to his father's throne, has commanded that we set a date for the wedding ceremony."

"We, not just my brother, are heirs to the throne. And I am already queen," she replied. "I assume that is what you meant to say?"

Pothinus said nothing but glared through his eye makeup.

"As for my brother, he wastes no time mourning the dead king, does he? But for myself, even I cannot plan a funeral, a wedding, and a coronation on the same day," Kleopatra continued. "Surely it would bring ill luck to us to set a wedding date on the day of the king's death."

"Nonetheless, it must be carried out according to your father's wishes." Pothinus had slipped into a tight-lipped, terse way of speaking that seemed completely foreign to his demeanor.

Kleopatra quickly took stock of her situation: Already she was queen; her brother required a ceremony to make him king. "You needn't remind me of my father's wishes," she said. "I was at his side at the drawing of the will. We are in mourning; an elaborate ceremony would be in poor taste. According to Egyptian law, a marriage is legal upon the signing of the contract. No public display is necessary. Have the papers drawn up for me to sign. As you are aware, I am of age and require no guardian."

She gave Pothinus a look that indicated that his business with her was concluded, whether he liked it or not.

"You may leave me now."

"Your Majesty," began Pothinus. "I do not know if your brother will accept these terms. He so looks forward to a ceremony. He believes it an important introduction to the people. For myself, I am certain the populace would be heartened at the sight of a boy king."

"Have my brother see me if he wishes to discuss the matter."

"But we are his Regency Council. I think it appropriate that we settle it here and now," said the eunuch.

"You said it was my brother who would protest. Now I find that you are confused. You must learn to delineate between your own wishes and those of the future king."

She dismissed them by returning her attention to the papers on her desk. The noise of Pothinus's adornments echoed in her head long after he left the room. She said nothing.

"You must accept this marriage, even if you escape the ceremony," Hephaestion advised.

"Must I?" she answered. "Must I really?" She had no intention of complying with any of them. Her plans did not include them, anyway, but she was not sure she should say this to Hephaestion, who could be so very conventional when it came to matters of form. Why, she asked herself, should I subject myself to a ceremony that demonstrates that I am aligned with my brother and his council of freaks?

"My Lady, you've had your way with your father these last years. You've all but ruled alone. But your brother has as much legal and blood claim to the throne as you."

"I can handle my tedious, schoolboy, Homer-quoting brother," she said. "But I cannot govern with his Regency Council. I ruled this country with my father and then alone when my father lacked the interest. Why should I share the crown with a pompous eunuch, a dandy general, a second-rate philosopher, and a little boy?"

"In point of fact, the law favors the male heir regardless of age," said Hephaestion, using his most reasonable tone.

"Laws are made by mortals and can be changed," said Kleopatra. There was precedent for solitary female rulers; she had confirmed that on her recent voyage.

"I must warn you that if you will not cooperate with the

Regency Council, you will bifurcate the government. You may threaten the peace your father established."

"Let us not fool ourselves. Neither my brother nor I rule Egypt. Rome and its demands govern us all. I intend to continue my father's policy, which Pothinus entirely opposes. I intend to secure the support of the Romans."

"But why would Rome support you against your brother? That would be against the terms of your father's will, which the Roman Pompey vowed to enforce. What is your strategy for getting their support?"

"The gods have not yet enlightened me," she said. It was something her father might have said. "I can tell you one thing. I will not be manipulated by that lot. Alexandria cannot contain us all."

"In that case, My Lady," replied the Prime Minister, "it will be interesting to see which of you leaves first."

Kleopatra had successfully avoided a ceremony, but custom and Auletes' will demanded the union of brother and sister. The estranged siblings were named husband and wife in all the official documents, and also, in accordance with the will, added "Lovers of Their Father" to their lengthy formal titles. After the documents were signed, Ptolemy the Elder, now King Ptolemy XIII, wielding a ceremonial scepter that he undoubtedly had fished out of the Treasury, leaned across the table and whispered, "May the Immortals bless our bed, dear sister. By the seed of my loins will many Ptolemies spring from your pretty thighs."

She looked into his eyes and saw Thea—Thea without any of the beauty. Kleopatra moved toward him as if she were going to kiss him. Instead, she hissed in his face, "This is the closest that your half-grown cock will ever get to my thighs, little brother. When it grows to full size, you may use it to pleasure your eunuch. That is what he wants—for me to be dead and for himself to be your queen."

The boy king slammed his scepter on the table, making a jagged scar in its perfectly polished surface. Kleopatra's servant, despite many attempts, was never able to entirely erase it.

Kleopatra had the kitchens prepare an array of foods and drinks for the two sons of Marcus Bibulus to sample while she and Hephaestion conducted business with them. It was always a delicate undertaking, entertaining Romans; it was important to appear not only stable, but prosperous. Demonstrating weakness to the Romans was an open invitation for occupation of one's country. On the other hand, demonstrating wealth was an open invitation for extortion.

"Your Majesty, we thank you for receiving us," said the elder Bibulus, a soft, portly young man with a serene face.

"And for receiving us so graciously," chimed the younger brother, taking in the dimension and the details of the great Dionysian reception room. "Our father sends his greetings to you."

"I regret that I did not come to know the eminent Marcus Bibulus during my stay in Rome. My father and I were sequestered in the suburban villa of Pompey and did not attend many social functions." Kleopatra wondered if they knew what she knew—that their father, Marcus Bibulus, had been the laughingstock of Rome. He had been Julius Caesar's co-consul, but was so intimidated by Caesar that he spent his year in office at home. He remained indoors for eight months under the excuse that he needed to search the skies for auspices before he rejoined the government. Bibulus's cowardly ways spawned the joke that the year had marked the consulship of "Julius" and "Caesar." But ineptitude did not seem to do harm to one's political career; now Bibulus was governor of Syria, the lucrative post vacated by Alexandria's greedy liberator, Gabinius.

"My father's province is in a state of emergency, Your Majesty, and he requires your aid," said the elder Bibulus. Though he addressed Kleopatra he faced himself to Hephaestion, who redirected his gaze toward the queen. Kleopatra wondered if the Roman had a difficult time conducting diplomatic relations with a woman, since no Roman female partook in government. No matter. He must learn. She cocked her head to the side, indicating interest in his speech.

"The Parthians have refused to leave the Syrian borders. We have tried to push them into Mesopotamia, but they will not budge. There is no Roman army in the region, so we are all in grave danger. The Parthians, as Your Majesty well knows, are unpredictable and warlike."

The younger brother, perhaps more sensitive to the power arrangements in the room, explained to Kleopatra that if the Romans lost the Syrian province to Parthia, all Rome's allies, including Egypt, would be in danger. "My father requests that you send him the militia left here by Gabinius to keep peace in Alexandria. Your kingdom is presently at rest, while our province is threatened. We know the army is still intact, and it's a Roman-trained fighting force. Can we count on your generosity?"

Kleopatra and Hephaestion exchanged quick glances. The Gabinians, despite the settlements made by Auletes, were still a menacing presence in Alexandria. The greedy mercenaries had quieted their reign of terror upon the citizens, but had not entirely transcended their brutish ways. They made the occasional unreasonable demand upon the throne, and the throne, intimidated by the presence of an army force that bore no loyalty to the ruling order, inevitably acquiesced. Hephaestion knew that Kleopatra would love to be rid of them altogether. But this was also an opportunity to ingratiate oneself to Rome, a chance to alter the balance sheet in terms of who owed what to whom. It would not do to reveal that Rome's request was a boon, rather than a burden, to Egypt.

The queen and her adviser knew each other's minds and said nothing.

"Will you honor the request of my father, and do this favor for the people of Rome?" asked the elder. Kleopatra could see that he was trying to subdue the arrogance in his voice but without much success. The younger was the better diplomat, waiting with a pleasant look on his face, confident that their demands would be met. Kleopatra did not want them to get their way by coercion. Far better that she appear generous and beneficent.

"Prime Minister, do you see any reason why we cannot fulfill the request of our friends? Do speak up if you have any qualms. The sons of Bibulus are our friends and will certainly understand if there is any reason we cannot accommodate them."

"Your Majesty," he said in a tone that she alone recognized as overly earnest and concerned. "We have had peace in the kingdom since your father settled with the Gabinians and ensured their loyalty to the throne. While we are not presently in conflict, I worry that the absence of the Gabinian army might endanger our security."

Kleopatra accepted this news with an affected slump of posture, as if someone had thrown a heavy weight into her lap. She remained silent, pensive. She cast her eyes into the air.

"Your Majesty," said the younger Bibulus in a gentle voice. "I do not speak for the Roman senate, nor for Pompey, nor for the present consuls. But I do speak for my father, who is an honorable man. Should any harm come to you in the absence of your army, my father will immediately come to your aid. He will vindicate you with all the resources of Rome that are at his disposal. And I assure you there are many. By honoring our request, you, like your father before you, will declare to the world that you are a Friend and Ally of the Roman people. Rome does not forget her friends."

How naive was this seemingly thoughtful man? Probably five years older than she, he was still spouting the idealistic rhetoric of his youth. Did he honestly believe what he said? Or was he better practiced at the art of diplomacy than she thought?

The queen looked imploringly at her Prime Minister. "How can we refuse these men in their hour of need?"

"If Your Majesty understands the risks involved and still wishes to proceed, then I shall have to be content and hope for the best," said Hephaestion.

"Go directly to the commanding officer and settle the matter. I will send word that they are to obey your instructions and accompany you immediately to Syria in whatever number and order you demand."

The men bowed to Kleopatra, and then spent the better part of an hour talking to her about the latest intrigues in Rome, and the threat of the upstart Julius Caesar, who had amassed far too big an army to remain benevolent. The elder son spilled his wine on the mosaic face of Dionysus as he recalled the insults his noble father had suffered during his year as Caesar's co-consul. Kleopatra said very little of substance, instead turning the conversation to more benign subjects such as the number of seats in the new theater

Pompey had recently erected in the city and the quality of the most recent productions. They argued gently about whether Roman actors had the grand stage presence of their Greek counterparts. It was an altogether festive end to the execution of a grave matter.

The next morning, Kleopatra awoke to the news that the sons of Bibulus were dead, murdered by two commanding officers who made it very plain that they had no intention of going back to Syria. They were very fond of the life they led in Alexandria, married to beautiful women, enjoying their salaries and doing little to earn them. Why should they march to Parthia to defend a Roman stronghold? Many of the Gabinian soldiers were Syrians, happy to see Bibulus attacked. When the brothers protested that the queen herself had made the order, the officers seized them and slit their throats.

Enraged at the soldiers' arrogance and disobedience, Kleopatra ordered an investigation into the murders. Fearless of her wrath, the two responsible parties admitted to the killings. Without delay, she ordered them arrested, enchained, and sent them to Bibulus for punishment. She told Hephaestion that she was unwilling to sacrifice relations with Rome over two hotheaded mercenaries.

"And what will the Regency Council have to say about these independent actions of yours?" the Prime Minister asked.

"It is plain that sooner or later a dispute between the Regency Council and myself is bound to erupt," she said curtly.

"You seem determined to make that happen," he answered.

"When it does happen, Rome will be the arbitrator between us. The senate might send Bibulus himself to settle the matter. Have you thought of that? He is the Roman official in closest proximity to us. It would not serve me to let those who killed his sons go unpunished." Kleopatra had thought the matter through. Hephaestion was not a man to take risks, so she had to override his advice when she thought it necessary. "Besides, those officers had no authority to murder anyone. How dare they? I thought it wise to make an example of them to the others."

"I believe we are about to get to the bottom of this entire incident," Hephaestion said ominously. "The Regency Council is waiting to see you."

"Must I?"

"Cooperation may behoove you."

"Very well. Send them in."

Pothinus entered, followed by Theodotus, King Ptolemy XIII, who had just passed his twelfth birthday, and Princess Arsinoe, who wore a bracelet on her upper arm that she had inherited from Berenike—a silver snake with an emerald for an eye. What audacity, to wear the heirloom of a traitor into the queen's office. The girl was, however, a striking beauty, resembling Thea in face and in the voluptuousness of her body.

Ptolemy the Elder wore a formal robe that should have been reserved for a religious ceremony. Kleopatra wondered how far the eunuch went in allowing the boy to play at his role of king. Short and pudgy, with small eyes and an excessively round middle, already he had a second chin. With none of his mother's good looks, he resembled his father to a large degree, though without the artistic bent that had made Auletes' quirky personality almost appealing.

"Greetings to you my sister and wife," he said, sneering. The two had not spoken to each other in months. Now he looked at her in what she could only interpret as bitter resentment, though a new smug quality had also settled into his demeanor.

"To what do we owe this visit?" Kleopatra asked. She would have liked to replace the word "visit" with "intrusion," for that was how she felt.

"Regarding the request of the sons of Bibulus for the Gabinian soldiers; regarding the acquiescence of the queen to that request; and regarding the punishment of the officers allegedly responsible for the unfortunate slaying of the brothers. We are here to protest that we were neither informed nor consulted by you." Pothinus made the complaint without taking a breath. He was well rehearsed. Theodotus nodded his head as Pothinus spoke.

Hephaestion was quick to answer the charge. "Her Majesty did not think it an issue grave enough to call a formal committee to discuss. After all, she did not—could not—foresee the consequences of sending the Romans to meet with the officers."

Pothinus ignored him. "We are here to inform you of the serious consequences of your actions that have grown to proportions of which you remain unaware."

"Is that so?" Kleopatra answered before Hephaestion could again intercede. Really, she had no patience for this castrated fop. And she did not at all like Arsinoe's icy stare. "Why is my sister present in this meeting? The princess holds no official office, does she, or am I once again misinformed about the hierarchy of my government?"

The young king raised his robed arm, railing at Kleopatra. He blurted, "She is here because she is my true sister and wife and companion. More than you."

"My dear brother, if necessary, I shall produce the contract of our marriage, signed by everyone in this room save your other sister. Have you forgotten the terms of our father's will?"

"Have *you*?" he screamed. "You think you're so smart."

Pothinus put a hand on his shoulder to quiet him. Theodotus pursed his lips in disapproval of the outburst. Arsinoe fiddled with a lock of her hair as if undisturbed by Kleopatra's challenge to her presence. What do they know that I do not? Kleopatra wondered. And what does the little imbecile mean by "his true wife and companion"?

"Your Majesty, I am afraid we are here to put you under house arrest," Pothinus said, nonchalant, as if he were announcing the most trifling matter.

"What?" Kleopatra jumped to her feet.

"How dare you talk to the queen in this manner?" said Hephaestion. "I am calling for the guard." He moved to the door, opened it, and two sentries walked in.

"Please sit down, sir," said one of them politely to the Prime Minister. "I do not wish to harm you."

"What is going on here?" demanded Kleopatra. She clutched the rim of her desk, suddenly the only solid thing within her grasp.

"Do sit down, Your Majesty," Pothinus said. "There is no need for a display of emotion. We must do this for your own good. You took it upon yourself to promise the soldiers to the Romans. You really should have called a formal committee. That much should be obvious to you by now."

"You are a puppet of the Roman mongrels, just like Father!" cried Ptolemy. "He sold us to the Romans, and you intend to do the same. Well I won't let you."

This time, Arsinoe put her arm around her brother. "We won't let you," she said.

A fury rose in Kleopatra that she wished she could squelch. She could not think clearly. She could not think at all. The blood had left her body and was pounding in her head. Her hands went cold. She tried to get up again, but did not think she would be able to stand.

Hephaestion addressed the guards. "I demand to be told by what authority you are here. This is your queen. You will be punished severely for your actions here today."

"No sir, we are here to protect the queen," answered the man. "The Gabinian soldiers are at the gates of the palace demanding to see the queen. They are furious that the queen sent their officers to Syria for punishment. They are threatening to raze the palace and burn the city. We are here to ensure that no harm comes to the queen or to her supporters."

"As I said, there is no need for hysteria," Pothinus said. "Our actions here today are in the best interests of the queen."

"The best interests of everyone," echoed Theodotus. "At this moment, Achillas is negotiating with the Gabinians to calm them."

"You are just like our father, aren't you?" said Ptolemy. "The people stood before the gates demanding his resignation, and now they do the same for you."

"And who put them there, you little fool?" she retorted. "Can you not see the handiwork of your cunning associates? You are the puppet, my brother, and your master will be your demise." Kleopatra looked at Pothinus, wishing she could slap the cinnamon paint off his cheek.

"Your Majesty," said Pothinus, rising. "You shall be confined to your quarters in the palace until the Regency Council determines that it is safe for you to once again have your freedom. We cannot allow anything to happen to the queen, can we?"

"You are a fool, Pothinus," she said, standing too. "I shall bring you down. I swear it on the memory of my beloved father. He is betrayed by his children even in death." She looked at her brother and sister. "Get out," she said.

"We are going," Pothinus replied, gathering his robes about him, wrapping himself in the starched floral linen as if it were his armor. "We are going, but you are not. The soldiers will be at your door to intercept you, should you try to disobey."

"Just let the soldiers have her!" shrieked Ptolemy, his fleshy young body shaking just like his father's used to do when he was angry. Arsinoe laughed.

"Come, Your Majesties," said Pothinus, putting a protective arm around each child. "Let us leave the queen to her own meditations."

Kleopatra turned her back on them and did not move until she heard the door slam. When she turned around again, the room was empty but for Hephaestion, who sat glumly in his chair, and two sentries, gleaming swords drawn, who blocked her exit.

TWENTY-ONE

He was always tired, yet he rarely felt the need for rest. Caesar pondered this paradox as he stared into the narrow river, swollen to dangerous levels by two days of ceaseless rain. The red, muddy water rushed by him, sweeping time and history past his heavy, bloodshot eyes. He thought of the Greek philosopher Herakleitos, who said that one could never step into the same river twice. If Caesar crossed the Rubicon, neither the river, nor Caesar, nor any of his men, nor Rome herself, would ever be the same.

In minutes, he and his men could be on the other side in Italy, a hostile faction touching home soil. He found it amusing that he was a quarter of a mile and five minutes from waging war on his own country. Would he do it? Would he cross the ever-changing river, leaving behind, once and for all, the world as it presently was known?

Though he was in the company of five thousand men, he felt alone. He was fifty-one years old, older than the oldest of his soldiers. He did not wish to wage war, particularly against his own people, but what choice had they given him? They had *trifled* with him, rejecting his numerous reasonable offers. The senate had recalled two of his legions—allegedly to join Pompey in a campaign against Parthia—and as a sign of his good faith, Caesar had relinquished them. But Pompey did not leave for the east. He remained in Rome, retraining Caesar's men and keeping them in the city, where they might do Caesar harm if he obeyed the senate, laid down his command, and entered Rome as a private citizen.

Did they think he was a fool? Demanding that he disband his legions while insisting Pompey keep his intact? Did they really believe that he would enter the city of Rome without protection, where he would immediately be entrapped, imprisoned, and put on trial for the abstruse constitutional violations they accused him of committing ten years ago?

In a final attempt to negotiate with them, Caesar had sent the tribunes Quintus Cassius and Marcus Antonius to Rome to deliver his very modest demands and his plan for peace. But the senate intimidated the two, refusing them their power of veto, and causing them to leave Rome in a hired taxi, disguised as slaves. A brilliant move on Antony's part, he reflected. Antony, who loved the company of actors, had played his role with relish. When the tribunes arrived at Ravenna and delivered the news that the senate had not only rejected Caesar's plans for peace but had also insulted the Tribunes of the People, Caesar stood before his men and gave a speech.

"They have seduced Pompey and led him astray, through jealous belittling of my merits; and yet I have always supported Pompey and helped him to secure advancement and reputation. In Rome's recent past, armed force restored the tribunes' power of veto. Now, armed force is repressing and overriding it.

"I have been your commander for nine years; under my leadership, your efforts on Rome's behalf have been crowned with good fortune. You have won countless battles and have pacified much of Gaul and Germania. Now I ask you to defend my reputation and stand against the assaults of my enemies."

The men rushed to the cause. He did not have to ask even one man twice.

"To Ariminum!" they shouted, referring to the town across the Rubicon where the tribunes had gone to begin to raise support for Caesar—the first stronghold Caesar might make in Italy if he was to cross the river and thus wage war on his opponents.

He was capable of this, capable of turning against the senate and prevailing, capable of marching these men into any foreign land and obliterating the current regime, even if that regime was the Roman government. All he had demanded of the senators were his rights. He had offered to disband the troops if Pompey would do the same. He wished only to be allowed to run for consul in absentia, as was the will of the people, and to return with dignity to the internal politics of Rome. But the senate would have him stripped of his legions, of his honor, of his rights.

In what dream world did they imagine he would cooperate with them?

"Sir, you hesitate." Asinius Pollio, one of Caesar's few officers who possessed both bravery and a scholarly mind, came to the commander's side, penetrating his solitude. Pollio's polite demeanor and aristocratic features and fair-mindedness were flawed only, in Caesar's mind, by his youthful friendship with the arrogant menace, the poet Catullus. But Caesar had forgiven him that and had spent more than one moment like this, reflecting on the possible outcomes of his commands, in the company of the pensive young man.

Rain came once more, beating down upon the heads of the two men as they stood in the muck of the banks and stared at the racing current of the river. "I am envisioning the horror wrought by the action I am about to take," said Caesar.

"The men do not fear it, sir," Pollio answered quickly.

"I am considering the misfortune the simple act of crossing the river shall have upon all mankind."

"It is true, sir, that Roman soldiers are garrisoned everywhere. If we cross the river, we challenge them all. They must either be seduced or defeated."

"But if I do not cross the river, I must consider the misfortune I bring upon myself. As you know, prestige has always been of prime importance to me, outweighing life itself. If I do not do this thing, I fear I cannot go on."

"As I have said, the men are ready."

This is what it came down to. The misfortune of mankind versus his own misfortune. He could do what the senate demanded— lay down his arms and walk right into Rome and into their trap.

And would all of mankind be better off if he did this? Perhaps it would avert war, but in the long run, why would that be better than war? Men loved war. He would not disappoint those who had supported him and believed in him despite the criticism he had taken in his long and illustrious career.

Who was to say that the fortune of Caesar was not to benefit all of mankind?

"Well then," Caesar said in a low voice. "The die must be cast. Let the game begin."

Kleopatra had not left the palace in two months. She had neither privacy nor freedom, leaving her room only to walk in the courtyard daily with Hephaestion or Charmion, followed by two vigilant guards.

She was prevented from participating in government, but Hephaestion reported to her the local horrors. The previous summer, the true Mother of Egypt, the life-giving Nile, had risen to only half its normal height. Now there was a food shortage throughout the land. Without her permission, the Regency Council issued a decree in the names of both her and her brother that grain should not be distributed in the provinces, but instead sent directly to Alexandria to prevent a famine in the city. The punishment to grain merchants caught distributing corn to the provinces was death. The people were deserting the provincial *nomes* and flooding the capital. Those who stayed behind were either starving, raising armies to revolt against the government, or both. What choice did the Regency Council give them? It protected the interests of itself and of the Greeks in Alexandria while pronouncing a death sentence of starvation on the native people. Kleopatra thought of her loyal supporters in Thebes, who surely believed she had deserted them. There was little she could do.

Charmion would not leave her side, watching with great suspicion as a slave tasted every morsel of her food, and inspecting her linens and garments that came back from the laundry for stealthily placed poisons or potions. Charmion even brought an old Nubian conjurer woman into the palace to tell the queen's fortune daily and to inspect all her belongings for curses placed upon them that might have gone undetected to the untrained eye.

She had not received so much as a letter. She demanded to know what messages had arrived for her from within and without the kingdom, but was told repeatedly that she had received nothing. For the first time in her memory, she was without access to the carefully constructed network of information that her father had established. No letters from Archimedes or Hammonius. Not a word from her contacts in the east. She was certain that the Regents intercepted her correspondence.

After months of cloister and bad news, Kleopatra was brought the message that Pompey's oldest son, Cnaeus, had arrived in Alexandria.

"So I am to be trotted out as if nothing were wrong?" she said to Hephaestion.

"I believe that is correct, Your Majesty," he said. "Perhaps we can use the unexpected visit to our advantage."

Kleopatra winced when she entered the Royal Reception Room where she and her father had passed so many hours. Her squatty little brother was flanked by his Regents. Pothinus wore his usual costume. Achillas had donned formal military attire, and Theodotus, with his wrinkled, disapproving mouth, wore the scholar's robes. What must the Roman think of this cast of characters running the kingdom?

Cnaeus had inherited his father's height, Roman good looks, and imposing air. Kleopatra was grateful that she had taken time with her toilette. With nothing else to do, she and Charmion had perfected the use of cosmetics that enhanced her looks. She still kohled her eyes and applied cinnamon to her lips and palms. But her body slave suggested that they wash the queen's hair with a rinse of henna to enhance its highlights, and cut short ringlets to frame her face, while the rest of her mane was swept into a graceful knot. With these improvements, her good features—the almost green eyes, the thick dark hair with hues of red, the lush full lips, the regal cheekbones—were brought forth, while her mannish strong nose seemed to recede. She wore simple, elegant gowns that highlighted the pleasing curves of her figure—now that she had finally acquired them. Unable to ride her horse every day, she had put on a few pounds, and they had landed in just the right places. She took pride in her new figure. She liked to set off a dress of exquisite fabric with long strands of pearls or chokers of dazzling emeralds. She had mixed for herself a special perfumed oil, making the chemist swear to keep the ingredients a secret. Whereas she had previously used artifice to hide her youth, now she used it to enhance her natural glamour. Though she was not beautiful, she knew that she was more than just a little bit appealing. She noticed now that eyes dared to linger longer on the person of the queen, and that the slightly uplifted noses of those she passed followed her as she walked by, as if doubly entranced by not only the loveliness, but also the unexpected fragrance of a beautiful flower.

She saw an appreciation of her appearance in the eyes of the Roman. She looked at her brother, who appeared shocked at her sudden sensuality. She saw that she had taken them all by surprise.

"How you resemble your father," said the queen, allowing the Roman to take her hand, looking charmingly into his eyes, and speaking to him in Latin, which she knew annoyed both her brother and the regents. "He is well, I hope?"

"He is as well as can be expected under the circumstances," answered the Roman.

"What do you mean? He is not ill?" asked Kleopatra.

Cnaeus waved away a tray of food and drink that was proffered. Kleopatra remembered that Romans sometimes did this to illuminate their stoical constitution, particularly in times of gravity. Cnaeus's bright face turned solemn. He stiffened and addressed the small assembly. "As allies of my father, and to repay him for his gracious hospitality of your father, the late king, in Rome, and for his tireless efforts to restore this monarchy to your family, my father asks that you furnish me immediately with a fleet of ships and ground forces to aid Rome's war against the renegade Julius Caesar."

"Rome is at war with Caesar?" Kleopatra asked. "We have not heard this news. Or have we? How is it that we have not heard of this?" She looked to the others in the room. They reacted with a polite veneer of interest, as if Pompey's son were updating them on the health of distant acquaintances.

"Your Majesty, as all the world knows, Caesar's goal is complete tyranny. The man is crazy. He has turned his back on the Republic and the Constitution and has become his own man," he said, indignant. "The senate came almost in its entirety to my father and begged him to defend the State against Caesar's menace. My father is the only power to stand toe-to-toe with Caesar, the only commander with an army that can defeat Caesar's legions. They are mad with their years of victories, you see, and in Caesar's thrall."

Pothinus and Theodotus began to mutter sympathetic words to Cnaeus, condemning Caesar's actions and offering their unqualified support to Pompey. Pothinus spoke up. "The queen remembers so fondly your father's generosity to the Royal Family in Rome. Does she not? Your Majesty?"

"Oh yes," she answered, realizing that Pothinus was avoiding a commitment of ships and men by making small talk. "I was just a girl, and your father let me ride his horse, simply because I wanted to."

"I am acquainted with the story, Your Majesty," he said, bowing low to her, lifting his handsome face and giving her a lingering smile. How did these Romans keep their large and dangerous-looking teeth so white? she wondered. Was it that the twins who founded the city had been suckled by a she-wolf? She did not know if Cnaeus was trying to seduce her or win her support, or both. She returned his smile, but asked herself: If Pompey is so mighty, then why has his son fled to Alexandria to ask for Egyptian support? One would think multiple Roman legions enough to defend Italy against a renegade.

"And how goes this war?" she asked. "What is the progress?"

"My father has left Italy to regroup his armies in the Greek lands. He awaits reinforcements from the governor of Syria. Caesar now invades Spain. He intends to take it away from the Roman people and have it for his own."

So, in the span of a few months, Caesar had ejected the mighty Pompey from Italy and had already turned his attentions to subduing the rest of Rome's provinces—that is, those he did not already control. And this was but March. "And what of Rome? Who controls the city?"

Cnaeus looked uncomfortable, as if he did not wish to be interrogated on these matters. "Caesar marched into Rome. On his
orders, his men broke open the temple of Saturn and took the treasury against the veto of the tribune Metellus, who attempted to stop
the crime with his own body. The renegade has confiscated the
entire Roman treasury for his war against his own country. He made
a speech threatening the senators, saying that if they were too timid
to govern with him, he would simply govern by himself. Then he
made off with the money, leaving his henchman, Antony, in charge
of the city."

"Dreadful! Treasonous!" Pothinus interjected.

"So Caesar has taken the city?" Kleopatra asked.

Ignoring the question, Cnaeus said, "Caesar underestimates my
father's power. It was foolish of him to let my father escape to
Greece. Pompeius Magnus shall emerge victorious from the eastern
lands just as he did thirteen years ago." Cnaeus seemed very protective of his father, a condition the queen could appreciate. "We shall
surprise Caesar if he is foolish enough to think he can win the war
on Greek soil."

Pothinus composed himself, putting on a pious air. "May Pallas
Athena, whose shield is thunder, protect your father in this war!
Tonight at dinner we shall give count of the number of our ships
and soldiers to be placed at your command."

Expressing gratitude and relief, Cnaeus left them.

"A magnificent person!" Pothinus exclaimed. "I don't see how we
could turn him down."

"Doing our own little part to help Rome destroy herself!" giggled Theodotus. Ptolemy joined his laughter. Achillas remained
aloof, eyeing Kleopatra all the while, waiting for her response. She
could not imagine what, if anything, was their plan. If the fools had
not cut off her communications, she would have been prepared for
this.

"Let us not hasten to the aid of Pompey," Kleopatra said. She
reminded them of Pompey's propensity toward inaction, remembering him fleeing to his garden as Cicero stood screaming outside
his gates; remembering the two crucial times he refused Auletes support.

"My dear girl, we have no reason to aid Pompey save that we were so politely asked. What care we if Pompey or Caesar prevail? If we help Pompey vanquish Caesar, so be it. Had Caesar asked first, I suppose we should have given him what he wanted, too. Though I dare say Caesar, at what—fifty years of age?—wouldn't cut the figure this young Pompeius does."

"It is insane to choose sides in this war," she said, feeling the impatience creep into her voice. "Did you not hear what he said? Do you not gather that Pompey is losing the war and that, in desperation, he sent his son to Egypt to secure reinforcements? Do you not understand anything of Roman politics? We must not choose Pompey over Caesar. If Caesar wins, he shall punish us. He shall bring us to our knees, no better than if we were barbaric Gauls."

"What do you know about Julius Caesar? You don't know anything. You just think you do," shouted Ptolemy.

Kleopatra did not even look at her brother, but addressed his regents.

"It is said that Caesar is lucid beyond ordinary human capacity, yet at times he falls to the ground in brief fits of madness during which he is touched by the gods. Then, minutes later, the gods miraculously release him and he is Caesar once more. How can you dream of challenging a man like this? If we bet, we must bet on Caesar. Already he has run Pompey out of Italy."

Ptolemy jumped from his chair and stood to face her, looking like a small version of Auletes, eyes bulging and fat face turning red. "Just because you went to Rome with Father doesn't mean you know everything," he sputtered. "We ought to throw you to the soldiers like they asked."

"What would you have us do, my brother?"

"We ought to do what Pothinus says. We ought to give Pompey what he wants so that he and Caesar can annihilate each other. If you weren't so bewitched by Rome, you would see that that is best." He sat down next to Pothinus, who smiled at his young charge.

Kleopatra laughed to herself. Undoubtedly the eunuch envisioned himself under Cnaeus's strong body that very evening, as if a good fuck was reason enough to align the nation with the party who is losing the war. To Hades with the lot of them.

A moment of prescience descended upon the queen, gifting her with the singular, obvious solution to her problems.

"So be it," she said and she left the room, leaving them with their mouths agape, stunned at her compliance.

The queen had not dined in the banquet room since the Gabinian uprising, but that evening she was escorted to dinner to give the illusion to Pompey's son that all was well in the palace. Cnaeus was not fooled by the little family gathering. Despite the place given to him between Theodotus and Pothinus, he insisted that "the young queen appears lonely," and seated himself next to her.

"What is occupying the mind behind so beautiful a face?" Cnaeus wished to know.

Would that she could have told him: Possible exile. Famine. A revolt against her brother. Civil war. Ptolemy against Ptolemy while Roman fought against Roman.

Kleopatra tried to maintain the flirtatious conversation the Roman wished to engage her in, all the while wondering how long she would have to spend at dinner before she could slip away to the Prime Minister's rooms and find out if he had recruited a small militia to sneak her out of the city.

"Your Majesty, please forgive my insolence, but I must know something," Cnaeus said, leaning very close to her, looking down the front of her gown and speaking his warm breath into her ear so that no one might hear. "How does a lovely young queen endure married life with a little boy husband? I do not understand your customs. I know the Greek affinity for very young males, but surely a woman, a formidable woman like you, needs a full-grown man in the marriage bed?"

He had all the qualities of his father that had made her blush as a girl. The size, the broad shoulders, the inviting eyes, the voice that soothed and enchanted. She let his question linger while she wished with all her heart that, at that moment, she was anyone but the queen of Egypt. She would have liked to forget duty and position and throw herself upon Cnaeus like the commonest of whores. But it was not to be. She reminded herself that after dark, her only illicit meeting would be with those who were risking their lives for her sovereignty.

"The marriage of brother to sister has always been the custom of the pharaohs, and my ancestor Ptolemy adopted it to please the native people. The Egyptians believed the pharaohs to be gods, with deified blood that could not mix with that of ordinary mortals. It seems strange, I know, but my family has successfully followed the tradition for almost three hundred years. I believe that when my brother comes of age, we will make many children together and live quite happily."

She wondered if she sounded convincing. All the while, her mind raced for any possible advantage in aligning with the elder son of Pompey. Was there any bargain she might seal in lust that might benefit her? It was tempting to use one so close to a source of power. But she simply could not convince herself Pompey would prevail against the intriguing Julius Caesar, as much as she desired to lean slightly forward and offer her lips to the glorious-looking man who sat beside her.

She took one more long look into the eyes of Cnaeus and, regretfully, excused herself to her chambers, where Charmion was packing her cosmetics.

"I want you to reconsider making this arduous trip," Kleopatra said. "This is no elegant exile at Pompey's mansion. You and I both know that you are a lady of refinement with no aptitude for rough travel or outdoor living. We will endure plenty of both. You will be guaranteed neither comfort nor safety."

"What?" Charmion said in a low, indignant voice. "I thought you cared for your Charmion. You wish me to stay here and receive Arsinoe's knife or Pothinus's poison?" She rose to her full height, which was not tall, but Charmion's Greek carriage and mien made her more formidable than her height.

"I do not want you to stay here, but I will send you somewhere— Greece, for example—until it is safe for us to return to the city."

"And who will see to your diet? Who will see to your wardrobe? At a time when you need appear most queenly, do you expect slaves and soldiers to care for your linens? To curl your hair? After a week without my care, you'd look like a ragged foot soldier. You'd be frail and thin for want of the proper foods. I know you. I raised you from a girl, remember?" Charmion, only eleven years older than the nineteen-year-old queen, still assumed the role of the stern mother.

A guard interrupted them to inform the queen that Achillas was outside her chambers, requesting a private audience. She avoided Charmion's face so that they would not exchange alarming looks that might alert the guard. She could not think what to do. To deny him would be to arouse his suspicions. To admit him would pose the danger of being found out. Did he already know her plan of escape? Had she been betrayed?

"Tell him I shall meet him in the antechamber," Kleopatra told the guard.

She realized that she had to calm herself, to transport herself, somehow, to a different state of mind, or else her nervousness would easily give her away. She needed to don a cloak of implacability. She sat quietly and closed her eyes, forgetting even the presence of Charmion. She pictured herself calm, revealing no thoughts and no emotions. She prayed to the goddess. *Lady of Compassion, let me wear this mask. Let it descend over my body like a sheath. Allow me to project only sobriety where I feel anxiety. Protect me from the suspicious and I shall continue to honor you now and all the days of my life.*

Still she felt nervous as she entered the room.

Mercifully, Achillas stood alone in the antechamber and not, as she had feared, with a guard to take her away. He wore formal military dress. Despite the severe attire, he was all perfume, oils, and smile. A beautiful man, no doubt, but so different from the Roman Cnaeus. Though he was a warrior of the first class, he had a certain Greek delicacy. He had been raised by his father, a Greek officer, and it was rumored that his mother was an Egyptian prostitute. Seeing him, Kleopatra had the thought that the Greeks and Egyptians should perhaps intermarry with more frequency, so exotic and lovely were their offspring. She gave him leave to sit but he remained standing. She sat, and he began to pace, circling her. The effect was disconcerting, sinister. Finally, he knelt before her.

"Your Majesty, I was very disturbed by your brother's outburst yesterday."

"Which outburst was that?" she asked, staring into his thick-lashed eyes.

"His threat to allow the soldiers to defile you. As long as I am in charge of the armed forces of Egypt, no harm shall come to you by my troops. I believe we should work *together*, you and I," he said.

She was torn between feigning appreciation for his gallantry and letting him know that she was not fooled. This was a lesson she was still struggling with: refraining from too quickly revealing her perceptions. What did he want? She said nothing.

"I've come to offer you my protection," he said. "I believe you need it." Still he remained on one knee, closer to her than protocol allowed. "You *are* in danger," he added.

"Not if you have assigned yourself to be my protector," she answered sweetly. "Then I am perfectly safe, am I not?"

"I see no reason why we cannot consider ourselves partners," he said.

"What would be my role in this partnership?"

Achillas put his hand on her knee. She stiffened, but made no move. She was not tempted to succumb to this man as she was with Cnaeus, but she did want to play out this scene so that she would know his intentions.

"To be my *friend*." It was a carefully considered and articulated word.

"Is my brother your friend?" she asked innocently.

"He is. But you would be a different kind of friend, a more intimate friend."

She remained detached from Achillas's seductive eyes, his hand on her knee, his coy smile, his gleaming white teeth that seemed ready to devour her. She swallowed her fear, calling again on the grace of Isis. These things must not be hurried. She could not be certain that he was not acting as a covert agent of Pothinus. She must repel him so that he would stay away from her long enough for her to escape.

"You are proposing that we become lovers. In exchange, you will protect me from my brother giving me to your army as if I were a slave whore. Is that correct? Instead, you would have the queen of Egypt as *your* whore?"

"I see that Your Majesty is caught by surprise and needs time to think," he said, standing. For one brief moment, she regretted not aligning herself with Cnaeus. She could have had him slay this insolent creature. Perhaps she would do it herself when the time came, after she returned to the city with the army that she intended to raise in the provinces where her brother and his regents were starving the people. When she rose up against Ptolemy and his monsters, she would remember to kill this one first.

"I shall come tomorrow night, Kleopatra. May I take your hand?"

"As you wish," she said. Perhaps if she gave him hope, he would not return until the appointed time, when she would be long gone.

He took her hand, turned it to face him, and kissed the inside of her palm, working his fingers up her arm until they stroked the flesh of her interior elbow. Then he put his mouth to it, kissing, sucking, biting. It was not unpleasant to her, though she did not wish it to be enjoyable. He discerned from the tiny gasp that she allowed to escape from her mouth that she was favorable to his advances.

"Tomorrow night, then? Will that be enough time for you to make a decision?"

"We shall see," she replied coyly.

"May I taste your lips?" he asked.

She feigned maidenly fear but did not reply. He leaned toward her face. She did not stop him. Gently he kissed her, letting his tongue linger on her lips. "Tomorrow, Lady." She watched his cape float after him as he left.

Charmion rushed in when she heard him leave.

"It appears that men are standing in line to relieve me of this menacing condition of virginity," Kleopatra said, catching her breath and projecting more nonchalance than she felt inside. "Little do they know that the god has already done so."

"He attempted to seduce you?" Charmion asked, incredulous.

"And he is coming back tomorrow evening to complete the act. If I join with him, I will be at his mercy. He will be free to report my adultery to my brother. If I fail to escape tomorrow, and I refuse him, he will surely find a way to destroy me."

Kleopatra picked up a hand mirror that Charmion had not yet packed and regarded her face. Her lips had filled out, becoming, apparently, the kind of lips men would like to kiss. She was nineteen years old, and ready for love, perhaps too ready. She worried that her desire would eventually overcome her good sense. She must learn more restraint, but she could tell that it would never come easily.

Kleopatra awoke to the murmuring bass tones of men's voices. She lay dead still. From the moment she left her bed and proceeded with this deceit, she would be a rebel, a renegade—a Caesar. Would that she had his reportedly dauntless disposition and indubitable confidence.

She calculated that it was less than one hour before dawn, the appointed time when the guard outside her chamber would change, replacing the two sentries with Hephaestion's men. She heard the rustle of fabric; when her eyes adjusted, she saw that Charmion was already awake and loading the remainder of their personal belongings into large laundry baskets. Quickly, Kleopatra left her bed, splashed water on her face, shed her fine silk sleeping gown, and slipped into a simple cotton shift. Without a word, Charmion put an Egyptian wig over her own head, adjusted it, and then settled one atop the head of the queen. Far from the mane of virgin girls' hair she had worn in Thebes, these were cheap horsehair wigs purchased at a stall in the marketplace, made for those who could afford no better.

The door opened and the guards let in the women who would accompany the queen into exile. Large women, capable of bearing whatever hardships might be encountered, they hoisted the baskets atop their heads and left. Kleopatra took a final look around the bedchamber of her childhood, the habitat of all the days of her life. Would she ever see it again? She tried not to think of all the things she was leaving behind. Why bother with material goods? If she remained, if she perished at the hands of Pothinus and her brother, these same belongings that she cherished would decorate her burial chamber. She turned her back on all she knew and walked out of the room.

The halls were dim and silent, the day still hidden behind night's dark sheath. They walked without lamps, unwilling to risk awakening the household. A squatting Egyptian hall attendant raised his head. He murmured, "Getting an early start, eh?"

The queen herself answered, in as humble an Egyptian dialect that she could muster. "It is the day I am allowed to visit my mother, but only after the queen's laundry is done."

He smiled knowingly and went back into his predawn musings. Kleopatra's blood quickened, remembering the days of her adventures with Mohama, when she had slipped by these same servants and successfully freed herself from the boring rituals of court life. She felt her fear turn into excitement. She was practiced at the art of escape, a master of the skill. But Charmion, who neither engaged in the art of disguise nor spoke Egyptian, walked tautly by her side, and Kleopatra wondered if Charmion's imperious posture would be the thing that gave them away. The two women walked arm in arm through the kitchens and out the door that led to the loading dock as the early morning staff coaxed the fires of the ovens so that they might begin the day's work.

Outside, in the darkness, Kleopatra did not see any members of her staff and retinue. The rear entrance of the palace was deserted except for a small caravan of merchants delivering food and supplies to the kitchens. The confidence drained from her body like melting ice. Which wagon was she supposed to approach? Where was Hephaestion? Where was her escort? Had they deserted her at the last minute?

The guard at the top of the platform eyed them suspiciously. Kleopatra did not wish to meet his glance. She could not be certain that he was not the same soldier who had rescued her from the mob on the day she and Mohama had gotten caught up in the incident of the murdered cat. Almost eight years had passed since that day. Surely the guard had moved on to another post.

Her eyes did not adjust as quickly as she would have liked, nor had the sun begun its ascent. She grabbed Charmion's hand as if she were still a little girl. Out of the darkness, a large man grabbed her elbow and whispered for her to follow him. She could tell by his cloaked physique that he was older, perhaps as old as her dead father would have been. Sixty, perhaps. Stout. Greek. He wore a low-brimmed hat. He led her to a wagon and helped her and Charmion into the rear seat. Soft hands.

The soldier on the platform called out. "Where are you going, girls?" A friendly, flirtatious question.

The man quickly answered, "I am giving them a lift. They wish to buy the first fish brought into the market today. By orders of the eunuch Pothinus, who adores fresh cod."

The soldier laughed and waved them on. The other wagons, five in number, with horses and camels now attached, pulled in line. So this was her party. She herself had not suspected a thing.

The old man waved to the guards as they passed through the palace gates. The wagons followed. How would they pull this off, she wondered, leaving the palace walls with so many of the possessions of the monarchy—livestock, wagons, and, presumably, copious supplies of food and weapons hidden under the blankets that covered the wagons? Yet no one stopped them, no one questioned why a caravan was leaving the palace at dawn.

"Hello, Kleopatra," said the old man in a taunting voice, reviving her fear.

"Hello," answered the queen, puzzled. He sounded so familiar, and yet she was certain she did not know him. The man removed his cloak and hat, turned around, and looked at her.

"Hammonius!" Her old friend, her father's faithful man, his most loyal and crafty agent. "Oh, I am so thrilled to see you. How is it that you were able to disguise yourself from me?"

"You were not expecting me. And it is dark. I would not have recognized you save that I was told to expect you and a lady slightly smaller than yourself, the unforgettable Charmion, to be at that door at precisely this hour."

"No wonder we had an easy escape," Kleopatra said.

"That's right. The guards are accustomed to seeing my wagons deliver goods to the palace."

Kleopatra dared not look back at the palace. She looked ahead. The sky cracked open at the horizon, giving birth to an unfathomable luminescent pink sky—auspicious weather for their cause.

"Dawn flings her glorious robe across the earth," said Kleopatra, her spirits lifting with the sun's golden orb that peeked over the white buildings of the city.

The caravan exited the southern gates of Alexandria, quiet, unharmed. The soldiers hidden in Hammonius's wagons emerged from under the tarps and raised their faces to catch the warmth of the morning sun. Outside the city, a small troop of foot soldiers and cavalry fell in with them. Words of encouragement poured from those who had chosen to cast their lots in with the queen. Kleopatra removed her disguise, standing to greet all who joined her.

Hephaestion, emerged from a wagon and now on his horse, had done a magnificent job of spreading the word of the queen's defection. It was a small band of soldiers and supporters, but it was a splendid beginning.

Hephaestion trotted to the queen's wagon.

"Are we prepared?" she asked.

"We have good men with us, and good men who have remained behind and will work for us on the inside."

To the south, at the dock at Naukratis, a ship awaited Kleopatra and her supporters. Hammonius left them, making plans to communicate with the queen regularly. "You shall hear from me, my dear girl, my darling Majesty. I shall send Archimedes to you at the appropriate time. He is with me always, now. I have ruined his life by introducing him to the business of export."

"I am very sad not to see more of my cousin at court," Kleopatra said. "Is he well? I am certain that his letters to me were intercepted by my brother's monsters."

"He is well. But I hate to go anywhere with him."

"Why?"

"Because all the ladies gather around him and ignore me."

"I would like us all to return to happier times," said Kleopatra, remembering the days when Hammonius and her handsome cousin would come to court and regale them with stories of Roman intrigue. "But I understand his reluctance to truck with the prevailing order."

"He was your father's man. But he is your Kinsman, and now that you require his services, he will be your man. Do not worry. He has become rather a genius at gathering information. Almost as good as myself. But not quite so. Not yet."

Kleopatra stood at the ship's plank and greeted her supporters, thanking each one for joining her. As they set sail for Thebes, Kleopatra descended to her quarters to check the condition of her belongings. She held her breath as she opened the latches of her trunks. Relieved, she saw that everything was in its place, which reinforced that those to whom she entrusted her life were unconditionally loyal. No one but Charmion, Hephaestion, and the queen herself knew of the treasures hidden in her personal luggage. She had learned from her father at a very early age never to leave home without ample money.

On the river, Kleopatra rose early. In the darkness of her cabin she would light a small saucer of oil and carry it above to watch the soft commencement of sunrise on the water. She liked to take the fresh morning air before the sun's punishing heat beat down upon the boat like a metal worker at his trade, forcing her back into her quarters where she would lay languid and depressed until the heat lifted. In fact, she found that her early mornings on the deck were necessary to survive the rest of the day.

Hephaestion often joined her, but this morning she was alone except for a few solicitous members of the crew. She had encouraged Charmion to remain below so that she might have this time to reflect and pray, and to strategize. She longed for her bedroom at home, with its windows opening to the fragrant sea air from the Mediterranean, and for Alexandria, with its palm trees, its parks, and its temperate climate.

Neither the queen nor her Prime Minister had been prepared for the extent of suffering that drought and famine had wrought upon the people, who depended on the annual inundation of the Nile when she blessed the crops with another fruitful layer of silt. This year the life-giving waters did not come. The Mother of Egypt, who nursed those fecund shores with her milk, this year withheld nourishment from her children. And the children of Egypt, confused, hungry, frantic, unable to imagine a way to survive other than the one they had known since time out of mind, went into a panic.

Everywhere in the countryside, people had deserted their villages. The mud houses on the riverbanks, once inhabited by farm families, were left cracked and empty, drying to dust under the eternal pummeling of the sun. Priests of some of the Egyptian cults had fled to Alexandria, leaving their shrines and temples unattended. Fellahin, starved, angry that their own portions of the very crops they had raised were taken from them and sent to feed the city population, had taken over the temples and other holy buildings, taking for themselves and their children the meager provisions left by the priests.

When the queen's boat stopped at the villages that lined the river, Kleopatra encountered their anger, for to them she was just another of the well-fed Greeks for whom they presently starved. Everyone knew that the government controlled the Nile. Its river workers and engineers measured the height of the water and kept record of it, built the canals that brought water to the crops, manned the waterwheels, the dams, the dikes. Some people believed that the government of the Ptolemies was purposefully diverting water from their lands. Kleopatra did not shy away from the people's wrath but talked to them in their own language and told them to be angry at those who levied the edict. Sometimes she met with success, leaving the village with the loyalty of whatever local regime had remained. But sometimes she failed. One man had looked her in the eye and said, "When I am fed, I will have the strength to direct my anger with more wisdom."

The native people who lived along the river had resorted to trickery and to the old forms of magic to provoke the gods. Even before sunrise, Kleopatra heard drumbeats imitating thunder, tormenting the deities into sending the rains. She had seen old men gather dust from the temple floors to scatter over their dying crops. "They must feed the frail ones who have been left behind," said the only priest who remained at a village they visited. "The young and the strong have left for territories where they believe there is food to be had."

This morning, the light of the ascending sun revealed a tableau of human misery. Women, pale and thin, bathed naked in the river, an ancient way to entice the river gods to make the waters rise. In the fields, emaciated peasant women—also naked—manned the plows of their crackling brown fields, pausing to stretch their arms to the sky, offering whatever was left of their bodies to the unseen Almighty. The queen wondered what god would succumb to seduction by these bony, sorrowful women. Small groups of fellahin and their children gathered in the shallow waters of the river to give whatever pathetic offerings they had to the river god. A little boy bravely flung his wooden toy into the river. A woman threw ears of discolored corn to the silent god, who had no inclination to heed these abjurations. Others bared their chests to the sky, beating their pendulous breasts, begging the sympathy of the mother goddess, from whose abundant fertility all life sprang forth.

Kleopatra could endure the pantomime of tragedy no more. She put her head in her hands and hid her eyes from the sight of the wretchedness.

"I am depending on the loyalty of a starving and dying people," she said to the tall man who appeared at her side. "If I wish to fight my brother with the bones of the dead, this is where I should raise my army."

"Today we will reach Thebes," said Hephaestion. "And you will see your friends at Hermonthis."

"I'm afraid we are going to find the temple of Sarapis deserted, the sacred bull with his ribs showing, and the people gone."

"Let us pray that it is not so," said Hephaestion. "The high priest Pshereniptah has promised us shelter and all of his power to add strong men to our army."

"If there are strong men in the Thebiad, they are the only ones left in Egypt," said the queen cynically.

When Kleopatra landed at Hermonthis, no phalanx of healthy, hairless priests lined up respectfully to meet her. Instead, the crowd gathered at the dock hurled angry words and epithets as the royal ship slid into harbor. Kleopatra saw the fists waving in the air like flags and dropped her head into her hands.

"Another angry mob, waiting to indict me," she said wearily to Hephaestion. "Another crowd to be won over. I am too hot and too tired. Perhaps we should wait until dark and then dock."

"Look again, Your Majesty," answered the eunuch. "Their shouts are directed at that Egyptian man, the one who appears to be the supervisor."

The uniformed Egyptian bureaucrat watched stiffly as workers wrapped in layers of white gauze against the hot sun loaded tall barrels of what looked like grain onto a barge. The area was cordoned by twelve armed guards whose faces remained stiff and mean as the people called them by their given names, and also by other epithets.

"Traitor."

"Coward."

"Puppet of the Greeks."

Two of the soldiers threatened the taunters with their swords, and the people backed off. The queen watched them mutter as they reluctantly retreated.

Kleopatra's small band of soldiers disembarked slowly, under intense scrutiny from the guard on the dock. The men walked heel to toe, forming a tense procession, like a pack of wolves huddled to ward off a common enemy. The queen and her retinue followed the men. Meeting Kleopatra on this very same platform was a frowning Pshereniptah and his wife, whose Egyptian name defied pronunciation. Kleopatra had met them during the ceremony of the bull and was grateful to see familiar faces.

"Do you remember me, Your Majesty? I am the one you called Happy Kettle." That is what the queen had called the woman in Greek, for that is what her name meant. Happy Kettle knew enough of the Greek language to be pleased with a special pet name given to her by the queen.

"You look well, if unhappy, my friends," said the queen. Both the priest and his wife were gaunt in the face, but neither appeared to have suffered too much physical damage from lack of food. The woman had purple circles under her dark eyes, unusual for the Egyptian complexion.

"Your Majesty, who could feign happiness in such times?" said the priest. "Who knows the wisdom of the gods? I apologize that no one is here to meet you but myself and my wife, but so many are dead and the rest have gone. And now what little food remains must leave us today, just as you are coming to grace our city."

"What do you mean?" asked Kleopatra.

"Your Majesty, the soil here is particularly fertile. We did not have a full crop this year, but, with the blessing of the god, we managed to harvest enough grain for our own people to survive. We might still survive the year if we were allowed to keep our portion of the crop. But, you see"—he turned his placid brown face to the barge—"what remains of our food leaves today for Alexandria. The people in the city feast while we who grow the food must starve. They are leaving us nothing. Nothing."

Happy Kettle turned her face away from her husband so that the queen would not see her tears. The priest continued. "In some villages, the people have resurrected the custom from the Old Time of sacrificing a young virgin to the river god. We have not seen this kind of desperation in our lifetimes, nor in the lifetimes of our fathers and their fathers' fathers."

"Can we not stop this travesty?" Kleopatra said to Hephaestion.

The priest leaned as close as he dared to the queen in order to whisper to her. "I know why the Nile does not rise, Your Majesty," he said solemnly. "When god is pleased with Pharaoh, the river rises. When god is pleased with Pharaoh, god gives us his gifts. God is not pleased with the boy Pharaoh."

Though her command of the native language was excellent, Kleopatra sometimes found the Egyptian manner of explanation utterly abstruse. But she knew what the priest meant. The people would believe that a proper pharaoh—a conduit between the deities and the people—would be able to protect them from such a disaster as drought.

"How do you know this?" Kleopatra asked.

"Because the god Sarapis, who loves the Egyptians and the Greeks equally, has told me. And I have spread his message."

"You mean that the boy king does not please the god?"

"Until the boy is deposed, the god will not bless us with the

waters of the river. The ones who starve the people must be punished."

"Is the god pleased with me, Father?" Kleopatra asked quietly,
aware that the support of the people of the district hung precariously on his answer.

"The god sent you to us. Just as you led the procession of the
sacred bull, so shall you restore the waters of the Nile."

Kleopatra was about to tell the priest that she did not know how
to control the flow of rain when she stopped herself. She turned to
Hephaestion. "Prime Minister, I now issue a new policy concerning grain raised in the Thebiad, to be implemented immediately."

"What does Your Majesty have in mind?" he asked.

"The food must stay. That is all. Go to that well-fed Egyptian
whose scribe stands at his side. Undoubtedly he is the district officer here. Tell him that the queen demands that the shipment remain
at the dock."

"He will say that the Greek military governor of the *nome* will
have his head if he does not obey the edict from Alexandria," said
Hephaestion.

"You may answer that the queen will have his head if he does not
obey her command now."

"Your Majesty," began Hephaestion in a low voice. "You are
bringing trouble to these people."

"How can I worsen their condition? What is worse than slow
starvation?" She waved to the captain of her guard. "Follow me. If
anyone makes a move against me, you know what to do." She turned
on her heel, leaving Hephaestion with his mouth agape and no
choice but to follow her.

The district officer's tense face slackened into a look of surprise
as the queen, the Prime Minister, and her guard approached him.
He looked to either side of himself to make certain he was the destination of this regal assemblage.

He stood stiff and frozen and then found refuge from the
queen's determined stare by bowing to the ground. His guard followed his example, all falling to one knee. The agitated crowd of
onlookers, too, quieted and fell into the submissive posture.

"Stand and face your queen," Kleopatra said, speaking to the district officer in Egyptian, not for his own benefit, for all district officers were well versed in Greek, but to make herself heard by his men and by the spectators. He raised his face and then came to his feet. All others remained on the ground.

He was younger than she had anticipated, perhaps not even thirty years old. He must have been very smart to have risen so quickly in the provincial bureaucracy. His face was set in the stern features of an older man, one whom experience had hardened. Yet there was a dreamy quality in his small, dark eyes. Perhaps it was that they were shaped like teardrops, round and then sharply upturned in the corners.

"I am Kleopatra, Lady of the Two Lands of Egypt, daughter of Ptolemy XII, descended from Alexander the Great, who many hundreds of years ago conquered this land and made it his own. I am your sovereign queen." The man fluttered his eyelashes at the young queen. He moved to bow again, but the queen interceded. "Remain standing. And listen to me. Command the dock workers to unload the food on the barge."

He stared at her as if he did not comprehend her words. He was not a man given to think for himself. She looked past him and saw the ubiquitous royal edict nailed to the dock: *No one may do as he likes; everything is organized for the best of all concerned!* Kleopatra tried to remain patient.

"What is the matter, District Officer? Do you not speak Egyptian?" she asked slyly.

Several of his men stifled snickers. The man looked imploringly at the queen.

"What is it you wish of me, Your Majesty?" he asked in a low, reverential voice, hoping that she would issue any request but the one she had previously uttered.

"I wish you, command you, to take the food off the barge. The food remains with the people who grew it. The food does not go to Alexandria, where there is already plenty of food. Command the workers to unload the food. Quickly, or we shall all be here in the darkness, working by the light of the moon goddess."

"Your Majesty, I am under direct order from the military governor. The penalty for disobedience is death."

"That is understandable," she said. She saw his chest sink with a sigh of relief. She prolonged a stare into his upturned eyes. Then she turned to her captain.

"Kill him."

The captain drew his dagger. Several of the district officer's men stood, not knowing whether to defend their superior against the queen's orders or to watch as the captain killed him. As the district officer's men moved, so did the remainder of the queen's guard. Within seconds a palpable tension encircled the assembly. The captain looked to the queen for final confirmation of her order. The queen folded her arms. "You men look rather well fed considering the circumstances," she said.

The district officer did not respond.

"Are you taking food off your own tables?" asked the queen, who knew very well the policies of her nation's bureaucracy. "Have you no family in this region whose welfare concerns you? Were you not sired by a man and born of a woman? Did you not have cousins with whom you swam naked in the river, or sisters who depend on you for protection?" The queen addressed her questions to the entire guard. As she spoke, heads bowed to avoid her eyes and her words.

"My brother, the boy king, and his regime do not care if your families starve, so long as they might fill their own bellies. But I will not have those loyal to me suffer. Unload the food. If the military governor insists upon starving the people in the district, I shall execute him with my own hands."

Though she spoke with complete authority, Kleopatra was amazed when she was not challenged. The officer sighed, and nodded to his crew to carry out the queen's orders.

"We have begun a civil war," said Hephaestion. "And we do not yet have an army to fight it."

TWENTY-TWO

Kleopatra regarded a small gold coin stamped with her image. The artist had rendered her face more grave, more mature than the visage she saw daily in the mirror; nonetheless, it was flattering. The nose was considerably smaller than its real counterpart, the eyes slightly larger, the lips a good resemblance to the full ones that the queen thought one of her finest features. She looked regal, imposing, and beautiful in a tragic way. If this is how the people view me, then so be it, she thought.

"This is a most hopeful sign," said Hephaestion. "Their decision to issue coins with your image means that the people of Askalon and the Sinai region are ready to accept you as their queen. Word will spread that you have great loyalty outside the city of Alexandria. And without using military might. Few Ptolemies, living or dead, could claim such."

She smiled at the eunuch's words of encouragement and returned the coin to him. They sat in a small room with narrow, shuttered windows closed against the day's heat, in the house given to her by the people of Askalon. She had fled there after her brother and his regime had had her officially deposed. They had wiped her name from the national documents and banned the use of her coinage. To make matters worse, Pompey had issued a decree thanking her brother for his support and declaring himself the boy's guardian. This terrified Kleopatra more than being deposed, because it might have meant that Rome recognized her brother alone as Egypt's monarch. But the fact also remained that, at present, Pompey was not doing well in his war against Caesar, who had just been named Dictator in Rome. Caesar had already run Pompey and those senators loyal to him off to Greece, and now, according to a recent letter from Archimedes, Caesar was in Greece with his army. It was assumed that Caesar would now vanquish Pompey once and for all. Archimedes assured Kleopatra that Pompey's decree would not carry much weight once Caesar defeated him.

"So it is actually better that Pompey has not named himself my guardian?" she had asked Hephaestion. The eunuch simply nodded his head thoughtfully. "Perhaps," he had said, with not enough enthusiasm to give her much comfort.

In any case, Hephaestion determined that Kleopatra was no longer safe on Egyptian soil and arranged for her to take refuge in the small city of Askalon in the Sinai territory, which her grandfather had liberated from the Judaean kings. She was assured that its population would receive her warmly. Besides, it was a perfect location from which she might raise a host of armies from the east.

Kleopatra's party had sailed up the eastern branch of the Nile, and before reaching Pelusium, had abandoned the ship and stole away to Askalon, resuming their disguise as a caravan of merchants. It was an efficient and appropriate masquerade in which to enter the region. Her new home was a one-story white rambling plaster structure, shaded from the undulating sandy mounds of the northern desert by a date grove. The queen had spent many mornings wandering about the grove with Hephaestion, watching in the distance as merchants in camel-caravans, wrapped in stark white layers of gauzy cotton without a morsel of skin exposed, carried their goods back and forth over the desert. Not far from the sea, the area held little else except the turquoise mines farther to the south. The coast was dotted with villages of peasants who made a living from the fruits of the ocean. Kleopatra longed for the sight of the great green of the Mediterranean, but she was not allowed to venture so far from her headquarters. She was only thirty miles from the Egyptian fortress of Pelusium, where Alexander the Great had accepted the surrender of the Persians so many centuries before, and where her brother's army was presently stationed.

"What is the news of the day, Prime Minister, who is now War Minister?" the queen inquired.

"Or perhaps Minister of Foreign Affairs is more appropriate?"

"You are my Cabinet," she answered, smiling at him.

"The news is the same, Your Majesty. The war between Caesar and Pompey makes raising an army impossible. I am afraid that every inquiry we have sent comes back with the same answer, a cordial but solemn response of regret from our neighbors that their armies have already been demanded by Pompey. His plan, of course, is to call upon the armies of the eastern territories he once conquered in the name of Rome. I believe the supply is inexhaustible."

They had hoped that Pompey's demand for soldiers would eventually work to their advantage; that he would call upon a large number of her brother's troops. Then, they would use the opportunity to strike. At that moment, Kleopatra possessed five thousand foot soldiers, three hundred archers, and five hundred cavalry—comparable to the size of a Roman legion, she thought with pleasure. But she did not have the money to keep such an army for long. If the gods were with her, Pompey would soon call away half of her brother's army, and she would challenge the remaining troops. If the gods were against her, she would eventually have to strike against the full force of Achillas's men—some fifteen thousand in all, with seven thousand at Pelusium alone—or reconcile herself to losing the kingdom. But the best possible solution, the one for which she most stridently prayed, was for Caesar to defeat Pompey and then to punish her brother and his regents for coming to Pompey's aid.

A servant interrupted her thoughts, allowing an unannounced party into the room. Kleopatra was about to reprimand him, but found herself staring at a face wrapped in white gauze, wondering if a creature living or dead resided within. He—she assumed it was a he—was bound tightly from head to toe, and walked toward her like a moving, breathing mummy, stiff, slow, and cautious. She expected to see the golden amulet of the vulture around his neck, meant to carry the protection of Mother Isis with the body into the next world. Despite the creature's laborious movements, alert brown eyes peered from the swaddled face and darted around the room.

"Identify yourself, man of the desert. You are standing before the queen," she said, annoyed that this person had gained entrance into the room that she and Hephaestion had converted into a war room. Maps lined the walls, correspondence from friends and allies was strewn about the desk.

The man continued to look about the room, but remained silent. Perhaps he spoke the Arabic dialect she had perfected lately to speak with the officials of Askalon and with the Nabataean kings from whom she hoped to receive more soldiers. She said to him in that tongue, "Tell me your name and your business or you shall be evicted from my presence and tortured by my men until you talk." Receiving no response, she repeated the same words in Greek.

"Have you no warmer greeting than that for an old friend?" asked the white figure in a voice muffled by the gauze around his mouth.

"You try my patience," replied the queen. "Reveal yourself or I will have my guard strip you naked."

The figure pulled the bandages away from his mouth and head. "It is not so easy or so safe for an ally of the dread Kleopatra to travel through Egypt, my dear," said Archimedes. "Precautions must be taken."

"Cousin!" Kleopatra threw her arms around her old friend, the loyal agent and Kinsman of her father. She felt his stiff, heavily bandaged hands on her back, holding her as if he were an animal with paws and not the man with the long supple fingers that she remembered. She wondered if his embrace was tense because of the wrapping or because she was no longer a girl but a queen.

"Undo these terrible bindings so that I may see you."

"Help me, Cousin," he said. He gave the queen one end of the cloth and spun himself around until his face, neck, and shoulders were revealed. His lengthy brown hair was matted against his scalp and hung in strings about his sweaty face. His neck was long and slender, but muscular. His shoulders were square and strong, and his body lithe and graceful. She had forgotten the extent of his charms, both his physical attractiveness and his nonchalant charisma. She had not seen him in years, not since before Auletes had died. Not since she was but a child. She moved to touch him again, but he withdrew from her.

"I wish to embrace you again, my queen, but as you can see, I am awesomely perspired beneath my costume. Forgive me for keeping distant from you. It is not for lack of happiness at seeing you," he said, smiling. "I could not forgive myself if I inadvertently bathed a queen in my sweat."

Kleopatra was relieved that the familiarity between them was not obstructed by her position. By his comment, he both acknowledged her role and dismissed that it should come between their closeness.

"Have you come alone, Cousin?" she asked him.

"No, I am part of a rather interesting travel party."

"Must you be coy with me, old friend? Who are your companions, and when do I meet them?"

"You shall meet them, my queen, for they are already in your service. They are not exactly fit for the presence of a royal. But I have enlisted them in our cause and I promise you that their services shall prove invaluable."

"Cousin, confess your associations before I have my men beat the information out of you," said the queen.

"You have not changed, Kleopatra," said Archimedes, removing the remainder of his gauze, revealing himself to be dressed in a short white chiton that showed his long and handsome legs. "You look like a woman now. That much is quite different. But you are still an impatient girl."

"And you are a very impertinent man," she said, not liking the haughty tone that slipped into her voice. She had welcomed his familiarity, but realized that she was not accustomed to it.

"I apologize," he said, bowing to her. "Please forgive me for taking advantage of the fact that in your childhood, I was given the liberty of being your familiar. May we speak alone?"

Kleopatra dismissed the guards. She did not sit beside Archimedes on the divan, but opposite him, on a stiff, square chair. She folded her hands in her lap.

"Kleopatra, I know you are aware that there are men who live in the shadow world outside the laws and structures of other men."

"Yes, criminals, outlaws, and the like. What are you getting at?"

"Outlaws are not necessarily bad men; they are simply their own men, and one can make excellent use of them. Your father, may the gods rest the soul of my benefactor and king, made much use of such men in his lifetime."

"I take no issue with my father's unconventional methods. His associations with the underworld saved his neck more than once," she said. "Remember dear Clodius?"

"Yes, an interesting man. A dead man, of course, but he did serve Auletes well. That is why I knew you would not object to doing business with my associates."

"Romans?"

"Not exactly. I have negotiated with a group of men who intercept merchant ships traveling from Roman shores to the eastern port of Tyre," said Archimedes.

"We are to do business with pirates?" She threw her head back and laughed.

"You seem so delighted, Kleopatra," said her cousin, teasing her. "Obviously you still have your romantic sense of adventure."

"Obviously," she replied. "What could be more romantic than an exiled queen, but an exiled queen who employs pirates?"

He had spent a long while thinking out the details of the plan. The men he hired were good men, men who began life as honest farmers and small merchants. But the Roman conquest and plunder of their lands left them poor and bitter. Being resourceful—and being unwilling to starve—they acquired ships and began to pursue commerce in their own way. Because he knew the famine was making it difficult for Kleopatra to feed her troops, he commissioned the pirates to provide them with supplies to sustain the army.

"I approve of your plan, Cousin, but who will pay for all of this?"

"When your father died, Hammonius and I were still in possession of a small fortune that he had left with us to carry out his business in Rome. I bring you the remains of that money. Hammonius sends his love."

What words might she say to thank him for this selfless gesture? "You and Hammonius might have kept the money and left me on my own. What made you come to my aid?" Kleopatra felt warm tears cloud her eyes.

"In my case, Cousin, it was memories of affection for the living and for the dead. In the case of Hammonius, he said, 'Tell Kleopatra it would not be possible for me to be much richer. Perhaps she needs this money more than I do.'"

"It is so rare to witness loyalty overcome greed and self-interest."

"Your father was good to me. I am an illegitimate, distant relative whom he elevated to Kinsman and Friend."

"Then why did you leave our service when my father and I returned from exile? Why did we not see you at court these many years?" she asked, trying very hard not to sound annoyed, remembering how hurt she was when her cousin had simply disappeared from their lives, never returning to visit. When she had asked her father why Archimedes was no longer with them, he had muttered, "He is a man and must make his way in the world. He needs an education. He cannot be your little playmate any longer."

"Do you really not know?" Archimedes asked.

"I do not. I was told that you had become a man and no longer needed us."

He said nothing, but assessed her with his eyes.

"Will you speak? Or are you dumbstruck from your long journey?"

Archimedes asked Hephaestion if he might have a private audience with the queen. He took the chair next to Kleopatra that the eunuch had vacated so that he might speak in a low voice. "Do you think I would have left on my own?"

"I do not know what you do on your own, Cousin." Kleopatra lowered her eyes. She did not like the way his gaze sent a quiver through the deepest part of her. She was a queen, and she did not have time for distractions.

"Forgive me what I am about to say, but it is the truth, and as a Brother in the Order of the First Kinsmen, I am sworn to the truth. Your father did not approve of our familiarity. He sent me away to school in Athens to study military strategy. When I finished my studies, he still would not let me come home and take a command with the army, but apprenticed me to Hammonius in Rome."

"He said this to you?"

"No, but Hammonius enlightened me. Auletes told him that you were the last hope of the Ptolemies, and you were not to be ruined by the likes of me."

"I see."

"I never would have left you, Kleopatra," he said. She believed that he wanted to take her hand, but he refrained, and she did not proffer it.

"But you have brought us company," she said, making her voice cold and formal and breaking the spell of his watery brown eyes. "Call for them. I wish to know them. The crown has had enough surprises for one day."

At first glance, Apollodorus the pirate was a disappointment. He was short, with an enormous square frame, more like the bottom part of a dead tree trunk than the body of a man. Yet his demeanor was gracious, and he seemed not a common thief but rather a gentleman disguised as a pirate for a costume party. He bowed low to the queen like a practiced courtier and waited for her to command him to rise. He had the wicked, dashing black eyes Kleopatra associated with men of Tyre, which he said was the place of his birth, though he also called himself a Sicilian.

He explained that he was an Italian by blood but without citizenship. His mother had fallen in love with a Roman soldier who promised, among many things, that he would take her back to Rome. Needless to say, he left with his regiment, never to return. "I am an international man. I belong nowhere but fit in everywhere."

"Apollodorus is a first-class gatherer of information," said Archimedes. "He knows every piece of gossip, from the birthplace of one of his parents to the birthplace of the other. I give the floor to him to tell the story of the war between the Roman generals."

"Your Majesty, I have traveled across many seas and a scorching hot desert to deliver to you this news: Pompey has overwhelmingly defeated Caesar at the Macedonian town of Dyrrhachium."

Like any good storyteller, he paused for effect, letting the queen absorb the information. "For a long time it appeared that the gods were with Caesar. He and his men had survived an impossible winter in Greece, cut off from food supplies and everything familiar, while Pompey and his men lived like kings in their exile. Caesar kept trying to engage Pompey in battle, but he would not be coaxed into the war. He was too comfortable taking food from the eastern territories, the lands of my people that he subdued and now extorts for every resource. Finally, Caesar engaged Pompey outside Dyrrhachium, but two Gallic deserters from Caesar's army sold information to Pompey, who was able to counter Caesar's attack and defeat him."

Kleopatra focused all her mental powers on concentrating on the details of Apollodorus's story but could not stop asking herself what this unexpected turn of events meant for her own condition. She looked to Archimedes, but her cousin was seemingly enraptured with the story and did not acknowledge her.

Apollodorus continued. "Caesar fled to Thessaly, where he met up with two more of his legions, but Pompey's army still outnumbers Caesar's two men to one. They say that Pompey's army is so large that even the gods, from their position of omniscience, would have trouble viewing the entire force at once. Now Pompey has set out for Thessaly, where he will surely finish Caesar off."

Kleopatra thought of the many times in her childhood she had thrilled to accounts of war, which always sounded so glamorous, but which had never concerned her in such a direct way.

"What does this mean for us?" she asked Archimedes.

"My friend, will you give us leave to discuss internal affairs?" he asked Apollodorus.

Apollodorus's absence was followed by a protracted silence, one that lingered for too long. Finally, Kleopatra said nervously, "My brother's guardian has defeated Caesar and will now rule the world. What does this mean for me, Cousin?"

"You know what it means, Kleopatra," said Archimedes gravely. "It means that we must strike. Your plan of counting on Caesar to win and to punish your brother for coming to the aid of Pompey has been foiled. We must quickly regroup, take count of the men in our army, and stage an attack on Pelusium."

"But now? I need more time. I need more troops."

"If you wait, you may very well find yourself at war with both your brother and Pompey. If you attack now and are successful, you can be in Alexandria before Pompey is back in Rome."

"But what then?"

"If your brother is defeated, Pompey will have no choice but to support you. What does he care who sits on the Egyptian throne, so long as the monarch has very deep pockets?"

"But Caesar is not yet entirely defeated," Kleopatra said. How could she have been so wrong? Who would have believed that the chronically inert Pompey would have bested one as vigorous and ambitious and favored by the gods as Julius Caesar?

"By all accounts, Caesar is finished. Must we wait for the body to be cold before we take action? It is not like you to dally, Kleopatra. You must either strike or go far away and retire to private life, and let your brother rule Egypt."

"Cousin, I am prepared to strike," she said, trying to summon up her courage. "But at this moment, and I hope this moment passes quickly, I am afraid."

Archimedes took her by the hands and raised her to her feet. He looked into her eyes and then took her in his arms, holding her tight, this time with unbound fingers that kneaded her back tenderly as he held her. The strength in his body and the calm beat of his heart steadied her nerves. He let her sink into his chest—for how long, she did not know—until she felt balanced. He whispered softly in her ear, "We must ready ourselves for victory."

Four miles from the fortress of Pelusium, the queen and her army encamped in the shadow of Mount Casius. She had marched from Askalon that very day with her troops, aiming to be settled by nightfall, where they could refresh themselves with sleep, and storm the fort at dawn. They had worked on the plan for two days and made the long march in one.

They were outnumbered. Kleopatra was almost two thousand

men short against Achillas's troops, but Archimedes and her advisers did not seem to worry about the disparity in their numbers.

"Your brother's men are mostly lazy Egyptians who despise their Greek king," said Archimedes. "Your troops are either men who have pledged you their loyalty or men who are well paid." She did not know whom to believe, so she decided to believe only her intuition, which dictated that she make war and defeat her brother as quickly as possible.

At sunset they made the proper sacrifices, and she and the officers dined on the kill under a moon that was almost full, casting a cold, stark light upon their banquet. She made short speeches to her army in the various tongues they spoke and then retired. She intended to put herself into the hands of the gods and go to sleep. But after the dinner, she realized she was exhausted and exhilarated all at once. She was prepared for victory, but she was also prepared to die.

"This may be my last day on earth," she said to Archimedes. The soldiers had set up a tent for her, large enough that she could stand in it. It contained a square table and two folding campaign chairs as well as a large mattress for the queen's slumber. Charmion, who insisted upon accompanying the war party, had furnished it with quilts against the chill of the desert night. Outside the tent, Kleopatra heard the sounds of soldiers readying for battle, swords being sharpened against rock, armor clanging as it was cleaned and polished, horses neighing softly as they were massaged and oiled to be ready for tomorrow's encounter.

"There is no reason to believe that we won't prevail," Archimedes said. "I cannot monitor exactly what numbers we face, but the scouts estimate that Achillas has stationed six thousand men at the fort. He could draw upon some fifteen thousand more. But that would take days and days. Weeks, actually, by the time he summons them from the provinces. For the moment, the odds are almost even, and we have the gods and all that is right and good on our side."

"And if we fail?" she asked. She did not wish to think of failure. She repeatedly calmed her fears with the long-ago prediction of the crones, with the dream in which Ptolemy Soter made her an eagle, with the declaration of the priest that the gods were on her side in the war against her brother. It was not that she lacked faith; it was just that her practical side groped for an alternative plan in the event that the battle was lost.

"We will not fail," he replied.

"I have been conspiring in my head, Cousin. If we lose but survive, I want you to help me finesse this plan. I will obtain an expedient divorce from my brother and offer myself in marriage to a number of eastern kings."

"Who?"

"I don't know. The king of Pontus. The king of Judaea. I will marry one of them, the one who agrees to join with me against my brother for the Egyptian throne."

"Cousin, those kingdoms are occupied by Rome. The Romans will not allow a war on Ptolemy. So let us prepare ourselves to win, not to lose."

"Archimedes, I fear you lack a practical nature. I must have an alternative plan. What do you think of my marrying into the royal house of Parthia, or of Bactria? Perhaps such a union might be the beginning of a kingdom larger even than the Roman empire. Perhaps such a union might challenge Rome and prevail," she said, her eyes wild and her heart racing with the grandiose plan.

"Now we are not merely negotiating with Rome, we are setting about to conquer her? Are you willing to live among the savage Parthians? Kleopatra, I believe you have battle fever. I believe you are going mad."

"What else to do with Pompey against me? How do I know how indebted Pompey might feel to Pothinus for fifty ships and five hundred Gabinian soldiers?" she asked, once again verbalizing the argument she had played out in her head a thousand times. "But if I married myself to a king of great resources, Pompey would have to take our demands seriously."

"I do not like to hear talk of your marrying some barbarian king," he said angrily.

"Well it may not come to that. Even if we do not prevail in this battle, even if my brother takes me prisoner, I still might find a way to expose Pothinus's anti-Roman sentiments to Pompey at the appropriate time. I could probably work through his son Cnaeus, who I believe is rather fond of me."

"Is he?" Archimedes asked darkly.

"Yes, he is. He attempted to seduce me when he visited the palace."

"Kleopatra, I have never known you to be naive. Do you think that a man's immediate sexual desires have anything to do with whom he may choose to support against his father's wishes? Particularly if his father is the most powerful man on earth? You are a clever young woman, but it is clear that you know nothing of men."

She felt the sharp sting of truth. He was not wrong; the accuracy of his comment hit her hard, flattening the confidence that moments before had begun to surge through her body. Yes, she had probably overestimated her power over Cnaeus. Hopelessness descended over her like a heavy shroud, eradicating any internal powers she had mustered. Had she overestimated her abilities? Was she, a young woman of twenty-one, and not an entirely beautiful one at that, foolish enough to think she could manipulate a man's desire into a political alliance? Or to think that she, with no military experience, could command an army and prevail?

"Perhaps this night should be spent in prayer and sacrifice to the gods," she said solemnly. "If this evening is my last, perhaps I should cleanse my soul before meeting the deities."

"I have a much better idea," said Archimedes. He pulled her to his chest and twisted his hand into her hair, throwing her neck back and forcing her upturned eyes to look directly into his. "If this evening is to be our last, then let us spend it together as a man and woman should."

He kissed her. Slowly at first, then with an open mouth, his tongue passing through her lips. Though her mind tried to argue against what she was about to do, her body, weak and tingling, was ready to surrender to his desire. A new feeling enveloped her, a thrilling but disconcerting sensation. She acquiesced completely to his lips and hands, feeling his body grow more tense and insistent. When he let her breathe, she said, very quietly, "This cannot be."

"Does it not strike you as an appropriate way for a queen, a woman, to spend her final night in mortal form?" he said.

"But I cannot be yours."

"Considering what may happen tomorrow and what we feel right now, doesn't that seem like a small concern?"

"But what if we survive? What will become of us then?"

"You cannot be my wife. But Kleopatra, my love, do you really believe the gods wish you to suppress your womanly desires? Do you really believe that the women of your dynasty have pleased themselves with their brother-husbands alone?"

"I do not know," she said, feeling the blood rush to her cheeks in embarrassment as she remembered Berenike and her tryst with the women who served her.

"Kleopatra, you are so brilliant, but you know so little of human nature. You can be mine in the way that you will never belong to whatever husband you next marry for political expediency. I have waited years for you to become a woman. Can you deny that Fate arranged this attraction long ago?"

"But my father warned against it."

"And I stayed away from you," he said. "But when you needed help, I came. As soon as I saw the woman you had become, I knew this was destined. Tell me, did you not feel it, too?"

"If we are to be lovers, we are doomed lovers. One way or another. Whether we die tomorrow or whether we live."

"Then let us enjoy the moment," he said, lifting her into his arms as he would a baby. "Have you done this thing before?"

"Only once. I am initiated," she said nervously as he laid her on the feather mattress. He sat beside her and stroked her body with his right hand, caressing one of her breasts and then the other. How could he do this so blithely, she wondered, when it was strictly forbidden to touch the queen? She understood the reason for the protocol, for to be touched so was to lose oneself, to forget everything—position, country, kingdom. And yet, she did not stop him, but let his fingers pinch her nipple until she arched her back in pleasure, reaching for something that she could not identify but was desperate to have.

She pulled his mouth to hers. It was time for her to know this part of life, to explore this dark cave that housed a beast of whom she had long been aware, but whose turbulent cravings she had staved off in the name of duty. And here was a man who loved her. Who would lay down his life for her the very next day if necessary.

He broke from her. "You are a queen, and someday you shall be a great and magnificent and wise queen, gods be willing. But just now, just for this moment, you are a maiden about to become a woman."

"Is the experience so transforming?" she asked.

"If done properly," he said, smiling at her for the first time that evening. "I am at war within myself at this moment about whether to ravage you the night long or to make love to you gently and then allow you a restful sleep."

"Be tender with me, Cousin, and save the more savage passions for our enemies. If we are alive and free at this time tomorrow, then you may ravage me the night long."

It was not the first time he had walked among the dead, but never had he viewed a vanquished enemy who had so forced his hand in war and destruction. He was grateful for his height, for it put him a good distance from the anguished faces of the deceased and the dying, some of whom he recognized.

"This they would have," Caesar said to Pollio, who walked soberly beside him. "They brought me to this necessity, did they not? After all my attempts at peace? See the dead, Pollio? I would be in their place had I listened to their demands and surrendered my army."

Caesar sighed, stepping over the body of one of the tall Thessalian soldiers who had been ordered by Pompey to defend his camp while Pompey himself had fled. He looked about at the lavishness of Pompey's deserted headquarters, at the gold and silver plate that, in grandiosity and optimism, had been placed at the senators' table. At the finely embroidered linen tablecloths. At the ceramic wineglasses meant for his enemies' lips. The arrogant fools had thought that they would, by this time of the day, be enjoying their victory feast.

Caesar thought of the hunger and privations his men had

endured all year long while the Pompeians lived in this well-stocked camp, enjoying the same opulence that they had in their Roman mansions. He was not one of them. He was not one to bathe in idle luxury. And that is why he was alive and walking over the bodies of the men his enemies had paid to guard their pathetic lives.

He would never allow himself to gloat, but his sympathy for the fellow countrymen he had humiliated and defeated quickly turned to a swell of satisfaction.

"It could not be helped, could it?" he asked Pollio rhetorically. "They asked for it."

It had been a horrible summer of veritable starvation, playing cat-and-mouse games with Pompey, who had refused to engage in battle. One terribly dry day in August, just when Caesar was sure his men would either murder him for putting them through this or simply desert out of hunger and malaise, one of Caesar's spies rode furiously into camp and announced that the senators who were encamped with Pompey would no longer put up with his inaction. They were so confident of victory that they insisted Pompey engage and, as the scout said, "finish Caesar off once and for all."

The scout reported a speech he overheard made by the traitor Labienus, who assured the Pompeians that Caesar's army was no longer the fighting force that had conquered Gaul, but rather a tired bunch of mercenaries ready to desert at any time. Further, the scout overheard the senators dividing up the spoils they would win in the wake of Caesar's defeat. The scout said to Caesar, "They squabble over your office on the Via Sacra, sir."

"Do they?" Caesar had replied, feeling his entire being rise to meet the senators' premature arrogance.

"Yes, sir. Every senator wishes to be Pontifex Maximus." To Pollio, Caesar's officer who was from the highest nobility, the scout reported that three greedy senators were squabbling over who would take his family villa outside the city. "They are fighting over it because of its lavish view of the ocean and its lovely baths that are reported to be the most rejuvenating in the land."

"Are they so contemptuous of me?" mused Caesar to Pollio. "Even after all these years? After I have demonstrated to them time and again what eventually happens to those who oppose me? Who insult me? We seem to have no alternative but to give them what they wish."

Later that morning, Caesar saw Pompey's men descend slowly from their position high atop the hill in Pharsalos—proof that the gluttonous senators had indeed cajoled Pompey into abandoning his logical scheme of letting Caesar's forces starve to death. Now Caesar would have a shot at full-scale battle. Sensing that this was his most auspicious opportunity, here in the hills where Pompey was completely cut off from his most excellent navy, Caesar immediately arranged his troops in the most advantageous lines, considering their weak numbers. He assigned the terribly diminished Ninth, who had suffered most at Dyrrhachium, to the left flank, under the command of Antony. The young officer's fierceness in battle and smooth way of speaking could hearten any soldier, could make ten men think they were as strong as an entire legion. The faithful Domitius took the middle, and he, Caesar, commanded the right, where he could fight at the head of the Tenth, the legion for which he held the most affection.

But upon further observation of Pompey's formations, Caesar realized that Pompey had congregated his entire cavalry on the left, aiming for Caesar's right. Moreover, Pompey had stationed all of his archers and shooters on the left as well. It became clear to Caesar that Pompey's plan was to upset Caesar's right with a barrage of missiles while the cavalry descended upon his rear.

Covertly, Caesar drew six cohorts, one from each of his legions, and formed a separate line. He instructed them to carry the rear of his right. In a moment of what he could only call divine inspiration, he commanded his javelin throwers to aim not at the legs and thighs of the cavalry, but directly at their faces, as a Parthian savage might do.

"It will be death by vanity," he told his men, who initially scoffed at Caesar's idea. "We must do something to compensate for their greater numbers. I promise you that these gaily dressed, longhaired prancing soldiers of the horse will be devastated at the thought of scarring their handsome faces and will retreat immediately." This earned a great roar of laughter from Antony, who was the master of all cavalry strategy, and was all too aware of the great pride such men took in their appearance.

Caesar, as was his custom before battle, singled out one of his best men, the great centurion Caius Crassinius, and asked, "What are our hopes today?" Crassinius looked at his general with a luminescent loyalty entirely in opposition to his fearsome appearance. He said, "We shall conquer today, Caesar, and this day, I will deserve your praises whether at the end I am alive or dead." Capitalizing on the momentum of Caius's fervor, Caesar led the charge, taking the grave risk of leaving behind his baggage carts and supply kits, which would mean utter defeat if the confrontation lasted very long.

But it did not. Pompey's cavalry put up great resistance to Caesar's initial charge, but soon the six hidden cohorts fell upon the cavalry with a tremendous force, casting their javelins directly at the horsemen's faces. Caesar's prediction proved so accurate that in the heat of battle, he let out a loud laugh. The vain cavalry officers realized the method of attack and turned around and fled, leaving a great opening for Caesar to enter and claim the day. Pompey himself was thrown into a state of confusion and made a hasty retreat back to camp, leaving Caesar to wonder if he had taken leave of his senses, for how was such behavior fitting of a Roman general? He, Caesar, would happily have fought to the death with the last of his men rather than scamper off like a scared child.

One of Pompey's officers appeared to change his mind about the retreat. He circled his horse around. Caesar wondered if the man was going to come over to Caesar's camp, as soldiers often did when it was clear who had taken the day. But the man did not ride toward Caesar. Instead, he took an unsuspecting Caius Crassinius by surprise and slashed him in the throat. Caesar rushed to his man, who was about to fall back off his horse. He grabbed him by the back of the head, and, looking into his dying eyes, said, "Today you have earned my praises above all men, my friend."

Now Caesar felt a tear well up in his eye when he thought of Crassinius. He had ordered a special monument to be put up for the faithful centurion, so that generations of men would come to this place and remember his courage. It was a fine gesture, but it was hardly enough. So many had come and gone from Caesar's service, even though he gave every thought, every ounce of his energy, to protect them.

Pollio interrupted his thoughts. "Sir, the scribes have an estimate on the numbers. I am going to record them should you wish to use them in your account of the battle. Apparently, Pompey had us outnumbered two to one. Forty-seven thousand to twenty-two thousand. Antony, who is very good at this sort of thing, agrees with the count."

Caesar looked about Pompey's deserted camp. Only slaves and the support staff of a long-drawn-out war were left behind, begging for mercy. Pompey, his army, and what was left of the Roman senate, had scattered to the wind like house dust a peasant throws out her back door.

"Where goes Pompey?" Caesar asked Pollio. "Do we know?"

"He is said to be heading over the foothills to Larissa with about thirty men, and from there, to the shore where his fleet is stationed. Undoubtedly, he will do his usual thing of trying to regroup in some eastern territory."

"Here are my orders. Let the men know that we waste no time plundering the camp. Fortifications are to be built around the hill by nightfall in the unlikely event of a surprise counterattack. I will divide the men between those who are to remain here, those who will go back to our own camp and ensure its safety, and those who will come with me in pursuit of Pompey and his army."

Pollio summoned the proper officers to carry out Caesar's wishes.

"General, we have a special souvenir for you," said one of the captains. He carried a basket of yellowing scrolls. "Here is the private correspondence of Pompey." He held the basket out to Caesar, who cocked his head and eyed it but did not take the proffered gift.

"Sir, the private papers of your enemy," said Pollio. "Surely there are multiple insights in those pages."

"Burn them," said Caesar. "Those are the private papers of a gentleman. Burn them right away, I said. And do not take a peek inside them yourselves. Burn every letter."

"But why, sir?" asked Pollio.

"Because it is the proper thing to do," said Caesar, nonchalant. He dismissed the officers.

"Of course, sir."

"I am going to take four legions with me, Pollio. But before we depart, I believe we officers shall indulge in a special treat."

"What is that, sir?"

"We have starved the summer long. Why should we waste all this food? Let us dine on the meal that Pompey's excellent cooks had prepared for his victory celebration. And let us not gorge ourselves like the fat men we have defeated, but let us savor every bite."

"An inspired idea, sir."

The meal was a capital success. Antony, who loved food, drink, and talk equally, made a long speech praising the high quality of the roasts, the fowl, the pork that was served by Pompey's very submissive cooks, who acted as though it was quite normal to be waiting on one army rather than the other. Treating the kitchen staff with extraordinary politeness, Caesar, usually unimpressed by fine cuisine, allowed that he had never had such a sumptuous, tasty plate of food in all his life.

Caesar washed his hands in a finger bowl and stood. Pollio jumped to his feet. Caesar motioned for the rest of the men to remain seated. "Finish your plates. You worked hard for this meal. But I must go."

Caesar's men groaned at his early departure. Some urged him to sit and enjoy himself. He smiled at them, at their loyalty and affection. But he indicated that he would not linger.

"I simply must catch up with Pompey and thank him for this delightful repast."

Caesar left his men laughing and applauding as he walked away from the table. He took Pollio aside. "How long will it take to spread the word that Caesar has prevailed?"

"As long as it takes men to travel, sir. If I go through the usual channels."

"They have been effective for us in the past, haven't they?"

"Yes they have. In two weeks, sir, the civilized world will know what happened here today."

TWENTY-THREE

Pothinus the eunuch stood on the shore looking out to sea. He had rushed to Pelusium the day before with the boy king to meet the threat of the troublemaker, Kleopatra, who had gathered a paid gypsy army and was encamped just a few miles to the east. They were certain she was going to strike that morning. His information, he thought, was infallible. He was so sure that his informers were correct that he had neglected his morning ablutions and left his breakfast sitting in its bowl in the city so that he could rush to Pelusium to meet the menace. And to witness her demise.

But she did not come. Probably because the very morning she planned to strike, the Harbormaster at Pelusium awoke to the fact that Pompey the Great, fleeing Julius Caesar, was lingering two miles offshore with a small flotilla of warships and merchant vessels, waiting for an invitation to quarter in Egypt. Pothinus received the news just before dawn. He estimated that it reached Kleopatra's ears at about the same time.

He hated the unexpected. But that was what he got. So instead of spending the day in the war tent, the eunuch and his council of advisers called an emergency meeting to decide how they would receive the defeated Roman general.

What an ordeal that was. And what patience it required.

Pothinus knew what the outcome would be even before the meeting convened, because he and Theodotus had already discussed it. But others were not as quick to see the inevitable. Some argued to make good relations with Pompey before Kleopatra got to him. She was just crafty enough to seduce him into backing her cause. After all, she had met him in Rome and had been a guest in his home. Pompey needed an Egyptian ally, and she could make good use of the troops he had managed to save from Caesar's wrath. That would never do, Pothinus agreed. Others said they should fight Pompey then and there. Confront him while he's down, they said. Yes, yes, quite right, Pothinus said again and again while he listened to their anxieties about the Roman general. He let them all have their say, sitting patiently through one erroneously constructed argument after another.

Then, he enlightened them.

Now he and Theodotus stood on the dock, where he would have a fine view of the events that he had been promised would happen, and happen according to his own plan. The stage was perfectly set. Achillas's officers were lined up at the harbor, not in fighting formation, but waiting to greet a dignitary, flanking the boy king, this latest Ptolemy, who was bedecked in his official purple robes. The child—fidgety, nervous despite his enthusiasm for the plan—stood out in the sunlight like some quivering, aberrant breed of orchid. Pothinus wished he would have stayed home, but it was not to be. The boy had insisted, and the eunuch had learned through the years to pick his battles with the headstrong, foolish thing. Pothinus was not certain exactly whom he could trust. But his co-regents had little reason to betray him. Not now, not when Pompey had been defeated and was floating in the bay, waiting for an invitation to bring him to shore where he could take over the Egyptian army and bilk the Egyptian treasury as he had done so marvelously in the past.

"Are you certain we are doing the right thing?" asked Theodotus.

"Your nervousness gives me cramps, Theodotus. You argued brilliantly on our behalf this morning. Why are you now acting so sheepishly?" Pothinus was losing patience with this paid rhetorician. "Please keep quiet. If you do not have the stomach for the decision we made, then go hide in your carrel in the Mouseion and comfort yourself with poetry."

"I suppose we have no choice," said the jittery scholar.

"Caesar will be here in three days' time. His boats have been spotted by the scouts at sea. Do we wish for the continuation of the Roman Civil War on our soil? Do you wish to face Caesar's army? Or his vengeance for helping his enemy?"

"No, no. You are right. Quite right."

"I am relieved that you think so."

"But Pompey has arrived with five ships. There may be a great army on those ships."

"We have made provisions for all that. Anyway, I do not believe they are filled with military men. The armies, for the most part, were left in Greece. I believe those boats are the vessels of the sixty fat Roman senators who escaped with Pompey."

"Oh dear," the scholar said.

"Do you remember the Romans who lived in Alexandria at Auletes' invitation? Do you think these will be any different? No, they will rob our temples of their holy artifacts, bleed our treasury, and rape our women. They will march into Alexandria, break into the Library, and steal the precious ancient texts that you so love to read. Now do please be quiet. You are making me anxious with your fidgeting."

"But what about his wife?"

"What about his wife?"

"Do you see her on the deck? I hear she is lovely."

"Yes, she is undoubtedly lovely. That means she will go back to Rome and quickly find another husband."

"Well, it's sad."

"She is also quite rich, Theodotus, and young, too. Please do not waste your tears on the lady Cornelia. Romans only marry for political reasons anyway."

"Still. She is so young."

"And he is so old. He is fifty-nine. He has lived long enough."

Pothinus clasped his hands together. He, too, was nervous, though he was not about to admit it to the scholar. It would not do to feed Theodotus's queasiness for the deed that was now unstoppable.

"Look at Achillas. How fine he looks in his uniform." Pothinus shaded his eyes from the sun to get a better look at Achillas, who was sailing in a small fishing boat to greet Pompey's larger vessel. Achillas had come up with the idea to fetch Pompey in the small boat—too small for any of his men to accompany him. He would tell Pompey that the harbor was much too shallow to accommodate his galley; consequently, the Roman should sail ashore alone in the small dinghy, where the boy king awaited him.

Achillas had dressed for the occasion, wearing his officer's uniform of royal blue that looked dazzling in the sunlight. He was accompanied by two men, one a former officer of Pompey's, Lucius Septimus, whom they had hoped Pompey would recognize, and Salvius, a former centurion. Both were presently mercenaries in the Gabinian army.

The dinghy met Pompey's vessel and Pompey waved to the men. But Pothinus saw two of Pompey's own men pull him back as if to prevent him from boarding the small boat. Then Lucius called out to him—hopefully, in the Latin as they had planned. He caught Pompey's attention, for the general pulled himself from his own advisers to answer him. Pothinus could not be sure, but he thought he saw Cornelia try to pull Pompey back by his cloak. But Pompey's sailors lowered a rope ladder, and Pompey descended into the smaller boat despite his wife's protests. The men pushed off from the ship.

"What is happening?" asked Theodotus.

"They are coming, that is what."

"Is that all? I do not have your eyesight."

"I don't know. It appears that Pompey is reading from a scroll. I suppose he's written out his speech to the king and is practicing it."

"Are they speaking to him?"

"No, it does not appear so."

"And he is not suspicious?"

"Apparently not. His face is buried in his book."

"Is he armed?"

"No. Now stop asking questions. It is time for us to do our part. See how close they are. We must step forward as if we are going to greet him."

Pothinus put one bejeweled arm in the air, waving each ringed finger separately like the legs of an insect propelling itself. Pompey lifted his head. He put his book away and stood, preparing to leave the boat. He steadied himself on the arm of Lucius, but instead of helping him, Lucius produced a dagger, and with a single thrust, stabbed him in the back. Pompey fell forward. Achillas and Salvius drew their swords. The cries of Cornelia could be heard on the shore. Pompey groaned and pulled his cape over his head, resigned to take the blows that would end his life and career. He did not fight back.

"I do not think he had time to contemplate his fate," said Pothinus, indifferent, as if the play he had been watching was over. Theodotus turned away.

The Egyptian vessels in the harbor that seemed to have no real purpose suddenly turned on the Roman ships, chasing them out to the sea. It was difficult to see, but it looked to Pothinus that a few would be caught. He had already given the orders, which he did not share with Theodotus: Kill whomever is aboard.

Pothinus kept his eyes on the dinghy. Lucius and the centurion frantically rowed it into the harbor, where Pothinus offered his hand to Achillas. "Well done," he said.

"Now what?" asked Achillas.

Pothinus regarded the dead Pompey. He could see where the son had gotten his looks. A fine-looking man in his day, to be sure. But now his eyes were open and staring blankly at the eunuch, who turned away.

He was taking a risk and he knew it. He wondered if he was being foolish, relying on reputation and not on real numbers of men, but when had that strategy failed him? It seemed that Mother Fortune encouraged him to take chances and rewarded his faith in the gods. He had set off from Greece with only three thousand two hundred men—hardly an impressive army if Pompey was successful in gathering reinforcements from the east. Caesar had sailed through enemy waters with this meager crew, where he might have encountered any number of Pompey's ships ready for battle. After all, he had defeated the old fox by cutting him off from his navy. If Pompey had been able to regroup his sea forces, Caesar would not have been alive at this very moment, breathing fresh Mediterranean sea air and sailing toward the legendary Greek colony on the coast of Egypt. But Fortune, his true love, had smiled upon him once again.

How was it that he had never been here before? What with his love for literature, art, theater, philosophy, and all things Greek? How had he neglected to spend time in the city of Alexandria, the home of the great Library that housed the world's accumulated knowledge, the Mouseion that hosted the world's most famous minds? Ah well, he had been busy. And the east had traditionally been Pompey's. Pompey had been a friend and benefactor to the old king. It would not have done for Caesar to saunter into Alexandria and threaten Pompey's hold on the place. Of course, that was before, when the two men were allies. Now that Pompey had been vanquished and was hiding out in the whitewashed Mediterranean paradise, everything was different. Perhaps he would be able to talk sense into his former comrade. Pompey could be such a practical, malleable man when push came to shove. Perhaps they would strike a deal. A man of Pompey's abilities and contacts could be useful in times to come. Pompey, when he had wanted to, could always make the senate go along with Caesar's plans.

Caesar braced himself at the bow of the ship. No one—not even a man who had conquered vast lands and laid waste to over one million lives—could see the Pharos Lighthouse for the first time and not have to catch his breath. The flame at the top of the three-story structure burned wildly, a second sun in the hot afternoon sky. Caesar found its blaze hypnotic, and he almost had to force himself to stop looking at it.

At the approach to the island stood two colossal statues of one incestuous Ptolemy couple or another—which two were these?— dressed in the Egyptian pharaonic style and sitting like sphinxes on either side of the tower, greeting every man, every ship that came into the harbor. The king and queen must surely be the son and daughter of the first Ptolemy, the two who scandalized the Greek world by marrying each other, and then, with their father's fortune, turned the little outpost into the center of the civilized world—well, at least until the rise of Rome. Still, Caesar expected to find remnants of the grandeur of the Greek world lingering about. He liked the shabby elegance of Greek cities; it gave them such a quaint ambiance.

He had no idea what he was to encounter, so he assembled the troops, making them ready for confrontation upon disembarking. Instead, Caesar and his landing party were met by a freakish-looking womanish fellow. A self-important eunuch courtier, he was sure. He could tell by the cosmetics, the jewelry, and the girth about the middle. Why the Greek monarchs had taken these creatures as advisers he did not know. The man was accompanied by a fat little boy wearing a crown; they were trailed by a large retinue, one fellow carrying a platter. Gifts, thought Caesar. What might they be? And where was Pompey hiding?

"Gaius Julius Caesar, we present you with this treasure," said the eunuch. He stepped aside, revealing a cowering Greek man in the robes of a scholar who held out a tray, all the while stretching his arms out as far as they might go to distance himself from what it held. It took Caesar a moment to discern the proffered matter. He would never have recognized the head, for it had been separated from its person for some time and was largely discolored. But the ring, he knew. He had held the hand that had worn it, had taken it in confidence, had faced it in war.

Caesar felt the bile rise to his throat. He turned away. His men had seen him cry before. There was no shame. He collected himself, not bothering to wipe away the tears.

"Who is responsible for this?"

"You see, great Caesar, you have no cause to remain here. We have done you the favor of vanquishing your enemy. You need only turn around and return to Rome," the eunuch said grandly. "Surely, there is now no reason for you to remain."

How *dare* he, this monster? Even he, Caesar, would not have moved to kill a great Roman like Pompey.

"Who are you to tell Caesar where he shall remain?" Caesar looked straight into the eunuch's eyes. The boy king appeared jittery, tugging at his robes as if they were not comfortable.

"You may not be aware of this, but there is famine in Egypt. The waters of the Nile are lower than ever before. We have no food for your troops. The king is at war with his sister Kleopatra, who would topple the government and replace it with her own. You would do well to leave us."

Did this man have no brain?

"We are here to collect the debt that King Ptolemy neglected to repay to the people of Rome. It is our intention to remain until we have been satisfied," Caesar said. "Besides, we are waylaid here by the etesian winds, which are not at this time favorable for sailing." He looked to the boy. "You are the son of Ptolemy?"

The boy nodded his head in the affirmative. "And you are at war with your sister, who is rightfully the queen?"

"Well she started it," he said, stamping his foot. "She ran away and raised her own army!" Caesar wondered if the boy was going to cry.

"Your father left his will and his kingdom in the hands of Pompey, but as you see for yourself, Pompey is dead. You and your sister must put yourselves entirely in my trust and I shall settle your dispute for you. If you listen to me, you shall continue to rule your kingdom."

The boy appeared calmed by his words, which only made the eunuch more flustered. Caesar said to Pothinus, "Send word to the queen that she is to appear before me."

"And where would you like to meet with her? May I suggest Damascus? She may be received there, but certainly not here in Alexandria, where she is considered a usurper and a rebel. She has been officially deposed."

"Well, we shall take care of that. Have her come to the palace."

"The palace?" said the eunuch, as if he had not heard correctly.

"Yes, that is where I shall be staying. Come, boy," he said to the king. "Let us go to your home. We must become acquainted. Which way to the palace?"

Caesar signaled for his escort to follow. The elite guard quickly assembled at attention, raising the conqueror's fasces—his personal banners. Those who did not carry colors raised their axes, the symbol of the victor.

Before they could leave the dock, Caesar and his men were rushed by a small militia of soldiers. What was wrong with these people? he wondered. And then he realized that the Alexandrian soldiers had taken affront to the fasces. They must have thought that he was asserting that Alexandria was his. Well, he was. Why not? But he didn't mean to start a ruckus.

Caesar moved to order his men not to react, but it was too late. Several of his men were already engaged with the Alexandrians. He saw one of his soldiers go down as a dark-skinned Greek slew him through the gut.

"Call them off," Caesar demanded of the king. "Call them off or you will die."

Caesar grabbed the boy and held him by the arms. Pothinus, alarmed, signaled for the militia's commander to cease fighting. The men stepped back.

"You see, Great Caesar, you are not safe here."

"Nonsense. I am Caesar, and all places are safe for me."

The eunuch had no response to this. He would learn, Caesar thought. That is, if he lived long enough.

"Attend to the wounded immediately," Caesar said to his commanding officer. He turned to the boy king. "Now then, where is your palace?"

"If anyone goes to meet Julius Caesar, it shall be me."

Kleopatra was adamant. She looked at her closest advisers, Hephaestion, Archimedes, and Apollodorus the pirate. Through her trials in exile, these three had been her most loyal and astute chancellors. Still, did they imagine that she would send one of them in her place for the most important meeting of her life? She looked about the table and wondered which of these men might communicate better than she with Julius Caesar. Which of them had her education or her command of languages, including Caesar's own? Who but she could converse so dexterously on the arts, or on philosophy, which she knew also intrigued him? Which of them knew the details of his history as she did, or had sat at the banquet table of Pompey the Great as he petted the pretty breast of Caesar's own daughter, Julia?

Archimedes interceded. "Caesar has already made his intentions clear. He wishes to make peace between you and your brother. He has already made himself a confidant of the king. Do you not think we should send him a representative?"

"Yes," Kleopatra said. "I believe we should send him the queen, just as he requested."

"That is much too dangerous," replied her cousin. "There is no safe route into Alexandria. I do not care what Caesar has said—if you are intercepted by Achillas's troops, you will not live to meet the Roman."

Kleopatra felt a surge of will rise up and take over her being. Her heart pounded with more ferocity than she believed it could withstand. She would have liked to have taken the organ out of her body and put it on the floor, where its maddening rhythm could not hurt her. She put her hand to her chest to stop the turbulence that had kidnapped her internal self. Reading her body's signals, Archimedes took her hands and put them in his, squeezing firmly as if trying to bring her back from some dark place without clutching her to him and giving away their intimacy.

This was the news they had heard: Julius Caesar made the boy king send two messengers, Dioscorides and Serapion, to Pelusium to convey the king's wishes that there be peace between the king and his exiled sister. Without delay, Achillas had them arrested and murdered. Now Caesar was at war with Achillas. But Caesar had only three thousand men with him in Alexandria, whereas Achillas could raise five times that count.

"You would do well not to put yourself in harm's way to meet Caesar," Hephaestion said. "He is outnumbered."

"Five to one is not good odds, even for Caesar," echoed Archimedes.

"I would wager that Pompey's supporters said precisely that before the battle at Pharsalos," countered Kleopatra. "I always said that Caesar would prevail against Pompey. Is there any chance that he can be defeated by a bloated eunuch, a punctilious scholar, and a foppish general?"

Kleopatra did not know if she was up to a game of chess with a master like Caesar, but she was willing to try. What choice did she have? It seemed to her that Fate had led her on a specific path to this distinct moment in time, and now she had little recourse but to go to Alexandria and confront Caesar—not as an enemy but as a potential friend in the sea of monsters into which he had docked in Egypt. She would lay it all out for Caesar—how her father had made her his queen while he was still alive, and how he had wished for her to continue to reign after his death. She would describe how her brother's Regency Council had banished her, in direct opposition to the will of the late king, who was, after all, a Friend and Ally of the Roman People.

She said, "It is crucial that I go to Caesar and speak on my own behalf. He has called for a meeting."

Archimedes protested. "Kleopatra, it is much too dangerous. Thousands of Achillas's men remain at Pelusium; thousands are on their way to Alexandria now. Who has control of the seas, we do not know. You must send an emissary. There are many possible emissaries and only one Kleopatra. If anything should happen to you—" He broke off. He could not say what he wished to say. He continued: "If anything should happen to you the throne would be lost to Caesar, to the eunuch Pothinus, to your brother, who knows? Which would be the worst for Egypt it is impossible to say."

She did not know if her lover had begun to suspect what was in her mind, or if he was merely acting the protective Kinsman. She hoped that she had concealed from him the plan that had begun to take form. It began with the recognition that she felt a mild thrill whenever she said the name Julius Caesar. She found melody in its syllables, and she found herself mentally repeating it time and again. She liked the discernible quiver of fear the mention of the name seemed to inspire in whoever said it. Even if the speaker attempted to demonstrate disdain, what was usually projected was awe.

She felt as if she knew him. Her fascination with him began when she was a mere girl of eight or nine, escaping to the bazaar and overhearing the tales of his prowess in politics, on the battle-field, and as a lover. She had paid strict attention to his actions in the world and listened for gossip about his private life whenever she had the opportunity. Soon it seemed as if all the world was fascinated with this man, for his private life was the subject of popular discussion everywhere, or wherever civilized people lived and kept abreast of important affairs. She had analyzed his actions, trying to put together the pieces of the puzzle of his difficult personality, and now she must meet him, if only to see if her perceptions about him had been correct.

"Who can get me to the city?" she asked.

Before Archimedes could protest, Apollodorus offered, "I believe I can promise you a safe journey to the shores of Alexandria, Your Majesty. We can take a small escort of your men—men who will not talk, that is—to the sea, where we will meet with my vessel. We will sail within a very short distance of the harbor, and at the moment when night is about to fall, lower the small dinghy and row into shore. I will send word ahead by land to one of my comrades, who can easily smuggle us past the harbor police as if we were refugees or merchants with small goods to sell at the market the next day. You must disguise yourself, however, or you surely risk being recognized. It is not easy to mask the greatness of a queen," he said with some pride.

"Then this is our plan," Kleopatra said. "Might you get a letter to Caesar?"

"Yes, it will be sent with the man who will ride to the city ahead of us."

"Scribe!" she said.

"Kleopatra, I know that there is no stopping you. But I just want you to know that I protest." Archimedes looked at her with much concern.

"Cousin, I believe I have no choice. I am going to introduce myself to Caesar. I want him to know that he will have to reckon with me before he makes any irreversible arrangements with my brother, who undoubtedly has told him I am a traitor to our father, or a lunatic, or worse.

"Write this down in your best Greek letters," she said to the scribe, who had jumped so fast to the queen's summons that his ink and paper juggled precariously as he approached her. He positioned himself on the floor and sat attentively as she began to dictate.

To Gaius Julius Caesar,

I have been informed of the ignoble murder of Pompey by Pothinus, my brother's regent, whose treachery sent me, the legitimate queen of Egypt, into exile for fear of my life. My father and I were the guests of Pompey in the days when the two of you were aligned in government and by the solemn marriage between your daughter and the Imperator. Julia was a wonderful companion to me in my exile. I can testify that she and the General were, in those happier early times, deeply content and in love. I hope that knowledge is a comfort to you now. As for the Imperator, I despise the odious methods by which he met his end. He came to Egypt for refuge because early in the war Pothinus had acted as his friend, giving ships and men to his cause. This action was against my wishes and better judgment. Unlike my brother's regents, I did not believe that Pompey, whom I had observed eight years prior in Rome as already exhausted with public life, could defeat the man who had subdued Gaul and Britannia. I was to be proved correct, but at that time my power had been usurped by the Regency Council, and as I feared for my life, I was even then planning my escape from Alexandria. I am returning to the city under cover, and I will find a way into the palace to meet with you. I wish to continue my father's legacy as Friend and Ally of the Roman People, and I am prepared to carry out my part in upholding that bargain. The stories told of the great Julius Caesar boast of his wisdom, his mercy, and his fairness. It is these noble qualities I look forward to meeting when we stand face-to-face and solidify what I hope will be a lifelong friendship.

Yours, Kleopatra VII, Queen of the Two Lands of Egypt

⌐⊸⋀⋀⧧◻⌐◉⌐⌐

Archimedes followed Kleopatra to her tent, assuming a lover's privilege.

"One week ago, we were prepared for war, death. We made a lover's foolhardy send-off to life," he mused.

Kleopatra did not want to meet his eyes. "This has been the lesson of my life," she said. "I can never make plans for myself or for my country, for our collective destinies are entirely intertwined with the designs of Rome. Her Fate dictates mine. I must bend to her will, as did my father and his father and so many of our fathers before him."

"The gods are cruel weavers, spinning the threads of grief and problems around us as if we were spindles," said Archimedes, taking her hand, pulling her to his chest. Kleopatra was relieved to hide in the shelter of his arms so that she could avoid his face.

"Perhaps this design may turn out for our good after all," said Kleopatra. "I shall pray to Athena, the master weaver, for a lovely outcome in this tapestry of seeming woe."

"Perhaps you should not pray to the goddess of war in a matter where you only wish for peace," said Archimedes, kissing her forehead.

"Then I shall pray to Aphrodite, who encourages love," said Kleopatra. She lowered her head, though she knew he wanted her to raise it so that he could kiss her.

"It is a risky business, involving the volatile Aphrodite in such a grave affair."

"Then let us pray to the god of Caution, whoever he is," she said, pulling away from him and closing the matter.

"You are very different this morning, Kleopatra," he said.

"I am preoccupied with my mission. I had prepared for war, and now I find that I must be a diplomat. And a very clever one at that."

Though she did not admit it, she knew what he meant. She knew that he was thinking of her behavior just twelve hours in the past, when she let him hold her breathless body and submitted to him utterly. But at this moment, there was not a thing she could do to recover last night's bewildering emotions. It was as if she had regained her balance, her power.

She was grateful to be back on solid ground, for she felt as though she had been losing herself in his love. Every night, at lust's furious conclusion, she prayed that there would be more; that the gods would allow her to have this exhilaration as a constant part of her life and not just mete it out in stingy increments. Archimedes had made her moan and gasp and reach for that ultimate pleasure, which to her prior self had been just a vague rumor, like a story that is told about people who live far away. Before they were to go to battle, she had prayed that they both might live and prevail so that they might repeat the glory of the moment. Every night since, she immersed herself in his passion and in the mysterious revelations she had about hers.

What oracle might have prophesied the events that she had learned of today? What god had primed her and Archimedes for love one day and then sent Caesar marching directly into her world in the next? Archimedes was right; they were merely the spindles the gods used to weave the threads of their ironies. But Caesar was a man who tempted the gods, who had made an apparent bargain with Fortune.

And it was a deal into which she, Kleopatra, intended to be admitted.

But what must she do now? Archimedes was in a state. He paced about the tent like a lion that had stumbled into the wrong den. She knew that he was wondering if Julius Caesar was going to usurp the privileges he had taken for himself the previous evening.

It had occurred to Kleopatra—as it would occur to any woman who had to negotiate with a man thirty years her senior—that Julius Caesar, the notorious lover, might attempt to make a conjugal union between them a condition of alliance. And what would she do? She loved her cousin, there was no doubt of that, and now, as she looked into his bewildered brown eyes, she felt herself drawn toward him again. But he was not the man who could save her kingdom. *In matters of state, let your blood run cold.* The eunuch Hephaestion had advised her thusly time and again. There was no choice. And yet Kleopatra felt ill at what she must do now to this beautiful and loyal man. Only last night he had told her that she was intoxicating, that she was an enchantress, a woman for whom men would kill for the privilege of being taken into the rapture of her intimacy.

"Woman, goddess, queen," he had muttered over and over again while he lost himself in her. If that was only a lover's heated speech, so be it. Perhaps that was what all men said as they pleasured themselves. She had no way of knowing. But in that moment, he had given Kleopatra the key to men. Or one of the keys, at any rate. Money certainly was another. And what would a man not do for power and position? What had Julius Caesar done already for these things?

Well, she had it all, did she not? She had the treasures of her ancestors, the riches of Egypt, the bloom of youth, and the knowledge that the Achilles' heel of a man was not necessarily in his foot.

This was her battle gear. It was not an army or a navy, but she had access to those things, too. She was as well armed as anyone Julius Caesar had ever faced.

Read the further adventures of Kleopatra

Volume Two: *Pharaoh*

available in bookstores in August 2002

Alexandria:
the 3rd year of
Kleopatra's reign

Kleopatra looked out the window at the scene that had greeted her all the mornings of her days before her flight into exile. There was little in the Royal Harbor to suggest Roman occupation of Alexandria. The pleasure vessels of the Royal Family rocked lazily at the dock. The morning fog had lifted, revealing a sky already white with heat above vivid blue waters, and she was grateful that she was no longer breathing the deadening summer air of the Sinai.

She did not know whether her country was in fact occupied or not. Caesar acted like a guest who had made himself overly comfortable rather than as the hostile commander who had entered the city with his standards raised, immediately engaging in a skirmish with the Alexandrian army. Kleopatra did not care what version Caesar put forth of the story. She believed he had entered her city with the intention of taking it. He had thought it would be easy; she was sure of this. Caesar had just defeated Pompey and was confident of his invincibility. But he had underestimated the Alexandrian hatred for all things Roman, the old Greek pride that the city's citizens still carried in their very veins. They did not lay down their arms for the exalted Roman general. Far from it.

Now Caesar and his men were virtually barricaded inside the palace walls, so angered was the mob at his presence. Yet he did not act at all like a prisoner. She had asked him if he was at war with her brother, and he replied that no, he was a friend to the Crown, as was all of Rome. He had come to Alexandria merely to chase down his former ally and old friend Pompey, whom he had had the unfortunate task of defeating in Greece in battle over whose policies would predominate in Rome. He had intended to reconcile with Pompey, to bring him back to Rome and to his senses, and to make Pompey see that the greedy Roman senators who had incited him to go to war with Caesar were acting in self-interest rather than in the interests of either Caesar or Pompey. "But your brother's eunuch Pothinus had already taken care of the issue for me. Upon my arrival, he presented me with Pompey's head." Caesar had looked very sad. "I may be at war with Pothinus," he said. "I may be at war with your brother's army but not your brother. We shall see what unfolds in the coming days."

How could a man be so casual about war? she wondered. Perhaps it was from a lifetime of waging it. And yet he seemed equally calm and dispassionate about everything, even those things that usually provoked the extreme emotions: debate, negotiation, money, sex.

She let her mind drift with the ocean's waves as she assessed the new order of things. She was no longer in exile, waiting for the right moment to attack her brother's army. She was again the queen of Egypt. Caesar had overwhelmingly defeated Pompey and the Roman senate, thus this made him the most powerful man in the world. And Caesar was now her benefactor and lover.

Could it have been just yesterday that she was in the middle of that great blue sea, stowing away on a pirate's vessel to sneak back into her own country? She had dressed herself as well as she could without her servants, knowing that the last leg of her journey would be a rigorous one and that she could not arrive in the harbor of Alexandria and be recognized. She had let Dorinda, the wife of Apollodorus the pirate, help with her toilette, fixing and bejeweling the locks that had been neglected while she was in exile. She would have done it herself, but her hands had shook with anxiety; she had fought with her advisers, rejecting their claims that it was too dangerous to reenter Egypt, and now she was faced with the task of using stealth to slip past both her brother's army and Caesar's army to meet with the Roman general.

At dusk, in view of the Great Harbor of her city, she had found herself with Apollodorus in a small vessel bobbing in the water. In the fading sunlight, she had seen the familiar Pharos Lighthouse, the landmark of her youth and one of the great hallmarks of her family's reign over Egypt. The tower was bathed in diffuse red light, which lingered as the sun sank behind her into the depths of the Mediterranean. The eternal flame in the top floor of the tower burned vigilantly. The imposing structure that had served as a marker of safe harbor for three centuries was the genius of her ancestor Ptolemy Philadelphus and his sister-wife, Arsinoe II, and now it welcomed her home. This had not been the first time she had approached her country from the vantage point of exile. But this was the first time she had returned from exile to find a flotilla of warships in a V formation pointing dangerously toward her city.

"These are not Egyptian vessels," she said, noting their flags. "Some are Rhodian, some from Syria, some from Cilicia."

"All territories from which Caesar might have called for reinforcements," said Apollodorus.

"Warships in the harbor? What can this mean? That Alexandria is already at full-scale war with Caesar?" said Kleopatra.

"So it appears. And now we must get you through Caesar's navy and the army of your brother's general Achillas before you can have a conference with Caesar. I do not know if my contacts at the docks can help us in these circumstances. As Your Majesty is well aware, in wartime all policies change to meet the dire times. I'm afraid that our simple scheme of disguising you as my wife may not serve us in these hazardous conditions."

"I agree," she said. Her heart began the now familiar hammering in her chest, its punch taking over her body and consuming her mental strength. *No, this cannot happen,* she said to herself. I cannot submit to this tidal wave of emotion, of fear that threatens to wreak disaster on my Fate.

Only I and the gods may dictate my Fate, she said to herself. Not a heart, not an organ. *I control my heart, my heart does not control me,* she said to herself over and over until the pounding in her ears gave way to the benevolent slurping of the placid waters as they slapped haphazardly against the boat, calming her nerves. She put her head down and prayed.

Lady Isis, the Lady of Compassion, the Lady to whom I owe my fortune and my Fate. Protect me, sustain me, guide me as I make this daring move so that I may continue to honor you and continue to serve the country of my fathers.

When she looked up from her prayer, she saw that they had drifted closer to the shore. Trapped now between the Rhodian flotilla and the Syrian flotilla, she realized that she must take some kind of cover. How could she have so foolishly thought that she could just slip into the city where she was known above all women? She must do something quickly to get herself out of sight.

She shared these thoughts with Apollodorus.

"It is not too late to turn around, Your Majesty—" he offered.

"No!" she interrupted him. "This is my country. My brother sits in the palace as if he were the sole ruler of Egypt. Caesar, no doubt, is in receipt of my letter and he awaits my arrival. I will not be shut out by these maritime monsters," she said, raising her hands as if to encompass all the vessels in the sea. "The gods will not have it, and I will not have it."

Apollodorus said nothing. Kleopatra made another silent plea to the goddess. She stared into her lap, waiting for inspiration to descend upon her. She was for a moment lost in the intricate pattern of the Persian carpet that the men had thrown aboard the boat at the last minute for the queen to sit on. An anonymous artisan had spent years of his life stitching the rows and rows of symmetrical crosses into the silk. Suddenly, she pulled her head up straight and focused on the rug, mentally measuring its dimension. Its fine silk threads would not irritate the downy skin of a young woman should she choose to lie upon it. Or to roll herself inside of it.

The sun cast its final offering of light. Her companion's square rock of a body sat helplessly waiting for the decision of the queen as his boat sailed precariously close to the shore.

"Help me," she said as she threw the rug on the floor of the boat and positioned herself at one end.

Apollodorus stood up and stared down at the queen, who lay with her hands over her chest like a mummy.

"But Your Majesty will suffocate," he protested, stretching out his palms to her as if he hoped they would exercise upon her a modicum of reason. "We must leave this place."

The sun had set, and the boxlike form that hovered above her was only a silhouette against a darkening sky.

"Help me quickly, and do not waste our time with questions," she said. "Julius Caesar is waiting."

When the squatty Sicilian had entered Caesar's chamber announcing that he had a gift from the rightful queen of Egypt to lay at Great Caesar's feet, Caesar's soldiers drew swords. But Caesar had simply laughed and said he was anxious to see what the exiled girl might smuggle through her brother's guards.

"This is a mistake, sir," said the captain of his guard. "These people are ready to take advantage of your good nature."

"Then they, too, shall learn, shan't they?" he replied.

The pirate laid the carpet before Caesar, then used his own knife to clip the ties that bound it. As he slowly and carefully unrolled it, Caesar could see that it was a fine example of the craftsmanship that was only to be found in the eastern countries, the kind he had so envied when he was last at Pompey's house in Rome. Suddenly, as if she were part of the geometrical pattern itself, a girl rolled out from its folds, sat up cross-legged, and looked at him. Her small face was overly painted, with too much jewelry in her thick brown hair, and a meretricious scarf tied about her tiny waist, showing off her comely body. The young queen must be a woman of great humor to have sent Caesar a pirate's little wench. She was not precisely lovely, he thought, but handsome. She had full lips, or so he assumed under the paint. Her eyes were green and slanted upward, and they challenged him now to speak to her, as if it were Caesar who should have to introduce himself to this little tart. But it was the pirate who spoke first.

"Hail, Queen Kleopatra, daughter of Isis, Lady of the Two Lands of Egypt."

Caesar stood—a habit, though he remained unconvinced that

the girl was not a decoy. She stood, too, but quickly motioned for him to sit. Surely only a queen would have the guts to do that. He took his chair again, and she addressed him in Latin, not giving him the opportunity to interrogate her, but telling him the story of how her brother and his courtiers had placed her under house arrest and forced her to flee Alexandria and go into exile; how her brother's regents were representative of the anti-Roman faction in Egypt; how she had always carried out her late father's policy of friendship with Rome; and how, most importantly, once restored, she intended to repay the large loan that her father had taken from the Roman moneylender Rabirius, which she must have guessed was the real reason that Caesar had followed Pompey to Alexandria.

Before Caesar might reply to her speech, the queen said, "Shall we converse in Greek, General? It is a more precise language for negotiation, don't you agree?"

"As you wish," Caesar replied. From there the conversation was held in her native tongue and not his—not that it mattered. He spoke Greek as if he had been born in Athens. He admired her ploy of simultaneously demonstrating her command of his native tongue while diminishing it in comparison to the more sophisticated Greek language. There was no pride like that of the Greeks, and this girl was obviously no exception.

But she had great charm and intelligence, so Caesar pledged her restoration, in accordance with her father's will and the nation's tradition. He would have done so anyway, but now he could do it with pleasure. Not only would it please the young queen, it would also irritate Pothinus, the dreadful eunuch whom Caesar despised. For Kleopatra's part, she pledged a great portion of her treasury that he might take with him back to Rome to satisfy Rabirius. A relief, he assured her, to have that clacking old duck paid and off his back. Kleopatra laughed, remembering the sight of Rabirius's great waddling ass as he was chased out of Alexandria.

"I do hope you are enjoying our city," Kleopatra said. "Are we occupying you as satisfactorily as you occupy us?"

Caesar felt he had no choice but to laugh. He told the girl about a lecture he had recently attended at the Mouseion, the center for scholarly learning that he'd heard about all his years. She had studied there herself, she said, and in her exile what she most had longed for was not her feathery bed nor the kitchen staff of one hundred who prepared for her the finest meals on earth, but the volumes of books at the Great Library and the visits of scholars, poets, and scientists who engaged her mind.

Now secure that she was once again at home and in charge, she called for wine, and before he knew it, they were discussing the philosophy of domination, and he was drunk and praising Posidonius while she disputed every point.

"Posidonius has demonstrated that Rome, by embracing all the peoples of the world, secures all humanity into a commonwealth under the gods," Caesar explained. "Through submission, harmony is realized."

A tiny laugh, almost a giggle, escaped Kleopatra's lips despite herself. "Does Rome *embrace*, General? Is suffocation not a more appropriate word?" she asked, her eyes wide and twinkling. He did not know if she was agitating him for the purpose of argument or to arouse him sexually. But with her enchanting voice which sounded almost like a musical instrument, and the way she moved her body with sensuous fluidity, she was succeeding more at the latter.

It was too much, really, but she said it so charmingly. He could afford to be generous. She was so young, one and twenty she had said, younger than his Julia would have been had she lived. "Surely the gods were drunk on the day they made an imperious Greek girl the queen of a filthy rich nation. Surely I must be intoxicated to insure the power of such a girl."

"The Crown thanks you."

"As you know, my child, as we have witnessed here in your own land, there must be a master. It's as simple as that. In accordance with the laws of the gods and the laws of nature. Otherwise, it's a muddle. 'The strong do as they will while the weak suffer what they must.' If I may quote a Greek to a Greek."

By this time, they were entirely alone. She had long ago dismissed the pirate, and Caesar, his men. They sat facing each other on two white linen couches with a table of refreshments between them. She regarded Caesar for some time, and he allowed it, enjoying the flush of color across her high cheekbones and the way flashes of inspiration seemed to leap from her eyes. "Is it not possible for the two civilized peoples, Greek and Roman, to rule side by side, one race of men of military might in cooperation with another whose strength lies in the world of the intellect, the world of art, knowledge, and beauty?"

"Possible, but not probable. If given the opportunity, men of means will always seek power and fortune."

"And women of means as well," she said.

"Yes, I have not seen that women lack ambition," he replied. "And if a woman of means has sufficient means, then perhaps many things are possible."

"I'm relieved you think so." She sat back, satisfied, her small hands folded in her lap, a quiet smile on her face as if she shared some lovely humor with herself alone. Caesar was sure that they had not exactly finished with this line of discussion. But he wanted, at that moment, to seize her mind in his hands as if it were another territory to be conquered in the name of Rome and of unity. Yet she was not a woman to be merely taken. *Here was a woman*, he thought, *who if giving herself of her own volition, would give the world.*

"But we have parried enough, Your Majesty," Caesar said, rising. "You've vexed an old man quite enough for one day. Now come to bed. You are under my protection."

But she did not rise with him. "General, just when I thought your command of Greek was beyond reproach, I find that you make a linguistic mistake."

"Caesar does not make linguistic mistakes," he replied. What now? More argument with this fetching creature? Was she determined to try his patience?

"You said, *come* to bed, when surely you meant *go* to bed."

Again, she looked at him as if she were either laughing at him or trying to seduce him. How could he, a man of fifty-two who had had hundreds of lovers, not rapidly discern which?

"No, dear girl. You know what I meant. I always make myself perfectly clear."

The chubby boy king burst into his sister's chamber. Though it was early morning, he was dressed in formal robes and wearing his crown. Kleopatra barely had a moment to pull the cover over her naked breasts. Caesar sat up quickly, the dagger under his pillow already in his hand.

"What are you doing here?" the young king screamed, his bulbous lips quaking as he yelled at his sister. "How did you get here?"

Caesar's soldiers followed the boy into the room; trailing them, Arsinoe, her panther eyes darting from Kleopatra to her lover. How old must the girl be now? Sixteen? She was the image of her treasonous, dead mother, Thea, only with marble green eyes instead of Thea's conniving brown ones. Arsinoe smirked but said nothing. She took her brother by the arm.

"Are you some kind of fiend or apparition? The entire city is on guard against you. How did you get into the palace, you ghost?"

Kleopatra did not answer but waited for Caesar to speak. Though he had just restored her to her own throne, he was dictator of Rome and she, at his mercy. At least for the moment.

"My good King Ptolemy," Caesar began, tossing the dagger aside, "I promised to repair relations between you and your sister and I have done so."

Caesar's men, ready to seize the boy, looked to their commander, but he waved them away from Ptolemy's benign presence.

"But I don't want to reconcile with her," the boy answered, pointing to Kleopatra, who tried to retain as much dignity as a naked young woman in a roomful of strangers might. "She's a monster! Has she poisoned you against us? Has she?"

"Come now, there is no need for this kind of upset," Caesar said. "Let us set a meeting for later in the day—perhaps some reasonable hour after breakfast—and I shall enlighten you and your regents as to the terms."

Caesar's calm voice settling over the room evaporated the anger Ptolemy had released into the air. But the boy king did not relent. "What do you think you're doing?" he stammered at Kleopatra.

"Is this how you welcome your sister back to Alexandria?" Kleopatra asked, trying to imitate Caesar's mellow tone. "I have not seen you for the better part of two years, my brother. How you've grown." He had not. He was no taller, as far as Kleopatra could discern, but had expanded horizontally, reminding her of the girth her late father had acquired in his last years.

Caesar leaned toward the boy. "You know the terms of your father's will. You and Kleopatra are to rule jointly. It isn't for you to question. You shouldn't have run her out of the country in the first place."

"Run her out? She sneaked away like a common thief and raised an army against me!" he sputtered.

Laughable, Kleopatra thought. She would not put one ounce of her energy into bolstering such a fool before the Roman general, before the Alexandrian population, or even before the gods themselves.

"That's all over now, and I insist that you make up. It's all been decided. No need to create another dispute when harmony is so easily attained." Caesar smiled at Arsinoe. "Is that not what the philosophers tell us, young lady? You have your brother's ear. You must counsel him to be reasonable. You do not wish him to get himself hurt."

"No, General. I do not." Arsinoe folded her arms, making a bridge under her voluptuous breasts and chilling Kleopatra with her glazed stare. It seemed to her that Arsinoe had been assessing the situation and had come to some dark private conclusion. "Shall we go, Brother?"

The boy grimaced at Kleopatra, but let himself be guided away by his sister; more regal than he would ever be, she held his elbow and led him out of the room as if he were entirely blind.

Kleopatra let out a sigh and fell back on her pillow, grateful to have awakened in her own bed, no matter what the circumstances, after two years of exile. She had not slept, really slept, in months and months, and even last night she and Caesar were awake almost until dawn negotiating and making love. Fortunately, her energy for both of those activities was of the torrential sort. She had had years of practice for the former, both in her father's government and in exile, where resources were limited. The latter, she was accustomed to with a man half Caesar's age, so that the passions of this older man, so distant, so polite, hardly troubled her at all. She thought of

Archimedes—cousin, lover, comrade—still in exile, of his eyes as deep and dark as Nile silt, of his strong square shoulders, of the way he lost himself in a private frenzy after he had done with pleasing her, of the way his cries while making love seemed like prayers to some taunting goddess, and she ached with her betrayal. But what choice did she have? For here was Julius Caesar, undisputed Master of the World, who had made it safe for her to be in this room once more, where the sounds and smells of the sea rolled into her window. How many times had she wondered if she would ever set foot upon Egyptian soil again, much less sleep in her own goose down bed? She had made a cold-blooded choice, but she had made the correct one. *In matters of state let your blood run cold.* Her most trusted adviser, Hephaestion, whom she had left back in the Sinai with Archimedes, had drilled those words into her head for so many years now that she chanted them to herself day and night. She must have no regrets.

A knock at the door interrupted her thoughts. One of Caesar's men entered, not the least bit embarrassed to disturb the morning intimacy between his commander and the queen of Egypt. How often did his men come upon such a scene? she wondered.

"Sir, so sorry to disturb you, but the boy king is speaking to an assembly of malcontents at the palace gates. He's torn off his crown and thrown it into the crowd. He is shouting all sorts of insults about the queen. He's getting them all whipped up out there. Shall we remove him?"

"No, no," Caesar said wearily. "Give us a moment. I'll fetch him myself and bring him in."

"We can handle it, sir," said the soldier.

"Yes, yes, but I've got a way with him," said Caesar. "Besides, I shall make a little speech to the mob. I'll tell them their queen is back, and that Caesar shall ensure peace in their kingdom."

"Have the wine sellers discount their wares to the crowd," Kleopatra suggested, remembering her father's old ploy for placating his people.

"Excellent," Caesar replied.

"As you wish," the soldier said. Bowing courteously to Kleopatra but not meeting her eyes, he left.

"My brother has always been a nuisance," Kleopatra said, leaning on her elbow.

"I imagine he has," Caesar said. "Not to worry. He shall be made to understand."

"General?"

"You may call me Caesar, my darling young queen, and I shall call you Kleopatra."

"Caesar. Do be careful."

"Never worry over me," Caesar said, waving his long fingers in the air, fanning away her concerns. "It isn't necessary. No one shall be hurt. At least not yet."

GLOSSARY

Consul The Roman consulship was the highest political office in the Republic. Each year, two consuls were elected, who presided over the senate and the military. They assumed the duties of the former kings (the Republic replaced the monarchy in 509 B.C.E.), but the fact that they shared power and only served for one year safeguarded against one man assuming supreme power.

Equestrian class The equites originally made up the cavalry in the Roman army, but later the term was applied to the wealthy citizenry beneath the patrician class. The equites were mainly businessmen or capitalists, while the patricians were a smaller group of large landowners.

Exegete A city official in Alexandria.

Fasces The Roman standards. When Caesar entered Egypt flying the fasces, the Egyptians took it as an act of aggression.

Fellahin The class of Egyptian peasant farmers who labored on small plots of land and shared their crops with the crown. They were responsible for producing the bulk of Egypt's grain crop.

Greek phalanx From approximately the eighth century B.C.E., the Greeks had organized their armies into the columnar unit of the phalanx, thus inserting discipline into what was formerly mass fighting. The soldiers were called hoplites, taken from *hoplon,* or "shield," which was carried in the left hand so that the right hand was free to thrust with the spear. Each soldier was dependent upon the man on his right to protect that side of his body.

Hetaira The Greek word for "companion," but used euphemistically for a Greek woman, slave or free, who traded sexual favors for money. Greek courtesans who were companions to men of rank were often educated, and sometimes had additional professions, such as hostess or entertainer. In the Greek world, the *hetairai* were more than tolerated—they were taxed.

Mouseion Literally a temple to the Muses in Alexandria, the Mouseion became the center of all learning in the Greek world. The Ptolemies funded the Mouseion, encouraging the finest minds to study and research there by giving them generous salaries and allowing them to live tax-free. Callimachus, Apollonius of Rhodes, Theocritus, Euclid, and Eratosthenes were just some of the scholars who lived and worked at the Mouseion. The tradition of research and learning continued well into the Byzantine period, until the Mouseion was destroyed by the Christians, who disapproved of "pagan" knowledge.

Novus homo A new man, or the first man in a family to hold the Roman office of consul, thus becoming a member of the nobility. Their descendants could then be known as members of the nobiles, the "well-knowns," an exclusive group of senators whose ancestors had held a consulship. Cicero was a *novus homo.*

Nome Under Ptolemaic rule, Egypt was composed of forty-two *nomoi,* or *nomes,* which were loosely comparable to states. The typical *nome* stretched along the Nile for approximately fifty miles. Its villages were governed by a nomarch, who spoke both Greek and Egyptian and was appointed by the king.

Optimates and **Populares** In Julius Caesar's time, politicians were either *populares,* those who worked through and on behalf of the citizenry, or *optimates,* or "best class," the senatorial conservatives who believed that the wellborn were best suited to govern. Caesar, despite his illustrious heritage, was a populare. Pompey was clearly an optimate.

Quaestor An official elected for a one-year term to serve as a financial administrator, usually to a general on a campaign or a governor of a client kingdom. Caesar began his political career as a quaestor in Spain.

Roman legion The Roman legion evolved over the years to suit the needs of the times, but in Julius Caesar's day it was a unit composed of approximately 4,800 infantry and 300 cavalry. The unit was further divided into ten cohorts that fought in a series of lines. The legion was more sophisticated than the phalanx; it allowed generals to command from the rear, and it allowed for diversity of weaponry and for greater reserves.

Talent A unit of currency, equal to 6,000 drachmas.

Tribune of the People Tribunes were elected from the plebeian class, historically, to protect the plebeians from the patricians. Nonetheless, many tribunes, such as Antony, were from very old and wealthy equestrian families. The tribunes had the all-important power of veto over the senate.

TIMELINE	(All Dates are B.C.E.)
3200	Begins Egypt's dynastic period
2700–2255	Egypt's old kingdom (the time of the great pyramid, built by the pharaoh Cheops, c. 2572)
2255–1570	Egypt's intermediate kingdom and middle kingdom
1570–1070	Egypt's new kingdom —Amenhotep I (r. 1551–1524) —Hapshetsut (r. 1504–1483) —Ramses II (r. 1279–1213)
1070–332	Egypt is ruled by a series of outsiders: the Tanis kings, Libyan chieftains, Cushites, Assyrians, Persians
753	Founding of the city of Rome
332–331	Alexander the Great (king of Macedonia) enters and subjugates Egypt, liberating the country from Persia —Founds the Mediterranean city of Alexandria at the site of the fishing village of Rhakotis —Becomes the first Macedonian pharaoh
323	Death of Alexander; Ptolemy I becomes ruler of Egypt
305	Ptolemy I becomes Pharaoh (November 7)
80	Ptolemy XII Auletes, father of Kleopatra VII, ascends to the throne
70/69	Kleopatra VII is born
60	First Roman triumvirate (Caesar/Pompey/Crassus)
58	Auletes in exile in Rome
55	Auletes reinstated by Gabinius, Governor of Syria; his troops are led by Antony
51	Kleopatra is named co-regent with her father —Death of Auletes —Kleopatra presides over the installation of the sacred bull in Hermonthis —Kleopatra marries her half brother Ptolemy XIII
49	Kleopatra flees to Upper Egypt
48	Kleopatra moves her headquarters to Askalon —Caesar is victorious in Pharsalos (August 16) —Caesar enters Egypt

KAREN ESSEX is an award-winning journalist, a screenwriter, and the coauthor of a biography about cult icon Bettie Page. Born in New Orleans, she is currently adapting her first novel, *Kleopatra,* and its sequel, *Pharaoh,* into a screenplay for Warner Bros. She lives in Los Angeles and can be reached at www.karenessex.com.

PHARAOH
by Karen Essex

In *Pharaoh*, volume II of *Kleopatra*, Karen Essex's magnificent saga reaches its stunning culmination, as the most celebrated woman of the ancient world finds turbulent love with the legendary Marcus Antonius. A decade of research pulls back the veil of myth that has obscured the real Kleopatra for centuries, and the natural gifts of a brilliant novelist make her subject's story come alive. The result is an enthralling retelling of history that will instantly take its place as the definitive portrait of a monarch and a woman like none seen before her time or since.

"Essex takes the beloved genre of historical fiction and works some major literary magic upon it. *Pharaoh* is thrillingly fun to read, but it is also full of serious delights—rich, round characters and lovely line-to-line writing. In every respect this is a splendid novel."
　　　—ROBERT OLEN BUTLER, Pulitzer Prize-winning author of
　　　　　　　Good Scent from a Strange Mountain